Praise for Denise Tompkins's *Niteclif Evolutions Series*

"A perfect blend of humor, suspense, and nonstop action kept me glued to the pages of *Legacy*. The intricate plotting made it hard to detect the villain which made for a surprise ending. I hated for this book to end and for a debut book, that is saying a lot. I urge paranormal lovers to run out and purchase this book..."

~ *Fresh Fiction*

"The world created by the author feels real, and the mystery is intriguing. And lest I forget, the romance while not the main point of the novel is still scorching! This is Ms.Tompkins's debut novel and all I can say is brava!"

~ *Romance Reviews Today*

"*Wrath* is book two in the Niteclif series and I enjoyed reading it quite a lot... There was no shortage whatsoever of conflict and surprises that I honestly never saw coming."

~ *Night Owl Reviews*

"This second book in the series (after *Legacy*) is easy to follow and impossible to put down. Add in wizards, warlocks, vampires, fairies, and dragons, and you have a truly spectacular story. Recommended to anyone who enjoys supernatural thrillers, as well as readers who have a taste for a good mystery with some flights of fantasy."

~ *Library Journal*

Look for these titles by
Denise Tompkins

Now Available:

The Niteclif Evolutions
Legacy
Wrath

Wrath

Denise Tompkins

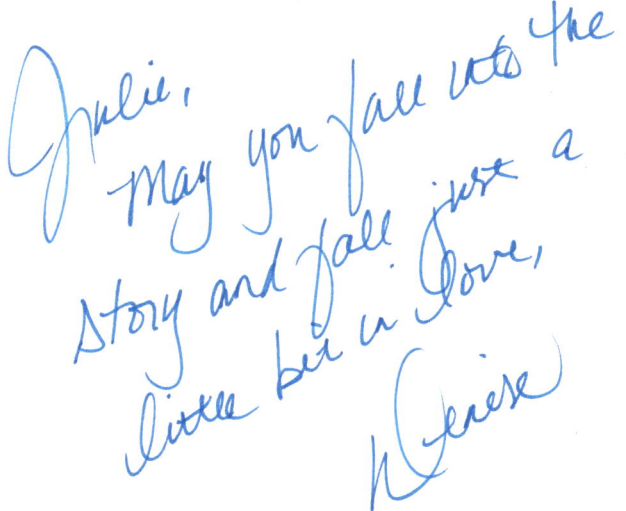

Julie,
May you fall into the story and fall just a little bit in love,
Denise

Samhain Publishing, Ltd.
11821 Mason Montgomery Road, 4B
Cincinnati, OH 45249
www.samhainpublishing.com

Wrath
Copyright © 2013 by Denise Tompkins
Print ISBN: 978-1-60928-946-1
Digital ISBN: 978-1-60928-723-8

Editing by Amy Sherwood
Cover by Kanaxa

This book is a work of fiction. The names, characters, places, and incidents are products of the writer's imagination or have been used fictitiously and are not to be construed as real. Any resemblance to persons, living or dead, actual events, locale or organizations is entirely coincidental.

All Rights Are Reserved. No part of this book may be used or reproduced in any manner whatsoever without written permission, except in the case of brief quotations embodied in critical articles and reviews.

First Samhain Publishing, Ltd. electronic publication: April 2012
First Samhain Publishing, Ltd. print publication: March 2013

Dedication

For you, my readers, whose faith in Maddy made her first story a success and enabled me to continue the series. You have my most humble, heartfelt gratitude. Thank you.

Prologue

Dreams can be cruel things, those nighttime reflections of the choices we make. Bitterly sweet, they are most harsh when you awake to find what you held in sleep was only a glimpse of what life could someday be or, worse, *infinitely* worse, what it might have been. How do you live with regret that is by its very nature terminally deep, aching within your heart like a fatal wound? I don't know. I wonder how long I can live with it before I'm done for. It seems that at every turn I look up expecting the Reaper to be standing there to usher me on. Why him and not Saint Peter? Because I don't believe the choices I've made—the most important ones— have earned me an angelic escort.

Women have died. They've suffered unspeakable violence because they were born with a specific physical build, a familiar face, even styling choices in hair and clothes. To whom were they all similar? Me. They were similar to me. Maybe if I'd been faster, smarter, more qualified, made better choices—left instead of right, look up instead of down—they wouldn't have died. I couldn't stop their murders, and I can't bring them back.

I have also been the direct cause of broken hearts. Plural. I have hurt the two men in my life by not knowing with whom my heart truly lies. Resentment flavors every conversation, taints every look and hangs on every touch. And the prophecy—that damned prophecy. It may be the death of me. Or worse, one of them.

The choices we make...

Chapter One

The trip from the bathroom back to the small twin bed had never looked longer. Torn muscles ached and screamed as I commanded my legs to shuffle forward, my bruised kidneys eliciting groans and curses with every tender step. Uncontrollable laughter tickled the back of my throat as I had a Hollywood moment, the distance to the bed stretching out tunnel-like, voices whispering through my head. Flashes of the brutal fight I'd been in three weeks ago threatened to bring on another blackout. I scrambled for a handhold on the wall, the dresser's edge, anything and anywhere that would help me stay upright. Bahlin might be here, capable of offering help, but *capable* and *willing* were two different things. I'd have to make the trip on my own.

The bed. I needed to make it to the bed. I pushed off the wall only to fall—literally—several feet short of my goal.

At least the oriental rugs are thick, I thought.

An involuntary shiver wracked my body, and the memories came faster. I couldn't shut them off now any more than I could yesterday or any day before or, truthfully, any more than I expected to be able to tomorrow. I could almost taste again the bitter smoke made by burning hair and flesh, smell the coppery, metallic scent of spilled blood and feel the blows as they landed on me with unstoppable fury. I unconsciously rubbed the mark on my chest, left where the curse that nearly ended my life had landed. Then there was the voice that hung in the air as Bahlin had spirited me away...

"Game on, Niteclif! Game on!" Hellion's angry words had echoed in my bleeding ears as I fled the apocalyptic battlefield where the supernatural had converged to take down Tarrek, the First Prince of Faerie and one of their very own. I could still see Hellion standing in the midst of the windstorm that was the thoughtless byproduct of his fury. Dark blond hair had whipped around his head like Medusa's own headdress, and his eyes blazed with wrath as I was rescued by my lover, Bahlin. A member of the Supernatural High Council and, arguably, one of the good guys, Hellion demanded reparation in the way of an eye for an eye for his lover's death. I had killed her. A strong proponent of justice, I still couldn't get behind his demand when it involved ending my life. It had been a legitimate fight, but he still felt compelled to challenge my version of events. Nothing I'd been able to say or do had convinced him otherwise.

It should probably be noted that Bahlin had rescued me by flying away with my person held firmly in his arms. He's a dragon. No, I'm not into bestiality. Yes, they really do shift into human form. I'm learning to look beyond the monster to see the man, though I still have moments when I struggle. It doesn't help that he has taken every opportunity to remind me he's a dragon first and a man second. Always. Watching your lover sprout a wicked tail from his literal tailbone, to see wings unfold from his shoulder blades as if they'd been hiding there just out of sight, and to watch his jaw elongate and realize he's lost the functions of speech and higher thought? It's a little rough. I've learned Bahlin and his dragon are two separate entities within his brain, two creatures of independent thought, though I'll only ever voluntarily wake up naked with one of them. The man is impulsive and passionate, driven by ardent lusts and his professed love. The dragon is equally impulsive and passionate, but he's a creature whose behavior is dictated almost entirely by animalistic instincts, primarily to defend his life and the lives of those he recognizes his man-half loves. His first means of defense is to kill the threat. It's effective. I can't help but wonder, though, what Bahlin's dragon sees when he looks at me. Sometimes I feel cherished. Other times I feel like an hors d' oeuvre. Uncomfortable, that.

Bahlin walked into the room while I was contemplating the flavor of cream cheese his dragon would probably spread all over me like a human cracker before devouring me. Pain medication does strange things to my mind. But I'd become a firm believer in better life through chemistry, so I'd take the stuff. Bahlin had used some of his own dragon's magic to help me heal the worst of the injuries, but he hadn't been able to cure the damage caused by the curse the desperate faerie had lobbed at me. The results of that curse had left me teetering on the edge of death and only my infinitely-great-grandfather, the Norse god Tyr, had been able to save me. One of the fae's healers had spent some time countering the physical effects, but the remnants of the dark magic were the equivalent of badly bruised internal organs. The eons-old magic of the curse was lingering, and nothing seemed to be able to fully and wholly heal me. Not even time. I hoped if I spent a couple more days recuperating I'd be recovered enough to start living again. One of us, either Bahlin or I, was going to have to put some effort into it, and Bahlin didn't seem interested—not in recovery, not in life and definitely not in me.

While I'd received help for my physical injuries, Bahlin was still emotionally broken. No healer of any species, no sympathizers in any quantity or level of sincerity, and no amount of compassion from any source could absolve him of his debilitating burden of guilt. He'd been forced to kill his own father and sister in order to save my life, and his split-second decision to choose my life over theirs had driven an undeniable wedge between us. I wasn't sure how to fix it. All I knew was that our fledgling relationship was fragmenting in front of me, breaking into so many pieces I couldn't hold it together.

I knew all about losing loved ones. My parents had been killed almost a year ago in a freak train derailment while on vacation. My heart hurt every time I thought about them. But whereas Fate had taken them from me, they hadn't died by my own hand.

"*Mo chrid*," Bahlin said, jarring me back into the moment.

I reached for him and he hesitated to touch me. "Just help me up, Bahlin," I sighed. "Get me back in bed and you can..." The final word, *go*, hung between us.

Bahlin closed his eyes, breathing slow and deep. "Maddy, I...can't—"

"Forget I asked." I rolled over and pushed, pulled and grunted my way halfway up the bedside. Hesitant hands settled on my hips and he picked me up, setting me on the covers as if I were combustible.

Bahlin settled himself on the edge of the bed to watch me tuck the blankets around my hips and shuffle pillows until all was as right as I could make it.

My heart hurt, and it had little to do with the curse.

As if nothing had happened, Bahlin asked, "How are you this morning?" The words were right, but his voice was flatter than a southern Arizona horizon, and his eyes were haunted.

I reached out a drug-heavy hand and stroked his face. He let me caress his cheek briefly before he turned away. That was the first time he'd let me touch him since we'd arrived at his flat.

I dropped my hand, and it made a muffled thump on the dense bedding. "I'm okay," I rasped. "You?" My voice was still hoarse from all the screaming I'd done first in rage during battle and, later, in pain while my wounds were being treated.

"I just got off the phone with my mum," he whispered.

Oh boy.

"She's still distraught, though she claims she doesn't blame me."

"How could she blame you, Bay?" I asked. "You did..." I had started to say *you did what you had to do,* but that would have been a lie, and we both knew it. He'd chosen me, and he hadn't had to. I sighed, unsure what to say or do to make this any better. "Have you talked to Aiden?"

He nodded but remained mute, refusing to meet my eyes.

"How is he?" I prodded gently, reaching over to touch Bahlin's arm.

He flinched but didn't move away. Progress? Or was it just my own desperate need to reconnect with the man I'd agreed to marry? I wasn't programmed to stay in a loveless relationship or, at the very least, one that was as seriously broken as ours.

"He's okay. He's torn up about Brylanna's death." Emotion choked his normally deep voice and made his speech sound forced and painful. "No one knew she was involved with that damned faerie until it was too late." Bahlin's sister and father had both defected to the dark side of mythology, the first for love promised by the First Prince of the Fae and the second for power promised by the same. None of us had known they'd switched teams until that fateful night. Their mutual desertion had cost lives on both sides, and the mythological world was still reeling from the near miss of all-out war. Tarrek's supporters were still being identified and hunted down.

"Bahlin, do you think it would help to see someone?" I had hesitated to broach the topic for the last two days to ask but felt I needed to know.

He looked at me, confused, then his eyes became impossibly cold and his lips thinned into a hard line. "I do not need some bloody shrink helping me dissect my feelings about killing my da and sister, Maddy. I know *exactly* how I feel." Standing, he pushed his hands through his shoulder-length, mahogany hair and fisted it at the back of his neck. I knew he was pulling it tight enough to hurt but I didn't say anything to him about stopping. In fact, I didn't say anything at all.

He looked over at me, a range of emotions racing across his face. "I'm sorry, Maddy." Then he left the room before I could ask what he was apologizing for.

"Bahlin? Bay," I shouted. No answer. I tossed the covers off, intent on getting up, but every time I twisted my torso there was a terrible, burning pain in my stomach. I eased back down and angrily flipped the covers back over my legs. Grabbing the remote, I turned on the television just in time to partially catch a breaking news story.

"...body was found this morning in the park near her home, the victim of a violent and murderous assault. Experts believe she was attacked from behind and her throat cut as she walked home following an evening out with friends. Both friends and family say that Annie Mendhel was a well-liked young woman with plenty to look forward to at age twenty-eight."

"I just don't understand it," said a weeping man, identified in the caption as Annie's fiancé. "Everyone loved her. It has to be random," he sobbed, turning to a maternal-looking woman at his side. The screen flashed to a smiling, pre-mortem picture of the victim, and I felt a rush of prickly heat up and down my spine. She looked an awful lot like me—tall, brown-black hair cut short, pale skin—but her eyes were brown instead of green.

Of course, the killer wouldn't have known that in the dark when attacking from the back.

The park she'd been found at was right around the corner from the apartment. *Coincidence, Niteclif. Stop being overly dramatic. The whole world isn't out to get you. Besides, she was a mundane.*

I closed my eyes to offer up a quick prayer for her family and must have dozed in the process. It seemed like it had been ages since I'd had a solid night's sleep. I dreamt of a soft-voiced man rubbing my head and speaking to me, though what he said was unintelligible.

My private nurse, Clay, knocked on the doorframe before walking into the room. Clay had been hired to come in and help me mend, and I adored him for the easy friendship that had developed in the wake of the multiple tragedies. As ridiculously handsome as the rest of the dragons, Clay didn't treat me with the same creepy deference other members of his weyr and, to some extent, the rest of the supernatural world did. Instead, this charming, witty dragon had coaxed me into opening up to him by using humor, sarcasm and general good will whereas my only other visitor and housemate, Bahlin, had been terse, cranky and morose. I'd clung to the kindness Clay offered as some type of unspoken validation that Bahlin's steady decline wasn't my fault.

Clay checked my temperature and vitals, forced a little more pain medication down my protesting throat, and took a seat on the edge of the bed. "Where did Bahlin go?"

"Go? He left the room earlier but I had no idea he'd left the apartment."

"He waited for me in the hallway and asked me to stay here for a couple of hours while he ran some errands."

Ah, I thought, *the infamous "errands."* Bahlin spent more and more time running these unspecified errands every day. If I didn't know better, I'd imagine he was having some illicit affair. But the guy couldn't stand to be touched anymore, and wouldn't accept even easy and familiar affection. Instead I assumed he was driving aimlessly, finding whatever reasons he could to be out of the apartment and away from me. As Glaaca, or leader of the weyr, no one questioned him.

Bahlin had issued a leadership challenge before the decisively terminal fight with his father and had been elevated to the leadership position of Glaaca by default. Dragons have some strange rules, but this was one I could get behind because now no one could challenge Bahlin for the position of Glaaca for twelve months. I was afraid if anyone challenged him at this point, he'd simply let them have the weyr. Not so big a deal, except most weyr coups were not staged as passive takeovers.

I sat up in bed, groaning softly at the heavy discomfort in my belly. My bruises had started to fade to that sickly greenish-yellow around the edges, though I wouldn't have called it a visual improvement. The hex mark over my heart was still black and blistered, and no amount of healing energy had been able to resolve it. I gently shifted my legs off the side of the bed and let them hang while I got my bearings. I was a little dizzy, probably a little dehydrated, and definitely a lot confused. Clay approached me and held out his hands.

"Bathroom break?" he asked.

"Yeah."

He helped me up and I shuffled to the bathroom, holding onto his forearms fiercely in an effort to stay vertical. We made it to the bathroom, and Clay pulled my pants down before helping me sit on the toilet. I blushed slightly. Humiliation has neither boundaries nor limits for the physically sick or broken.

"I'll be right outside," Clay murmured, pulling the door shut behind him.

I sat there, not so much for relief as for the few private minutes I could steal.

What's going on with Bahlin? I wondered. Obviously he'd killed his father and sister, and now he felt guilty about everything. But why would that drive him out of the flat? There was only one answer, and it wasn't "why" but rather "who": me. *And you're supposedly some super sleuth?* I snorted then bit my lip at the pain caused by clenching my abdominal muscles.

It wasn't so farfetched to assume Bahlin might regret choosing me over his family. That would leave him stuck in an engagement he probably didn't want to honor. My heart sank and I shuddered, moaning softly at the pain in my stomach. I nearly choked on the lump of emotion caught in the back of my throat. If this was true, it complicated things. Regardless, I didn't like feeling stuck here, in Bahlin's apartment, with nowhere else to go.

What about the room at the hotel? I wondered, letting the thought coalesce.

Okay, I could go to the hotel. There was my out. I'd just put a little space between us and see how things played out. But first I had to get my pants back up.

Clay helped me back to the bedroom, then went to grab me a bottle of water from the kitchen. I began to slowly gather some of my belongings that were scattered like the leaves of fall around the room: bits here and there, no real logic to their placement, they'd just stayed where they'd landed. I found a pair of socks on the nightstand, a book on the chair, jeans on top of the dresser, and a bra at the foot of the bed. I'm such a slob.

I stuffed my meager belongings into the trusty messenger bag that had followed me all over England and Scotland, and I shuffled back to the bedroom door.

"Hey," Clay exclaimed when he saw me in the doorway. "You're not supposed to be up. What gives?"

"I need to get out of here, Clay. Now."

He scanned the room, his eyes shifting to the familiar icy blue that Bahlin's turned pre-shift. He scented the air. "There's no one here.

What's the rush?"

"Just trust me on this. I want you to take me to the Pemberton and get me back to my room."

"Sure. But you know I've got to ask, Maddy. Why?"

I looked at me feet, unsure how much of my and Bahlin's angst to reveal. "It's really private, okay? I'll consider it an enormous personal favor if you just get me there."

He snapped a mock salute and said, "Aye aye, ma'am."

Despite it all, I couldn't stop the small smile that tugged at one corner of my mouth, and he grinned in return.

He grabbed my meager belongings and offered me his arm for support. Clinging to him, I ignored the beads of sweat popping out at my hairline. I wasn't going to let pain get the better of me. After all, big girls don't cry.

Chapter Two

The trip by car was a bitch. Every bump seemed to make my liver wobble, and I thought my spleen was going to rupture from the tightening and releasing of the seatbelt. It was miserable.

Pulling up under the *port cochère*, I recognized the valet and smiled at him. He did a double-take at my present condition but said nothing about the cuts and bruises decorating my topography. I made it through the lobby with the predictable stares and behind-the-hand whispers, grateful to reach the bench in the elevator car. Rapid movement caught my eye as I turned, and I swore I saw a familiar face in the crowd—long hair, androgynous build, pixie-like face. Definitely fae, but he—or she—was gone too fast for me to be sure I recognized him. We rode up to the twenty-second floor and Clay helped me into the room. I still thought it was too lavish, with its electric fireplace, bedroom-bathroom combo located behind leaded glass French doors that separated it from the living area and the million-dollar view of Big Ben and the Thames, but Bahlin had insisted. I wasn't proud I had, predictably, caved to his wishes.

Stripping to my T-shirt and underwear with Clay's help, I crawled into bed and was grateful for the man's medical indifference to my state of undress.

He settled the covers carefully around me. "Need anything else for the moment?"

"No, I—" The phone rang, interrupting me.

Clay reached over and answered, and his side of the conversation was made up of mostly grunts and "uh-huhs" and finally a "see you in a minute."

"Who was that?"

Clay looked at me, face studiously blank. "You have a delivery at the front desk. Are you expecting anything?"

The skin on the back of my neck crawled, and I shook my head slightly in the negative. I was back to what was becoming my standby line: "No one knows I'm here."

"Obviously *someone* knows." Clay pulled a Walther PPK semi-automatic handgun out of the waistband of his jeans and checked the chamber. "It's loaded," he said, handing the gun over butt first. "Don't hesitate to shoot if anyone other than me comes through that door."

I had a flashback to my time in the fae's sithen when Bahlin had offered almost the exact same advice. My lips twitched with a smile. "Aye, aye," I said, giving him the same answer he'd given me.

"Smart ass," he mumbled, turning away, but not before I caught the grin on his face.

Clay's departure marked the first time I'd truly been alone in days, bathroom breaks notwithstanding. I closed my eyes and reveled in the small sounds that infect silence so gently it's never really truly quiet: the drip of the faucet, the clicking of the thermostat, the hum of the heater, the distant sounds of traffic, the murmur of voices in the hallway. None of the sounds was threatening, and they kept me from feeling lonely.

My traitorous mind shifted back to Bahlin. I was both angry and hurt. The distance between us seemed self-explanatory now, and I felt incredibly foolish for not having seen it earlier. I didn't know how to help him heal, and it felt like our disconnect could become a permanent thing if I pushed him at all. I hated feeling so ineffectual.

The electronic lock *hummed,* and I shifted slightly so the gun was hidden in the bedding, only to relax after Clay called out. My eyes nearly bugged out of my head when he walked around the corner carrying what had to be two dozen red roses in a cut crystal vase.

"You weren't expecting these?" he asked skeptically.

"I have no idea who they're from, so there's no way I could have expected them, Clay."

He set the vase down on the dresser and pulled the card out from the small holder nestled deep in the arrangement. He looked at it carefully before walking it over to me.

I took it from him and opened the sealed envelope, carefully extracting the card. The little I'd learned of magic had made me leery of such unexpected events. A lock of hair fell out of the envelope. I lifted it and thought with a sickening feeling that it was the same color as my own hair. The card read:

19

My dearest Maddy,

A typical mundane's casket blanket has 144 roses. Here are your first 24. Be sure to lock your windows, love. You're beautiful when you sleep.

I dropped the card and began feeling all over my head. It only took a second to find the small area at my temple where my hair was shorter than normal. He'd cut my hair as I slept. *Holy shit.*

Clay watched me carefully, taking in the signs of panic undoubtedly crossing my face. "Want to tell me who sent the flowers?"

I held the card out to him with a steady hand. Bully for me. I leaned back against the pillows and shut my eyes, my breath raspy and my heart tripping double-time in my chest.

Clay read the card and grasped my chin, turning it to look at the small area of shorn hair. Letting out a low string of curses, he dropped the card on the bed and grabbed the hair from my open palm. He sniffed it, eyes closed, before turning to put it in the discarded envelope.

"I don't know what the hell is going on with you and Bahlin, but I have to call him, Maddy."

"No!"

"Yes. No discussion."

"Screw you, cinder breath. I'm not dragging him into this just because you feel the need to play pigeon. No."

He pulled his cell phone out of his pocket and began dialing. "If you can stop me, crip, bring it on. Otherwise? Sit back and shut up."

What the hell had happened to my mild-mannered nurse?

"Listen, you sorry son of a—"

"Bahlin? We've got a situation." He turned away from my squinty-eyed glare and listened to the response. I could hear yelling. "No, man, I know I shouldn't have let her weasel me into taking her out." More yelling. "We're at your hotel—" Silence. Clay flipped his phone shut and turned to me, eyes flashing that otherworldly blue. "If you get my ass kicked over this, woman, you and I are going to have problems."

I just laughed. "What are you going to do to me that hasn't already been done in the last three weeks?"

He grimaced.

"Come on, Clay. You like me and you know it."

He shrugged. "So? That's not news. This," he said, waving a hand toward the flowers, "is. He's pissed, Maddy."

I was certain it would only get worse when he saw the card and the flowers. And the shorn lock of hair? I didn't even want to think about it. But no matter how angry Bahlin was, I didn't think he'd wish death on me. That was a little extreme. "He'll get over it," I said, distance between me and the enraged dragon enhancing my bravery.

"Tough talk for someone who can't take a piss on her own." He smirked, and I flipped him off.

Asshat. What's worse was he was right.

Bahlin showed up a half hour later, the door slamming open without warning. I jumped and groaned at the pain brought on by the reactionary movement. Clay flew to his feet ready to defend me until he figured out who it was. Then I was on my own.

"Glaaca," he said, making a slight bow. "Should I stay?"

"Wait in the hall," Bahlin growled, his voice deeper than normal. This was more life than he'd shown since the big fight.

Clay went outside and pulled the door shut behind him with a decided *click* as the latch and lock reset.

"What's the meaning of you leaving the apartment?" Bahlin demanded, shoving his hands in his pockets and pacing back and forth at the end of the bed. The flowers on the dresser stood like a bright red beacon, and he stopped in front of them, brow furrowed as he took them in.

I chewed over the words to say, to explain why I'd left, but he took my silence as something else entirely.

"You've no answer for me, Maddy? All right then. Care to tell me who's sending you flowers?"

I sighed, hand slipping to cradle my side at the discomfort. "It's not what it looks like, Bahlin. I left because, well, I thought it might make it easier."

"Easier to what?" He gestured at the flowers and shook his head, a miserable smile pulling at the corners of his lips. "Move on?"

"Move on," I repeated stupidly. "Look, Bay—" He never gave me a chance to finish my thought.

"So you'll admit this—leaving the apartment, the flowers—is about moving on." He turned to glare at me. "With all that's happened, this is probably for the best."

I stared at him, dumbfounded. "With all that's happened *what's* for the best?" I croaked out, confusion settling over me like a veil.

"Seeing as it's obvious you aren't clear on how you feel about me, and now I'm in a similar situation, I think it's best that we call off the engagement." He looked pained but resolute. He turned and stalked toward the door. "It's over, Maddy."

I just sat there for a long moment. *Huh?* "Bahlin, wait." The implication of his words sank in slowly. I tried to stand and just barely made it, but I couldn't get my bearings to go after him, to force him to listen to me. "Don't leave me alone!" I yelled, ignoring the pleading in my voice.

He never slowed down and he never looked back. Yanking the door open, he said something to Clay before disappearing.

The other dragon hadn't even made it back inside the room before my scream of frustration tore through the air. Grabbing for the bed, I pulled the covers to the floor as I collapsed. I lay there, the nylon carpet rejecting my tears so they formed a small pool at my temple. Clay tried to get me up off the floor, but I swung out at him, clipping his jaw.

"Leave," I croaked, gathering the fallen sheet below my chin. "Just leave."

He backed out through the bedroom doors, pulling them closed behind him. As they were about to latch he said, "I'll be right here, Maddy. I'm not going anywhere."

I lay there for hours, unaware of anything but those small sounds of silence which were no longer comforting but instead were just ambient noise. I counted the stripes on the bed skirt, let my fingers trace the knobby hem of the sheet and contemplated the presence of dust bunnies under the bed. I tried to think of anything except Bahlin. Sadly I wasn't even remotely successful. Despite my initial distrust of fairytales and the concept of one true love, Bahlin had spent all of our time together coercing me into believing in happily-ever-after despite life's long odds and the damnable prophecy. But his efforts appeared to have been pointless. It was ironic that, for all he espoused believing in us, he was the one to walk away from the commitment.

Maybe you were you just in love with the idea of being in love,

Niteclif. Otherwise how could you claim to truly love each other and then both accept it's over so easily? There were no easy answers.

I pulled more covers off the bed and burrowed into them there on the floor, propping my head on my folded arm. There was no noise from the living area but I suspected Clay was still there. He'd only pulled the French doors shut to let me have a private rage then cry. He was a good man and an even better friend.

The sun had begun to set before he opened the doors and came in with more pain medication. I shook my head, but he continued toward me.

"You've got to take it, Maddy." He held the bottle out like a shield.

"No one's paying you anymore, so you don't have to stay," I croaked, my throat raw.

"This isn't about payment, sweets. It's about right and wrong. You need someone with you right now." Setting the bottle on the bedside table, Clay gently scooped me up, covers and all, and deposited me back on the bed.

I pushed myself to sitting, and Clay adjusted the multitude of pillows behind my back.

"But, Clay—"

"If it bothers you that badly, I'll tell you Bahlin's still paying me."

"What? Why? I don't need his pity," I snapped, my eyes daring him to argue with me.

"It's nothing to do with pity, Maddy. It's because you're the Niteclif."

Okay. That was an infallible argument. "Oh yeah. The High Council." It figured it wasn't personal. This was business. Had the whole relationship been a farce? Just business?

He got what he wanted from you, Niteclif—power. What did you *get?*

Clay interrupted my thought process just before it got really ugly. "Look, Maddy, if you repeat what I'm about to say, I'll deny it then fry you like a crisp first opportunity I get." He stared me down and I nodded slowly. "Bahlin loves you, and he's made a huge mistake today. I think he believes that by punishing himself he's atoning for, particularly, the sin of patricide."

"That makes no sense. He'd challenged his dad for the position of Glaaca and would have killed him anyway."

"Not necessarily." Clay handed me the bottle and, without thinking, I took a swig, grimacing at the sickly sweet, artificial cherry flavor of the syrup. "He could have let his dad live and just forced him out of the weyr. Winner's choice."

"Wouldn't that have been just as bad?"

"Sure, but it allows room for reconciliation, doesn't it? He could have, probably *would* have, reintroduced his da to the weyr at some point. Whereas death is just death, and there's no undoing it." Clay sighed, set the bottle on the nightstand and motioned for me to scoot over.

I did, curious, and could only gape at him when he stripped to his plaid boxers and slid under the covers with me.

"Don't look so shocked, Maddy. I'm tired, this is the only bed, and I'm not leaving you alone any more than I'm sleeping in my jeans. I promise you, though, that I'll keep my hands to myself. You look a bit, uh, *haggard* today." He snuggled down under the covers and closed his eyes.

The pull of the narcotics was stronger than my disbelief at Clay's actions, so I lay down beside him and turned on my side, giving him my back.

"Rest well, Maddy," he said softly just as I felt him begin to gently stroke my head.

Sleep pulled me under so quickly there wasn't time to answer.

I woke up comfortably warm. The sunlight shone softly through the window, a kaleidoscope of rainbow patterns shining through the cut glass of the French doors. I could see small patches of blue sky beyond the curtains that had remained open through the night. Realizing I'd slept all night, I did a mental celebratory shimmy. I snuggled under the covers, and a strong arm tightened around me.

Bahlin.

But he didn't smell right.

Uh oh. Not Bahlin.

I rolled my eyes up and found Clay still sleeping. At some point we'd wound ourselves together like lovers. I put my hand on his ribs and pushed back a little, and he slowly opened his soft brown eyes, looking down at me. He closed the distance I'd created and dipped his head in one swift motion. Our lips met, his soft and persistent as they

Wrath

moved slowly back and forth over mine, coaxing. He nipped at my lower lip and I pulled farther back, confused but not angry.

What the hell was it with me? I'd spent my entire life in relative anonymity but once I entered the supernatural world, everyone wanted a piece? Gaah.

"Clay, you need to back off, buddy," I murmured into his lips. He didn't stop. "I mean it, Clay."

He tilted his head back, his dark eyes assessing my intent.

"Don't try me on this, Clay. Move back. Now."

I could tell the moment Clay fully came awake and realized what he'd been doing because surprise darted across his face like a fast-moving comet. He'd started to move away when he was ripped out of bed, arms and legs flailing for purchase.

"The lady said to move the fuck back," Hellion said, throwing Clay to the floor. Hellion stood beside the bed, his face mottled with rage, his flat black eyes like unpolished chips of obsidian beneath sculpted brows. This ruggedly handsome face had scared me shitless more than once, and today was sadly no different. He was still huge, still well muscled and still scary, but somehow with his rage turned on someone else he seemed less menacing despite the two-dozen roses decorating my dresser. What settled uncomfortably over me was that same inexplicable feeling of familiarity I had every time I looked at him.

"Wait. You openly threaten me less than a month ago and you're here to kill me, but you're going to protect my honor before acting on that threat?" Disbelief colored my tone. The only weapon I had at hand was sarcasm, and I'd be damned if I wasn't going to wield it. Of course, swinging it about with wild abandon probably wasn't wise.

Clay jumped up, his eyes flashing as he turned to face Hellion. He leaned forward on the balls of his feet, muscles trembling and fists clenched, his fury tightly—but barely—controlled. "Leave the woman alone," he hissed, his voice guttural and deep.

Hellion wandered casually over to the flowers, effectively putting distance between himself and Clay before dismissing the younger man. "You won't shift in the room. It's too small to contain your dragon form. And you can't take me hand-to-hand, no matter what you think, so stand down, boy." Clay glowered as Hellion turned to me. "Actually, I came to see if the news reports were true and our newest Niteclif was, indeed, dead by near decapitation." He let his eyes roam over me with open insolence. "Obviously, the newsmen have reported in haste. At least you're alive to enjoy your gift. Do you like them?" He reached out with his massive hand and snatched up a rose, crushing it and letting the destroyed petals fall to the floor before turning to me for my answer.

"Frankly? It's damned creepy. Look, is there something I can do for you? You had the perfect opportunity to kill both of us but you didn't. Why are you here?" I challenged. Okay, it was admittedly more like I asked him firmly. After all, it's hard to really challenge anyone while you're so bruised you look like an eggplant and you're sitting in bed wearing nothing more than a T-shirt and underwear.

Hellion took a quick step toward the bed, but Clay moved toward him at the same time.

"Back off, lizard boy," Hellion snarled in his low baritone.

Clay growled deep in his chest but paused to look at me before jumping the other man. There was something to be said for those who respected leadership, no matter how poor it was. I figured I'd take what I could get. Shrugging, I shook my head, and Clay went back to watching Hellion closely.

Hellion looked at me, his eyes carefully assessing. "How hurt are you?"

I thought about how to answer. I was definitely too hurt to defend myself against him. "I suppose hurt enough isn't a sufficient answer?"

"Can you walk?"

Huh. "Yes, but I still need someone to help me when I first stand."

"Works for me." He lunged for the bed. Too fast for Clay, he had his hands on my throat before the dragon could get to me. Our skin touched without interference.

My ears popped and the world went black before immense pressure everywhere pushed my skin into my bones. I screamed, but the sound seemed restricted to the inside of my head. I was suspended in space and time, Hellion in front of me with his hands wrapped tightly around my throat. We hung there like abandoned marionettes.

"Odin," Hellion whispered, his eyes going wide and glazing with shock.

Immobile, I had no way to know what was behind me. All I could do was listen.

A smooth, deep voice filled the void. "The prophecy foretells a love of the ages between the Niteclif and an unnamed man."

No, no, no. Not this. Not now, I screamed wordlessly.

"I hereby name that man. Hellion, son of Markalon, you are destined to love this woman, to serve her well, and to fight for her in every sense. You will cherish her above all else, and—"

No!

Hellion looked pained, and he closed his eyes.

"—she will love you as she has loved no other."

Chapter Three

I felt a shift, and Hellion's arms came around me just before I was blinded by a flash of light. I shrieked and reached up to cover my eyes.

"It's over, Madeleine," Hellion whispered into my ear. "We're here." His arms were around me, his front pressed to my back, and for all the sense it made it felt like he was cradling me as we lay on the floor.

I was breathing hard and shaking like a flag in the wind, great, wracking tremors that hurt. I grabbed my stomach and retched. Hellion tightened his hold and put one hand to my forehead. The nausea eased with his touch though the pain in my stomach was fierce.

"Please," I whispered in agony, "please let go of my stomach."

He dropped his hand quickly and I rolled away, coming to rest on my side on the carpeted floor. I lay on the floor, eyes closed. *It can't be Hellion.* Desperation pushed my fight-or-flight response into overdrive but I was too hurt to do anything about it. *It can't be Hellion.* I opened my eyes slowly, my heart thundering in my ears and my breath coming short. I lay there shocked and scared, even if I only admitted the latter to myself. Apparently a divine prophecy had been rendered on us when we had touched each other. *It can't be Hellion.* Now the man who had demanded my life as preferred coin for repayment had me at his mercy, and I had no way to call for help. *Why did the room look—*I blinked out for a minute and when I opened my eyes I was lying on a bed that looked very similar to the one I'd left in my room only minutes ago. I shifted to adjust the covers to my waist while Hellion took the seat nearest the door. "Where exactly are we?"

"About four floors up from your hotel room. They'll never think to look for you here." Hellion's eyes were closed and he was shaking his head, his face devoid of any emotion. Apparently he was confident that I wouldn't—or couldn't—attack him, the smug bastard. I had to give him this, though—his plan was really a product of pure genius. No one would consider checking the hotel when the search for my now missing person began, and I couldn't exactly dial zero for assistance. Personal history what it was, I thought it safe to assume that the concierge service wouldn't cover this type of dilemma anyway.

"This changes everything." Hellion ground the words out, his voice tight with some unidentifiable emotion.

"I'll say," I muttered. I dug around in my battered heart and there, there was what I feared. I looked at Hellion and I *felt* different. The confusion I'd experienced upon meeting him increased by a thousand fold. But truth was truth. I still experienced that undeniable feeling of familiarity, now adding comfort to the mix, despite having spoken to him on less than half a dozen occasions. Terrified, I pulled the covers tighter around my hips.

Hellion gently banged his head against the wall. "Fuck." He ran his hands through his pelt of hair, pulling it from his face harshly. In relief, his bone structure was almost too perfect, his face almost too handsome. "How in Odin's name... I mean, seriously, what am I... Shit!" he bellowed, launching himself out of the chair and spinning to punch the wall. The drywall buckled under the pressure of his fist, and small red dots marked the places his knuckles had split on impact. Breathing hard, he turned and sat down again, this time seeming more composed. He laid his head back against the sheetrock, and I watched with dispassionate interest as his little movements dislodged dust and debris so that it drifted down into his hair. His eyes were closed, his face drawn tight. "I suppose the one consolation I have is that life with you will never be boring."

"So you're just going to accept whatever this Odin guy says?"

Hellion opened his eyes and sat up, his movements stiff. "'This Odin guy' is the head of my pantheon, Niteclif. He's my Alpha, the one the greatest holidays center around, the one my prayers are issued to, my divinity."

All the hair on my body stood up. *Odin.* "I get it," I whispered. "Who is Tyr to you?"

"He's the god of justice. Why?"

"I guess you should know he's my many times removed great-grandfather and my Niteclif mentor."

"Bullshit," Hellion snapped.

I gaped at him, then fury took over. "Look, you cauldron-sniffing, branch-waving, mumbo-jumbo-spouting man-witch! I don't lie! So you can just take your attitude and shove—"

He laughed and his face seemed to relax some. "I get it, I get it. Nice imagery too. So Tyr is really your ancestor? Very cool." Then his face went back to its cold mask. It was like he didn't know whether to talk to me or threaten me. "I have some questions to ask, Madeleine, and I need you to answer me honestly."

I sighed and snuggled down under the covers. Looked like I'd be here for a while because there was no possible way I could fight my way past him to get to the door. "Ask away, and if I can, I'll answer you," I said, the picture of nonchalance as I snuggled down under my nest of blankets. That's me, the Goose Down Badass.

"I'm sure you're curious—" he began and I immediately interrupted him.

"Furious is more like it," I snarked, not even remotely sure how he'd intended to finish his sentence.

"I'll ask you one time, Madeleine, to keep your voice civil or I will silence you. Understand that I don't make idle threats."

"Please, go on," I said through clenched teeth as I wadded the sheet in my fists, out of his site.

"Tell me what happened with Gretta."

I sighed to myself before answering. "Hellion, I swear to you I didn't get a chance to issue a formal challenge of any type that would have made the killing sanctioned or whatever. I was busy defending myself from her seriously spunky, sword-swinging self. For your sake, I'm sorry I killed her. But it was her or me, and I was intent on it being me."

Leaning back, Hellion crossed his hands over his stomach and laced his fingers together. His hands were clenched together so tightly they pulled the skin harshly over bone, making the skin white there and mottled elsewhere with forced circulation. Looking closer I could see his pounding pulse visible just beneath the skin of his throat. He tapped his foot softly.

"Tell me why you don't believe me when I tell you I had no choice but to defend myself from her attack," I said before realizing how harsh I sounded. "Please. I mean, *please* tell me—"

"I know what you meant." He bit the words out, looking around the room, focusing on anything but me, before answering me. "I know you didn't kill Gretta unjustly," he whispered.

I think I sucked all the air out of the room. "You do?" I whispered back.

He closed his eyes and nodded, and I wondered if he was going to dislocate his fingers, he was pulling on them so hard. "I do. I know now, anyway. Odin's made several things very clear." He actually tugged at his collar before he said, "You should know Gretta was having an affair with Tarrek."

I was silently shocked, amazed at how many women Tarrek had lured into his web of lies and deception, as well as his bed: Gretta, Hellion's mate; Imeena, High Council vampire; Brylanna, Bahlin's sister and the daughter of the Blue Weyr's Glaaca. And he'd tried with me. "How do you know she was, um, *seeing* Tarrek?"

"I appreciate your delicate handling of the discussion, but there's no need. I found the e-mails she exchanged with him."

I looked down quickly to hide my reaction. One of if not the most powerful wizards in the known world had resorted to simple technology to track his partner's clandestine behaviors.

Irony, you have a wicked sense of play.

I did my best to mask the inappropriate amusement on my face when I looked up but it didn't matter. Hellion wasn't paying me any attention.

He'd slid down and tipped his head back to rest on the chair, eyes shut tight. He must have felt me looking at him because he slowly opened his eyes and sat up to face me, squaring his shoulders and taking a deep, shuddering breath.

"What?" I demanded. My mind flashed back to the news story from earlier this morning and the murdered girl who looked so much like me. "Hellion, in my official capacity as Niteclif, I have to ask you something."

"Go ahead. I figured you'd get there eventually, particularly because I showed up in your hotel room right after the murder was reported." He shook his head and said, "The picture they flashed on the news this morning *did* look very much like you. I held out hope that it wouldn't come to your death at my hand, but..."

"You did? She did. Why were you watching the mundane news? Wait. But what?"

"Do you really expect me to make sense of that gibberish? Great Odin, Madeleine, the Council was under the impression you were at least remotely intelligent," Hellion spat out, shifting in his chair to cross an ankle over his knee. His total disregard for me as any type of threat stung.

"Screw. You." I tried to get up and he sighed, leaned forward and pushed me back down. I gasped and grabbed my abdomen.

"I thought you weren't that hurt," he said, his gaze considering.

"Forget it. You're not changing the subject. Did you kill—"

"I didn't kill the girl. Why would I wield a knife when I have much more creative ways to kill? As for the mundane news, I watch it because I have a variety of investments in the mundane world, not unlike many inhabitants of the mythological and paranormal worlds you now inhabit. Where do you think we get our money?"

"You're really a little creepy, you know that?"

He smiled faintly. "If I'm only a little creepy I suppose I'll have to try harder."

"Funny guy," I muttered. "You'll give me your oath you didn't kill the girl?"

He looked at me long and hard, and just as I was about to insist he answer me, he volunteered, "I give you my solemn oath that I am innocent of this crime."

"I'll have to look in to it when I get up in a couple of days. Understand that."

Hellion nodded then stood, walked to the in-room vanity and filled a glass with water. Carrying it to the bedside table, he set it down and took a seat on the edge of the bed, twisting to face me.

The hair on the back of my neck stood up, and I inched further away from him, unconsciously seeking distance. Something was wrong—very, very wrong.

"About the prophecy..." He reached out and traced a cold finger down my cheek.

I flinched and he dropped his hand, my mind racing as I watched him carefully. The prophecy had foretold that I would bring into power the first male to take me to bed. The price of that power was that he would be cursed to truly love me, but I would love another. The first had been Bahlin.

"No." I shook my head rapidly. "I can't, Hellion." Shock and gut-wrenching grief gripped me. "I won't betray Bahlin."

"He's left you, Maddy. Love or no love, he's ended the engagement."

"How do you know?" I whispered harshly, never taking my eyes from his. "You can't know, not for sure."

"I'm relatively certain you're no longer tied to Bahlin because Clay was in bed with you. He never would have risked his Glaaca's rage if the engagement stood."

I blanched and Hellion sighed, standing and walking to the window to pull the curtains tighter.

"As much as it infuriates me, we are predestined to love, Madeleine. Ours is to be a love of the ages. I was there for the original delivery of the prophecy by the limnae."

I just stared at him, mouth slightly agape, until he walked over to me and gently lifted my jaw.

I jerked away and snapped my jaws together with an audible *click*. I stood slowly, still in my T-shirt and underwear. I was embarrassed, but it seemed worse somehow to have this conversation while lying in bed with him.

He offered me the glass of water, and I shook my head. "My choices aren't made yet, Hellion. No prophecy can foretell every choice, and mine *aren't made,"* I yelled. I gasped and clutched my stomach but managed, just barely, to stay standing under my own power.

He rose and walked toward me, his magic only loosely reined in. I'd forgotten his edict to not yell but he'd have to kiss my brass balls on this one. He stopped in front of me and I looked up, forgetting he was as tall as Bahlin. He gently clasped my jaw in his hand and murmured a few words. *Latin maybe?* I wondered, though his voice was too low to be sure. My throat tickled and before I could ask, he bent forward ever so slowly, pulling me into his embrace as he went, until he was wound around me. Then, and only then, did he begin to lower his head to mine, his eyes focused on my lips.

Up close I realized what a perfect set of lips Hellion had—soft and full on the bottom, sculpted and firm on the top. He brushed his lips over mine tentatively. The chemistry between us was dynamic, and I gasped into his mouth as his lips touched mine. We fit together perfectly, his firm lips over my soft ones, our hips brushing against each other and our thighs intertwining so we were vertically melded together. He raised his head from mine and looked so serious, so sad, and in that moment I inexplicably wanted more than anything to make his hurts go away.

I leaned forward and wrapped my arms around his neck, pulling him back to my face. He gave over, bending toward me again, and we met in the middle, our kiss unhurried and fragile as few kisses ever are—the first kiss, the last kiss, and a truly healing kiss are the only ones that have ever fit the bill for me. This first real kiss was everything it should have been, with the exception of the fact that I wasn't in love with Hellion.

"*Yet,*" Odin whispered through my mind unbidden, and I turned a deaf ear. My choices weren't made.

Hellion broke away, turning from me in one harsh movement that left me wobbly and reaching for support. I collapsed onto the edge of the bed. He waved a hand over his shoulder and said something that sounded like *edictum vox vocis,* and my throat burned for a moment.

"What the hell did you just do?" I croaked, massaging my throat.

"I gave you your voice back. That spell would have lasted indefinitely so don't bitch and make me regret my decision already," he said through gritted teeth. His shoulders were rigid and a fine tremor passed down his arms.

"I—"

"I mean it, Niteclif. Don't push me on this." He stalked back to the room's chair and sat down, dropping his head in his hands. "I can't," he whispered beseechingly. "Anything but this, Odin. *Anything.*" He shook his head slowly back and forth, anger and despair warring for prominence on his partially hidden features. "It would have been so much easier if it the news had been right this morning."

I wasn't sure what to say that wouldn't come out as simply "fuck off," so I sat there, silent, grinding my teeth and twisting little pieces of hair around my fingers.

Hellion finally looked up. His eyes were a flat, cold black again. "What?"

"What do you want me to say?" I always seem to resort to the most direct honesty when cornered. "I can't hope for your sake that tomorrow's outcome is more favorable for you."

He stared and me and then dropped his head and snorted, his laughter brief but superficially sincere. "No, I don't suppose you can."

"And just because she looked like me doesn't mean I was the intended victim. I mean, seriously, who wants me dead?" I was massaging my throat when he lifted his head.

"You aren't serious?" He stared at me in open disbelief. "Great gods above, you are. Madeleine, there is a list of people who likely want to see you dead, some of whom I'm quite sure would see to it themselves given half the chance."

My hand froze at my throat. "Who?" My voice drifted out on a single note.

"First, I'd have to assume Tarrek's parents are at the front of the line. Their motives would be understandable but royalty doesn't carry out their own dirty work. Remaining members of the fae, royalty or not, see you as a seductress and murderer and could come for you in any form at any time. Any of Tarrek's remaining lovers, particularly the vampire Imeena, would gladly see you taken out, just as Gretta tried to do, for revenge. Females of the blue weyr resent you—hell, any of the female dragons of *any* weyr resent you—for taking the Glaaca out of the dating pool. They seem to believe that with you out of the way they stand a chance with Bahlin. Smaller sub-groups believe you're in league with the larger groups in plotting their demise because you've already sided with the dragons. The Atlanteans will be interested in your preservation until Bahlin's godmother Sarenia finds out you've broken his heart, then your survival will be of less interest to them. I think the only group you're safe from is the witches and wizards, but many of them are employed by the other groups. So while they may not want you dead personally—yet—they may be paid to carry out your execution." He stood and shoved his hands in his pockets, looking at the wall over my shoulder instead of facing me directly. "Are you really so naïve?"

I must have turned green because he stepped toward the bed and I cringed, gasping at the pain it brought in my stomach and chest. He came forward more slowly, laid a hand on my forehead, and the nausea passed even though the pain stayed. Oh, and the terror. It *definitely* stayed.

"You really are green, aren't you? And in more ways than just your complexion," he teased.

I flipped him off and rolled onto my side, panting. "Either kill me or get the hell away from me, Hellion." I hurt so badly that, at that very moment, I think I favored death as the more humane option.

"You're going to need Bahlin's help to survive this political shitstorm and come out alive," Hellion murmured. "I suppose I can be of some assistance—"

I interrupted him without apology "Why bother? If my death is what you were really after, seems you can simply hang out and wait for one of the other groups to step forward and swing the blade."

"Because... Well, because I'm apparently the third part of the prophecy, Madeleine."

"Just Maddy, Hellion. You know I prefer it, so cut it out."

"I wish I'd never unblocked your vocal cords." He began pacing back and forth at the foot of the bed. "We're destined to experience an epic love story, Maddy." He emphasized my name and looked over at me, quirking a brow. I nodded in acknowledgment and he went on. "Odin has spoken, and I won't defy the head of my pantheon, so I must believe it's true. I may not like it, but destiny is destiny. Besides, I know you felt what I felt when we kissed." He stopped and turned toward me, and he smiled, truly smiled, for the first time. It was like the scary Hellion melted away and was replaced by a Greek sun god. He was bright and warm, and all I could do was stare. The removal of the worry lines, the softening of the black of his eyes and the emphasis of the sooty lashes surrounding them, the shape of his lips, the square of his jaw—it all worked together, and he was suddenly physically remarkable. I reached out to him, compelled to trace these inexplicable changes, and he came willingly to my hand. I looked on him in wonder and he laughed, a rich-bodied sound that made me smile in response. He leaned in to me and kissed me gently. My heart tripped painfully in my chest.

He sat back, the small smile still playing at his lips. "It hasn't ever been like that for me, not even with Gretta. It's never felt so, well, so perfect."

"Not knowing exactly what you felt, I can't answer that. I *will* tell you I've always been cautious by nature, and Bahlin's dumping me has only made me more so. The word of a god just pisses me off as a reason, so don't use it." I laid my hand on his heart; he automatically mirrored the gesture. Neither organ was behaving rationally but instead the two were pounding out similar staccato rhythms. He smiled down at me and I continued. "I also won't lie to you and say I felt, or feel, nothing. I feel something very intense and it scares me. My very short, very volatile engagement only ended hours ago, and here you want to talk about long-term commitment, not because you love me but because someone told you to. It doesn't fly for me. I'm bound to Bahlin as a detective's partner for twelve years. That's a long time to be stuck with someone who hates you, so I need to sort this out. I won't get involved with someone who dislikes me equally as much and commit my life, however long—or short—it may be, to him because his god says it's supposed to be so." I dropped my hand and sat back.

"I understand, Madeleine." Hellion bent his face to mine and kissed me gently, leaning into me and overwhelming my senses all over again.

I sighed into his mouth and settled into his embrace. He hugged me and I grunted a little.

"I'm so selfish sometimes. I can heal most of this. Lie down on the bed," he said, stripping off his shirt so he was wearing only the black slacks and boots.

Whoa, baby.

The man was built beautifully when he was in his shirt, but out of it? He was a visual orgasm. More muscular than Bahlin, he wasn't muscle-bound but rather seriously ripped. There wasn't a stray hair anywhere on his chest and only the thinnest stripe from his bellybutton running into his trousers.

He caught me looking and I blushed. He didn't laugh but came over to my side of the bed and knelt on the floor beside me. Taking my hand, he kissed each knuckle "May this body please you in any way you see fit to use it, Madeleine Niteclif, be it for sword arm, shield arm, lance, magic, or love." He looked stunned at his own words. He scrubbed his hands over his face and muttered an unintelligible oath before getting back to business.

I pushed myself to sitting, grimacing with the movement and ignoring the unexpected oath of devotion. "What are you going to do, Hellion? Bahlin's tried, and the fae healer did a little, but nothing's finished the process."

"Oh, I'll do a bit of this and a bit of that." He cracked his knuckles and eased me back onto the bed so I was lying flat. He lifted my shirt up so my stomach was bared. He pulled a small dirk from his boot top and, without pausing, sliced his palm open. I gasped. "Shh, you'll distract me." He took the knife and laid it across my stomach so it pointed north to south, then he began to drip blood around the knife. He scrubbed the wound to keep it open and, when he had enough blood gathered, he began to trace runes onto my skin, using the blood as paint. The patterns were impossible to discern. The one thing I could say with certainty was that they were interconnected. He got to the last rune at due north, and he said, "This is it, Madeleine. Do you

37

want me to take your voice? This is going to hurt, and I can't have you scream."

I nodded, and he did the same thing as earlier, leaving me with a scratchy throat. He finished the last line in the rune, and my stomach lit up, the runes blazing gold and red. Black smoke seeped from around the knife and seemed to come from my skin. I screamed but it was nothing more than a hiss of air. The sheer pain was ripped straight from my gut. I cried and I thrashed, but Hellion held me immobile, pressing down on the hilt of the knife with one hand and laying his other forearm across my shoulders. He ended up nicking me, and when my blood joined his, the runes burned even more intensely for an interminable second, and then it was over.

I lay there panting, fighting nausea. It hadn't taken more than a literal minute though it felt as if it had passed on a time-lapse camera, each frame sliding by at a third its normal rate.

Hellion laid his hand over my forehead, and again the nausea faded. He said, "Stay here." I nodded, and he murmured the releasing spell for my voice. He went to the sink and grabbed a washcloth, wet it and came back to clean my stomach off.

"What *was* that?" I panted.

"It's a rather complex, arcane piece of magic that has been all but forgotten. It's used for healing when one is dying and for, ah, well, death itself. Different order for the runes and a few different words, and you'd be pushing daisies before you knew what had happened."

"What do you mean dying? I wasn't that bad."

"Days more and you would have been."

I sat up and realized I wasn't sore. I looked inside my T-shirt, and all the bruising was gone. I scrambled off the bed and Hellion let me go. I raced to the bathroom and shut the door. Lifting my T-shirt, I twisted in front of the mirror: the bruising over my kidneys was gone. I looked closely at the area over my heart where Tarrek's curse had taken me, and the black blistering was gone. I felt really good. I walked quickly back into the bedroom. I stopped across from Hellion and smiled a true smile, and he gave one in return.

"Better?"

I nodded. Then my smile faltered. "I have to go back to Bahlin, Hellion. It's not a choice for me right now. You understand that, right?"

"I do and I don't." He moved farther onto the bed, propping

himself up on the pillows and watching me. "But I do believe it's for the best, at least until we sort out how you and I are going to proceed." He let his head list to one side, and his eyes closed gently before he asked, "My god has deemed us a mated pair and all but ordained it. I must ask, do you think you could love me, Madeleine? Or spend your life with me?"

Why do the supes always go straight for the kill shot? I wondered. "I don't know, Hellion. There's something between us, and it's only the second time in my life I've felt this type of connection, and the first didn't end so well. I want to be careful, okay?" I took the chair he'd vacated earlier and watched him a bit warily. I knew he wouldn't hurt me at this point, but I also knew he had the potential for a wicked temper and the means to back it up.

He shifted again, settling the covers around his hips. Without his shirt, he looked like a model for the cover of a bodice-ripping romance. I was staring at his torso again when he asked, "Is what you feel for me the same as what you felt for Bahlin?"

I thought about it. "No. And I don't like that. I'm not like most women, Hellion. Emotions scare the ever-loving hell out of me."

"Why?"

"I've never had luck in relationships." I struggled to find the words to adequately explain and finally just gave up, shrugging. I would have to use what I had, adequate or not. "I'm just not that woman, the one who dreams of the fairytale ending, or the one who runs off with a man because he professes to love her, or even the one who generally accepts happily ever after." I thought back to the wish at the stones, and my bitter thoughts about love being an add-on to life. "I'm not your storybook heroine, Hellion, so how can I just accept a storybook life?" I stood and rolled my head around on my neck. Man, I was tense.

He threw the covers back and stood, a small smile playing across his face. He shoved his hands in his pants pockets, the muscles on his stomach bunching. "I'm truly glad you're not that woman, Madeleine."

I took a small step toward him and he reciprocated, moving only when I moved and only so far as I went, until we met halfway and faced each other. "You say that now, but you'll undoubtedly learn that I won't have my hand forced, not by threat or magic or fear or, sadly, even love. I make my decisions in my own time, so don't get too excited about finding the perfect minister to officiate just yet." Though it still surprised the hell out of me, I admitted, "I like you, but that doesn't a marriage make. Let's see how this goes and also see how things with Bahlin work out before we go jumping from any bridges." I laid my hand flat on his bare chest, and the feel of his heart was soothing to me. I jerked my hand back.

He reached out and traced my cheek with his thumb. "I understand the fear of what might be, but why not celebrate what is? You respond to me, I respond to you. For now, it's enough." He shook his head, and a crooked grin graced his lips. "It's amazing to me, this shift, but I'll accept it at face value. I wish you'd consider the same so we could at the very least see what lies between us."

"Seems like you weren't listening." I smiled to lessen the sting of my words. "I don't trust anything like this, Hellion, particularly anything this easy. I just don't. And you sound like you're trying to get into my pants, nothing more." He opened his mouth, undoubtedly protest, but I held up my hand to stop him. "You've done an emotional one-eighty— first wanting me dead before declaring me your true love because someone told you to. I'm skeptical, no matter what I inexplicably feel. I'm disappointed I let things get as far as they did this morning." I stepped back and he followed me. "Back off, Hellion." I sighed. It felt like I'd spent the morning telling men to give me some space.

He took a step back and reciprocated my sigh but his was followed by a sudden grin. "This will be great fun."

"What?"

"Convincing you to follow your heart."

"And are you so sure of the answer?"

"Odin's spoken. Besides, the true answer will be what's best for all, even if it hurts initially."

"How can you be so stoic?" I demanded.

He shrugged and beamed. "I'm Irish."

Chapter Four

I pulled the hotel bathrobe from the closet and slipped it on. Guilt settled over me like a strand of spider's web, swirling around me as I moved, sticky and impossible to shake off. I turned back to Hellion and found him leaning against the bathroom door, arms crossed over his still-nude, muscular chest, an intensely brooding look on his face. "I thought you managed so well because you're Irish?" I teased.

He made a *harumphing* sound and shrugged, his emotions barely contained. "We've no method to speak to each other. How will I reach you?" A frown tugged at his lips, and his fingers dug into the muscles of his crossed arms.

I smiled gently. "You'll call me on the phone like a normal man," I said. I walked over to him and gently bumped his chest with my shoulder. "Do you have a cell phone?"

"Not with me. I rarely carry it."

"Get one that you'll keep on you," I suggested. "Then we can keep in touch. I've got this niggling feeling about the murdered girl, and we've got to elect new Council members. You'll need the phone regardless."

"Fine." He stared down at me, impassive. And then the sun came out in the way of his smile. "For you." He dipped to kiss me quickly before I could object.

I backed up hard and fast, bouncing off the wall. "No more of that, Hellion." I cinched the robe tighter against his lustful gaze and the physical response he seemed to wring from me. "I have to go."

"So you keep saying. I'll be out of here as soon as you close the door. Any parting wisdom from the Niteclif?" He pushed to standing and slid his hands back in his pockets, rocking slowly back and forth on the balls of his feet.

So he didn't entirely trust me not to run out of the room screaming. I wasn't the only cautious one. Still, my gaze ran over his body, head to toe, and I licked my lower lip. "Oh, yeah."

He quirked an eyebrow in question, a small smile tugging at his lips.

"Put your shirt on before you leave."

He threw back his head and laughed long and loud, the rich baritone sound pulling another genuine grin out of me as I turned and fled the room.

I walked slowly down the carpeted hallway until I got to the elevator. I didn't want to go back to my room, but clothed in only a T-shirt, underwear and borrowed robe, I had little choice. I strongly suspected my return would bring about chaos, and I was worried. Would Bahlin be able to read the guilt in my face if he was there? Because guilty I was. No, I wasn't still formally bound to my dragon, but my heart had been his and his alone until last night when he gave it back. Now it was divided and I found myself conflicted. I was also feeling very adrift, as if I'd been cut loose from all who cared about me, from parents to friends to lover, and all I wanted was to belong, to be genuinely loved by someone. What if Hellion... No. I'd not explore that just yet.

That damned prophecy, I grumped, kicking at the front of the robe just as the elevator car arrived with a soft *ding*. I boarded the car and did my best to ignore the stares from the elderly couple who already occupied the car.

"Floor?" asked the gentleman.

"*Hmph*," said his octogenarian partner, taking in my bathrobe and disheveled hair.

Unable to help myself, I turned to face her when I answered. "I believe I left my other lover on twenty-two."

He smiled and she glared at me. I glared right back. She reached around her partner and pushed the next floor button.

"But Genevieve, that's not our flo—"

"It is now," she hissed, and dragged him off the elevator as soon as it stopped.

I'm not usually such a snark, but her attitude had empowered the bitch in me to make an appearance. Oh well. It would give them something to talk about over dinner.

The elevator arrived at my floor and I exited to a flurry of activity. There were people rushing about, two men were posted in the hallway outside my room, and the door was propped open. I heard Bahlin bellow something along the lines of, "I don't give a flying fuck *what your excuse is, find her.*" I cringed. This was going to be ugly.

Just as I was contemplating getting back on the elevator, one of the guards spotted me.

"Hold it," he ordered.

I stumbled backward and fell into a table holding a fresh flower arrangement. It crashed to the marble elevator foyer and splintered. I sat there among the scattered flowers, water and shattered glass and watched the other guard disappear into the hotel room as the first guard closed the distance. His eyes were dragon blue, and I knew he had to be a member of the weyr.

"You are..."

I sighed. "The Niteclif."

"I thought so. Glaaca," he shouted, then he turned back to glare openly at me. Hellion's words came back to me that the killer could be anyone in the weyr, and I shivered. Suddenly complete strangers looked like potential murderers.

Bahlin swung around the corner of the door and, seeing me sprawled on the floor, broke into a sprint. Clay was hot on his heels. The lesser dragon sported a massive shiner and a nasty split lip. It didn't slow him down.

Bahlin slipped and slid through the mess and snatched me up off the ground, crushing me to his chest.

"*Oomph.*"

"Maddy, Maddy, Maddy," he chanted into my hair, briskly rubbing my back.

"It's a good thing I'm not still wounded, you know." I pushed back on his chest so I could see his face.

His midnight blue eyes peered down at me and his brows drew together. "What do you mean you're not wounded? I just saw you yesterday—"

"Right. When you dumped my ass. Put me down." I struggled, and he set me down just outside the halo of broken glass.

"Clay explained—"

"Only because you wouldn't give me an opportunity to do it myself." I shoved him back and he let me. "You arrogant *ass*. Did you think to give me a minute to explain before jumping to conclusions?" I

43

stormed away from him, the robe flapping in the breeze of my righteous fury, and I spun to storm back. " No, you didn't. Instead, you called off the engagement and left me to be abducted." *And to get a personal message from a god.* My chest was heaving and my heart hurt. I knew this was unfair but I couldn't seem to stop myself.

Sensing a cataclysmic fight in the making, Clay jumped between us. "Maddy? Maddy." He grabbed my shoulders and shook me, and Bahlin growled. "Listen. It was my fault you were taken. I wasn't, uh, doing my job when Hellion broke into the room. Where did he take you?"

"Is no one going to ask if I'm okay?" My question was met with total silence. "Nice. Very nice you arrogant, overgrown, winged geckos. He took me to the twenty-sixth floor. You never think to check your own house first, do you?"

I wrenched myself out of Clay's hands and stalked into my suite, intent on getting some clothes on.

"Maddy?" Clay called. "Before I forget, there's a message for you."

I paused, looking over my shoulder. "Yeah?"

"Gaitha, Queen of the Fae, would like to speak to you about the Council vacancy." He looked disturbed.

"I'm sure she would." I sighed and ran my hands through my hair. "Not today, though. I'll send a messenger…how? How exactly does one get in touch with the fae, Clay?"

"I'll make sure she knows you'll be in touch."

Bahlin followed me into the suite and turned to the other man. "Get everyone out," Bahlin said softly but firmly. "Clay, arrange four men on the door and elevators, six men in the lobby. Someone watch the window. I need some time alone with my…" He paused.

I looked at him over my shoulder. "Your what?" He didn't answer so I turned to face him head on. "Am I still your fiancée? Your *trékkar?*"

He scrubbed his hands hard over his face, then clutched his temples with his eyes closed. He stood that way for a lifetime before he finally opened his eyes and dropped his hands to his hips. "What do you want from me, Maddy?"

"Nothing more than you're willing to give."

"I just don't know," he admitted, staring at me intently.

"Fair enough. When I thought you wanted me, all I wanted was you in return. Now I'm not so sure either."

"I thought you were—wait, what do you mean you're not sure?"

I laughed but it was a bitter sound. "Don't like the sound of that, do you? So it's okay for you to decide you might not want to be married to me, but I don't have the same luxury? You and your damnable prophecy, Bahlin. It's going to ruin what would have been a good thing."

He paled in front of me, swaying so that I thought he might actually fall down. He staggered to the sofa and sank into the cushions, all his normal grace gone. "You've met him, haven't you? You've met the third leg of this cursed triangle."

"We've known him all along, Bahlin." My back was now to him, and my voice carried on little more than a whisper. "Think. With Tarrek gone, who is the only other male member of the Council? It's been that simple from day one. We just didn't see it, didn't *want* to see it."

"Hellion," he snapped, leaning his head back on the sofa's headrest. "Damn it, it's Hellion."

"Give the dragon a prize."

I left Bahlin stewing on the sofa, gathered up some clothes and headed into the bathroom to grab a quick shower. The hot water sluiced over my skin but I still felt cold. *Hellion.* Just the name evoked a strange feeling in the pit of my stomach. I thought back to the first time we'd met at the sithen. It had felt like, at the very least, we'd met before. But I'd dismissed the feeling, taken it for a fluke. Now I wondered if past lives were coming into play. And did I even believe in past lives? I wasn't sure. What I was pretty sure I *did* believe in was free will versus destiny. Difficult as it was, the choice between men had to be mine. The concept of destiny seemed like a cop-out, a chance to blame every poor choice as inconsequentially preordained by the Fates. That made me, in effect, nothing more than a thread in their greater loom. No. I was Madeleine Niteclif, and I had an unchangeable history and a future of my own design.

I have choices to make, I thought, scrubbing at my skin with a vengeance that left it glowing pink. *I am no one's pawn, and I don't accept destiny as an excuse.*

The dark voice in my head said, *Ah, but then how did you get here?*

There was no easy answer.

I shut the water off and stood there dripping. The room outside was quiet. Running my hands through my hair, I shook like a dog emerging from a deep body of water. I grabbed my towel and dried off, dressed, and brushed my hair into some semblance of order. I was stalling. I didn't want to face Bahlin. Knowing that pissed me off, and I hurled the brush across the bathroom. It hit the door with a bang and a clatter, and I heard movement in the room beyond.

"Maddy?" Bahlin's voice was muffled through the door but the concern rang loud and clear.

I sighed. I couldn't put this off any longer. Opening the door, I moved past him and grabbed my sneakers. "Sorry. I'm just having a small temper tantrum."

"Your socks are in the top right dresser drawer."

I pulled it open and, sure enough, there were my socks. Someone had kindly unpacked my belongings. Apparently I'd be here instead of living with Bahlin. One more nail in the coffin of our relationship. Good to know.

I sat on the floor to put them on, not wanting to sit next to Bahlin on the bed.

He perched on the edge of the mattress, watching my every move. "We need to discuss this."

I hunched my shoulders at his words. Maybe I could convince myself destiny was responsible after all because I sure as hell didn't want to tell him what had gone down in the room upstairs.

"I agree." I finished tying my shoes and got up, walking into the living room and sinking into one of the sofas. "But not in the bedroom."

"Uncomfortable?" he asked, menace weaving effectively through the five syllables of that one simple word.

"Maybe. Why are you being an ass when you're the one who left me?" I fidgeted with the decorative pillows, straightening tassels and fringe. I froze. This had been a nervous habit of my mom's. I put my hands in my lap and watched Bahlin walk to the big picture window, his back to me.

"You're right. I did call off the engagement." He turned to me, his face grave. "I want to take it all back, Maddy. Even the part where I killed my da and sister. But what's done is done."

It sounded like he meant it as a whole. The engagement was off.

My guilt over Hellion eased just a bit.

"Do you believe in free will or destiny?" It was out of my mouth before I could stop myself. In for a penny and all that, I continued. "Because here's what I think. If you believe in free will, you chose to save me at the cost of their lives. If you believe in destiny, your actions were preordained by the Fates or your goddess or whomever you hold to that higher power. So which is it?"

Bahlin was shocked into silence. He walked over to the opposite end of the sofa I sat on and sank down, some of his grace returned—or forced—and he leaned back, lacing his hands behind his head. "There's no real right answer, is there?"

"I don't know. I'm asking what you believe."

"I'm not sure. I don't feel like there's a right answer for this conversation."

I sighed. "It's not about right or wrong, Bay. It's a matter of personal belief, of what you believe to be true."

"What do you believe, Maddy?" His voice was rough, and he cleared his throat. "Because if it's a matter of free will, then you'll choose either Hellion or me. If it's a matter of destiny, then what I say or do doesn't matter, and the prophecy stands."

I hadn't consciously thought of it in such a basic way, but there it was. "I don't know," I answered, shaking my head before dropping it into my hands and closing my eyes "I think you do have a strong opinion but you're afraid to acknowledge it because either way you're stuck between us."

Bahlin turned his head and looked at me, his eyes heavy with knowledge. "What happened between the two of you that you don't want to tell me, Maddy?"

Oh crap. Here we go. Once again, give the dragon a prize.

Chapter Five

"Why do you ask?" What didn't happen would have been a better question. I sure as hell wasn't telling him about the little visit from Odin or my shift in feelings toward Hellion. Not now and maybe not ever.

Bahlin snorted and stood, walking over to the fireplace. "You're working too hard at avoiding this conversation. You have little tells yourself, lover." The last was said caustically.

"No need to get nasty, Bay." Sitting made me feel smaller and more vulnerable so I stood, sticking my fingers in the back pockets of my jeans to keep from fidgeting.

"You actively avoid every question I ask, Maddy. That's the biggest clue." He leaned against the mantle, all cultivated nonchalance. "Did you screw him?"

"Get out. Now." I turned and walked back to the bathroom and slammed the door, locking it behind me. I closed the lid to the toilet and sat, shaking with fury.

The lock snapped open, and I belatedly remembered Bahlin's skills with telekinesis. *Shit.*

The door crashed open, bouncing off the counter so hard he had to throw out a hand to keep from having it hit him in the face as it rebounded. "Did you?" he asked, his voice no more than a breath on the air.

"No, I didn't." I put my elbows on my knees and my face in my hands. "Jeeze, Bahlin, what do you take me for?"

He dropped to his knees in front of me and wrapped his arms around my shoulders, but I was stiff and unyielding. "I'm so sorry, Maddy. It makes me nuts to think he might have had his hands on you. You can tell me anything, okay? Anything." He rubbed his hands up and down my back and sides gently, trying to convey support but only further rubbing in my guilt with every pass.

"Give me some space, Bahlin. Please."

He sat back on his heels and, thankfully, stopped touching me. "What is it, love?"

I shook my head and stood, brushing past him to walk out of the room. I stopped in front of the picture window, not missing the irony of our switched places.

Bahlin followed me out and stood behind me, not touching me but still invading my personal space so effectively that I felt his aura cross into mine.

"I will say this once," I murmured, "and then I need to talk to you about business. Are you okay with that?"

He briefly set a hand on my shoulder before turning and walking to the nearest sofa. He propped a hip on the back and said, "Go ahead."

"I kissed Hellion. It was definitely more than a peck and barely less than foreplay. It was voluntary, Bahlin, so no retaliation. I feel something for him that I can't explain, but I'm nobody's bitch, particularly not Fate's." Or Odin's. "So I'll make my own decisions in this, and the universe can kiss my ass." I turned to look at him, my arms wrapped around my core. I was cold, and his gaze did nothing to relieve me.

"Did you enjoy it?"

"Yes. But if it's any consolation, I stopped myself because of you, even though you'd kicked me to the curb. I don't know where I'm at in all this, Bahlin, but there's work to do, and we don't have the time or the luxury of letting this control our lives."

He nodded tersely and swallowed hard, his throat convulsing around the emotion he forced down. "Fine. But it won't be long before we have to talk about this in detail, Madeleine."

"Fine," I echoed. We could argue definitions of *"it won't be long"* some other time.

"Are you aware of the woman who was murdered yesterday in the park near your apartment?" I moved to sit across from him.

"She was only the first." He held up a hand to stop me from interrupting him. "There was a second woman murdered on the Tube near the hotel's stop early this morning, and no one saw a thing. The victim profile was nearly identical. She looked suspiciously like you, Maddy. In fact, if we're going to practice honesty, I have to tell you that hearing about it is what brought me back here. I had to know for sure it wasn't you."

I ignored both the invisible stab to my heart and the creeping fingers of fear that stroked my spine with sharp nails. "Method?"

"The same. Her throat was cut deep enough to nearly sever her head. The press picked up this tidbit and is clamoring for more information. They're speculating the killer is a modern day Jack the Ripper targeting tall, shapely women with short, dark hair, age twenty-five to thirty."

I closed my eyes and shuddered, feeling a great deal of empathy for the women who had died because they looked right—or wrong. I heard Bahlin move closer then felt him sit down next to me. "Both victims had their throats cut from the back, left to right, with a fair-sized blade."

"Serrated or non-serrated?" I asked in a flat voice.

"Non."

"Bahlin, what are the odds, do you think, that the victim profile is a fluke?" Those sharp fingers of fear skittered up and down my spine with increased speed and pressure, and I broke out in goosebumps.

"I'd say slim to none." He shifted closer and put an arm around me. "Your take?"

"I agree." I sighed and leaned into him, but the original comfort that had existed between us was gone, replaced by wariness and hurt and a freshly wounded love that might not survive the injury. "I'd have to assume, again, that the killer is someone I might recognize. Why else attack from behind each time?"

He hugged me tight and kissed the top of my head. I sighed again, and he pulled me in even closer, tilting my chin up with his free hand. We stared at each other. He dipped his head to kiss me, and I turned in to the kiss. His lips sought an answer I couldn't provide, but I'd try to offer what comfort I could.

I went to my knees beside him and cradled his face in my palms. He followed where I led him, and I recognized it for what it was. Insecurity. I withdrew from him, unsure how to reassure us both that the prophecy was simply a suggestion and not a firm future. Remembering the feel of Hellion's lips on mine and my body's response to him, I realized I couldn't offer any guarantees. The world was too full of what ifs right now. What if the killer was seeking victims who looked like me? What if the prophecy was firm and not to be influenced? What if Hellion was my heart's match? What if I failed as the Niteclif? What if

I didn't survive my legacy? What if I broke my dragon's heart? What if he broke mine?

A grief-laden sob broke from my throat, and I buried my face in Bahlin's chest, breathing hard and trying to hold it together. My life was out of control.

He wrapped his arms tight around me and held on. The only indication of his heightened emotion was his whispering nonsense into my hair in Gaelic, not English.

I nodded quickly and moved to sit on my side of the sofa again. "Will you turn on the TV? I want to see if there's any more information, maybe some new stories, about the murdered girls."

Bahlin silently moved to grab the remote and fetch a small foot blanket from the bedroom. When he sat back down he was close enough we could have held hands, though we didn't. Instead, we surfed the local channels looking for morbid news about murder.

The sun had just set in a cloud-muted blaze of oranges and pinks on the metropolitan horizon when the sound of conflict in the hallway reached us. Bahlin and I stood, and he physically set me behind him toward the corner of the room. Irritated, I moved to stand shoulder to shoulder with him. Without looking, I reached across and pulled the dirk from the top of his boot. It helped knowing each other as well as we did.

There was a sharp knock at the door and the guard, Jenks, called out, "Glaaca. You've got a Council member here to see the Niteclif."

I rolled my eyes. I had no illusions about who was at the door. "No one makes those decisions for me, but me, Jenks," I called back. Do it? Don't do it? To hell with it. "Let him in." I moved in front of Bahlin, and it wasn't lost on me that I was physically putting myself between the two of them for the first time.

The door opened and Hellion stood there, fierce in his arrogance. Bahlin moved up behind me and put his hand on my hip. Hellion stepped inside and casually waved his hand at the door, slamming it in Jenks's face.

"What can I do for you?" I looked down and saw the bandage on his hand and the blood crusted around his fingernails. I knew Bahlin scented it because he stopped breathing for the briefest second.

"I actually came to give you my new number, just as you asked."

He reached into his pocket and withdrew a cell phone.

"Stay here," I muttered to Bahlin. More loudly I said, "Both of you behave."

I walked quickly into the bedroom and retrieved the pad of paper and pen by the phone. "You could have called," I said to Hellion as I jogged back into the living area. Nervous? Me? Distrustful of the angry dragon and indifferent magus was more like it.

"Sure, I could've. But where's the joy in that when I have the opportunity to see you again?"

At this point Bahlin was breathing hard through his nose. Without any further warning than that, he charged at Hellion. The two began pounding on each other, grunts of pain coming from the fray when one or the other made contact with ribs or a kidney. The guards rushed into the room with the first crash, but they couldn't seem to get the two separated. An unidentified guard stumbled back, holding his bleeding nose. The group of men tumbled over the back of the sofa, knocking the lamp to the floor with a crash. Bahlin was on his feet first and landed a particularly vicious kick to Hellion's side. Hellion absorbed it and, grabbing Bahlin's foot, wrenched his knee. The sickening crunch convinced me he'd probably destroyed the joint. Bahlin bellowed and went to the ground. Hellion grabbed him by the front of his shirt and threw him against the picture window and it cracked.

I sprinted for Bahlin as hard as I could and watched as the window caved outward and began to crumble under his weight. Hellion charged him and the two crashed through the window in an explosion of glass. I couldn't slow my momentum, and I hit the open air, backpedaling as I tried to stop. I had a total moment of vertigo as I hung suspended in the air before beginning to fall.

It was twenty-two stories to the ground, and we were all observing Newton's Law, falling at an equal rate of descent one to another.

Everything happened too fast. Bahlin spun end over end, his destroyed leg flopping uselessly as he tried to gather his bearings and determine up from down. Hellion was falling with his back to the earth, and his eyes widened perceptibly when he saw me follow them out the window.

I could hear him shouting something, and he spread his arms and legs out so he looked like he could be mounted to a St. Andrew's cross.

His fall slowed dramatically, and he reached out for me, snagging me around the waist as I raced past him. He wrapped his arms around me and twisted; I lost sight of Bahlin. Everything went black, my ears popped and with a flash of light I found myself mashed into an Oriental carpet that didn't belong to the hotel, trapped beneath a great weight.

Hellion pushed himself up and I choked, gasping for air. He flipped me over and crushed me to his chest.

"Holy hell, woman." His limbs shook, though whether it was from restraint, fear or fury was beyond me.

"What happened to Bahlin?" Tears coursed down my cheeks. "Tell me," I screamed.

"I don't know, lass."

I pushed against him, scrambling out of his arms. "You son of a bitch! You did it on purpose! You threw him...you threw him—" I huddled on my knees, arms clenched around my middle, and rocked back and forth as shock settled over my body.

"Maddy—"

"Scry, damn it," I screeched, hysterical. "You find him."

Hellion pushed himself to standing and went down a long hallway off the living area we'd materialized in. He came back, holding his side, and sat on the ground. He unfolded a map of England and Scotland, went through the centering ritual and took the crystal hung from horsehair out of a velvet bag. He began with small circles, ever widening, until he'd moved more than a hundred miles in any direction from the hotel.

Head down, he mumbled something unintelligible, then asked, "Is there a chance he cloaked himself?"

"He told me he was bound to cloak in darkness. And I don't know if he could cloak when he hadn't shifted. I'm going to say no, he didn't cloak himself."

"I'm sorry," he whispered, looking up at me with flat black eyes. "I'm so sorry, Madeleine."

I shook my head. "No. He's not dead." I choked on that last word. "Until there's proof, absolute and irrefutable proof, I won't believe it. I need to get back to the hotel, see if he's there. In the meantime, hand me your phone."

Hellion moved slowly to dig his phone out of his pocket and hand it to me. Our hands touched. I jerked away.

Dialing Bahlin's number, I waited. It rang once, then went straight to voicemail. Closing my eyes and breathing slowly, I waited for the beep. "Bahlin, it's me. I need you to call me, let me know you're okay. I don't have my cell but I'll get it. In the meantime, call the number that showed on caller ID. It's Hellion's. Just...let me know you're all right. Please." I didn't care that the message sounded like pleading.

Hellion reached for me. I shrugged his hand away and clung to the phone. He'd call back. I knew he'd call back.

"Madeleine." Hellion's voice was gentle, too gentle in the given situation, and I flinched.

"You don't understand. I can't be sure, absolutely sure, until I see the—" I stumbled a bit, unable to say the world "body." I just couldn't. It would be too much like accepting this at face value, which I refused to do.

"I'll take you to the hotel," Hellion began, and I scrambled to my feet. He shook his head. "Not now. I'll take you tomorrow, when the dragons will have either vacated or calmed down. To walk into that mess now would be akin to calling for war, and I won't do that."

A cold weight settled in my chest. "I need to go now."

"You'll stay here, with me, until we get this sorted out." He held up a hand to stave off my indignant protest. "Listen to me. There's a killer out there targeting women who look like you, the weyr is going to be angry one way or another, Imeena is still unaccounted for, and frankly you've made quite a few enemies. You've nowhere else to go that's safe."

That cold weight in my chest intensified, making it hard to breathe. Rubbing between my breasts didn't help, and my panting became more noticeable as I fought for air. Hellion reached for me and I flinched, but it didn't stop him. He turned me gently and traced fingers across my back. The weight dissipated like mist in the sun, fading to nothing in a few seconds.

He laid both hands on my shoulders and turned me to face him. "Better?"

"Yeah. Thanks." I looked up at him, and that pull of familiarity, that sense of belonging, flared. I stepped back, breaking away from his touch, but the feeling lingered.

"You need rest, Madeleine."

"It's just Maddy. And no, what I need is to go find Bahlin, but thanks." I looked around the room for the door.

"Stay here tonight and I swear I'll help you look for him tomorrow. Give the weyr time to tend their own—" I jerked at his words "—regardless of what that may mean."

The phone in my hand rang, startling me so badly that I dropped it. Hellion leaned in and picked it up, answering smoothly. The conversation was short, his face blank of any emotion. Hanging up, he turned to me, and his face went from blank to compassion.

"No," I whispered, backing away from him and shaking my head. "Don't say it."

"I'm sorry, Maddy. A few things were found below the window—a broken watch, some blood, a single shoe they believe is his—but no...body. It's missing. The weyr's afraid he may have somehow survived the fall only to have been grievously injured. If so, they believe he may have hauled himself somewhere private to..." Hellion looked down, rubbing the back of his neck. "He's not checked in with anyone, his brother's frantic—"

"How can they just assume the worst?" I demanded. "They can't be sure. If he *did* 'haul himself off,' it could be to get help or else to treat himself on his own. You can't just assume he's dead without proof."

"He would have reached out to the weyr healers for help. And where would he go that his own people, his personal sentinels, wouldn't have checked, Maddy? They're as desperate to find him as any but you, I'm sure. And they have access to magic of their own, whether it's truly theirs or simply purchased." He paused, running his hands through his hair. "Between what they've said and the fact I've yet to find a trace of him, you've got to brace yourself for the likelihood he's dead."

The word rocked me back on my heels. *Dead.* I couldn't rationalize it. "But I have to see him. I have to *know*, Hellion." My voice sounded small, uncertain. I sank to my knees and buried my face in my hands.

Hellion gathered me up in his arms and took me into what had to be his bedroom. He laid me gently on the bed, unfolding a quilted silk coverlet over me. Kneeling next to me, he took off his shoes and shirt and crawled under the cover.

"No," I whispered. Bone-chilling numbness was spreading through my body at an alarming rate. *Shock*, my mind whispered gently, *you're in shock.*

"I only seek to offer you comfort. I never would have done him permanent harm, Maddy, particularly knowing it would cause you heartache. I'm so sorry."

I nodded. His acceptance that magic proved Bahlin was gone began to seep into me, and I felt a massive wave of grief roaring up from deep in my soul. Needing ease from any source I could find it, I turned and let him tuck my face into his bare shoulder. I jumped at the heat emanating from his body.

I couldn't stand having my nose pressed into his skin when it smelled so different from my dragon. I turned my back to him, and he spooned against me, wrapping me tightly in his arms. It was an awful comfort.

Sleep, elusive sleep, didn't find me that night.

Chapter Six

I was staring at the same wall I'd watched all night when the sun broke over the horizon. Hellion's breathing was slow and even but I didn't think he was asleep either. The night had seen me swing back and forth between despair and rage, shaking with each emotional shift, as I waited. All night I clutched the phone, mentally willing it to ring. The silence had been an unkind companion.

Hellion had held me tight, never making it a matter of sexual interest but rather human support. Not once did he complain.

"You need to get some breakfast," he finally said, speaking into my hair, his breath was hot on my scalp.

"I'm not hungry," I croaked.

"It's not a matter of hunger, Maddy, it's a matter of survival. Your body needs fuel. I'm going to the kitchen to make you put together a smoothie. It's not open for debate. Any flavor requests?"

"Strawberry." I ignored the command and gave in to the practicality. What was the point in fighting?

"Done." He got up and tucked the coverlet around me while I continued to lie there.

"Then you have to take me to the hotel," I murmured.

He traced a hand down the back of my head. "As I promised, so I'll do." Then he was gone.

I could hear him rummaging around in the kitchen, pans and such clanging as he dug out whatever he needed while muttering to himself. I felt like such a traitor, having spent the night with Bahlin's potential killer... No. I couldn't think that way. I'd seen the whole accident, and logic had to rule my thoughts. Bahlin had started the fight despite my admonition about no retaliation. True, Hellion had continued the fight, going so far as to even follow Bahlin out the window. I'd lay no blame anywhere. But that didn't mean I wouldn't grieve the loss, whether it proved temporary or more permanent.

The sound of the blender ripped through the silent morning, and I winced at the obnoxious grating noise. Burrowing farther under the covers, I realized I was cold without Hellion.

He walked back into the room carrying two smoothies and I sat up, folding the coverlet to the side. He smiled gently and, setting the glasses on the night table, he scooped me up in his arms and folded the bedcovers back before setting me down on the mattress. I propped myself up on the pillows and he crawled back in bed, handing me one of the glasses. I snuggled up to him for his warmth and drank.

"Thank you for this." I didn't know if I meant breakfast or the night just passed. I didn't intend to look too closely at it.

"I'm so sorry, Madeleine. For all my new and unexpected jealousy, I never meant to seriously hurt him."

I turned in slow motion, a horrible thought crossing my mind. "Did you kill him to satisfy your debt against Gretta's life?" If he had, I'd kill him myself.

His eyes flared with shock before settling into outrage. "No. I told you, that debt is long past, particularly with our situation. Had Gretta lived, I would have left her, if not for cheating with Tarrek then because I've found you. Gretta is done, history."

I nodded, settling back into numbness. I had new empathy for how Hellion must have felt when I killed Gretta. "I don't think I've ever told you I was really sorry for killing her. I was, you know."

"Not so directly. But I know well enough now that you're not comfortable with killing, Madeleine. Your job will force you to handle it, but you will never kill indiscriminately."

"Thanks, I think," I muttered, finishing my drink. I lay under the covers, shifting to my side so I faced him. Hellion slid down with me so we were lying with our noses only inches apart.

He kissed my forehead gently and I pulled back, too broken to rail at him for a simple kiss, too scared if I didn't move he might try to take it somewhere I wasn't ready for it to go.

I rolled over and stared at the ceiling. "I need to get it together and go to the hotel."

"Give me a few minutes to get cleaned up, and we'll go. For now, rest. I know you didn't sleep last night."

I shoved pillows up behind me, displacing him and forcing him to move back some. "Will you turn on the news so I can watch for any additional information on the murdered girls?" I asked. "I have to get my mind off this while I wait on you. Work might help."

He nodded and flipped on the TV with a wave of his hand. Surfing to the local station, he settled down to wait with me. I was about to ask him to get moving so we could leave when a local reporter came on with a news update. "Again, today's victim was found outside the Pemberton Hotel, near the valet entrance, her throat slit ear to ear. The victim profile seems to be the same. Panic is beginning to take hold as Londoners wonder exactly who it is targeting these similar young women. I'll bring you more information as it's available. Back to you at the station." Hellion switched off the TV and I lay there, the smoothie a heavy block of ice in my stomach.

I wondered about Imeena, the rogue vampire and former member of the High Council who had defected with Tarrek. She'd also been intimate with him. Imeena was vicious and hated me with a passion I hadn't recognized until it was nearly too late. My hand unconsciously caressed the small scars her fangs had left on my neck. "That's three in three days. No one's found Imeena yet, have they?"

"No, no one's seen her since she escaped the night we took Tarrek down." He shifted to lean on one elbow and look up at me. I fumbled with the edge of the comforter, feeling like I had with Bahlin weeks ago—uncomfortable, uneducated, unprepared. "I suppose...well, I suppose she could be biting the victims and then slicing their necks to hide the evidence?" I posed it more as a question than a statement, so if it was foolish I had an out.

Hellion pushed himself out of bed and began to pace around the large room. He was irritated, his steps choppy and unbalanced. "What concerns me the most is that the newest victim was taken down at the Pemberton without witnesses and that she, again, looks like you. We have to assume someone is trying to kill you, Maddy."

He hadn't answered my question, so I forced my mind to slow down, consider the facts and apply a liberal dose of logic. I knew each woman had looked similar to me, at least from the back. Each murder was moving the killer closer to my last location. Bahlin had said their throats had been slit from left to right. Slicing is a pulling activity whereas stabbing is a pushing activity. Logically, this meant the killer was right-handed. Bahlin had also said the blade was non-serrated, and I had taken him at face value, though I had no idea how he'd obtained this information or, when combined with the other facts I had, what it might mean. And, most importantly, I knew each victim had been killed at night. The murders had been fast and efficient, or else mind control was at play, because there were no witnesses.

Hellion stopped and looked at me. "What are you ticking off on your fingers?"

I hadn't realized I'd been labeling each item with my fingers, but he was right; I had. "Facts I'm sure about." I covered all my points, and he agreed with me. It looked like I was the target.

Hellion took a quick shower and, while I waited on him, I thought about the events of the last twenty-four hours. I couldn't cry anymore, and I couldn't be any more fearful or angry or confused. After a long debate, I had agreed to let Hellion go back to the hotel room alone to get some of my clothes and things and to scavenge for any information he could find on Bahlin. If the dragons were there and on the warpath, Hellion wanted me far away from the potential violence. I had grudgingly agreed.

Hellion walked out of the bathroom with a towel slung low on his hips, water droplets decorating his chest and arms, and his damp hair darker and heavier, hanging just past his shoulder blades. I openly stared, unable to look away. Guilt wound its way around my legs, whispering, "*Bahlin, Bahlin, Bahlin,*" and I couldn't move.

Hellion noticed me watching him closely and he stopped. The dripping water made little pools on the hardwood floor, and still he didn't move. His eyes were so alive, hungry. He raised a hand and trailed it slowly down his chest, sliding it between his pectorals, and my eyes were glued to his every movement. He swirled a thumb knuckle around his nipple and it rose slightly, his breathing shifting to shorter, harder breaths. He dragged his hand lower, pausing at his bellybutton.

I didn't look away.

He hit that sexy, narrow strip of hair from bellybutton to groin, and his fingers played in the hair lightly before sliding lower, hooking the edge of the towel where an impressive, twitching bulge was starting. It demanded attention like a living thing.

I swallowed hard.

"Madeleine?"

"No." I turned away from him and closed my eyes, breathing hard. I didn't know if I'd ever wanted anyone so badly as I wanted him. But wanting and loving were two different things. I'd wanted Bahlin, had broken all my rules about fast sex, started truly falling for him and he'd broken my heart. It left me questioning whether or not it had ever been, or had the chance of being, real love. And didn't that just make me feel horrid about myself. "No," I said again, more firmly this time, though I still didn't look at him when I said it.

"I'll not push, but I'll remind you that the prophecy is what it is. We're predestined, Maddy," he said, emphasizing my name. I looked back at him and he smiled. My tiny, answering smile trembled with uncertainty.

"Is that what you believe? That life is predestined?"

He thought about it before answering. "I wouldn't have thought so before meeting you, but I must admit my viewpoint is starting to evolve some, yes. There are things we're meant to accomplish with each life we're given, and what could be better than realizing an epic love is at least a part of our purpose?"

I thought about that, disturbed. I turned away from him and rubbed the headache forming at the base of my skull.

Hellion moved up behind me and wrapped his arms gently around me, laying his chin on my shoulder. A slight tightening of his embrace warned me he had a hard question to ask, but a little more query foreplay would have been good. "Are you worried about what Bahlin would think?"

I thought carefully about how to phrase my answer. In the end, I just answered as honestly as I could. "Yes and no. I'm pretty sure that, on some level, Bahlin loved me--*loves* me--and he'd want me to be happy. He said as much before, just...just before. But now I can't help but wonder, you know? He absolved me from all guilt yesterday morning, but it wasn't with the knowledge that this would happen."

Hellion turned me to face him, holding me away from him by my shoulders. When he answered me he proved he was a far better man than I gave him credit for. "Worry a little, *anamchara*, then leave it go. He'd not want you to live your life looking back and missing what was right in front of you."

"Are you so sure?"

"I knew Bahlin for years, Maddy. He wasn't one to live with regret until—"

Right. Until he'd killed his father and sister to save my life. And what had I done to repay him? Thrown myself out the window of a thirty-story building after him. Now there was a brilliant way to convey unmitigated love.

I sighed and pulled myself out of Hellion's arms. "I'm going to shower while you go to the hotel. Please look—"

"I will. I'll be thorough, Maddy."

"Thanks," I said, struggling to speak around the emotion lodged in my throat. "I'm keeping the phone. In case he calls."

Hellion casually nodded.

"I'm going to have to start looking at finding the Ripper impersonator and schedule a meeting with the remaining Council member to start the election process for new leaders. It'll wait until you get back, though. Until I know."

Unable to finish the thought, I turned and willingly walked away from what I feared was my destiny.

Chapter Seven

It took me a while to actually work up the energy to shower. Eventually I made it to the bathroom, ignoring the elegant landscape of marble tile and elaborate lighting. The only thing I really got into was the heated floors. I was only slightly apathetic as I went through the motions, wondering what Hellion would find when he went back to the hotel. I thought about Bahlin's face as he'd told me to be happy. *No. Not going there.* I hunched my shoulders in an unsuccessful effort to deflect the painful assault of memories. His smile, his smell, the feel of his hair running through my fingers...the look on his face the last time I'd seen him, freefalling. *No!*

I slammed my fist into the tiled wall, and the door crashed open. I shrieked and snatched up a towel as Hellion stormed into the bathroom. He swiftly assessed the space, determining there was no threat. He looked at me, and the flat black of his eyes creeped me out again until they softened.

"You yelled?" He reached in to turn the water off.

"You scared the shit out of me?" I snapped, dripping wet and only marginally covered by the small piece of terrycloth.

"No cause to get bitchy, love."

He was right, but my galloping heart didn't feel particularly forgiving yet. "You weren't gone very long."

He looked uncomfortable and sighed, a small sound issued in harmony with the dripping faucet. "The window had already been repaired—no need to draw attention to ourselves—but not much else seemed to have been changed."

"No sign of Bahlin anywhere?" I reached back and turned the water off, pulling the towel tighter around me.

"I went to the concrete pad below the window. As the weyr said yesterday, there was a small amount of blood but nothing more. Everything had been cleaned up and the area swept for glass. I searched for him again and still can't find him. I even went so far as to question one of the dragons there. No one has heard from him. After his brother sent out his frantic call, the weyr went silent. If they're locking down this tight, it may well be in an effort to prevent a hostile faction from taking over their weyr while they're without a leader. It wouldn't be unheard of for them to hide the body in a situation like that. I'm sorry, Maddy. I just feel you need to know the truth so you don't fill yourself with false hope."

I choked on the tears that clogged my throat. Hellion reached for me, and I slipped and stumbled away from him. "No. I need...just, no." A small sob broke free, dense with grief. Sucking in air, I stood and faced him at the same time I swiped single-handedly at the tears coursing down my face. "What else?"

"I was frankly surprised to find no one in the room on the off chance you came back." He leaned against the far wall, watching my reactions carefully.

"Why would I? Go back, that is." I busied myself with a large bath sheet, situating it carefully around my body before letting the smaller towel fall away. "There's nothing there for me." *Not anymore.*

He surprised me by pulling me roughly into his arms, wet hair and all. "We'll seize our own bit of happiness and the world be damned."

"How can you be so sure?" My voice was muffled by the folds of his shirt.

"How can you not?"

I smiled into his chest but said nothing. I was a little worried about what I felt for him, but more worried about the enormous vacancy that felt permanent in my heart.

The next two weeks passed in fits and starts of mind-numbing misery and strange, budding camaraderie. I left several more voicemails for Bahlin and had Hellion send a note to the hotel, but none of my messages were answered. As much as it hurt me, I was beginning to accept the fact he must be gone. Somehow, he had completely disappeared. It was the only thing I could piece together, because he wouldn't have ever let me hurt this way, not if he could stop it.

Bahlin's name wasn't mentioned but his shadow seemed to hang between Hellion and me, particularly early on. Guilt kept me trapped in the spare bedroom at Hellion's flat where I'd taken up temporary residence at his insistence. It diminished a little with each passing day, aided by the development of a tenuous friendship. The more time I spent with the wizard, the more I found I truly liked him. He was charming, witty, intelligent and very compassionate.

After I'd fallen off the paranormal map, the killings had stopped. More than once I found myself wondering if I was bearding the lion in his own den, but my emotions dismissed every attempt at logic my mind made.

It was the end of the fifteenth day after the accident when Hellion came to me and said he'd been in touch with Sarenia, the last remaining Council member. Nominations and elections had to be made to fill the Council vacancies. I winced at the mention of vacancies but Hellion went on as if I'd not reacted. We'd leave after lunch, giving me plenty of time to pull myself together. I was going to need it.

Hellion and I rode the elevator to the underground garage to retrieve his car. Hellion had advised Sarenia of Bahlin's death and asked her to come to us at Avebury Henge in Avon. Sarenia was Atlantean, as in from Atlantis, and while I had no idea where the Lost City was or how he called her, it was apparently reasonable to expect her to show up at the stone circle within six hours.

We dumped our stuff in the trunk of his Mercedes and settled into the coupe for the three-hour trip. It wasn't possible for Hellion to materialize somewhere he hadn't physically been before or somewhere he didn't have an effective safe room waiting. It would suck to get snatched up by scientists for showing up at the right place at the wrong time—with witnesses—so we were driving.

I thought about my last road trip across England only a few weeks ago with Bahlin. The memories were new enough to still be painfully bright. Ironically, Hellion had tracked us down and made himself part of that trip too. *Don't think about it.*

The day was typically overcast and a soft rain fell. The sweep of the windshield wipers was hypnotic. Hellion reached across the console and held out a hand. I took his giant paw in mine, seeking only comfort. His hands were work-roughened, and I asked him why.

"It's from the gardening and harvesting I do at my country home in Ireland. It's not all city living and funds management for me," he teased.

I looked over at him to find him staring at me, a soft smile playing around his lips.

"Watch the road, please," I murmured. He turned back to traffic and I said, "I should be able, and I'd like, to visit Ireland once these murders are solved." The thought of putting some distance between me and current events was appealing.

"We can go for a night if you'd like. I can just materialize at home."

"That would be nice."

"Let's plan on that tonight. I'll find a place in the woods for us to dematerialize, and we'll spend the night at my home. I'll send one of my coven members after the car, and they can return it to me in London. We'll materialize at the London house tomorrow morning and begin working on the murders."

I thought about it briefly. The idea of some more casual privacy in which to get to know this man felt important. And the opportunity to get out of England and Scotland was truly priceless. "Before we go, can we take a minute to see Stonehenge since we'll be so close?"

He smiled over at me. "Of course, *mo chroí.*"

I flinched and couldn't control a small intake of breath. I took my hand back gently.

"I'll find my own pet names for you, Madeleine." He rolled his eyes up to the roof dramatically and said, "Maddy," as if he were put upon.

I forced a watery smile and realized that was all he'd been after. He offered me his hand again, saying, "If I may offer you any ease, Maddy, take it. I'll not push you in any way." I took his hand and he was right, it was comforting. We held hands for the rest of the trip, with Hellion occasionally lifting my fingers to his lips and murmuring to me in Irish. There was almost enough difference in the language that it wasn't too painful to hear...almost.

We arrived in Avon long before our appointed meeting with Sarenia, but we went to the stone circle anyway. Any stone circle with five or more standing stones, one for each Council member's sect, was a safe haven among the supes. No violence could occur within the original circle, thus explaining why the megaliths were all over Europe. I'd snorted with laughter when Bahlin had explained this to me, debunking the ageless extraterrestrial theories. He hadn't been entertained.

Wrath

The circles were governed by magic dating back to the days of creation. Anyone attempting violence on another within a circle was marked on the cheek with a symbol similar to mathematical Pi and subject to an immediate death sentence and execution by the High Council. Getting to and from the circles was the tricky part since ambushes weren't unheard of. Hellion had picked a very public circle, the largest in the UK, to give us room to maneuver without too much tourist interruption. He wanted to be well seated when Sarenia arrived because she and Bahlin had been allies for over two thousand years and, as I'd recently learned, she was his godmother. It would be easy to strike first and pretend to ask questions of his flaming pile of ash later. She struck me as much more level-headed than that, but this was based on a single meeting with her.

We parked the car at the car park and walked to the small vegetarian restaurant near the circle for lunch. I wasn't hungry, but Hellion again insisted I eat something to keep my energy up. We'd been sitting in the small diner for about half an hour, our food just delivered, when I realized we were being watched by a small man wearing a bulky jacket and having a hard time sitting still. The man looked somehow out of place in the restaurant. I probably would have figured out what it was that set him apart if I'd been able to get past his gaze. If a pair of eyes could speak, his were issuing me threats of violence and promises of pain. I looked away and shivered, unnerved by the level of malevolence held for me by a complete stranger.

"Hellion?" I leaned forward and spoke low. "We've got an audience."

"Aye, we do. He's a member of the Tuatha Dé Danann, Maddy." Hellion took a big bite of his tabouli and said, "He's been following us for about an hour, love. He picked us up outside Avon as if he knew we'd be here."

"Why didn't you say anything?" Setting my fork down while still looking at Hellion, I missed the edge of the table and dropped it to the floor with a clatter. I had to bend toward the faerie to pick up the fallen utensil. I thought it over before sighing and beginning to move very casually. He shot out of his chair and ran out of the restaurant.

"Oops." Obviously my mad stealth skills still sucked.

Hellion smiled. "I'd imagine he was supposed to deliver a message to one of us, but finding us together threw him. The fae know of the prophecy, but their king and queen had hoped you would bond with

67

Tarrek. Beyond their wishes, they'll be as surprised as any of us to find we've been cast together."

"Oh. I, uh, had no idea they'd wanted that. That's a little awkward." The sentiment seemed insufficient in the wake of their son's death, but I couldn't find it in me to regret his demise. "Should we go look for our messenger?"

"The little fellow? No. He'll either show up again or we'll be approached by another of the fae. I would imagine the king or queen, or both, seeks an audience with one of us."

That reminded me—the queen had asked to speak to me. I opened my mouth to tell Hellion about Clay's message when I realized the couple at the next table were listening unapologetically to our conversation. They'd gone so far as to give up their meals in order to lean closer. I glared at them, and the man sat back, but the woman couldn't take her eyes off Hellion. I cleared my throat and she didn't flinch so I leaned forward. "Boo."

She jumped back as if I'd yelled at her instead of spoken softly. Standing, she gathered her tourist flotsam and stalked out of the restaurant, muttering about the rudeness of the locals.

I laughed out loud and leaned over to her partner. "Tell her I'm from the States. The locals here are much nicer than I've ever been."

He gathered his coat and dropped some bills on the table before scampering after his table partner.

Hellion laughed softly "That was brilliant, Maddy! They'll likely remember your attitude and not the topic of conversation. Good thinking, chit. I'm typically more conscientious, but I'm a bit distracted today. Apologies."

It hadn't been thinking at all, which I wasn't going to tell him. Instead it had been pure, unfiltered jealousy at the woman's interest in Hellion. Okay, it was prefaced by concern, but the knee-jerk reaction was in response to the jealousy. I shoved my plate away. "I'm done."

"You've hardly eaten a half dozen mouthfuls."

"And you're not my keeper, so can the attitude. One father was all I ever needed."

"Where are your parents, Maddy? I'd like to meet them."

I closed my eyes and felt the hot burn of tears in my throat. "They died," I rasped. Two traitorous tears fell over my lower lashes and raced for my jaw. A roughed thumb beat them there and brushed them away.

"*Ta bron*, Madeleine."

I opened my eyes and looked at him, laying my cheek in his hand. "Taw broin?"

"I'm sorry."

"Oh." Again. "I'd say it's okay, it'll be fine, but it's not and it may never be. Some things never really seem to heal."

"I hope that others will." He stood, took his wallet out and dropped a few bills on the table before coming around to pull out my chair for me. I sighed. My status as an independent, modern woman seemed to have caved under the force of these western European men. I smiled, sure it had something to do with their accents. Oh, and rugged good looks didn't hurt. Bahlin would be happy to know he'd influenced me and created in me high expectations.

We walked out of the restaurant companionably, my hand tucked in Hellion's arm.

We sat in the fast-diminishing sunshine on thermal blankets designed to keep our rumps dry. Hellion had his arm slung casually over my shoulders, chatting about his childhood and his Irish estate. I gradually relaxed and enjoyed this new open, easy manner of his.

It wasn't long before the creep of power swept into the circle and almost forced us apart. Sarenia wasn't happy. Mundanes in the area began to wander away without seeming to notice they were more interested in leaving than in staying. I stood and turned to face her as she walked into the circle, her rage palpable.

"Sarenia." My voice was cooler than spring water. I only inclined my head to her in deference to her status.

"Niteclif," she bit out. Oh yeah, she was pissed. She looked over at Hellion, who was just getting to his feet. "Wizard."

"Come now, Sarenia. I've known you for more than two centuries and you've never called me simply 'wizard.' Let us discuss this like rational beings."

She sat and we followed her lead. "Tell me what happened," she commanded.

So I did, beginning with the prophecy and Odin's little interruption, my conversation with Bahlin, the conflict and fight and, ultimately, our plunge out the window. I made sure to explain that

Bahlin had instigated the fight against my express desire. It mattered to me, if to no one else.

Sarenia took it all in, tears coursing down her face at the mention of Bahlin's plunge and my account of his death. "Did you see his body?" she asked.

Struggling to maintain the little bit of control I felt when Bahlin's name came up, I answered her. "No. But Sarenia, I've left messages for him everywhere I could think he might be and he hasn't answered—his cell, his brother's cell, the hotel, with several members of the weyr. Hellion has looked at the hotel. We've scried for him. And I've pleaded with the gods to interfere." My shoulders slumped. "There wasn't time for him to change. I don't think there's any way he survived the fall."

"So you don't believe he could have flashed to dragon and saved himself?"

I shook my head, mute with the loss of him.

Hellion listened carefully, his face a study in careful neutrality. "Is it possible he could have cloaked that quickly? Because no one reported anything. In fact, no one reported seeing us all fall."

Sarenia waved a hand. "He probably cloaked you on the way down, meaning he may have had time to shift. So you never saw the body?"

A spark of hope seated itself in my heart. "No. No body."

"Then you've no proof he's dead, Niteclif." She started to add to her answer then stopped. "Yet you have come together anyway." She looked at us, gesturing to our joined hands and our togetherness.

Hellion answered her, but instead of denying we were lovers he said, "Sarenia, you know the prophecy better than any, as your daughter was the one to deliver it. It's been verified by three sources, as required by the Council. Maddy and I are predestined, and no amount of anger will change that."

I looked back and forth between the two. There was that word: predestined. Did Hellion really believe in true love or was he just accepting his fate? Most likely it was a little of both. I myself had acted on both, believing Bahlin was my One and then accepting pieces, but *only* pieces, of the prophecy as fact. Add into the mix the feelings I had of having known Hellion somehow before all of this, and it was one huge damn mess.

Sarenia turned to me and asked, "Did you love Bahlin?"

I was so thrown by the question I answered quickly and honestly. "Yeah. I still do." I quickly looked over at Hellion. "I'm sorry, Hellion. You know how I feel."

He smiled gently and said, "I do. Yet you will love me too, only differently than you ever loved him. We are fated, you and I."

Goosebumps ran up and down my arms. Bahlin had said the exact same words to me weeks ago.

"We are." I wasn't sure who it was that I was answering...or remembering.

Sarenia sighed. "As much as it pains me, I must admit I believe this is right."

My head snapped around. "What's right?"

"The two of you. Your connection is visible, like one heart split between two bodies, one soul reunited. I fear that if Bahlin finds out, this will pain him greatly, prophecy or no."

I nodded in agreement.

"Be gentle with him, Madeleine Niteclif. He will need your patience and understanding through all this."

"So you believe he's alive?"

"I believe the odds are in his favor."

"Why did he not show when I scried for him?" Hellion chewed on his bottom lip, the action an undoubted holdover from youth, then smiled. "Ah, if he was cloaking himself with his full magic, he would have been invisible to me."

I nodded. "He could also have gone to his den. If he made the shift, he would have headed there. He told me it's a magical place of safety for him."

"Did he take you to his den?" Hellion and Sarenia asked at the same time, both incredulous.

"Yeah. Why?"

"It's a huge sign of commitment from a dragon," Sarenia answered, glancing over at Hellion. He was scowling and picking at the grass.

I reached over and laid a hand on his arm to still his destruction. "You're taking me to Ireland. Isn't that kind of the same?" I moved my hand to trace the edge of his lips, and they twitched in response. Sarenia looked so sad.

"What?" The belligerent word came out like a challenge.

"He will take you home and seat you in his place of power. You're right. It's significant as well, Niteclif. You are well-mated, but at what price?" She stood, dusting herself off, and prepared to leave. "We will convene here again tomorrow evening so that all may come safely. I will spread the word. The king and queen of the fae will wish to attend."

"Oh yeah. We had a visitor—"

"Follower," Hellion interrupted.

"Okay, a follower. He was fae. Do you think that's what he wanted—to ask us to meet with the king and queen?" The thought made me nervous. I wasn't looking forward to meeting with Tarrek's parents. How do you express remorse for, essentially, arranging the murder of their psychotically deranged son? Hallmark doesn't exactly make a card for that.

Sarenia watched the different emotions cross my face before answering. "I'm quite sure the king wants to recommend a replacement fairy for the High Council. He is disqualified from serving because he is a ruling monarch. It would be like asking your president to serve on your Supreme Court, yes?"

Why couldn't all explanations be so simple? I wondered, nodding in understanding.

"The vampires and shapeshifters must also recommend their replacements, so I will coordinate that. Unless, of course, you'd like to do so, Hellion?" Sarenia watched him carefully.

"My interest in serving the Council has never run toward leadership, but thank you for the vote of confidence," he answered formally. He slipped an arm around me and pulled me close, silently daring her to suggest otherwise.

She inclined her head to him and walked away. Stopping, she turned back to me and asked, "And what will you do, Niteclif, if you find Bahlin has survived?"

Self-doubt washed over me. "I don't know, Sarenia. He left me and sort of affirmed it was for the best. Do I love him? Yes. Is it enough? I don't think it's enough to carry the whole relationship, no."

"And besides, Sarenia," Hellion said, his voice resonating so that it carried across the distance effortlessly, "I ask her only to share the burden of love, not to bear it alone. Odin has spoken, and she is my heart. I will not let her go willingly."

"Odin means nothing to me." Outside the circle, she disappeared.

Chapter Eight

Night crept in from the shadows, finally falling around us as a blanket of stars covered the blue-black sky. Hellion drew me close and kissed me, and the stones seemed to hum their approval. "What's that?" I asked, gently pulling away. I wasn't entirely comfortable with the easy intimacy that had developed between us today, appealing as it was.

He wrapped his arms tighter around me and raised his brows. "You truly do not know?"

"Wouldn't have questioned it if I did." I ducked my chin, trying to buy the time I needed to regain control of my facial expression following the tenderness of the kiss.

He lifted my face to meet his. "Will you kiss me, just once, as if you hadn't a care in the world?"

I shrugged. It wouldn't be the first time, and it wasn't like I was cheating. *Except on his memory,* I thought. Before I could convey my change of heart, Hellion kissed me more enthusiastically.

Throwing caution to the wind, I kissed him back. The stones quivered with energy, nearly singing their praise. It felt like my heart was vibrating with the intensity of their sound.

It sounds joyful, I thought.

Hellion broke the kiss but kept his hand on the back of my neck. "It's a lover's henge, Madeleine. When lovers come together inside the circle and kiss, the stones answer them if their love is true. If it is not, the stones remain silent and the lovers are cast apart."

My stomach plummeted to my feet. *So this is it.* I was surprised I wasn't any more terrified than I was. I didn't run screaming. I didn't have a panic attack. I stood and stared at him, feeling the beat of his heart and seeing it echoed in his eyes. Seriously, they seemed to pulse.

I looked away. "Why do your eyes do that?"

"What? Oh, the pulsing? It's power. When I feel some strong emotion they change, just as they do when I channel magic, large or small. It's a consequence of my power and the same reason they're truly black. They're a mark of my standing in the magical community."

"What color were they?" I pulled back more strongly and, after a brief moment, he let me go.

"Plain brown," he answered softly. "Do you know you're the first person to have asked me that since they changed?" He stroked my face and laid his forehead to mine.

I thought back to a discussion with Bahlin, and it became relevant all over again. "How long will you live, Hellion?"

He shrugged but was much more direct than my dragon had been. "The level of magic I carry slows the aging process. It's impossible to know exactly what my lifespan will be since my power only increases with practice, but I would guess another three to five hundred years."

"How old are you?"

He laughed and said, "I guess it's fair since I know your age. I am three hundred thirty-eight years old."

I flinched. Seems I really had a thing for older men. "You look good for your age," I said, and he squeezed my hands.

"Very funny, chit. Shall we go on to Ireland?"

Suddenly the whole thing seemed funny, and I laughed out loud and nodded.

Laughing with me, he picked me up and spun me around, the world blacked out and we were gone.

I opened my eyes to a lovely living room in what looked like a very old house. The walls were plaster and the hearth was stacked fieldstone. A fire blazed and the lights were set low. Large, masculine furniture lined the room. Floor-to-ceiling bookshelves were set into opposing walls. It was the kind of place that made me feel as if I could curl up and read for hours with a glass of neat whiskey at my fingertips and a hunting dog curled at my feet.

"Oh, Hellion, it's lovely." I stepped out of his arms to look around the room. I walked the perimeter, picking up and setting down knick-knacks and running my fingers along the spines of the classics—Dickens, Frost, and Brontë among them. More modern books were held on another shelf—Gabaldon, King, Butcher, Hamilton. I could definitely stay here for ages.

He moved up behind me and slid his arms around my waist. He dropped his chin to my shoulder and I sighed. Why was he so comfortable to me? No idea. A small kernel of self-doubt still existed, wondering, *Why me?* But I wasn't sure if it was a question for the moment or the question of the ages.

Sliding his hands down my sides, he grabbed my hands, and soft music began to play on the stereo.

I looked over my shoulder and into his black, pulsing eyes. "Did you do that?" My voice carried softly across the short space between our lips.

"Mm-hmm." He kissed me gently, still swaying back and forth to the eerie, sexy Celtic crooning.

I leaned back slightly, breaking the kiss. "No kissing. In fact, we probably shouldn't be dancing."

I made to step away from him and he said, "Just relax for a moment, Maddy."

I tried to relax my stiff shoulders. "What about the lights and the fire?"

"The house is staffed, and they prepare for me each evening on the off chance I pop in."

"Bad pun."

He shrugged and spun me out and pulled me back. I ended up facing him, his arms holding me gently. "Years to perfect romancing the ladies is turning out to be beneficial for me," I teased.

He grew still and serious. "Madeleine, prophecy or no prophecy, I believe we would have ended up together. What I feel for you surpasses everything I've ever felt before."

My heart contracted but any response I might have offered hung up in my throat. I put my hands on his chest and pushed away gently, needing space. *Too fast, too fast,* screamed my head, while my heart whispered, *Maybe.* I couldn't so blindly accept the prophecy as he did. I was a creature who should be ruled by logic, but logic held no place in the deepest corners of the heart. It was like being blind, moving ahead without any reassurance of what was around the corner or, more immediately, right in front of you.

He watched me struggle and bent to kiss me softly despite my earlier warning.

I turned away and his lips brushed my cheek. Taking his hand, I led him to the sofa and sat down. "I wanted tonight to get to know you. I need to feel more connected to you than the prophecy affords, Hellion." I realized I'd put myself in yet another strange country with a man I hardly knew, with no knowledge of where exactly I was, or how I'd get away from him if I needed to. Not the wisest thing I'd ever done. It ranked right up there with punching my dragon in the face. *Can't think about that.*

Hellion sat down with me and leaned back on the sofa, putting his feet up on the ottoman and pulling me close. "Of course, *mo shíorghrá*. What do you wish to know?"

"First, what does that mean?"

"It means 'my eternal love.' But surely you're not here to learn the Irish?" he teased.

"No," I answered so quietly the exhalation of breath was louder than the word.

"Don't worry, Maddy, love. It will be fine. You'll see. Odin wouldn't have paired us if it were not to be so."

"I don't know how *not* to worry," I admitted. "I'm such a practical soul, Hellion. I don't buy mysticism and messages from gods."

"Not even when they are personally delivered?"

"I didn't firmly believe in any of you until Bahlin finally fully shifted in front of me, and by then I'd seen each of you up close. Hell, I'd been in the sithen." I shrugged, and the weight of his arm around my shoulders was heavy. Suddenly I felt stifled, like I couldn't quite catch my breath. I stood up and walked to the window and stared at my own reflection, the darkness outside barely separated from the light within by the thin skin of glass. Profound, that.

The glass reflected Hellion's movements, and I saw him stand and walk up behind me. He didn't touch me but I could feel the power roiling around him. It was like being buffeted by a commanding wind without a hair on your head moving. Very strange.

"Maddy?" he asked tentatively. "I have a favor."

"Sure," I answered without thinking.

"Come to bed with me."

"That's a bit more than a favor, Hellion," I snapped out.

He dipped his head but not before I caught the flash of teeth and the smile. "Not for sex, Maddy, but for contact. It seems we're easier with each other when we're touching. I'd hold you while we talk. Of course, if you'd prefer sex, I'm fine with that."

I relaxed a little and turned to face him. "I'll go to bed with you only if you promise to not try to seduce me. Okay?"

He closed his eyes and took a deep breath before answering. "I suppose," he groused, but he finally touched me and pulled me close.

I leaned back into him and laid my hands across his forearms.

"Come to bed, my Madeleine."

What had happened to my moral compass? I shivered, not sure who I thought I was fooling with my talk of abstinence. It wasn't working. I knew in that moment that it was inevitable that some night soon we would end up in bed for more than comfort. And if I wanted to add logic to the mix, there were two options for me: I was either the whore of Babylon or following my destiny. I could suddenly see with disturbing clarity why people used destiny as an excuse.

Morning dawned bright and clear, and I had my first look at the grounds. They were unbelievable. Hellion's cottage was more historic manor house with beautiful flower gardens surrounding it. I yanked my jeans on and rushed down the stairs only to meet him coming up.

"You're an early riser," I said almost accusingly.

"Only today. You're a cover hog." He smiled, and I did my best not to think of the time Bahlin had accused me of the same thing.

I'm not going there.

"Sorry." He quirked an eyebrow and I attempted a grin. It came across as pained-looking, I'm sure. "Okay, I slept like the dead. I'm not really sorry, but I'll try to be better." It was out before I could stop myself.

Hellion moved on as if I hadn't just admitted there would be a next time. "What would you like to do this morning before breakfast? Because I know you're not going to go rushing back to London to begin the investigation without breakfast."

"It's all about food with you, you know it?" I demanded, moving passed him to look out the mudroom door. "I want to wander the gardens and have you tell me about the flora and fauna. I'm absolutely enamored," I said, looking over my shoulder.

His eyes pulsed. "As am I," he said gently.

Uncomfortable with any kind of intimacy in the light of day, I opened the door and stepped out into the warm morning. I was so tired of it being dreary that the sunshine was like a celebration, and I'd never seen anything so green as Ireland in all my life. The rolling hills, the grass around the house, the bushes. It was vibrant, with splashes of color everywhere the eye looked. There were primary colors and pastels, bright and soft mingled together, with crisp interjections of white here and there. Every color of the rainbow was represented, and it was all done so well that it didn't feel overwhelming to the senses, but rather earthy and organic. The multitude of flowers gave off a combination of scents, some spicy and some predictably floral. It was heady just to stand, eyes closed, and breathe in the smells.

We walked and talked the morning away, discussing nothing to do with flowers but about everything else. I learned more about his childhood in the 1600s and the changes he'd seen; we talked about the United States and the things I missed of home. He learned that I loved English and hated math, while he was an alchemist at heart and couldn't write terribly well. We shared many of the same likes and dislikes, though he couldn't fathom that I didn't like seafood. Nothing was too small to discuss, dissect, consider. We held hands, and he cradled me gently under the rose arbor. He lifted me over a small mud puddle to keep me from getting dirty. He laid me down on a bed of clover and held me close, my head resting in the depression of his shoulder, the silence comfortable. It was the single most beautiful morning of my life.

As was his wont, he demanded food early that afternoon. We went back to the house, and I blushed when the staff met us at the front door.

"Maddy, they want to meet you. Let me introduce you?" I nodded, and he led me to the doorway where they'd gathered. We went through the formal introductions to each individual—there were eleven people total—and then he shocked the shit out of me when he said, "Ladies and gentlemen, allow me to introduce you to the new lady of the manor, Madeleine Niteclif."

Stifling my indignation at his presumption that I'd come around to his way of thinking, I found myself unsure whether to bow or curtsy. For the second time in only a handful of weeks, I did a combination of both and they all just stared. Hellion choked on his laughter, and I glared at him.

"Say something to them," he whispered, red in the face.

I just thanked them for their service and asked where the dining room was. At this they all chuckled, and Hellion roared with laughter. But I got lunch, and the service was stellar.

We had just finished eating when his butler, Conor, came in and cleared his throat softly. "Sir, I'm sorry to interrupt but there's a young man here who claims to urgently need to speak to the lady."

Hellion laid his hand over mine. I looked up and met his concerned gaze. We hadn't told anyone I was here.

"Did he give a name?" I asked, lifting my wine glass to my lips.

"He did. It's Aiden Drago, member of the Blue Dragon Weyr."

I choked on my drink, and Hellion rushed to pound me on the back. "Bahlin's little brother is here?" I croaked.

"You don't have to see him, Maddy. I'll send him away," he snapped and turned to deal with Aiden.

"No! No, Hellion. I'd like to see what he wants. Please." His hands tightened on my shoulders, and I nearly begged him to let Aiden in. I turned to him and asked again, "Please."

Hellion's eyes pulsed differently, dangerously. "He'll no be takin' ye from me, *mo chroí*," he snarled, "and I'll no apologize for callin' ye so."

It was the first time I'd heard his accent so pronounced. "I won't leave with him," I promised. "Just let me find out what he wants."

He stalked away from me then turned and came back toward me, the rage still plain on his face. I had a brief, irrational moment of fear. He saw it and slowed, and I relaxed.

"I won't hurt you, and I'm sorry you thought I might." His voice was stiff and formal. "I'll see you into the living room and fetch him for you. But I insist on being there, Maddy."

"I wouldn't have it any other way." Surprisingly, I meant it. I wouldn't be alone with a dragon from Bahlin's weyr for all the gold in a wealthy dragon's den.

His eyes pulsed again, and this time it was his heart I saw in them.

I took his arm, and we walked through the lower level to the same living room we'd come into last night. The room was entirely different in the daytime, with beautiful views of the gardens and soft natural light bringing out the deep reds and browns of the mahogany woodwork.

Hellion left me seated on a loveseat and went to get Aiden. There was a brief, heated exchange, and I imagined young Aiden trying to force his hand with Hellion. Of course, young Aiden was older than Hellion, but his power was nowhere near formed yet. I worried for his wellbeing. The voices simmered down, and I heard approaching footsteps. I stood just as the two men entered the living room.

Aiden looked older, aged with anger. He sneered at me and took in the room in one motion. "Didn't take you long to move on, did it, dear sister?"

Hellion stood to his full height and glared down at Aiden. "Ye'll keep a civil tongue in her house, boy," he rumbled, his manner full of unspoken threat.

Aiden's eyebrows shot nearly to his hairline. "*Her house?*" he choked. "Great goddess, Maddy. What have ye done?"

I shrugged, unsure what he was asking.

"Are ye handfasted then?" he demanded.

Before I could answer, Hellion said, "That's none of yer concern, Aiden. Why've yeh come?"

The verbal volleys combined with the Irish and Scottish accents had my mind reeling. "I—"

"Ye owe no one any answers, Madeleine," Hellion said gently.

"So does yer man speak for ye then?" Before I could answer, Aiden shook his head and sighed. "There's nothin' here for the blue dragons, Maddy. I was wrong to come."

Trying to regain a little of my slipping composure, I stood and smoothed my shirt. "How did you know where I was?" I was pissed at having been stuck between two men again when my heart was bleeding for Bahlin. And Aiden looked enough like Bahlin that I couldn't look away from him. I felt Hellion move closer to me.

"You're not the only one with a magician, Niteclif."

"Fair enough." I swallowed hard. "Aiden, can you tell me what happened to Bahlin? I need to know." The pleading in my voice embarrassed me, but not enough to stop me from asking again. "Please."

"You've no right to either weyr or family business," he said, lifting his chin defiantly. "This is both. You've clearly chosen your side, Niteclif."

"This isn't about politics, boy. Her heart's breaking. Bahlin wouldn't want her to hurt." Hellion stepped closer to me and laid a comforting hand on my shoulder.

"You have no idea what Bahlin would want. Neither of you does." Aiden was visibly trying to gather himself and leave with a good parting shot.

"Fine. You've made your point." I stepped forward and reached out a hand beseechingly. "Please don't leave me without something, okay? You can either end the false hope or the false heartache. Do that for me, if for no other reason than that your brother cared for me at one point."

"What Bahlin felt doesn't matter—not anymore. I'll see you at the meeting tonight." He turned and walked out without a backwards glance.

As parting shots went, he'd scored a bull's eye.

Aiden's reference to Bahlin in the past tense had taken me to my knees as he left the room. Hellion picked up the pieces silently, pulling me into strong arms.

I needed to get my mind off the heartache, so we prepared to immediately return to another of Hellion's London homes. We were both quiet, neither willing to share what was going on behind shuttered eyes. I would have willingly bet our thoughts centered around the same dragon, though they were probably as far from similar as they could get.

Our plan was to go to London and poke about a bit, see what we could learn about the murders, then take that to the meeting tonight. We'd have to materialize inside the circle, so the two coven members who had gone after the car were going to set up a protective circle for us to come into that would hide our activity from prying eyes. Only luck had hidden us when we'd dematerialized the night before, and I knew enough not to count on her benevolence twice.

Hellion and I came back together in the master bedroom of his Lees Place home. It was still disconcerting as hell to me when we popped in and out of places. I took my jacket off and tossed it on the chair near his bed. My overnight bag had been delivered here at some point, and it was both comforting and foreign—the familiar in the unfamiliar place.

Hellion went into his closet to change out of his heavy sweater. He emerged in a soft, plaid flannel that looked like it had seen no less than a hundred washings. I was about to touch the shirt when I heard footsteps along the hallway's wood floor, and the bedroom door opened.

"I apologize, sir, I had no idea you had, er, company," stammered an average, forgettable young man.

"She's not 'company,' Mark. She's my... She's my..." Hellion was truly stumped about how to introduce me.

"I'm his partner," I answered for him.

"No, she's more than that. She's my..."

I was honestly a little amused at Hellion's discomfort, and held out a hand to Mark, who seemed genuinely startled at my greeting. He shook it tentatively and looked at Hellion.

"She's my *anamchara*." He stood up straighter and made a sweeping gesture with his hand, clearly proud to have come up with some type of titled introduction. Mark, who was obviously British, looked confused. "My soul mate, man," Hellion groused, disgruntled to have to spell it out.

"Don't let him insult you, Mark. Hell, I'm American, and half the time I don't know what he's spouting off about in that strange brogue of his." I smiled sweetly and Hellion just glowered back.

"Pay the woman in compliments—"

"And get your ass handed back to you as change. Probably a lesson best learned early with me if we're going to be spending much time together."

Mark snorted with laughter and had to step out of the room for a moment, presumably to compose himself. I could hear him guffawing just outside, and his sincere laughter set me at ease. But that was short lived when I realized what I'd said. "If we're going to be spending much time together." It was a shock to realize Hellion's faith in the prophecy was wearing me down, that a small part of me was busy hating myself for being so inconsequential with my affections while another part of me was relieved to have at least acknowledged I was alive and Bahlin's death hadn't killed me. The prophecy, that horrid prophecy, had rocked my entire belief system, and I was irrationally angry. The longer I thought about it, the angrier I got.

"Damn you, Odin," I screamed.

Hellion jumped and clapped a hand over my mouth.

I bit him and tasted blood.

"Sod it all, Madeleine," he roared and shook his hand. Blood flew in a fine arc from his hand and I watched, temporarily transfixed, as it splattered against the pale wall and begin to slide slowly down. He muttered under his breath, and my voice was gone again.

I flipped him off and stormed into the bathroom, slamming and locking the door behind me. I turned on the water to the shower and screamed in silence. Not the first time I'd reacted like a bug nut.

The door flew open and Hellion stormed in. I slipped as I turned to face him, cracking my head against the edge of the counter. I grabbed my scalp, feeling for blood before I stood and started to fling things at Hellion—hairdryer, toothbrush, brush, towels, anything I could reach.

He reached out and snagged me around the waist and hauled me back to the bedroom, tossing me on to the bed and falling on top of me. I was mutely cussing him actively and creatively when he gave my voice back.

"... stupid, fucking toad spawn, I'll rip your balls off and boil them in your damn cauldron and make dick soup to feed the dog you son of a—"

"Dick soup?" he asked, calmly, pinning my hands over my head. We were both breathing hard.

"Get the hell off me," I panted, unable to quit struggling despite his superior strength.

He shifted to his side and rolled me with him, keeping my arms pinned. Dumbass forgot about my legs.

"You're one good push from singing soprano, asshole," I spit out, shoving my knee between his legs and into the soft sacs of his testicles. He clamped down with his thighs. I reared back and head-butted him. Unfortunately he was so tall I only reached his chin, and I split my forehead open. "Son of a bitch!"

The door banged open and Mark the butler stood there staring at us, unsure whom to aid first.

"Out," Hellion bellowed. The door shut quietly again.

"Slam the fucking door, Mark. You'll feel better, trust me," I yelled after him.

"Don't encourage the staff, Madeleine," Hellion growled. He rolled away from me, and we both lay there breathing heavily.

I swiped the blood out of my eyes but it wasn't enough. I got up with a groan. That I was going to be sore all over from such a brief tussle was embarrassing. I had to get back in shape. I rolled off the bed and stumbled into the bathroom. Grabbing a hand towel to hold to my head, I rinsed the blood from my face one-handed in the sink. I looked up into the wide bathroom mirror to check the split and saw Hellion standing behind me.

"Let me see," he said softly. I turned to face him, and he lifted the edge of the towel from the wound. It was minor.

"Can you fix it?" I asked.

"Yes, but I won't." He laid three fingers across my lips to stop my response. "I won't for two reasons. First, you got what you were after, which was a fight. I swore I'd never fight with you over him. Second, it would cost me something to heal a self-inflicted wound you earned while fighting with me, and I need all my power for tonight."

"What's the big deal about tonight?" I asked.

He looked at me funny. "The Blue Dragon Weyr will be there, Maddy."

"But there's no fighting inside the circle, right?"

"No, there's no fighting. But if I get physically pushed outside, it's considered a legitimate tactic and I'll have to fight."

"That's not fair!"

He shook his head, dabbing at the wound on my forehead. The bleeding had almost stopped so he reached under the counter and grabbed a small case, extracting a tiny butterfly bandage. He smiled as he stuck the bandage on. "No, love, it's not fair, but fighting rarely is." He tapped my forehead gently, and I grimaced at the obviousness of it all.

I laid a hand across his wrist and met his eyes in the mirror. "I'm sorry."

He paused briefly then went back to cleaning up the counter. "For what?"

Embarrassment flushed my skin with color. I stepped aside to give him access to the trashcan. "This. All of it. I'm not sure exactly what pushed me over the edge. Just...all of it, I guess."

"Understandable."

"Is there anything I can do to help? Tonight, I mean." I asked. Fear made my stomach hurt. So many things to juggle, politics to interpret and vaguely mapped responsibilities to take care of.

"Stick by me, no matter what."

"Is there anything I need to know before we get there?"

"Nothing I can predict with certainty. If it comes to a fight, though, the gloves will be off and things will get dirty fast. "

"Good to know."

It was lost on neither of us that I hadn't promised him anything.

We went down to an early dinner. Mark met us in the dining room, his actions careful and measured as he set plates in front of us.

"I'm sorry, Mark." He jumped at the sound of my voice, making me feel even worse about fighting in front of him. "Forgive me?"

He blushed, stuttered and left the room.

"What did I say?"

Hellion chuckled under his breath. "You don't owe him an apology, Maddy."

"That's rude! Of course I do. Otherwise he'll think I'm horrible."

"So?" He continued to cut up his grilled chicken, indifferent to the situation.

"So? Are you always this insensitive?" I grumped. "And why can't you put ice in anything you drink? Coke is meant to be cold."

He smiled and called loudly, "Mark."

"You asshat," I said just as Mark came through the door. He backed out. "What did he... Not again. Mark!"

He stepped through, looking at neither of us. "Ma'am?"

"I'm sorry. That last was for Hellion."

Mark's eyes darted to me and back to the floor. "Yes, ma'am."

Hellion snorted. "She'd like some ice."

"Yes, sir." Mark quickly turned to leave.

"I'm also sorry about you seeing us fight earlier. It's, um, I'm not always like that," I said to his retreating form. He stopped and turned to offer me some small platitude.

Before Mark could reply, Hellion paused and opened his mouth, and I just knew something foul was about to come out of it. He swallowed and said, "No, usually we're not fighting, unless you count—"

"You pig," I yelled, throwing a roll at him.

He fielded it nicely. "Years of lacrosse, dear. You'll have to do better than—ouch!"

The spoon hit him in the head.

"Years of watching Major League Baseball, chump, so I will."

Mark backed out of the room and burst out laughing.

"The staff won't respect me any longer if you keep this up," Hellion said, sounding pained. "Mark."

Mark stepped back in the room yet again, his face red as he tried to keep from laughing. "Sir?"

"You came into my room earlier for a reason. What was it, man?"

"Ah, it was about the, ah, news, sir. You asked me to watch for further news..."

"Maddy's aware of the murders, Mark. You understand she's *the* Niteclif, right?"

Mark's eyes grew wide, and he looked between us both quickly. Then he leaned out the door and called out, "Kendall, Stearns, Mary." Looking back at me he said, "That's the maid, the driver and the cook, ma'am."

The two women and one man walked into the dining room and froze, obviously unsure what to make of Hellion dining with a woman.

"Ladies and gent, this is the Niteclif, the master's new mistress."

I flinched at the word, and Mark stumbled over himself trying to undo the offense.

"I'm, um, not exactly a mistress."

"I apologize—"

"No, no." I waved my hand as if clearing the air. "No worries."

Hellion reached over and took my hand, rubbing my knuckles with his thumb. "Madeleine is my heart's blood, my trial and temptation, and the prophesied love of my life. She's nobody's mistress." He smiled, and his face went from handsome to beautiful and all the women in the room, including me, sighed just a bit. He wiped his mouth, and Mark stepped forward quickly to draw out his chair. Hellion waved him off and stood to pull my chair out for me.

Rising, I turned back to Mark. "What was it you came in to tell us? Hellion. I mean, Hellion and me. I mean—"

"For the love, Maddy, just stop. He's really going to think we're sleeping together if you don't quit."

I rounded on him, ready to tear into him only to find him pinching his lips together behind my back.

"Your face. Odin save me, you have murder in your eye over such a natural thing." Laughter won out.

"Ha. Ha. Now I've laughed, and your Irish ego should be soothed." He sobered and it was my turn to chuckle.

"Mark?"

"Oh! Right. Sorry, sir. It's just, you've never laughed this much—"

Hellion cleared his throat and blushed. I was charmed and reached out to touch his hand. He jerked it back, and I felt comforted by the knee-jerk reaction. *Finally*, I thought, *something I understand*.

Mark strode out of the room and returned with an envelope. "This came for you this afternoon, sir, before you returned."

It was a letter addressed simply "H."

I leaned forward to watch Hellion open the letter. A lock of long, blond hair bound in blue string fell out, and black spots danced in front of my eyes.

"Too coincidental to even be funny," I whispered. Hellion's hair was so thick it would take forever to find where it had been clipped from, if the spot could be found at all.

He never flinched, never blanched, just opened the letter and read it, leaving the hair lying on the floor. He refolded the letter, handed it over to me and walked out of the room without a word.

I unfolded it and, sitting back down, I read.

Hellion.

Steer clear of the American whore. I realize she's a rousing good romp with Gretta gone, but the traitorous bitch is slated to meet a suitable end just as the fair Mary Stuart did.

Mary Stuart, known as Mary Queen of Scots, had ruled France and Scotland in the 1500s before being tried for and found guilty of treason. She had been beheaded. The girls who had been profiled and killed had nearly been beheaded. It took practice to get someone's head lopped off. *Shit*.

Hellion walked back in, his face flushed and his knuckles bloodied on his left hand. "Madeleine?" he asked, holding his good hand out to me.

I rose and walked to him, handing him the letter. He turned to Mark and said, "Put this in the library safe. Not a word to anyone, even the other staff, about what was in that letter. Set some basic wards while we're gone and open the door to no one. Use the hair that was cut to bind and strengthen the spell. Understand?"

"Perfectly, sir." He held his hand out for the letter and then bent to pick up the hair.

"Can I see it before you go?" I asked, holding out my hand for the small bundle of hair. One end had been cut with a sharp blade of some type because all the ends were even and smooth, though whether it had been done with a knife or scissors was anyone's guess. I handed the hair back to Mark, who tucked it in the envelope and silently left the room.

"Who are these people?" I asked, slightly stunned at the efficiency with which they all followed orders.

"All the houses are staffed with long-time members of my coven. Now, what are you thinking, Maddy?" Hellion moved to stand behind me and rub my shoulders.

"I'm thinking this is the first time the killer has screwed up. It's the first real clue we've got, Hellion." I reached back to pat his hand. He let me go and I turned to face him, my eyes fierce. "There's something in there—I just need to think it through. Give me a day or two, and in the meantime, find me somewhere else to stay."

He immediately protested. "I won't consider it. I can't help you if I can't protect you."

"Let me be very clear. I don't want you to protect me. If you intend to help me with this case, then help. But don't assume I'm some incompetent, male-dependent damsel who needs to be rescued. It just isn't the case." His face closed down, eyes cooled to flat black, his features taking on a hard edge. "Look, I realize you don't know me well enough to know I'm not waiting on my knight to arrive, but I'm not. It's just not my speed. I've had three years of martial arts training, I'm learning to be proficient with a dirk and dagger, and I intend to get better with a gun. And I've managed so far to survive a couple of serious fights. So it's up to you. Either be a partner in this or don't. Your call." I held my breath. It was a tough speech from someone who would have to ask to use the phone to call a cab if he gave me a fare-thee-well.

A bundle of muscles ticked at the hinge of his jaw. "Fine. It's after eight. We need to be off, Madeleine."

I involuntarily looked at the clock above the mantle. Where had the time gone?

"If it's not too heroic of me, I'd suggest you take a jacket tonight. Will you go and fetch it yourself or should I have Mark retrieve it?"

I ignored the sarcasm. No need to pick an unnecessary fight. "I'll get it. Be right back." I ran up the stairs, my mind in a totally different place. I walked into the bedroom and sniffed, smelling something strange, like singed hair. I followed the smell to the bathroom where it intensified. I'd have to mention the odd smell to Hellion. Before the idea could cement itself there was a scratching at the windowpane, and the hair on the back of my neck stood up. Turning, I caught movement from the corner of my eye. I looked toward the window but there was nothing there. I crept to the windowpane and looked out. I couldn't see anything except darkness. I retreated to the chair by the bed and retrieved my jacket.

"Maddy," Hellion yelled up the stairs.

"Coming." I raced down the stairs away from the creepy feeling of being watched, the odd smell long forgotten.

Chapter Nine

Hellion materialized with me in a small circle within Avebury Henge. There were about twenty witches and wizards already gathered within the stone circle, and to the last person they went down on bended knee and bowed their heads. I looked at Hellion, confused, only to find his response baffled me further. He looked impossibly moved, as shocked at their response to our arrival as the day Odin had delivered his message in person.

"What are they doing?" I asked quietly.

"Declaring their oath of fealty to you."

I stared at all of them and cleared my throat. "Please." With my voice still raspy, I had to clear my throat again. "Please stand. I'm no different from any of you."

Hellion stepped in front of me and gently lifted my chin so he could search my face, finally settling on my eyes. "You're wrong, *anamchara*. You're quite different. I'm the coven master of all of Europe, and you're both the Niteclif and my proclaimed soul mate."

"Oh." I'd known Hellion was near the top of the world of magic's hierarchal pyramid. I hadn't known he was the pinnacle. I was as shocked about that little revelation as I was about the "proclaimed soul mate" statement. *Too much, too fast.*

The coven members rose as one body and moved forward to congratulate us. Gossip apparently traveled fast among members of the coven if they knew I'd parked my stuff at his place and we'd had a visit from Odin.

We were still receiving well wishes when I felt the first brush of cold power, a creeping thing that made me search the darkness. I turned to the south before I could see anything. How I knew without a doubt the power was approaching from that direction was beyond me, but I was sure. "What is that?" I rubbed my arms to ward of the chill, but it was ineffective. It wasn't that kind of cold.

"Your sensory powers are developing, Maddy." Hellion seemed

pleased. "We'll discuss what I know of this after the meeting. For now, open your senses and pay attention, but say nothing."

Open my senses? I hadn't been able to open my wallet at lunch with him around. *Open my senses*, I snarked to myself.

Hellion took my hand and closed his eyes, and I felt him unfurl something gigantic. Unseen yet overwhelming, its impact was felt by everyone inside the circle. All eyes shifted to him, even if only briefly.

"What you feel, or sense, are vampires," he said. "Stay close to the center of the circle until we're sure how many there are."

I swallowed hard and nodded. I didn't have a good track record with vampires, so I'd follow orders like a good little soldier. The key would be to keep my mouth from making runaway promises or asinine threats.

A dozen or so pale faces emerged from the darkness, moving in a blur of speed. They stopped just outside the circle. It felt as if they were assessing prey, and I didn't like where that put me on the food chain.

"Darius. Good to see you, man." Hellion raised a hand in welcome.

The vampire, Darius, stepped into the circle, and I looked at him closely. He was beautiful in the way of vampires, with pale skin, deliciously dark brown eyes, chin-length dark hair and a body that moved with fluid grace. I was disappointed he wore all black, no matter how well-suited he seemed to the color. Darius approached us and nodded to Hellion, shaking his hand and passing him something shiny. Hellion never reacted, never moved, but the object was gone. Simple magic, probably, but I was curious.

Seeing me open my mouth, Darius reached out and took my hand and squeezed. As far as warnings went, it was both discreet and effective. "Madeleine Niteclif, it's a pleasure to meet you." His voice was reminiscent of great sex and dirty secrets.

"I hope to be able to say the same of you, Darius."

Hellion winced but Darius laughed, clapping the other man on the shoulder. "Don't worry about honesty. I'd want nothing less from the Niteclif."

"Who is your nomination for Imeena's position on the Council?" Hellion pushed his hands deep in his pockets, and I wondered if he was depositing the mystery object.

Darius looked almost pained. "I am."

Hellion shook his head and smiled ruefully, a dimple gracing his left cheek. "You avoided it as long as you were able. You'll be affirmed, Darius, I'm sure of it. Welcome aboard, Voyyah of London." They exchanged more newsworthy information and, as they were talking, I let my mind wander to the murders. I'd have to Google them when I got home tonight and check out the latest news for public consumption.

Sarenia showed up next. She wove through the clusters of people quickly and came straight to us. Her eyes gleamed with some sort of fanatical light. "Maddy? You are well?"

"I'm fine. Why?"

"Good, good." She walked away without answering me, moving to take a seat near the edge of the circle. She kept scanning the darkness, her hands folding and unfolding the silk of her dress until it was a wadded mess.

It only took a few minutes of watching her agitated behavior before I started after her. Hellion snagged the sleeve of my jacket, stopping me before I took more than a couple of short steps. I started to ask him to let me go until I saw the worry on his face.

"The shifters are here but they're hanging back, Maddy. Stay close, please." He bent to me under the pretense of kissing my ear and said, "Darius has left most of his people in the hills surrounding the circle."

I turned into his lips. "Sure." To anyone but the vampire at our sides we appeared to be nothing more than lovers.

As we waited, time took on a surreal quality. It was punctuated not by seconds or minutes but rather by snippets of overheard conversation, the fluid movement of people in and out of the circle and the laughter of flirtatious maneuvering, both sexual and political. I felt the dynamic shift in the group just before the heat crawled over my skin. Hellion stayed next to me but freed his hands and made sure we both had room to maneuver. He bent and pulled a small dirk from his boot and handed it to me. I took it without comment. Eventually I was going to have to get my own damn knife or, preferably, a gun.

"Dragon," he said, confirming my worst fears.

Aiden and his mother, Adelle, walked into the circle. They were followed by about twenty dragons of various colors. Overhead movement caught my eye, and I saw three forms lazily circling in the air. The dragons on the ground, both males and females of several weyr, glanced over at me. A disproportionate number of them wore openly hostile expressions. I opened my mouth to say something, but

Wrath

Darius grabbed my hand and squeezed just as Hellion bent to kiss me.

"Sorry," he whispered against my cold lips. "I need you to be very quiet."

I nodded. I definitely needed someone to walk me through this maze of strategy and politics.

Sarenia stood and moved to greet the dragons. They exchanged warm words with her before they turned as a group to face Hellion and me. "Patience, my friends," Sarenia cautioned.

Never one to take advice from the other team, I called out, "Aiden, good to see you again." I stepped in front of Hellion slightly, and I felt him move directly up to my shoulder and drape his arm casually around me. "How was your afternoon after you left Hellion's place?"

Aiden looked pained as his mother hissed something at him that was too low for us to hear. Darius stepped up behind me and said very quietly, "I don't believe the boy's mother knows what he's been up to today."

"Good to know," Hellion murmured.

Sarenia's voice cut across the clearing, effectively hushing the social chatter. "Vampires, who is your nomination for your Council seat vacancy?"

Darius stepped away from us and met her gaze. "Darius, Voyya of London."

"Very well. Are there any challengers?" No one stepped forward, and she left the answer hanging long enough that people began to shift and whisper. "The nomination shall stand unchallenged." Her breathing changed. Looking back, that's what I would remember—that her breathing changed, her chest rising and falling faster than normal, one hand fisting at her stomach while the other settled over her breastbone. Sarenia looked across the clearing at me and met my gaze, blinked slowly then raised her voice over the murmur of the crowd. "Representatives of the shapeshifters' faction, who is your nomination for your Council seat?"

"There is no vacancy," came the reply from just outside the circle.

I swear my heart stopped for the briefest moment before beginning to pound. Blood thundered in my ears as Hellion's arm tightened on my shoulders.

Bahlin.

I felt light-headed and thought for certain I was going to be sick. "Hellion," I choked out.

He urged me to sit, squatting next to me to easier reach my forehead and manage the swell of nausea. It passed, and I could feel the tremors running through him. He hadn't known Bahlin was alive either.

I scrambled to my feet, ready to run to Bahlin, but the fury in his look stopped me. I actually tipped forward and took an involuntary step toward him, so intent had I been on rushing into his arms.

"Nothing to say to me, Hellion? Not even after trying to kill me?" Bahlin stepped into the circle. His right leg was in a brace, and he leaned heavily on a walking stick, but otherwise he looked fine. "And what of you, Maddy? Nothing to say to your former *trekkór*? Not even a kiss for old time's sake?" He kept talking as he approached us slowly. "You know, the last I saw of you, Hellion, you were racing after me to confirm my death. But to protect Maddy, I cloaked us. Convenient the sun set as you arrived. No need to have her caught up in a mundane investigation if I couldn't pull out of the dive in time. Then she leapt after you. I was sure it was a mistake—right until you two disappeared into thin air. Together. I had the sense to shift before hitting the ground, thus saving my knee which, by the way, I owe you for nearly destroying." He stopped five paces in front of us. "I made it to my den. Aiden called, frantic. He'd been in touch with Sarenia and had heard about the incident from one of her Seers. We discussed it and decided it was best if another member of the Council was aware I'd survived so I called her back. She agreed to meet you when the call came in."

I turned to look at Sarenia, the hatred contained in my gaze open for all to see. "You knew he was alive. You met with me, left me with that lingering doubt when you could have put an end to my misery by telling me the truth?" My lips trembled so violently that I had a hard time forming my words. "You hurt him on purpose, you *bitch*."

Hellion put a warning hand to my throat and I objected, pushing at his hand at the same time I stepped clear of his reach.

Sarenia looked at me without remorse. "He had a right to know what was going on, Niteclif."

"Going on?" I was incredulous. "There was nothing going on. Tell me, though. Did you decide he had a right to this presumed information before or after you declared Hellion and I a good match?" I demanded.

She blanched and Bahlin turned to look at her. "Sarenia? Did you say this to her?"

"I did," she said, "and I'm sorry for it, Bahlin."

"It's irrelevant." He turned back to me and Hellion, venom lacing his next words. "Simple locator spells helped me track you two down. You were in Ireland. Together. Aiden went to check on you and reported you two were already handfast. Awfully quick, don't you think, Maddy? Hardly two weeks after I die, and you've moved on so thoroughly as to be lady of the manor? Impressive." He tucked his walking stick up under his arm and clapped his hands slowly, derisively. "Unwilling to take even my own brother's word for it, I went to Hellion's home tonight and saw you retrieving your jacket out of the bedroom."

"That was you at the window," I surmised, feeling sick all over again. I waived Hellion back and stepped farther forward. "Why did you leave?"

"I saw all I needed to see."

"Then you missed me coming to the window," I said slowly.

His face registered a pain so raw my heart bled for him. But then he ruined it. "Interested in a threesome, love? Because I'm sure I could be enticed to share that deliciously fine ass of yours." His tone vibrated with unfiltered rage even as he schooled his face to reflect nothing but disdain. Not even his eyes changed color.

Hellion took a step forward, and I threw out an arm to stop him before he got any closer to the other man.

"Why are you doing this? You're responsible for this as much as he is, Bahlin." I felt the whole of the circle's inhabitants wait with baited breath. "I told you there would be no retaliation, and I told you that day to leave it alone. But you couldn't, you *wouldn't*, and you started the fight. It was your pride you fought to defend, not my honor. You're just mad because you lost. You lost the fight and, if you don't cool it, you're going to lose the girl."

He glared at me, and I took a step back at the sheer look of frigid animosity on his face. "She's already lost to me."

I heard an internal crack, like a wrong step on thin ice, and wondered at it before I realized what it was. My heart was breaking. "Then you've betrayed more than one promise to me, Bahlin. But the biggest, the biggest by far, was your promise that you'd love me forever. Looks like it was all just to get me on my back and gain yourself the Council's leadership. Congratulations. I hope it's warm company on cold nights." My chest ached. I stepped back to Hellion's side and took his large, warm hand in mine. "Can we vote on Darius's seat? I want to go home."

Hellion never corrected me or questioned where home was to me. He just rolled with the punches. "We're waiting on the fae."

"We're here," came Kelten's voice. The King of Faerie held his wife Gaitha's hand as they stepped into the circle. "We hesitated to interrupt the fascinating proceedings."

I stiffened, and Hellion pulled me close as the fae approached. I looked around and saw they had brought only one woman with them besides the queen; the rest of their escorts were male and of the warrior variety. Queen Gaitha looked horrible—unwashed and generally unkempt. Her long, blonde hair was knotted, her clothes dirty, her fingernails ragged and dirt-filled. There were scratches on her arms and bruises on her neck. Her eyes were wild as they landed on me and she keened, scaring the shit out of me.

"Is this your recommendation for your Council seat?" Hellion gestured toward the other woman—a petite creature with a pixie-like face, tiny hands and perfect, white teeth. Her blonde hair hung to a waist small enough to have been fashionable when boned corsets were all the rage.

Gaitha protested with a smaller noise, but Kelten answered, "She is. This is our niece, Praen." The king turned to face us as he spoke, and I noticed the oozing scratch marks on his face and hands. Before I could comment, Bahlin spoke.

"Then let us vote."

"Any tie-breakers go to the Niteclif," Hellion said, "as per the Law of Olde."

I started, but Hellion held me steady. Everyone agreed.

The vote was fast, and both candidates were appointed without discussion. Apparently one of the biggest requirements was a willingness to serve. Good enough. I wanted out of there. I turned to Hellion to ask him to take us home, but Bahlin's cold voice stopped me yet again.

"There's also the matter of leadership of the Council. I am the prophesied leader, and I will be claiming my right at our first official meeting."

So that's it. You're so naive, Niteclif. This has been all about power and nothing about love. I hadn't thought I could get any colder inside, but I was wrong. "We'll discuss it at the next meeting, Bahlin. Tonight is neither the right venue nor the time for it, and you know it."

"Fair enough, for now. But know that I *will* be claiming what is mine by rights, Niteclif." Bahlin stared at me hard, eyes flashing to icy blue.

My skin seemed to crawl all over my body and I shivered. Hellion laid his large hand at the small of my back, and his touch steadied me.

Bahlin stepped closer and I watched him warily. "Before this meeting adjourns, I have a charge to bring to the Niteclif's attention."

I realized I couldn't ask for his help any longer, and I had a moment of sheer terror. I had nothing to work from, and I was scared I'd make some critical error. Of course, that's what he was counting on. He was discounting the fact he was still my familiar, and that Tyr and Hellion were still available to me.

"On the day of my attempted murder," he began and I protested.

"On the day you picked a fight with Hellion, which you legitimately lost," I corrected.

"Semantics, Madeleine. On that day, the same day a mundane was murdered by near decapitation, I saw Hellion in the Niteclif's room with a knife wound to his bandaged hand and fresh blood around his fingernails. I allege he has intimate knowledge of the crimes. Further, he is manipulating the Niteclif to gain her affections and to unduly influence her investigations."

"What?" Hellion and I exploded at the same time, and chatter started among the witnesses.

"What answer you, Niteclif?" he demanded.

"Besides that you're a prat?" I asked.

"So you concede—"

"Nothing. I concede *nothing*. You should have asked me about this. I would have answered you. But now all I'll say is that your complaint is lodged, and I'll give the accused a chance to answer."

Hellion began speaking almost before I finished. "I hereby swear on my life that I did not commit the crime as alleged."

"I can affirm his statement because I was there when he cut himself. He sliced open his hand when he healed my wounds. He did not attack those girls."

Bahlin shifted his stance on his walking stick and sneered. "And the girl outside the hotel?"

"He couldn't have done it, Bahlin. Leave it alone. I'm warning you."

He stumped closer to me and let loose a wicked sexy smile that had made my heart falter in my chest since the first night I'd seen him in my dreams. "Defending your lover as always, Madeleine. Good to know." His eyes were cruel and his mouth twisted into a hard frown. It was heartbreaking, as if I'd never known this man at all. "Now I want to know his innocence or guilt regarding the last murder."

"He couldn't have killed her because he was with me, all night."

"You never slept?" Bahlin asked, confused.

This was going to sound bad. "No, we never slept." The crowd snickered, and I cast a wide-reaching glare. "It was the night I believed you had been killed and I couldn't sleep, so Hellion stayed awake with me all night and offered me compassion, not intimacy. He's innocent of that allegation." I had a moment of inspiration. "Can you tell me what hand was cut?"

"His right," Bahlin answered quickly.

"I saw Hellion perform magic, write, eat, and scry with his left hand."

"No, Madeleine. You have to investigate—"

"Unless I have firsthand knowledge pertaining to how the injury came to pass or possess firm and undeniable knowledge of a party's innocence and/or whereabouts during the course of the crime." How did I know this crap? Tyr. I smiled. "Isn't that correct, Wats—"

Bahlin's anger was like a wildfire that was fed with every word I uttered. He raged in front of me, deadly angry, and I took a small step back, clutching my borrowed dirk. "Fine. It's correct. But will you be investigating the murders of these women since they are likely being profiled then killed based on similarity to you?"

I didn't think it was my imagination that the crowd sucked in air and waited for my response. It hurt me to do it, but I had to ask, and he'd chosen the venue for persecution. "How do you know for sure they were killed because they looked like me?"

"I'm assuming—" he began, but the doubt was cast.

"Bahlin Drago, I will need to discuss these murders with you on a formal level." The crowd waited. "I agree to formally investigate, but only if you agree to willingly answer any and all questions regarding the murders. Assuming you're cleared, you'll then act as my familiar. You'll willingly help me and give me your very best effort, personally, at all times, until these crimes are solved." Hellion stilled beside me. I hated to spring this on him, but I needed to secure Bahlin's whereabouts somehow and get him to back off Hellion. Now the ball was in his court, because if he refused he looked guilty, and if he agreed there were more than fifty individuals, including Council members, to serve as witnesses.

"Fine," he ground out. "This has all been a misunderstanding," he announced to the crowd, "and circumstances are being used to manipulate me." He stepped closer and I held my ground, fine tremors making me appear to shiver as I fought not to step away from his rage. In a quiet voice filled with malice he said, "I'll see you soon and we'll clear this up, all of it. It was a misunderstanding, and you know it."

Hellion stepped closer to me and said in an equally low voice, "We sleep in, so don't show up too early. In fact, we're not sure which house we'll use tonight, so allow us to contact you in the morning."

I looked at Hellion and frowned. He didn't know me well enough to announce my sleep habits. Then I realized he was trying to keep from being alone with Bahlin at any time. With me as a witness, Bahlin couldn't bring false charges against him. Without me as a witness, anything Bahlin reported as a crime I'd have to investigate, and Bahlin could bog the system down with allegations. I'd killed two bad intentions with one well-worded promise. I'd pat myself on the back later.

Chapter Ten

The meeting adjourned quickly after the last confrontation. Bahlin and the blue dragons left first en masse while Darius hung around to keep us company though I was aware of him as more than a strictly conversational companion. His eyes scanned the circle, watching the night as if it had ill intent all its own.

We waited as the fae began to leave, but it was the king and queen who interested me most. King Kelten came forward alone, leaving his wife with their niece and guards. Gaitha glared at me and, if she had been able, she would have brought me down with a look and nothing Hellion could do would cure me. She seemed to be memorizing my face, blinking long, slow blinks every few minutes.

"Niteclif," said Kelten. "A word, if you please."

I looked at Hellion, and he nodded so slightly I wondered if I'd imagined it. I was fighting to hold it together at this point. Still, I nodded to the king. "Please, go ahead, sir."

Kelten inclined his head and very softly said, "The deaths of our son and her uncle have left my wife scarred. She is not the same woman she once was. I would caution you to stay clear of the fae directly tied to her, at least for a while." He wiped a sheen of sweat from his upper lip. "Should you need anything from the fae that Praen cannot provide, please contact me directly. Hellion might help you with that?" He looked at Hellion, who nodded. "Good, good. She is not well, Niteclif. I'll do what I can for her, but..."

The implication hung suspended between us.

"But what?" I asked.

Kelten shook his head and backed away, never taking his eyes from mine.

He's aged, I thought. *Not as scary as the queen, though. Not by half.*

I looked over and found Hellion sticking his cell phone back into his pants pocket.

Hellion hooked an arm around my waist and pulled me tight to him, leaning to kiss me gently on the temple. "We must leave, and quickly."

"Okay, but—"

"Ask me anything you'd like about Chaucer after we get home," he said, stroking a hand down my cheek.

We were headed back to the manor house, and he didn't want anyone to know where we were. That hadn't worked out so well last time, but I'd play. Nodding, I said, "I'll wait until we're in bed, reluctantly. Will we drive?"

"No need," he said smiling, pleased I had picked up the subtle hints he'd dropped—Chaucer on the bookshelf, we wouldn't be driving, where we'd shared a bed reluctantly—to let me know we'd return to Ireland. He looked over my head at Darius and said, "Tomorrow, my friend?"

Darius smiled and nodded. "By the first hour of the night."

I glanced over my shoulder at him, and he had his total poker face going like only a vampire can. It said nothing.

Hellion called his coven members together and said softly, "I'll trust you to make breakfast. Scramble the eggs and make some toast?"

They nodded.

What the hell? He was hungry again?

They stood close and, under the guise of conversation, several began to chant. Magic swelled and I clutched Hellion. Something was wrong.

"Hang on," he said. He barely turned and we were gone.

I opened my eyes and recognized the room we were in. A man moved near the fireplace, and I squeaked in alarm. It took me a moment to place him. Conor, the butler at Hellion's Irish estate, waited patiently. He looked me over quickly but carefully before he turned to Hellion.

"Good, man, you've arrived," he said, striding forward to clasp Hellion's shoulder. "News arrived just ahead of you. The blues are gathering, Hellion."

I looked back and forth between the men, confused.

"Did the coven understand my instructions well, I hope?" Hellion asked, releasing me and running his hands through his hair. He walked to the big sofa and flopped down, then immediately stood and walked to the window. Turning, he moved back to the fireplace and grabbed the poker to stir the coals in the hearth.

"What's wrong?" I asked.

"The blue dragons are gathering, and I believe it's to take you back to Bahlin by force. That's what he meant when he said he'd see you soon, and the two of you would clear everything up. He's claiming his rights to you as a dragon's mate. When he took you to his den, did he commit to you?" The fire sparked merrily, the coals eating up the oxygen in the room—or so it seemed.

I had to think about it. What had he said to me? *"What's mine is yours, from home to hearth to lair."* But it had been after the visit to his den. I said as much to Hellion, and he looked so discouraged.

"So he proposed."

"Yeah."

He pinched the bridge of his nose, and then asked in a pained voice, "Did you accept?"

Anxiety climbed up my back and settled, uncomfortably hot, between my shoulder blades. I shrugged, trying to dislodge it. "Yeah, but we were never bound or married or anything."

Conor looked between us, some strong emotion tightening his mouth and drawing the corners down. "There's only one solution, sir, and I believe you know that, yeah?"

Half listening, I thought back to the stone circle and the object Darius had slipped Hellion, then his strange message to his coven. I clasped my hands behind my neck and pulled, feeling the stretch in my neck and shoulders. It did nothing to alleviate the building tension. "What did Darius hand you, and what did you say to the coven? How did Conor know we'd be here?"

Hellion looked up from where he was still squatting in front of the fire. The muscles in his thighs pushed against the denim of his jeans, and his shirt pulled tight across his shoulders as he flexed to stand. He rolled his head around his shoulders then dug a leather strap out of his pocket and tied his hair back. His hands yanked at his hair, twisting harder than necessary.

Hellion rubbed his lips hard and then dropped his hand. "Darius handed me this." He dug in his pocket and pulled out a gold coin. It looked familiar. "It was taken out of the neck of the first victim. A similar coin has been taken out of each additional victim's neck. They've all been embedded deep enough that it took an autopsy to find it. I never thought to say it, but thank the gods Darius has a man inside the morgue to help cover up vampire killings."

I blanched. Another urban legend confirmed. Shit. I turned the coin over in my hands. It was heavy. And gold. I knew I'd seen it before.

Hellion barely paused for breath. "I texted the coven while we were standing in the henge and told them we were coming here. I asked them to scramble the eggs and toast, or have conversation to mask the noise of the spell casting, or toast our leaving, and to scramble the trail we left when we dematerialized. All magic is traceable, and I wanted our path as obscured as possible. Most of them chatted while some cast spells behind us to confuse anyone trying to track our disappearance." He looked down at me, and the intensity in his eyes gentled. "You did good discerning what was happening overall. I was proud of you." He leaned down to kiss me, and I turned away before our lips met.

I was feeling very vulnerable following the verbal exchange with Bahlin but was still amused. *That could be their slogan*, I mused. *Faster than FedEx, more reliable than AT&T*. Conor cleared his throat. "With all apologies, sir—"

Hellion grunted but stepped back. "I know." He looked worried. "Conor knew we were coming because one of the coven members sent a message ahead of us."

Drawing my attention back to the conversation, Hellion said, "Maddy, dragon law is quite different than human law. When you agreed to marry Bahlin, it sealed a contract between you."

"But he broke it." I stalked to the window and looked out at the night through the living room window for the second time in twenty-four hours. My eyes were too large, my skin too pale. I watched Hellion move to the sofa and sit more gently this time. He met my eyes in the reflection and patted the seat next to him. The clock chimed one o'clock.

I turned to go to him and squeaked in alarm at the vampire sitting in the chair opposite Hellion. Darius had arrived right on time—by the first hour of the night. I, obviously, hadn't seen his arrival by reflection in the window. Urban legend two confirmed tonight. *Double shit*, I thought, coaxing my heart down from where it had lodged in my throat.

Darius grinned. He was in total metrosexual mode, and his suave factor was through the roof as he took me in.

Down, girl, I thought and I snorted. The men looked at me, and Hellion raised a brow. *I hope he doesn't read minds.* I looked at him and thought very hard, *You're hung like a chicken.* No response. Thank you, Odin.

I crawled into the deep sofa beside Hellion but refrained from snuggling close to him.

"Where were you in the conversation before my arrival interrupted you?" Darius asked, crossing an ankle over his knee and stretching a long arm across the back of his chair.

"I was explaining that Bahlin broke our engagement."

Darius shook his head gently. "Unbelievably daft of him. Were there by any chance witnesses to his idiocy?"

"No one was in the room with us, but his guard was outside the door." Hellion looked so dejected that I reached up and turned his face to me. "What?"

His skin was warm and dry, slightly flushed from the heat of the fire. "I'm afraid you're going to be furious. Know I only tell you the truth, all right?"

Everything in my body tightened as tension paralyzed me, causing me to mumble through numb lips, "Okay."

"Bahlin believes we've been handfast already. He's claiming he didn't break your engagement and therefore we are not legitimately wed by the customs of the coven."

"We're *not* wed," I said. "That assumption was on Aiden. And Bahlin *did* break our engagement. Clay held me while I cried, and then you showed up and saw Clay kissing me while he was half asleep and unaware it was me, and you witnessed me trying to get him off my face."

"Ah, but Bahlin punished Clay for touching you. He claimed a misunderstanding between the two of you and accused Clay of inappropriate conduct with the Glaaca's *trekkár.*"

This had happened *before* he knew about Hellion? Bahlin had lied? "What, exactly, does this mean?" I clutched at Hellion's hand. "I don't belong to anyone."

Hellion looked at me, his deep eyes pulsing with emotion. "No, and that's the problem." He lifted my hand to his lips and kissed it. "The only way I can deny his request to return you to him is to marry you, Maddy. A formal ceremony, with witnesses, is the only thing that will trump his claim."

I choked and looked back at Conor, who nodded grimly.

I looked at Darius and he shrugged. "He's right, my little chick. It's the only way to keep from having to observe the dragon's claim, even if you know it's invalid."

I pushed away from Hellion and stood. "I belong to *no one*." I turned to look at Conor. "You were here this morning. Aiden left because he thought we were handfast?" I asked, gesturing between Hellion and myself.

Conor nodded. "That's the excuse he used to get the information back to his brother more hastily. But I believe he knew you weren't declared. That's why the dragons are moving so quickly to reclaim you."

I felt sick. My independence meant nothing in this world. The one ally I might have had, Sarenia, wouldn't help me at this point. "So what are my choices?" I asked. My voice was decidedly flat and emotionless and left no clue to the brewing fury within.

"Marry Hellion, officially, or be returned to the dragons," Darius said.

"Bit blunt there, *mate*," I snapped, courtesy choked out by my anger. "We just need to look harder to find a better solution."

Hellion stood and walked out of the room without a backward glance. My dark mood stumbled at his abrupt departure. I looked at Darius, who eyed me coolly. Conor's face was blank, but he couldn't hide the tension around his eyes and lips any more than he could coax his hands to relax and stop fisting at his sides. I'd acted irrationally yet again, pissing off the very people from whom I needed to obtain help. Fan-damn-tastic.

I sank to the sofa and dropped my head in my hands, my anger quickly replaced by despair. I heard Conor move into the hallway. He had a brief discussion with someone before moving farther into the house. Darius was silent by nature but I suspected he too was gone. I was poor company right now.

I heard soft footsteps and refused to raise my head and face any more problems right now. The steps came to a stop near the fireplace, and curiosity eventually got the better of me.

Damn if that ain't always the way.

Hellion stood there, hands in his pockets, a serious look on his face, backlit by the fire so he appeared to glow. "I apologize for the events of this evening," he said formally. "They truly are beyond my control."

"It's okay." I dropped my face back into my hands. I shook my head and, when I finally spoke, it was around a knot of emotion lodged high in my throat. "I don't want to be forced to deal with Bahlin right now, Hellion. I can't, not and survive it. I don't know the man I met in the circle tonight." It was just one more case of life proving love couldn't last. Everyone I'd ever loved had been taken from me in some form, leaving me alone and lonely.

Hellion moved closer to me, and I heard his knees crack as he sank to the floor beside me. "Come to me?" he asked, reaching out a hand.

I slid off the sofa and curled up next to him, leaving just enough space that we weren't melded together but close enough I could enjoy his heat. I laid my head on his upper chest and sighed. The feelings he was coaxing from me through patience, camaraderie, humor and lust were terrifying, and I didn't trust them. *Fool me once, lover, shame on you. Fool me twice, love, shame on me.* But just because I didn't intend to get permanently involved with him in a way that involved falling in love didn't mean I couldn't enjoy the physical comforts of companionship in the moment. I'd just guard my heart, viciously if need be.

With that decided, I rolled my head up toward Hellion's face only to find him watching me with somber eyes. "What's going on in that brain pan of yours, oh great and magical grand poobah of Europe?" I asked, lightly teasing.

He smiled and ruffled my hair. I started just a little and realized he was treating me solely like a good friend. What about the prophecy? Forget the prophecy. Why was he being friendly, as in *friend* and not interested, as in *male to female*? I was disappointed in myself. The realization that I never seemed happy, but instead always skeptical with the moment at hand, was hard to swallow.

Sensing some discord in my thoughts, Hellion closed the gap between us and wrapped his arm around me, pulling me close. "What bothers you, *mo grá?*"

I felt awkward, unsure how to convey my thoughts. "It's silly really. I'll leave it alone and—"

"I'd like to know," he interrupted. "I'd like to know much more about you, things that take a lifetime to figure out. Unfortunately, tonight is not our night." He sighed deeply and moved away from me.

"Because of the blue weyr?" I asked, reaching up to touch his face.

"That's the one. Their intent is to take you back, and I don't want to let you go, so we've a dilemma on our hands." His smile was as far from happy as the East is from the West. "Do you want to go with them? Because if you do, we can avoid another skirmish. There are enough of us here to make their lives difficult, but not enough to win should they come en masse. So what you want matters very much and holds influence on the lives of others."

Even if he'd dropped an anvil in my lap I couldn't have felt more surprised or bogged down. How was I supposed to know what was best? Bahlin hadn't made me... And then I realized a hard truth. Bahlin had made the majority of the decisions for me. He'd led me around by the nose and I'd just followed blindly, using the excuse that I was new, that I needed a mentor, that I couldn't do what needed to be done alone. The thought made my stomach hurt. How capable was I *really*, and how much of it had been him?

"I don't know what I want," I whispered into the room.

Hellion nodded. "Then because you are undecided, I will further complicate things," he said with a sardonic smile. "I will give you one other option."

No. No, please. I can't—

"Maddy," he rasped, looking at me with wildly pulsing eyes. "I care for you deeply and want for you only what you want."

I panicked and tried to push to standing. He held me firmly in place so that I was only able to force my way to my knees.

"I will ask only once, and you are free to refuse. Madeleine Dylis Niteclif, will you marry me? Will you be mine for all that eternity holds for us?" He looked up at me, so serious, and I searched his face.

"Why are you asking me?" I whispered.

"First, because I am falling in love with you and I want to spend my life with you. Second, I believe we are predestined. Third? To be honest, I want to keep from being forced to give you up. It's one thing if you choose to go to him. It's another if you're torn from me unwillingly." He pulled me into his lap so I was facing him, his thumbs making small circles on my abdominal plane. They moved in a hypnotic rhythm.

"Would you have asked anyway?" My voice was shaky, belying my fear, and I hated that.

"But I already did, love."

"No," I said, shaking my head, "no. It's not the same thing. I need to know you would have asked me to marry you for all the right reasons, not because Odin willed it or Bahlin forbids it or the universe demands it. Do you think you would have ever asked only for love?"

"I'm asking now. If you believe it's because of anything other than true love, say no. But if you are beginning to have feelings for me as I believe you are, there's only one answer. Regardless, I'll respect your decision." He stilled his hands and gave me a small squeeze.

Bahlin had said the same thing. He'd promised me he would love me no matter what, and now it seemed he was more interested in possession than love. I said as much to Hellion and his eyes quieted. "If you think so little of me as to lump me in with that type of behavior, then these past weeks amount to nothing, and you don't know me at all." He moved to shift me gently off his lap.

I managed to hang on, giving him pause.

"Maddy?" That one word combined with the tone of his voice to issue a sexy warning. "You're fooling yourself, *mo chroí*, if you think I'll not press my advantage." He shifted so his hips were pressed into my pelvis. He was quickly becoming aroused.

In a split second I made my decision to pursue physical comfort over emotional demands. Here was hoping I could keep the two separate. "Take me to bed, Hellion."

"Pardon?" His head snapped back, shock widening his eyes.

I blushed. "You heard me."

He pulled back, settling me on his thighs instead of his groin. "I'll do nothing of the sort until you tell me why. Because this is out of character for you, love, and I'll not do anything that will ruin what we're building, nor will I take advantage of your fear of the moment."

"You forgot one thing," I said.

He just quirked an eyebrow. "And that is..."

"Desire," I murmured, running my hands through his thick hair. I leaned forward and kissed him gently, our height difference meaning he had to lower his face to mine and make the decision to give himself over to me.

Hellion wrapped me in his arms and shot up off the floor with impressive strength, carried me past the curious staff and strode straight up the stairs to his bedroom.

He slammed the door with his mind, and with one yank he shed the covers from the bed so that only the fitted sheet and the pillows remained. He wrapped an arm around my waist and crawled onto the bed, sinking to the middle with me beneath him.

I arched my back as he came down on top of me. The press of his hard groin into my aching cleft was electric, and I gasped.

He leaned back and pulled my T-shirt off over my head. He unbuttoned and unzipped my pants, running his hands around my hips. I writhed on the bed, reveling at the curious confidence in my sexuality, scared to look at it too closely. Hellion leaned forward and kissed his way up my front, beginning at the V of my opened zipper and nipping, licking and sucking his way up to my mouth. I was absolutely on fire by the time he made it to my lips. I grabbed his head and laid waste to his control, kissing him with every ounce of skill I possessed. I nipped his quivering lower lip and sucked at it until his eyelashes fluttered against his lower lids. I ran my hands across his abs and pulled at his shirt until he let me dispose of it, pressing our upper bodies together. Fine sweat was already collecting between my breasts, and he drug a finger through it, drawing it down until he circled my bellybutton.

A loud crash sent us both scrambling apart. Hellion raced for the closet and came out with a dirk for me and both a scary-ass sword and a gun for himself. Sounds of fighting floated up the stairs, getting louder with every breath I took.

"Stay here," he shouted as he sprinted from the room.

"Like hell." I got up to run after him and realized I should probably put some clothes on.

If only I hadn't paused for clothes, I probably wouldn't have had to kill the dragon.

Chapter Eleven

I had just pulled my shirt on when the door crashed open. I grabbed the dirk and recognized Clay, my only friend in the weyr and my former nurse, as he came through the door, followed by Bahlin's little brother, Aiden. Holding short swords, they were both bleeding. Each man had tucked a gun in the waistband of his pants.

Aiden stood smirking at me, blocking the only exit from the room. He looked a far cry from the sweet kid that had chased me down to beg me not to leave his brother weeks ago.

Clay, on the other hand, looked miserable. "You have to come with me, Maddy. I've got to take you with us."

"I'm not going, Clay."

He advanced on me, sword hung at his side, dragging the floor and leaving a deep gouge in the hardwood planks. "Don't make this worse than it needs to be, Maddy. You're coming."

I lifted my little dirk and shook my head. "No. Don't make me do this, Clay." I was terrified it would come to blows, and I held no illusion over who would win the scuffle. I backed up until I was in the doorway to the bathroom.

"Don't take another step, Niteclif," Aiden said, pulling his gun out and leveling it at me.

"Put the damn gun away, Aiden," Clay barked. "He never should have given you the thing."

"*Bahlin* gave him a gun?"

Clay nodded and rolled his eyes. "Look, Maddy, don't make me disarm you. Drop the knife and come with me."

"No."

"Damn it, Maddy! You're coming, and that's final. Drop it now or I'll disarm you!" Clay shouted. The sounds of fighting rolling up the stairs were getting closer and more violent. It had gone from a simple abduction to a full-fledged battle. Metal clanged on metal, men grunted as fists met flesh, and a single gunshot sounded, temporarily masking the noise as my hearing rang.

Clay rushed me while I was distracted. I instinctively raised my knife hand and swung out with it. He hadn't been anticipating it, and I caught him in the gut, ripping across his lower abdomen. I screamed and watched him fall to his knees, surprise replacing the intensity of the moment. The shock of hitting the floor knocked his hand away from the wound, and I saw that I'd laid his lower gut open. The smell of perforated bowel hit my nose, and I knew I'd killed him, whether he bled from the gut wound or died from infection.

I threw the knife down and skidded across the floor on my own knees, grabbing his arms as he sank further to the floor. Blood was pumping from the wound with his every heartbeat so I knew I'd cut something major, and the intestine and bowel roiled like snakes in a pit as he sank lower.

"Maddy?" he asked, confused. Shock was setting in.

"Clay!" I screamed. "Aiden, get Hellion."

Aiden stared at the dying dragon. Clay's heels dug into the floor and he arched his back, his body recognizing what his conscious mind couldn't grasp.

"Get Hellion, you malignant asshole!" I screamed. "Move!"

Aiden started, and it was like he came back to life. He dropped his sword before vomiting all over the floor. I crouched over Clay, trying to protect him from the splatter. Aiden righted himself but didn't move to get help.

"Forgive me," I whispered. "Oh, Clay, I'm so sorry."

We sat there for a few minutes staring at each other while Aiden blocked the door and did nothing. *Nothing.*

Clay's wound was bleeding less, his skin cooling, and I knew we were minutes away from death. Then he surprised me.

"Kiss me, Maddy."

I bent toward Clay and made the softest contact with his lips and he opened his mouth, kissing me gently. His lips were turning blue, his eyes going glassy. My salty tears wet our joined lips, and he tried to lick them away. I sobbed. His breathing changed, becoming intermittent as his heart fought to hold on. His last breath eased into my mouth. He was gone.

Aiden crossed the floor and shoved the gun under my jaw, lifting me painfully to my feet with the muzzle.

"I fucking hate you," I spat. "You could have saved him."

"Don't put that off on me, bitch. Your knife, your kill." He shoved me with his free hand, and I stumbled forward. He snatched the short sword off the floor as we headed for the door. "Stay in front of me, no fast movements. You're leaving with Bahlin. No discussions."

"You're too late," I said, my own shock beginning to settle over me like miasma. "Hellion proposed tonight." What the what? Where had that come from?

"Same event, different groom," Aiden said cryptically.

I went icy cold. "If your brother thinks I'll marry him now, he's delusional." My feet felt like lead as I navigated the stairs. I was almost to the bottom when I saw Hellion lying on the floor in a small pool of blood.

"No!" I darted forward, sliding toward my second body in less than five minutes. Scrambling, I felt for his pulse. It was there but thready. I looked up and found Bahlin standing over us, a gun in his hand.

"You should have just come to me, Maddy. It would have saved his life."

"Not just his," I snapped.

Bahlin looked around and realized Clay was missing. "Where's Clay, Aiden?"

"She killed him," Aiden said, his voice rough, and I realized then he was trying not to cry.

"I'm not leaving with you, Bahlin. You threw me over for your guilt and then you treated me like offal tonight. What in heaven's name makes you believe I would marry you?"

He stood proud and arrogant and never more lethally beautiful. "You were the one who convinced me to damn the prophecy and make what we wanted out of our lives. I want you, Maddy, more than he does." He gestured toward Hellion with his gun and shoved him with the toe of his boot. "I'm giving you an out here, Maddy. Come with me and let's fix what's broken. We'll go away, sort things out—"

"Wanting and loving aren't the same, Bahlin," I said, and I laid a soft hand on Hellion's. I pulled my T-shirt off and pressed it to Hellion's shoulder wound. "I'm not like your treasure, something you obtain, possess or own."

Hellion's eyes fluttered open, and he had a hard time focusing on me. "Don't go. Please."

My choice was made. I glared at Bahlin. "Leave," I snapped, my voice like the crack of a whip. Hellion winced and I stroked his head. "I need to take care of him. If he dies, I swear on my own life I will hunt you down and..."

Bahlin stood there watching me care for the man in my arms. Turning on his heel, he let out a screech I recognized as dragonish. Men emerged from the shadows and followed him to the front door. Aiden, however, stood there.

"Get out. And...take Clay's body home." I choked on my tears. "Shift on the way out the window if you have to, but don't bring him through here. Go."

Bahlin wasn't out of the house before I heard another groan from behind the sofa.

"Stay still, Hellion," I whispered. "I'm right here." I crawled around the corner of the sofa and gasped.

Darius lay on the floor, his right arm partially severed at the shoulder, a puddle of dark blood under him. He lifted his head, and his brown eyes took on an amethyst edge. "I've got to have blood to heal this before sunrise," he gasped, "and you're going to help to gather the people to save Hellion."

I looked around for any other volunteers, but I was the only hale person in shouting distance. I could hear groans from the hallway too.

"Can you stop it from hurting and make it damned fast?" I asked, crawling closer to him and shooting one last look at Hellion, who was still breathing.

"Oh, yeah. It won't hurt a bit, flower, so long as you relax and let me in your mind. Can you lie beside me? That's it," he said, encouraging me to lay my neck nearly over his mouth. I supported his head and took two deep breaths. I felt the strangest sensation come over me, but instead of riding it, I fought it. His fangs pierced the skin, and I grunted in pain. It burned ferociously, and I had to draw him closer to keep from dropping him altogether. He took several long draws before pulling away. He sliced his finger on his fang and rubbed it over the twin wounds, presumably to heal it.

I stood up and, woozy, immediately sank back to the floor. I crawled back around the couch only to feel myself lifted. Darius had picked me up with his good arm and moved me toward Hellion.

Hellion's eyes were closed and his breathing was too shallow. He'd turned gray in the short minutes since I'd left him.

"No, no, no," I chanted, struggling toward him.

His eyes fluttered open but they couldn't focus.

"Help him, please just...don't let him die, Darius." Tears clogged my throat and made it hard to breathe.

Darius came to my side immediately and looked Hellion over. "The only thing I know to do is get a coven member or change him." He raced down the hall and came back with Conor in his arms. The man had a broken leg but looked otherwise untouched.

"Hellion," he gasped, the pain and longing in that one word holding more anguish than that of a mere friend. Conor was in love with the Coven Master. "Put me down beside him. Maddy, do you have a dirk?"

I nodded. "In our room."

Darius raced off and was back before I could have made it to the top of the stairs. He handed me the dirk, still stained with Clay's blood.

I remembered what Hellion had once said to me, "*It's an arcane piece of magic...*"

"Heal him, and I'll grant you anything you ask of me," I pleaded.

"Anything?" Conor asked as he ripped Hellion's shirt away. Hellion didn't make a sound.

"My word of honor. You don't leave me, Hellion. Do you hear me? You stay. *You. Stay.*" I held his hand and wondered how I'd gone from foreplay to death in under thirty minutes. Conor started to slice his hand and I shouted, "No!" I held my hand out and he looked at me. "Do it."

He cut my palm deep and I grunted in pain, but Darius was suddenly there, supporting my shoulders. Conor placed the blade on Hellion's stomach and began drawing the runes in my blood. Hellion's skin was cooling.

"Hurry," I ground out.

Conor got to the last rune and hesitated.

"Do it—now!" I shouted.

He finished the last rune and for a moment nothing happened. I began to sob. "Tyr! Odin! Don't do this to me."

Hellion's body shook once, hard, and Conor scooted back, eyes going wide as the runes sank into the skin of Hellion's bare stomach.

Hellion arched his back and screamed, his fingers scrabbling against the wood floor, looking for purchase. I started to reach out but Darius shoved me roughly aside.

"He'll break your hands, Madeleine," he said. He grabbed Hellion's hands and pulled them above his head. "Efein!" Another vampire darted into the room, a huge gash still healing across his stomach. "Across his legs, man."

Hellion was thrashing about, bellowing in pain. Tears coursed down his temples and I cried with him, knowing how badly it hurt to come back from a date with death. It felt like it went on for ages when, in all likelihood, it was under ninety seconds. Then it was over. He lay there trembling like a flame in a breeze. His eyes opened and sought mine, relaxing only when he found me.

"No more of that," I whispered, leaning forward to kiss him softly. His voice was raw, and all he could do was nod weakly. I crawled to Conor and, taking his face between my hands, I kissed him tenderly and briefly on the lips. "Anything."

He nodded, never breaking eye contact with me. "Anything."

"Darius." I turned to the vampires still kneeling by Hellion. "Will you and Efein—nice to meet you, by the way, though circumstances couldn't be much worse—please carry Hellion up to a different room than ours? I need to see to Conor and see who else needs help."

Conor pushed himself to sitting and leaned against one of the bookcases, staring at me as the vampires carried Hellion away. "You don't worry they'll make a meal of him?" he asked. I must have looked confused because he said, "The vampires. Hellion's blood. *Our* blood." He looked pointedly at my neck.

I slapped a hand over the puckered, healing skin. "Of course they won't. Don't be ridiculous. Darius and his people are allies, and if you've not figured that out after tonight, you're warped. I'm guessing because you accepted my offer so quickly that there's something in particular you wanted from me. If you'll let me know now, I can begin working on it as soon as I know Hellion's well."

Conor narrowed his eyes and his gaze cooled radically. "I want you to leave."

"Huh?" I asked stupidly.

"Leave, you stupid bitch. Go away. Immediately."

I just stared at him like he was speaking in tongues. It took a minute for my synapses to start firing again. "No."

"You said, and I quote, 'My word of honor'," he snarled.

"Where is this coming from?" I pushed myself up so I towered over the slight man.

"You're bad for him," he said, holding firm. "He's had nothing but heartache since you showed up. He tried to be a benign observer, helping you by giving you your family tree. Did you figure that out, oh mighty Niteclif?" He laughed once, a short and bitter sound I never would have equated to the quiet man. "No. You're just a dumbass American with no right to be here beyond an obscure bloodline the prophecies herald as true. You've gone back and forth between him and Bahlin, and all you've managed is to hurt both of them and set two friends against each other."

I wasn't sure my mouth could fall any farther open. Was this all coming from the fact that he had feelings for Hellion or was there something more there? "I'm not leaving him," I said. "Anything but that."

"Then your honor is worth nothing."

And there was the rub. What *was* my honor worth? Did it have a price tag? "No." My voice was soft and pleading, a hair's breadth from begging. *Anything but more heartache.* But by my pleading he knew he had me.

"Go now, and I won't say anything to him. Stay and I'll tell him I witnessed you and Bahlin together tonight after the fight."

Shocked, I reached down and slapped him hard enough to crack his head against the wood of the bookshelf. "You son of a bitch," I hissed. "I did no such thing."

"Then it becomes my word against yours, doesn't it? He's known me longer, Niteclif. If I tell him in confidence, you won't persuade him otherwise. Lying is the least of what I'm prepared to do to get you to leave." He licked the split lip, delicately retrieving the trickle of blood with his tongue. He began to push himself up with his one good leg, using the wall for leverage.

"It's really irrelevant, Conor," said a furious voice just behind me, "since you just forfeited your life for hers." Darius radiated malevolence. He stepped around me and kicked Conor's broken leg.

The man screamed and collapsed back to the floor, clutching the knee above the broken shinbone. Fear had his eyes rolling in his head.

"Niteclif! Mercy, Niteclif!"

Darius stepped on Conor's leg and it snapped the rest of the way, making a sickening sound like dry kindling being broken for a fire.

My stomach heaved but I held. Flashes of the last few days began to pass by, and the pieces fell into place. Grabbing my dirk off the floor, I squatted down by Conor and said, "There's no mercy, now or ever, for traitors, man."

"I haven't betrayed you. I swear it."

"Lies aren't becoming," I said. "I couldn't figure out how our position kept being compromised. First here, with Aiden, then in London with Bahlin, then here again with Bahlin and the blue weyr. You're the only person Hellion told where we'd be. You first called Aiden, thinking Bahlin was dead. You were assuming the little brother would take over the Council seat, and you knew Aiden to be easily influenced. You invited him here so he could see if you were telling the truth about me being here with Hellion. When he came and told you Bahlin was alive, you offered to throw your support in with him. Anything to not have to watch Hellion fall in love with someone else." I went to my knees beside him, Darius at my back. Truthfully, I'd forgotten about the vampire. Not necessarily a good move, but in this case I thought I could be forgiven. "Then you called Bahlin when we returned to London." His eyes flared and I smiled. "How can I be sure? Because we never told Aiden where we were going. Bahlin came to the house and saw me in Hellion's room retrieving my jacket. Was it you who sent the letter?"

Conor said nothing.

"Tell me, you sorry sack of rat shit." I slid my dirk under his chin and pierced the skin, a small line of red snaking down his neck and wicking into his shirt collar.

He cringed, but didn't break.

Working to control my breathing, I shoved my free hand through my hair and closed my eyes. "Then you were waiting for us tonight, the coven having sent word ahead of our arrival. We were here a short while when you left the room, and I heard you talking to someone in the hallway. I assumed it was another member of the house, but I was wrong. The moment Hellion expressed his intent to propose, you called the dragons. They got here much too fast not to have known for sure where we were." I laid my palm over the compound fracture and pressed.

He grunted in pain.

"But the kicker was tonight. You opened the door to the vampires and realized Hellion had aligned himself with Darius, so you pointed the weyr right to me and Hellion. You let the weyr have their way with everyone here, and we never had a chance to call for help, you sorry fuck."

"I'd do all this and worse to see you kept from him," he snarled, leaning forward.

I grabbed his face and roughly kissed his forehead. "Hellion recognized one of his worst fears tonight. May the same fate be delivered upon you." I made to stand and felt a hand on my elbow helping me up. I looked over my shoulder at Darius. I hadn't realized four members of his voyyah who had come with him had joined us, watching the cowering man with cold expressions. I looked each vampire in the face, finally coming to rest on Darius. I nodded.

Conor realized what was about to happen and began to scream for Hellion, pausing only long enough to draw a shallow breath before beginning to scream again.

I never looked back, not even when they began to feed. Justice was served.

Chapter Twelve

I trudged up the stairs, one heavy foot at a time, my hand pulling me forward on the banister. It felt like it had been hours since I'd been in the bedroom. I nearly ran into Hellion at the top of the stairs. I was so tired I didn't see him standing there.

"Did you kill him?" he asked softly.

"No, I—"

He pushed past me and set one bare foot down on the first step very carefully.

I grabbed his arm. "No. Yes. I didn't kill him, but I passed judgment. Darius got the job done for me. Had Darius not been here, Hellion, I would have done it."

"It was for me to do, Madeleine!" he bellowed and I jumped back, nearly going ass over teakettle down the stairs. He grabbed my arm and swayed as I regained my balance.

"I'm going to pretend you didn't just yell at me for doing my job," I said, eyeing him carefully. "I need to lie down." I only breathed the last, my voice wavering. It had been an overwhelming evening. I was reeling inside, careening wildly from emotion to emotion inside my head and heart. I had uncovered an ugly part of myself tonight that I didn't care for. I'd learned that my honor didn't have a price, but my love might. And I'd learned that violence was an easy solution to embrace when I was pushed into a corner. I needed to hide away from everyone and lick my wounds.

Hellion grasped my arm hard enough to bruise.

"Get your hands off me, Hellion. Now." I wrenched my arm free and shoved him back a step. See? Violence. Easier than rationalizing with someone who didn't want to hear it. I shouldered my way by him and stomped down the hallway, intent on crashing in any other room than the master bedroom. I'd never, ever go back in there if I didn't have to. Clay's blood would always stain that floor for my eyes, no matter how well it was cleaned.

I opened the first door I came to and found a small smoking room. I walked in and began to shut the door behind me. Hellion's fist stopped the door before it could latch. "I mean it, Hellion. Give me some space or we're going to go rounds."

"Understood. At least go to the adjoining room and sleep in a real bed."

I looked around before it dawned on my cotton-candied brain that there wasn't a bed in the room. "Fine. Now leave."

He bent his head in acknowledgment and went without another word.

I walked through the adjoining bedroom and went into the bathroom, dropping clothes behind me as I went. I turned on the shower, letting the steam fill the tiled room while I folded down the bedding, removed extra pillows and kicked my clothes into a small pile near the foot of the bed. Naked, I padded back into the bathroom and shut the door, making sure it latched and locked. I'd brought my dirk with me into the shower stall, rust be damned, and I stood under the hot water watching Clay's blood rinse away from the blade. I knew I'd never forgive myself for the loss of the blue dragon. It wouldn't matter who said what. Forgiveness was unfathomable.

I sat on the floor of the shower and propped my forearms on my bent knees, laying the blade next to my hip on the water-warmed floor. Resting my cheek on my arms, I shuddered. I was so tired. The sound of the water softened, and I found myself staring down at, well, myself. It had been a while since I'd seen Tyr but I recognized this separation of physical self and astral self as one of his visits.

A muscled arm held out a towel, and I realized I was naked. "Aw, damn it," I sighed, grabbing the towel and covering up. "Can't you *ever* choose to visit when I'm wearing clothes?"

"And what, exactly, does it say about you that I'm always finding you naked?" he bit out.

I blushed furiously and took a step back to the water, intent on waking up.

"Hold it right there, Niteclif," he thundered, and I froze like a small animal in the bracken. "You will tell me what you've been doing about these murders. Now."

I turned slowly, mouth agape. "Are you *blind*?" I yelled. "I've been falling out thirty-story buildings, getting my heart broken with shocking regularity, electing new Council members, moving through time and space with freakish determination, getting offers of marriage and abduction, and killing an innocent dragon!" I took two large steps to him and shoved. Following him, I got in his face. "Besides, when did the mundane world become my responsibility?"

He was so shocked he stumbled back.

"Tonight is *not* the night to screw with me, Tyr. You knew about the prophecy and you did nothing. You let me get blindsided, knowing all the while. Well yuk, yuk, wasn't it a laugh? And where were you when you could have told me Bahlin wasn't dead? I might have made different decisions," I yelled, bumping my chest to his.

This time he held his ground.

"And where were you when you knew Bahlin was going to be raiding my new home and nearly killing Hellion?" I demanded.

"'Yuk, yuk'? You think I found any of this *funny*?" he snarled, pushing back at me. I stumbled but he persevered. "I demanded Odin tell you *both* of the prophecy before it got any further out of hand. Where was I when you thought Bahlin was dead? I was standing next to your fucking bed, Madeleine, waiting for you to go to sleep so I might reassure you." He grabbed my shoulders and shook me, and my physical body rocked with the force of it. "But you stayed awake all night mourning the dragon. And tonight? I violated Odin's directive and pulled Hellion back from death because I thought you'd suffered too much. *That's* what I've been doing—waiting on you to find time to involve me in your jaunty love life. Meanwhile, another girl has died, guilty only of looking like you and you've done nothing, *nothing*," he roared.

I whimpered in my sleep. My astral plane self was righteously pissed, and I opened my mouth to argue with him.

"Silence," he bellowed, and beyond the bathroom window a shower of stars fell from the night sky.

It was at that moment I remembered Tyr was truly the Norse god of war, known for his wisdom, fair play and administration of justice. Sheer folly to forget it, but I had. I snapped my mouth shut and glared at him.

He was breathing hard, his pupils had become pinpricks, and his non-gloved hand clenched and opened as if he seriously toyed with strangling me. "What are you doing, Maddy, to protect these women?"

My guilt quotient for the week apparently hadn't been met yet, because here he was loading me up with more. "Nothing yet, though I have some clues. I promise I intended to get back to them after tonight. I did," I asserted when he just stared at me, straight-faced. "I did," I said more softly. I *thought* I'd intended to, but without Bahlin's support, I wasn't sure what to do.

Seeing my discomfort, Tyr took a deep breath that filled out his barrel chest and let it out through his nose. Doing this twice more, he leaned forward and pulled me into his arms. "I was scared for you, Maddy. You've had the worst start to the Niteclif position. Anyone else going through this much trauma has been mercifully killed, and tonight when you turned your back on the vampires? I nearly manifested as a corporeal deity and laid waste to the room. You make it hard to watch over you," he said, resting his chin on top of my head.

I hugged him and he hugged me back. "*Dýrr barn,*" he whispered into my hair, "oh, my precious child. My heart has hurt so for your over the last few weeks, just as it has rejoiced for you in finding your true *félagi*, or partner." I'd never heard him slip into the old language, but the familiarity with which it rolled off his tongue could make it nothing else. "You have scared me, daughter mine."

"Do you know who's killing the girls?" I asked.

He nodded but said nothing. "I do, and I fear you must hurry if you are to stop h... the killer from reaching you. That or keep moving every day to stay in front of the killer, but then the question becomes who is chasing whom?"

I nodded at this sage observation, not sure we weren't already at that point. "What about Bahlin? Is he still going to help?"

Tyr looked sad and he shook his head. "He's your familiar, but he won't offer you assistance for a while. It will be up to you, me, Hellion and—" Thunder rumbled across the astral plane and I winced. Tyr wasn't fazed. "I swore I'd give you what I could, and Odin will just have to accept it," he mumbled, scratching his short beard. "How about this: include in the group your new friend, made tonight with a blood exchange."

"Darius?"

"Craps!"

"Huh?"

"The game you call out when someone is right. Craps, it's not craps. What is it?"

"I think you mean bingo," I said, grinning.

"Bingo." He smiled back at me. "Darius is a strong ally, someone you will do well to align yourself with. I've been aware of him for years. Don't blindly trust anyone, of course, but you would do well to get to know him and foster the friendship. I don't trust all his people, and neither should you, but you'll navigate those waters just fine."

Tyr sighed, clenching his head in his fists. He looked up, no longer smiling. "Maddy, you're going to need to give Bahlin some space. His world has been shattered, and his belief that he could manipulate the outcome of the prophecy has been decimated tonight. He thought you'd leave with him—"

"Even after his behavior at the stones?" I thought about his little spy session at Hellion's London home. "Was the burning smell I picked up at the hotel and Hellion's London house related to the dragons?"

Tyr tapped his forefinger to his lips. "I can tell you it was related to your killer. For now, let's leave it at that. For what I've told you tonight, Odin is near to ripping me back across this plane to the divine—and that hurts like a son of a bitch. I'll space out my punishments, thanks. I will caution you against tempting Odin, though, Maddy. Not your wisest move to date."

I ducked my chin to hide my anger. *Odin can kiss off.*

Tyr sighed and said, "He can hear that, Maddy." He leaned back against the bathroom wall and crossed his arms over his chest and his feet at the ankles.

"So no private thoughts?" I asked, biting my lower lip.

"Hellion is hung like a chicken?" He grinned widely.

I blushed like mad. "Thankfully you're the only one that knows about that little experiment. Um, where should I focus my energies? Is that all right to ask?"

He cocked his head to the side, seeming to listen to some otherworldly answer. Turning his face back to me he said, "I'll tell you the killer is stalking you, even interacting with you. Have Hellion cloak your activities and tell no one where you'll be. I mean it when I say no one. Be seen in public, then dematerialize to another location and be seen again before moving on for the night." He sighed and stood up, stretching. "This will keep the killer chasing you, but it will keep the focus off the innocents."

I looked over and realized my physical body had begun to shiver.

The hot water must have run out.

"Take a day, tomorrow maybe, and lay low here, but have Hellion bring in more of his people tonight and ask Darius to bring in more vampires to leave behind. It's important you become proactive in protecting yourself because I can't pull either of you back again without consequence." Tyr stepped up to me and wrapped me in his arms, and for just a moment I smelled my dad's old pipe smoke. It was a relief to find that memories like this were happy.

"Back you go, sweetheart." He turned me back toward my physical self. "Oh, and don't sleep alone tonight."

I spun back around. "What else is going to happen?" I asked, ashamed of the higher pitch of fear that leaked through.

"Nothing, love. Just don't miss this time to reinforce your destiny."

And he was gone before I even thought to ask him about my internal debate over destiny and free will.

I awoke in the shower, pruny and cold. I unfolded my frozen limbs and stood up, stretching and turning the water off. I toweled myself dry, thinking of what Tyr had said to me. I needed to spend some time with Hellion and work on healing together; probably wise, but I still couldn't sleep in that room. I needed to talk to him about cloaking immediately, and I needed to coordinate a small army of backup between the coven and the vampires. *How bad could this killer be?* I wondered. Not reassuring to know the god of war was encouraging me to rally the troops. I was rubbing the dirk down when I walked into the adjoining bedroom in nothing but my skin. That's how I found Darius.

Chapter Thirteen

I screamed. Darius rushed to me and slapped one hand over my mouth and the other around the back of my neck. One push and he could snap my neck.

"*Shh*, pet, *shh*," he whispered, his cool skin firmer than a normal man's against the softness of my mouth. "I want to talk to you, nothing more. Dawn is close, so I'm pressed for time. Okay?"

I couldn't nod my head so I let out a muffled, "Gluck," and he slowly removed his hands.

He looked uncomfortable and I sighed, wrapping the towel around my chest.

"Thank you," he said.

His voice was sorrowful, and I wondered what had happened. "Hellion? He's all right?"

"He's fine." Darius rolled his shoulders and walked to one of the wingback chairs situated near the room's fireplace. Sitting slowly, he gestured for me to do the same.

Relieved, I nodded. "Just let me grab some clothes." I started for the foot of the bed where I'd left my clothes before I remembered that all I had were the clothes stained with Clay's blood. Once again, I was left with a towel and nothing more. To hell with it. I walked to the bed, stripped off the top sheet and went back into the bathroom. I wrapped it around myself like a toga and came back out to sit with Darius. "What can I do for you?" I asked.

His lips twitched, and he waved a hand toward my improvisation. "Very nicely done. I would ask you to model it for me but you're still wielding the dirk, and I'd hate for you to take the request poorly."

It was true. I had the dirk clenched in my hand and had only put it down to tie the toga. This wasn't what I had imagined for my life. I sighed.

"Is it all that bad, Maddy?" Darius asked, leaning forward and putting his elbows on his knees, his hands dangling loosely between them. He looked at me so intently I could only listen as I blurted out my fears.

"I've got to get my shit together, Darius." I waved the dirk around for emphasis. "I've done nothing about the murders of these women short of gathering a few clues and accepting a threat on Hellion's behalf, I've killed a very good acquaintance if not a new friend, men seem to be coming on to me every time I turn around, I'm breaking one man's heart as I seem to fall in love with another, I feel like I've been inconsequential with my love and let's not discuss my body, there's a prophecy hanging over my head, and I can't figure out what the right thing to do is in all of this." I gasped the last as I ran out of air. "Oh, and I watched a very ugly part of myself I hadn't known about come out to play tonight with Conor. I don't like myself very much right now." I slumped back in the chair, feeling better for having purged my guilt with this veritable stranger. It was the old adage "a burden shared is a burden halved" come to fruition.

Darius grabbed the arms of his chair and scooted it closer to mine. Reaching out slowly, he took the dirk from me and set it on the floor. He grabbed my hands and squeezed gently, and I looked at him. He looked flush and healthy. *Ah, the color of Conor.*

I half smiled at the thought, and then grimaced at the morbidity of it all.

"Maddy, I must confess why I'm here."

If he wants to take me to bed, I'm embracing the violence without apology and cutting out his heart, I thought.

"...worried about it," he said.

"Can you say that again, please?" I asked, unsuccessfully stifling a yawn.

He smiled. "I know you saw our baser nature tonight—vampires—and I was worried about it." He watched me for some reaction, to which I proudly gave none.

Inside I was shuddering, but that was private.

He nodded and went on. "It's the first time in eight hundred years that it has mattered to me whether or not someone thinks well of me. I want to assure you that, while a vampire, I'm not necessarily cruel by nature. A large part of the man remains, and I'm left with free will. I choose what type of man to be every night when I awake."

Free will. "Do you believe the choice is entirely yours?" I asked. I knew both curiosity and skepticism showed on my tired face. I could feel the transparency of emotion but I didn't seem able to school my face into submission.

"I believe I influence the outcome of my destiny with the choices I make, but I do believe we all have a destiny, a calling. Is the choice entirely mine? That's a debate for another night when you're not weaving with exhaustion," he said gently, and I realized my eyes were closing.

I stood up, abruptly ending the conversation. "I'm so sorry. I *am* exhausted. Darius, will you bring some more vampires to watch the house? I think we need a little extra reinforcement in case the dragons come back again. And I hate to be such a bad hostess, particularly when the house I'm offering isn't mine, but the only rooms that are light-proof are probably in the basement."

He nodded. "I agree it's necessary, and all of us have slept in worse than a basement at one time or another, so don't fret about it. I'll send for...?" He left it a question.

How many more did I want? How many could we reasonably feed?

He smiled. "We'll find a place to hunt, so don't worry about how to feed us."

I groaned. "You read minds too?"

"'Too'?"

"Nothing. Just forget everything you heard tonight."

"You were broadcasting the chicken dick comment so loudly I nearly lost it right there. Don't test my humor like that without a little warning next time." He smiled big enough I saw his fangs and oddly I wasn't scared of him. "Oh, and I am *not* a metrosexual."

Darius was a good man, or monster, and I felt comfortable with him. I nodded my head. "Yeah, you are. But you wear the look well, so don't worry about it." I stood and stretched. "Will you do me a favor, Darius?" I asked, looking around the small room. I'd have to have a larger bed or we'd smother each other in sleep.

He nodded. "Anything, my friend."

Warmth spread through my body, and I realized he was the first friend I'd made independently since I arrived. My conscience whispered, *Hellion has offered friendship and what have you done with it?* Ignoring that nagging voice, I held out a hand to Darius, and he came to me willingly. I stepped up to him and kissed his cheek softly.

127

"And a worthy friend I hope to be," I said softly. "I need to find a larger bedroom, particularly a larger bed, and then I want you to bring Hellion to me, even if you have to carry him. I need him tonight, Darius." Emotion balled up in my throat and choked me, and I looked away.

"I'll tell you that the bedroom two doors down is ready, and it has a king-size bed. Settle yourself there and I'll go get Hellion. Ten minutes?"

"Perfect."

The room was just what I was looking for. It was like another master suite with attached bath and large closets and a huge bed. I piled the decorative pillows on the floor by the footboard and folded the sheets back. Seconds later there was a knock on the bedroom door.

"Maddy?" called Darius.

Shit. Hellion hadn't come. "Come in," I said, unable to hide the disappointment in my voice.

He opened the door and leaned his head in. "Hellion's here," he said, then pushed the door in the rest of the way, fading back so the shadow of the man I so badly wanted filled the door.

"I'll leave you two to each other's company. I'll see you both later tonight after sunset," Darius promised. He moved silently out of the doorway.

Hellion stood just inside the open door. "You asked to see me." His voice and his eyes were flat, his posture rigid and wary, his uncertainty broadcasting clearly.

"I'm not good at apologies, so bear with me as I fumble through this. I know I owe you one. An apology, that is." I walked toward him, stopping several feet away. "I sent you away when really I should have been pulling you closer. I struck out when it wasn't justified, but you shouldn't have pushed me quite so hard or grabbed me quite so tight, literally." I lifted my arm and showed him the bruising. He winced. "I needed a little space, then a little comfort. You gave me demands and criticisms on the heels of me killing a friend, realizing Bahlin wants me but doesn't love me and, finally, acknowledging that there's some dark part of me that's good at violence." I stopped and shook my head, as if clearing it from the sticky web of guilt and anger and confusion.

"To ice that cake, I had a visit from Tyr tonight. It made several things clear to me, not the least of which is that I've acted like an ass and I've been neglecting my job. I'm sorry, Hellion." I turned and walked back to the bed slowly, unsure how to get beyond this one moment.

Hellion's soft voice carried across the room. "As far as apologies go, I'd rate that one sufficient." I heard him move and the door close, and I sagged. He'd gone. I wanted to cry. When his hand landed on my bare shoulder I instinctively jerked, and his hand fell away. I turned to face him and found him staring at the fireplace, looking bereft.

"I'm sorry," I said, "again."

He smiled a little and turned toward the door.

"Don't go. Please. I'd like you to stay with me tonight."

He stopped, putting his hands in the pockets of his lounge pants. "Why?"

And then I realized what part of the problem was. The proposal. I'd never answered him. I still didn't know what to do, so I left it alone and focused on the now. Taking a fortifying breath, I said, "I want to pick up where we left off before the dragons arrived." My stomach clenched in fear, and I worried that this decision wasn't the right one. I'd never been casual with sex or my body, and I was proposing to offer both to him tonight. The only consolation I had was that I knew I cared for him on some real level; I just didn't know exactly what it meant. And I believed, honestly believed, he cared for me, prophecy be damned.

Hellion turned back to me and rocked back on his heels, biting his lower lip. He stood this way for several moments before he asked, "Why now? What's changed? I didn't ask before, but I should have. You've disregarded the prophecy, have only just accepted my friendship, you've turned from the little affection I've shown you, and you've acted guilty about the few times we've touched. What's different now?"

Fair assessment, I thought, if a hard one to answer. "You're right. I was torn between you and Bahlin, and to a point I still am. I don't know how to change that immediately because I believed I loved him. I agreed to marry him—it was only a few weeks ago. I can't just let that go, even if it was a whirlwind romance. He betrayed me and broke my heart at the same time you and I went from enemies to predestined lovers. I've said it before and I'll say it again: it's all just been overwhelming," I whispered in a rush that could barely be heard above the crackle of the fire as I slumped on the edge of the bed. Aware Hellion was studying me closely, I tucked the sheet tighter around me before continuing this admission of desire. "But still I want you on some basic level that defies reason and understanding and logic. This 'want' disregards my personal boundaries, my morals and my general fear of commitment. It's not something that's easily put into words." I stood again and moved passed him to the fire. Like the other room, there were two armchairs before the fireplace, and I sank into one feeling as fragile as spun sugar. "I can't tell you what's different, exactly. It just *is*. Maybe it has to do with the prophecy, maybe it has to do with Tyr's endorsement, maybe—"

"I don't hear the reason I need, Maddy. Love. It has to have something to do with love."

"Can you give me some more time? Love me now, physically, and we'll nurture the emotional together. Because I feel strongly for you. I *do*," I said with emphasis when he looked at me, fine lines and flat eyes marking the guardedness of his thoughts. "It's just, I don't trust it yet. I did that with Bahlin, and it left me brokenhearted. I need a little help here, Hellion." I moved to sit in a chair by the fireplace and give him a private moment to sort out his thoughts, to accept or deny my proposition.

He moved to sit in the chair opposite me. "All I've wanted was a chance, Maddy. I know, *I know*, we are fated, you and I. I've come to believe it with my whole being. So while I won't settle long-term for a chance at love, I'll settle for a chance at long-term love. Does that make sense?" he asked, concern drawing his brows together, "because it made sense in my head."

I nodded, my heart in my throat. I think we had just negotiated sex with an option on love.

Hellion rose and moved to face me. I couldn't help but notice he was already becoming aroused. I stood up to meet his approach, and he gently reached for the tucked edge of the sheet-toga. I nodded, and that was all the encouragement he needed. He tugged and it fell to the floor. Arms like steel bands wrapped around me, and I felt safe for the first time since...the last time I was with him. Hellion's head dipped toward mine, and I turned my chin up and away, offering my neck. He nibbled a line from my collarbone to my ear, sucking on my lobe and groaning so slightly I wasn't sure what I'd heard. He ran hot hands up my back then down, caressing the soft upper swell of my buttocks, teasing the skin with his work-roughened hands. I fought the urge to rush this, leaning into him and lifting my face to his. He bent down and kissed me, gently at first and then letting the passion grow with unspoken consent. He lifted me up, and my legs went around his waist instinctively. He reacted quickly to my positive response, ravaging my mouth, and I did the best I could to give as well as I got. He gripped my thighs and walked me to the bed, letting me slide down his body just before we reached the platform.

Hellion sank to his knees in front of me as if in worship, and I bent down and pulled his T-shirt off over his head, my nails raking his sides as I pulled. Hissing slightly, his breathing increased in depth and rhythm, mine voluntarily matching his in measure and intensity. Firelight gilded his body, and he seemed elemental and raw, a ripple of muscle and restrained desire. I stumbled into him when he grabbed my ass and yanked me forward, my hips pressing into his chest and my hands grabbing his shoulders for balance. He held me steady, working his lips up from my lower torso until he reached the nipple on my right breast.

I moaned as he bit it, almost too hard—almost, but not quite. I grabbed his head and pulled him closer. He drew great, laborious breaths around the breast, and his hot breath skated across the skin like a mirage.

Finally he released the nipple, and it pebbled even harder in the cool air, glistening with moisture. I stood bare before him, totally unembarrassed at my appearance for the first time in my life.

"Oh great goddess," Hellion moaned, standing and holding me at arm's length so he could look at me. "You're a miracle."

I flushed a little with the praise and reached out tentatively to pull loose the drawstring on his pants. They loosened and fell, hooking on his erection. I was uncertain how to handle this, and I looked up to find him watching me. He hooked his thumbs around the waistband and pulled, his erection springing free.

What was it with the supes going commando? I smiled up at him and he chuckled. I guess the smile could be interpreted several ways. He *was* impressive.

Together we sank slowly to our knees so we were closer to each other. I leaned into him, trapped his blazing arousal between us and lifted my face for a kiss.

Hellion bent down and captured my mouth without pretense. I worked hard to keep up with the aggressive pace he set and to not let my mind get between me and my physical desires. We kissed and touched and caressed, learning the topography of each others' bodies, the tender points and those spots that brought a hiss or a groan of satisfaction. Finally, bracing his hands under my arms, Hellion stood with me, and I wrapped my legs around his waist again.

Locking my arms behind his neck and sucking his tongue into my mouth, I bit it gently and pulled back. His hands flexed into my ass. I ground my hips against his, and he involuntarily thrust forward in response, setting himself at my opening. I was thoroughly aroused. At this point, consequences could be damned. I wanted this man like I'd never wanted anyone in my life.

Hellion was panting hard. He lifted me ever so slightly and looked at me, his eyes bottomless pools of black. "Are you sure—"

"No talking," I whispered into his mouth, licking at his lips. I bit his bottom lip hard, and his eyelids fluttered and he moaned. "No thinking." I reached between us and adjusted the head of his rigid erection so he was well positioned. I sank down on him slightly and he breached my outer folds. "No consequences." I sank farther, and he grabbed the back of my head, took three large steps to the wall and slapped my back against it, driving himself home. I gasped at the invasion that stretched me to the point of discomfort.

"I can't stop," he warned and I nodded. He began to pound into me, the slap of flesh on flesh an erotic background noise to our grunts and moans of pleasure, small words of encouragement, praise and challenge pouring from both of us.

Leaning forward, I licked the shell of his ear and breathed, "More." He shouted, grabbing my hips to drive me down his length and oblige me. I grunted at the impact, but it was what I needed, this borderline violence. It was like flipping the bird to the universe. Arching my back, I pushed against him again and again until sweat ran between us in rivulets and made it hard for him to hold on to me.

"Close, Maddy, I'm so close," he ground out and I clutched him tighter, throwing my head back right before my own climax took me over and I was shattered, bucking and writhing with pleasure. My sheath clenched and released, pulling his orgasm from him without apology. Hellion shouted and I felt him let go. It seemed to go on forever, this circle of mutual gratification. Finally, finally, Hellion sank to the floor and fell backwards, taking me with him. His heart thundered in his chest, and I shifted to roll off him but he tightened his arms and held me still, forcing me to stay where I was.

"You called me Maddy instead of Madeleine when you weren't thinking about it," I said, lazily running a hand through the sweat on his chest. "I much prefer it, you know. So keep it up. Look at the rewards."

"Don't get used to it, chit," he replied. "Of course, it didn't exactly hurt anything." He was silent then, running a hand up and down my spine. He whispered something, and I paused mid stroke, playing the phrase over in my mind.

"What did you say?" I asked.

"*Táim i ngrá leat,* Madeleine," he said softly.

"And it means what?"

"I'm in love with you, Madeleine." I froze but he didn't stop his gentle caresses. "Does it scare you?"

"Terrifies me," I admitted. I struggled to move off him and he let me, but refused to completely release me. "How can you be sure you really love me and it's not just about your expectations based on the prophecy?"

"Life offers no guarantees, *anamchara,* so we must make the best of what we're given."

I was petrified that he suddenly seemed so serious. I'd convinced myself I'd been looking for comfort and affirmation of the decisions I was making for my own life. What could really be more affirming than post-coital bliss?

We lay in the floor until the sweat started to cool on our bodies and the air became uncomfortably chilled against our skin. Hellion shifted me to the side and sat up, grabbing the discarded toga to wrap around his waist. "I'm going to the kitchen to fetch some snacks. Get settled, and we'll talk when I get back."

I scrambled up and ran to the bathroom, quickly cleaning myself up. I went back to the bedroom and crawled into bed, pulling the sheet up and tucking it under my arms. I waited like that for at least fifteen minutes, watching the sky lighten as dawn broke behind the cloud cover of the Irish sky. One minute I was contemplating the chance for rain, the next Hellion was scooting me over in the bed and sliding in beside me.

"Sorry," I mumbled. "Must've fallen asleep." I let loose a jaw-cracking yawn and looked at the tray of meats and cheeses he'd brought up. I was too tired to be interested.

"Sleep, love. The food will wait. Rest easy, Maddy. I'll be here."

His words were so reassuring. I settled down in bed, snuggling next to him. I didn't even have time to realize how immediately comfortable I was with him beside me, naked, before sleep claimed me. Fortunately, even Tyr left me alone and let me get some dreamless sleep. I was grateful.

I awoke to a bright room and the sounds of soft *whuffling* in my ear. Hellion had fallen asleep with his chin tucked into the crook of my neck as he spooned me. We fit together like puzzle pieces. I shifted and he jerked awake.

"Sorry," I said, patting the arm around my waist. "Didn't mean to startle you."

"No, no. It's okay. I must have fallen off just after you." He yawned and stretched from head to toe, shaking with the effort before relaxing against me. "I haven't slept that well in ages," he said against my neck, kissing me softly behind the ear.

I rolled over and laid my head on his chest, listening to his heart beat solidly beneath my ear. My traitorous stomach growled loudly. Hellion chuckled, the sound reverberating through my skull. Setting me gently aside, he rolled to the bedside table and hauled the tray of meats, bread and cheeses to the center of the bed. We ate in silence, sharing small caresses or covert glances when our hands would touch. The comfort of darkness was only partially lost in the light of day which was—historically—remarkable for me and my sense of propriety. The charming way he was behaving made me feel that much less conspicuous.

Finishing the meal, I curled up under the covers while Hellion scrounged around for clothes I might be able to wear. He came back with a pair of his lounge pants and an enormous T-shirt. I'd obviously have to grab better clothes when we got back to London, but for today this looked perfect. I pulled on the pants and shirt and admired his physique as he tended the smoldering fire, watching the muscles move on his back as he hoisted firewood and encouraged the flame. The hollow of his spine between the columns of muscle was just deep enough to cast a shadow in the uncertain light of the room.

"When do you want to go back?" he asked, turning on the balls of his feet to face me as I lounged in the bed.

"Back?" I asked dumbly.

"To London, love. We'll need to get you back there so you can start putting together the pieces of this puzzle. Another girl has died, this time a waitress from the small café we had lunch at near Avebury Henge."

I blanched and Hellion moved toward me. "I wasn't even near there," I murmured, a chill settling over me that had nothing to do with the temperature of the room. "I was here last night."

"Ah, but not for the whole night, Maddy. Think."

"I—okay, I need to sort this out. Who was at the henge last night that might wish me ill?"

"Besides all the dragons?" Hellion asked, crawling back into bed and drawing me to his side.

I scooted over, settling in against him with a sense of familiarity that hadn't yet been earned. "All right, all the dragons. But who else? Let me think." I pushed my nose into his chest and breathed deeply of the scents of linen and laundry detergent, a faint remnant of cologne and the musk of male. "There was Darius and members of his voyyen, the dragons—though it wasn't restricted to the blue weyr, a handful of fae, Sarenia, members of your coven and me. I think that covers it." I lifted my chin and met his eyes, arching a brow. "So, roughly, we've got about a hundred people to exclude that were *inside* the circle. Outside? No way of knowing."

Hellion sighed deeply, running his fingers up and down the back of my skull and making me want to purr. "We've got to be able to pare it down more, Maddy. Who are the primary suspects and why?"

Considering, I sat up and wrapped my arms around my knees. "Do you have some paper and a pen? It might help if we write this down."

He crawled out from under the covers and disappeared from the room. I heard a door open and, moments later, close again. Hellion padded back into the room, his long, loping stride covering the ground quickly. He tossed the pen and notebook on the bed and crawled back under the covers, propping himself up against the headboard.

I grabbed the notebook and flipped it open to the first blank page, intimidated by the vacant paper and energized to finally be doing something.

"Here's what we know for certain," I said. "The killer is purported to be right-handed based on Bahlin's report. He also claims the knife used was non-serrated, so it's probably something like a dagger or dirk, right?"

Hellion nodded. "It would have to be something that could be easily handled yet sharp enough to get the job done. Magic leaves a trace, so if we can get in to see a body, I can determine whether or not it's just brute strength behind the violence."

"Darius," we said together.

Hellion nodded and gestured for me to go on.

"We'll get Darius, or his inside morgue man, to get us up close and personal with one of the bodies. Then there's the letter. Could you tell anything about the handwriting?"

Hellion looked at me, amused. "I'm a wizard, not a bloody forensic specialist, sweetheart."

I glared and shifted around in the bed to face him, tucking the covers around my bare feet. "No need to be snide. What you do is 'bloody' complicated, and I'm unfamiliar enough with it that I don't know what's reasonable and what's not."

He grinned. "You're cute when you say 'bloody'."

I rolled my eyes and moved on. "So we know nothing about the letter except it was delivered to your London home and, somehow, the killer was able to snip a lock of your hair. If you haven't been sleeping that well, it should have been difficult for someone to sneak up on you and steal your hair. Unless, of course, the hair isn't yours."

"Brilliant!" Hellion exclaimed. "We'll go to London, retrieve the hair, and I'll perform a spell of revelation. It should be able to give us at least a cursory idea what flavor of individual we're dealing with." He scrambled from the bed, grabbed the covers and yanked me toward him. Scooping me up, he spun in a circle and I flinched, not prepared to dematerialize, but he was just being slightly exuberant. Recognizing my hesitation, he set me down gently. "Does it bother you, what I am?"

"What you are... Oh. No. I'm just, um, a little unnerved by the casualness with which you pop in and out of places. Can all witches and wizards do that?"

"No." His brows drew together as he contemplated a reasonable explanation. In the end, he went with basic truth. "It's a highly specialized skill, and to be able to carry a passenger with you is even more difficult. There are four, maybe five of us in the world who can do it. Two of us, Amaly and I, are in my coven."

"Amaly?"

"She was at the henge last night, but she went back to London so you've not had a proper introduction. She's the most powerful witch in Europe and my second."

"Oh." I felt uneasy, and it took me a minute of digging around in my own psyche to understand that the emotion I was having a hard time identifying was jealousy. I sighed, slightly disgusted with myself.

Understanding the variety of emotions dancing across my face, Hellion leaned in and kissed me gently. "You've nothing to fear, Maddy." He sat on the edge of the bed and lay back, pulling me down with him so I straddled his hips. Shifting beneath me, Hellion smiled up at me so harmlessly that I had to laugh.

"That's far from innocence I'm feeling from you despite the look on your face," I said, leaning forward to brush my lips over his.

He snaked his tongue out and traced my lower lip, and I shivered. "What would it take to talk you out of your clothes?" he murmured against my lips before laying kisses across my temple, down my neck and stopping just over my heart. He bit me through the T-shirt and I gasped, involuntarily responding to his physical suggestions if not his words.

"Less talk," I responded.

Hellion flipped me over on my stomach, and I shrieked with laughter. "Less talk it is," he promised. He delivered.

Chapter Fourteen

We gathered our things and left Ireland. I had to get busy with the investigation, and too many interruptions—imagined death, near death, death—had diverted my attention. Hellion and I materialized in his London home. More specifically, we ended up in his bedroom. I recognized some of my personal belongings sitting on his dresser. I stepped over to the chest and pulled out a drawer; there were my underwear.

"It seems you expect me to stay...to, ah, live here with you at this point." My voice was unsteady as my mind ran through a gamut of emotions—fear, frustration and anger.

"And why shouldn't I, *mo shíorghrá*? We're together now, not to be separated. In my mind that means we live together. Am I wrong, then?"

"I'm not sure. That isn't the point, though. Not really." I stumbled around, searching for the right words, but blurted out, "I'd like to be asked, Hellion. Don't presume to know me well enough to know what I want."

"You're right, my love. I should have asked if you wanted the same thing, not just assumed. I apologize. Do you want to stay here?" He wandered up behind me and his hands snaked around my waist, his chin resting on my shoulder.

"For now. I'll stay for now." He moved to cup my breasts. "Don't assume I'm here because I've nowhere to go at the moment. I could get another hotel..." He laid small kisses along the side of my neck. "Or an apartment."

"I'll buy you your own house if you'll stay here. Then every time you get angry with me, you'll have somewhere you can go."

I sighed, distracted from my displeasure by pleasure. He was stroking my nipples through the thin material of the T-shirt and they, along with other things, were tightening in response to him. How could I want him so much? I wondered. It hadn't been this fierce with Bahlin... I was distracted momentarily until Hellion nipped at my neck and, settling himself in the crevice of my ass, gently rocked back and forth.

There was a knock at the door and we both paused.

"Bloody fucking hell," he muttered, reaching to adjust his impressive erection. "Come in!"

Mark, the butler, entered the room. I squeaked and turned my back to him, hiding my erect nipples against Hellion's chest.

He stroked my back and said, "Mark, what is it?"

"I'm sorry, sir, ma'am. I didn't realize you'd come home together. Is everything to your liking?"

"Sure," I said, uncomfortable with the fact that this strange man was catering to my every need. I just wasn't cut from the stock that expected the custom service, or butlers, that wealth could buy. My family had been the servers, not the served.

"There's nothing to be uncomfortable with, Maddy," Hellion whispered. He turned my chin to face him, and I jerked away from him, stepping out of his arms.

"Give us a minute, Mark."

The butler left the room quietly.

"What is it, love?" he asked.

Good question. "I feel like I'm failing everywhere and fitting in nowhere. A few weeks ago I was engaged to another man, and this morning I find myself post-coital cuddling with another whose expressed intent had been to see me dead. What is it with me, Hellion? I'm floundering like a drowning woman, and people are dying because of it." I slapped a hand against the wall and thumped my forehead against the cool plaster. I felt his arms come around me and I sagged into him, needing just for a moment to be supported. He caught me, just as I'd counted on him to do.

"Maddy, you're new at this—" he began.

"And that doesn't mean jack shit to each and every dead woman's family," I countered.

"Families who have no idea you exist."

I jerked and realized that that was probably the biggest rub. I was fulfilling the prophecy without even trying, walking between the worlds of the mundane and mythological, a foot in each reality and a place of belonging in neither. I rubbed my forehead, the worry lines feeling like little mini-ridges under my fingertips.

"Do you want to talk to Tyr?" he asked.

"It might help," I answered. "But I'll save it for tonight when I hit the sack. For now I need a shower and my own clothes."

"Of course. I'll just run downstairs and see what we've missed in the last night. I need to take care of some business anyway." He turned me around and I went slowly, slipping my arms around his waist and laying my head against his chest. His voice rumbled under my ear when he spoke. "Don't hold yourself accountable for the murderer's actions, Maddy. We'll catch him, or her, and we'll see justice meted out."

I nodded, feeling inexplicable tears building in the back of my throat. I pushed away from him gently and turned for the bathroom.

"Maddy?" he called.

I shook my head and kept going. Any more empathy and I was going to begin to unravel, and right now I needed to keep it together. I had a murderer to stop in a world that, as Hellion had said, didn't even know I existed.

I wandered downstairs after my shower and found Hellion in the study poring over the letter that had been delivered to him before we'd left for the Council meeting.

"Anything new?" I propped a hip on the edge of his desk.

"Nothing." He sighed, leaning back and pushing his hands through his thick, blond hair. His black eyes were flat with frustration, and he stared at me carefully. "Have you had any new thoughts on it?"

"I'm wondering about the blue thread." I reached over and picked it up, rolling it between my fingers. It was silky but heavy, almost like embroidery floss. "Do you think it could mean it's from the blue dragons?"

Hellion shrugged. "I wondered the same thing, but it seems too obvious."

"Maybe." I sniffed the thread and smelled nothing in particular. "Think back to the note. They refer to me as the traitorous Mary Stuart. Could be that they're English, or of English persuasion. That would rule out the leaders of the weyr." My chest constricted. *Bahlin.* "Who does that open up, in particular?"

"You're thinking in modern terms, Maddy. What if the killer actually *knew* Mary Stuart?"

I blanched.

"He knows her, thinks she turned traitor to her family, and ended up getting what she deserved. That would be right in line with what the blue weyr has been to you: potential family, then you turned traitor—"

I made a noise of protest and Hellion held up his hand.

"—you turned traitor and sided with someone outside the family, someone from foreign soil. It could very well be the blue weyr, Maddy."

"Aiden could have killed me last night when he had the gun to my jaw," I argued.

"For all his tough talk, he's just a boy. And he had his orders to return you to Bahlin."

I thought about it, rubbing my temples at the developing headache. Could it have been Aiden? Was it that simple? Somehow I doubted it. Aiden was angry, and he'd lost his father and his sister, but he wasn't a killer. The opportunity to take me out last night and then change the story of the surrounding circumstances convinced me he wasn't my focus. Shaking my head, I stood and walked to the sideboard to pour up a neat whiskey. I raised my glass and offered Hellion a drink. He nodded but came to retrieve his own. I took a generous sip and it burned going down, the artificial warmth spreading immediately into my torso and arms and making me relax slightly.

"He's just not the right focus, Hellion. I'm sure of it."

"What about Bahlin's mother? She's arguably lost the most in this, and she stands to have her family scrutinized closely due to the murders. Could she want to take you out?"

"Undoubtedly," I said. "But not for that reason. I could be considered indirectly responsible for the deaths of her husband and daughter. *That* would make her want to kill me. But I don't know that she's the type to act on it personally. She's been in power, or related to those in power, too long. She'd find someone to do it for her." The thought sent chills up and down my spine despite the effects of the alcohol. If someone had been hired to take me out, I was working against someone I wouldn't recognize. I sighed and walked over to the sofa, sinking down into it and setting my drink on the side table.

"And Imeena?" Hellion asked, rolling a pen back and forth in his fingers as he watched me.

"Imeena is a possibility. The attacks are at night, no trouble with the brutality, she's got the strength and she's definitely got the motivation. I just don't know that she'd waste the blood. And her sense of smell—wouldn't she be able to determine if it was me before killing?"

"I'm not sure every vampire has a distinguishing sense of smell. Yes, they can smell blood and hear heartbeats and such, but we'll have to ask Darius about the general improvements they undergo after the rebirth." Hellion walked over and sat beside me, setting his drink with mine. He opened his arms to me, and I was struck by the kindness of the gesture. He was offering me the choice to seek comfort, not assuming I needed to.

I pushed off the back of the sofa and crawled into his lap.

Hellion held me close, breathing in and out with slow, deep breaths that ruffled my hair. " *Tá grá agam duit,* my Madeleine," he whispered. *I love you.*

I nodded, unable to answer him. My heart seemed to have lodged itself in my throat, bound equally by joy and fear at Hellion's profession of feelings.

His arms tightened around me then released me, and I crawled out of his lap to stand in front of him. "When will Darius be here?"

Hellion stared at me, his eyes pulsing, before answering in a soft voice. "He should get here later this evening. As fast as he is, it will take him a bit. Two hours after dark, I'd assume."

"Let's—"

"I don't expect you to answer me right now, Maddy."

I looked up sharply.

"But I do expect you to answer me someday."

I nodded, mute with fear. I couldn't speak.

Hellion smiled gently. "There's nothing I can imagine that's more important than hearing the words from you, but I won't push you. You'll come to me willingly or I'll not have you at all. You understand this, right?"

I shrugged so stiffly it must have appeared I was cast of stone. "What do you mean 'not at all'?"

Shaking his head, he rose to stand in front of me. I instinctively reached up and smoothed his hair back from his forehead. He dropped his forehead to mine and laid a light kiss on my upturned face. "I won't coerce you and I won't push you, but I also won't hide my own feelings. You'll come to me or you won't. If you don't, then we'll have nothing between us but the physical, and that's not enough for me. So consider that, Maddy. I love you, but I'll not tolerate heartbreak just for the sake of suffering some emotion."

"Sounds sort of like you're pushing," I stammered.

"No. Don't misunderstand this. There's a difference between pushing and honesty. I'll give you honesty. Don't ever doubt that."

My recent history with Bahlin led me to believe that every oath could be broken, but I didn't want to fight with Hellion so I just nodded. "Okay." I stepped back and turned toward the clock. "So we've got about three hours before Darius shows up?"

Silence. I kept my back to him so he could have a minute to either strangle me or compose himself. "That's about right," he finally said. "What would you like to do?"

"I'd like to leave the testing of the hair for later. I think it's best if we use the daylight to visit the sites where we know the girls have been killed, at least locally. We can look at the approach, the places someone could hide, the lighting—things I don't have a freaking clue about but that I'm willing to take a stab at."

He winced.

"Sorry. Bad pun. Unintentional, but still bad."

Hellion reached for my hand and I reached back. It was the most I could offer. We headed for the door.

We started at the Pemberton because it was closest to Hellion's home. The sidewalk had been washed down well by the daily rains, but there were still slight rusty-looking stains on the concrete. My stomach plummeted, and I fought to hold on to the remainders of my lunch.

Feeling like a complete fool, I looked over our single page of notes that covered all the crimes. According to this, police believed the woman had been walking toward the hotel entrance. She'd been taken down at the valet entrance, located between street lamps on a relatively dark side of the building. The only immediate sources of light that had been available were security lights along the side of the building. The killer would have been able to steal up behind her with ease, but had she turned at the last moment—before the killer could either hide or reach her—she would have seen the killer's face without difficulty.

I stood facing the entrance and had Hellion walk down the sidewalk, ducking into doorways and moving as quietly as a large man can. It was surprisingly easy to see how she might have been snuck up on in the dark.

"So what do you think?" I asked as he made his way up to me.

"She would have been far enough from the entrance, and it would have been dark enough between security lights, that no one would have been likely to see anything. If you add supernatural abilities of cloaking or stealth, she never knew anyone was there." He looked as disgusted as I felt.

"She never had a chance," I repeated, frustrated. "Is there any way you can trace the magic that might have been used?"

"No, sweetheart. Magic fades like a scent on the air. So after this long, there's no way to know what was here with any certainty. I would if I could."

I reached out to him and we grasped each other's hands, the sensation of being anchored in each other a comforting one. "It's all right. I'm just floundering here, hoping for some quick fix to the problem and knowing it's not going to happen." I took a deep breath and nearly had to chew the London air to get it down. There was something to be said for the Irish countryside.

I took my hand back and walked down the sidewalk, looking for something, anything, that would give me a damn start on this nightmare of a case. Lying in the crevice between sidewalk and street, its color darkened from rain and grime, was a long piece of blue thread. I snatched it up and held it out triumphantly to Hellion. I had no idea what to do with it, but it was a start.

"What do you want to bet it matches the blue thread that bound the hair in the letter?" I asked.

"Chances are good you're right." He held out his hand and I gave him the thread. He mumbled something, and the grime and dampness disappeared, leaving only the vibrant blue thread in his hands.

"You're pretty handy with this stuff. Can you handle red wine stains?" I teased.

"Funny girl. It's all elemental—water, dirt, cotton thread—or it wouldn't have worked."

I thought about what he said. *Elemental.* "So if it had been man-made..."

"I'd have had to get the Tide pen just as you would have," he responded dryly.

Shaking my head, I reached out and took the thread back,

wrapping it around my finger to make a small bundle before shoving it in the pocket of my jeans. "Let's try another site. Maybe the one...maybe the one near Bahlin's." His name hurt to hear, and I did my best not to show any emotion, but I'm pretty sure I failed miserably.

Hellion said nothing, just held out his hand to me and said, "I'll drive."

We rode the short distance to the park near Bahlin's apartment. The back of my neck felt hot and my stomach hurt. If we ran into him, I was pretty sure I'd just walk away, but only if I could keep from running. Cowardly? More like self-preservation. Scanning the area for any sign of the blue weyr or their leader, I crawled out of Hellion's coupe and began walking swiftly for the park. "Do you know where she was found?" I called out over my shoulder, never breaking my stride.

"Maddy? Slow down, sweetheart. He's not here."

My pace faltered, and I stopped. "Are you sure?" I asked softly.

"I'm positive. He's been seen at his family's home in Scotland since he tried to enforce his claim to you."

"Are you sure?" I asked again, a little more firmly. "Because I'd hate to have to brawl in the streets." I smiled at him, trying to soften the blow my initial fear had caused him.

Hellion's lip twitched and finally broke into a grin. "I'd like to see you brawl."

Remembering Clay and the price he'd paid for forcing his hand, I looked away and shook my head. "No, you wouldn't. Trust me."

Hellion took three large steps, caught me by the elbow and spun me around to face him. Crushing me to his chest, he spoke to me quickly and quietly in Gaelic. I had no idea what he was talking about, but I nodded my head as if he made sense. He released me and stepped back, holding me at arm's length. "Let's check out the park and go home."

I nodded and twin tears rolled down my cheeks. I swiped at them angrily, scrubbing my face and breathing deeply, blowing out through my lips. *Enough feeling sorry for yourself, Niteclif. Life sucks and then you get dead, one way or another.* It was tough talk. I needed it.

The sun was setting. Shadows crept toward us with the unspoken malicious intent of swallowing us and the light as a whole. People think darkness descends from the sky but it doesn't. It creeps out from under trees and bushes, the shadows growing dense and dark at the same time. Small animals were bedding down for the evening to avoid the night's predators, and foot traffic along the path was quickly thinning out as the mundanes followed the eons-old primal instincts to get inside to the safety of home and hearth before dark fully set in.

We walked wordlessly through the park, sticking to the path, all the way to the point where the girl's body had been found. It had been seven days since she'd been killed. With the human traffic in the park combined with the foraging of animals, I didn't anticipate finding anything in the way of clues. I was right. But the setting was suspiciously like the hotel in that the lamp's light was spaced out just far enough to provide shadowy hiding places between the yellow glow of the gaslights. There were plenty of ways the killer could have approached and hidden, approached and hidden, until she, or he, was close enough to move in for the kill.

"Maddy?" Hellion called.

I jumped and spun around, instinctively throwing my hand to my throat. Knowing the things that went bump in the night were real and, on occasion, interested in my jugular, made my reaction more a defensive move of self-preservation. I could feel my heart thundering beneath my fingertips.

"What?" I hissed, forcing my hand down to my side and taking a deep, shaky breath.

"Step over here, love."

I strode toward him as if he hadn't just scared the ever-loving shit out of me.

Stepping into the halo of light, I noticed for the first time what he was pointing at. There were deep gouges cut into the ground about twenty feet off the path. They appeared to have been dug by a set of vicious tines or claws. The dirt had caved in at the edges with the passage of time and rain, and the grass was yellowing, but the ground had yet to heal its wounds. I bent down and ran my fingers along the dirt but there was no divine revelation; it was just disturbed earth. The gouges were also well concealed enough that the average path patron wouldn't have seen them.

"What do you make of this?" I asked.

Hellion shook his head, staring at the ground. "I suppose we could take a sample of the dirt and see if it reveals anything back at the house."

Wrath

"What's so special about the house? And what's dirt going to 'reveal' anyway?"

Hellion stuck his hands in his pockets and stared at me in disbelief, shaking his head as if to rid himself of my ignorance. "I'll be able to spend some time—private, uninterrupted time—and cast a couple of revelation spells. The dirt is organic and, therefore, belongs to no one, so it shouldn't be magically warded in any way. Whatever scored the earth will have left a physical imprint behind, a sort of psychic, or metaphysical, signature. Does that make sense?"

"So you'll do that voodoo you do and shazam. You'll have an answer? Seems too easy."

"No, Madeleine, it's not voodoo. We're talking very technical magic, difficult spells that focus on elemental and personal disclosures," he snapped, rocking back on his heels and losing the easy-going façade. His hands made lumps in his pockets where he'd shoved them with force, the fabric straining against the continued downward pressure.

Truthfully, I didn't know what he was capable of other than the dematerialization thing. And while it was impressive, the novelty had worn off after the sixth or seventh trip we'd made together. I said as much to Hellion and he sighed heavily, closing his eyes and rubbing the bridge of his nose. I've been known to have that effect on people.

"Obviously you have no concept of whom you're dealing with," he said, his voice serious. Holding out a hand, he breathed across it, and a flame sprung from his palm. With the other hand, he extinguished it.

I watched his little performance in silence but it was impossible not to comment. "If you'd ever been a Boy Scout you would have undoubtedly earned your fire-starter badge with no trouble."

Hellion gaped at me, his mouth hanging open just a little, his brows arched and bared hands falling to his sides. "I can call down the stars from the heavens, cause the earth to quake and split, destroy someone where they stand with little more than a thought." He stepped closer to me, leaning over me enough that I was forced to either step back or lean away from his building fury. I did neither, craning my neck to meet his gaze but holding my ground. "I travel through space and time and heal death blows in others with my *will*, and you compare me to a Boy Scout?" he hissed, seething with rage. His eyes had gone flat black, the irises eating at the whites, and a fine wind blew around him, whipping his hair about and stirring his clothes.

"Sorry," I whispered, and I was...mostly. But the intimidation act was pissing me off since we both knew he wouldn't physically hurt me. "Really. It's just that I've never seen you do anything other than move me around and cure the tail end of that curse, so I *don't* know what you're capable of. Maybe instead of getting mad at me for my lack of understanding you should show me what to expect. I never even saw you fight at the big showdown with Tarrek." He opened his mouth to object and I quickly continued. "No. That's not what I meant. I *know* you fought, I just didn't witness it myself."

Hellion nodded tersely before turning to storm off, his movements jerky and uncoordinated as his anger drove him away. I stood in the fringes of the lantern's glow and shivered in the damp, cooling air. The noises of the night seemed louder, more threatening, the minute I was alone. They seemed to feed on the all-encompassing dark and my escalating heart rate, the scent of my perspiration, the twitching of my fine muscles. The implied threat of that darkness circled without apology or compassion. The sudden cessation of noise transcended everything I thought I'd known of fear in that space: the crickets stopped chirping, the rustling noises of prey mammals ceased, the wind held its breath.

A figure shoved me as it rushed by, swiping at the back of my head as it passed me from behind. It was so sudden I didn't even have time to gather a breath to scream, but instead grunted in pain as I slammed shoulder-first into the dirt. I pushed myself up, gritting my teeth against that initial blow. I was getting really tired of getting my ass kicked as the Niteclif, and this newest fight had just begun. Regaining my feet, I turned on unsteady legs to face my assailant. There was no one there.

I was slammed again from behind, my head snapping back, the impact so hard my teeth clacked together and I bit my tongue, the coppery taste of blood flooding my mouth as the fight-or-flight response kicked in post-shock. I raised a fist and swung out, connecting with a shadowy mist. It was like a blast of nitrogen to the skin, and I involuntarily jerked my hand back. Following the retreat of my hand, the mist knocked me off balance with a blow to the solar plexus, and I gasped for the air I couldn't convince my lungs to retrieve. I stepped into the ruts and fell. The shadow flung something at me but I was too slow to roll out of the way before it pelted me on the forehead.

Wrath

The assailant rushed me just as Hellion broke through the brush at a dead run. He shouted something and cast out a hand in my general direction, and the shadowy attacker dissolved into wisps of smoke. I rolled onto my hands and knees, and my breath came in short gasps. I was shaken, and the shock of recognition the gold coin evoked only added to the riot of emotions clamoring for my immediate attention. Settling on nausea as the most relevant physical feeling and anxiety the domineering emotion, I studied the coin closely. I'd seen coins like this twice before: first, weeks ago in a dragon's den and, more recently, when Darius passed a mate to Hellion at the henge.

How could I be sure they were the same? Because they were distinctive, and I'd studied the first one very carefully, admiring the monarch's likeness and the raised horse on the back after the dragon had tossed it at me. That time I'd caught it. In a rush of cognition, I put the pieces together—the member of the blue weyr who could cloak himself in night, who would fight dirty when the situation called for it, who in dragon form could have easily gouged the earth or...*oh shit*. He could control even a partial shift and turn his hands into claws, and what better to behead a woman with than dagger-sharp claws? *Bahlin.*

I pushed myself to standing, promising my body that if we got knocked down again we'd just stay there. It was the best I could offer my aching shoulder and bruised chest. I held out the coin, and Hellion snatched it out of the air as I dropped it. "How did you know I was in trouble?" I asked, my voice wheezy with the rasp of my breathing.

Hellion pocketed the coin and, kneeling in front of me, began going over me very carefully to assess the damage. I protested at his fussing but when he lifted my shirt to look at my sternum, I really balked.

"Hush," he said, moving my hands aside gently but unrelentingly and pushing my shirt up so my chest was revealed. "I'd already turned to come back to you when I heard the scuffle. I got here as fast as I could but it wasn't soon enough." He traced the bruise forming between my breasts, the points of knuckle contact deepening faster than the rest of the fist-shaped discoloration. Making a fist, Hellion laid his knuckles against the bruise, and I started. His fist was almost exactly the same size as the imprint on my chest.

His head was bent so close to me that I unthinkingly reached out a hand to stroke him. He grabbed my wrist just before it made contact with his mane of hair. I gasped and jerked my hand back, and Hellion

149

let go to continue his triage.

"Hu—" I cleared my throat. "How did you know I was going to touch you?"

"You forget, love, I'm a wizard and, under the right circumstances, a warlock. The first uses magic for the right reasons while the second uses magic as a means to an end. There's little I wouldn't do to protect you, right or wrong." He lifted his eyes up to me and they were black...*all* black. The whites had been consumed by the black pupils, and the depth of soul they opened up to me was terrifying. Seeing my reaction, Hellion stood and spun away from me. "Let's get back to the house where I can better protect us and help you with your current condition." And he walked away.

Chapter Fifteen

We rode back to Hellion's flat in an uncomfortable silence. He parked the car in his regular spot and turned off the engine, and I reached over and grabbed his hand. "Thank you," I said. "I wasn't handling having my ass handed to me so unexpectedly. You saved me a seriously worse beating at the very least."

He nodded in a short, jerky movement, his eyes avoiding mine as he stared at some point over my right shoulder. Sighing, Hellion turned away and moved to get out of the car but I yanked on his arm, hard, to get him to face me and see me.

A muscle ticked in his jaw and his eyes were flat and cold, guarded, when he met my gaze. "What do you want from me, Maddy? I'm still angry with you, but I'm angry at myself for leaving you alone, as well. Nothing's supposed to be happening the way it has with you, from working with you to falling in love. I'm not a qualified detective or even a detective's assistant, so I'm not sure what I'm about, but it seems I'm working with you more and more, and it has me out of sorts. Had anything happened to you tonight after I lost my temper, I wouldn't have forgiven him—ever. I'm half inclined to go after him myself and solve this once and for all. Great Odin," Hellion bellowed, slamming his fist against the steering wheel.

"So you're thinking of Bahlin too." I studied Hellion's face in profile, the corded muscles standing out in his neck, the flexing jaw muscles, the fingers of one hand wrapped around the steering wheel and the others clutching his knee. The empath in me hurt for his insecurity and rage. In a split second I decided to share with Hellion one of the few true secrets I had about the paranormal world. "You know how I'm related to Aloysius Niteclif?" I asked, to which he nodded. "Want to know why Bahlin seems so good at this stuff?"

He nodded. "It might help me maintain some semblance of sanity. I feel like I'm always one step behind him when it comes to you." His voice seemed to leak sorrow the way an old pipe seeps water, slow but persistent.

I searched his face looking for some clue to his ricocheting emotions. Dishonest or not, I'd never intended to share with Hellion any of my lingering doubts about the two of us but obviously I was doing a piss-poor job of keeping my feelings to myself. I took a deep, shaky breath, and the next words rushed out in a blur of sound. "Aloysius was Sherlock Holmes. When he was fictionalized as Holmes, his partner was, too. Bahlin was Watson. He lived next to Aloysius. That part was true. But the story left out that Watson was not only a doctor but a dragon. So he's had years and years of experience working with the greatest sleuth of all time. Of *course* he seems more adept at this shit."

Hellion's jaw relaxed, and the nervous tapping of his fingers slowed and finally stopped. "I knew Bahlin worked with the other Niteclifs, but I had no idea his level of help was that intensive." He glanced over at me and looked away again. "Are you serious or are you placating me?"

"Dead serious. Which, uh, brings me to one other thing."

Hellion waved me on but said nothing. He turned in his seat to face me squarely, bracing one hand on the headrest of my seat and looping the other over the steering wheel.

"My job is to walk between both worlds, to keep one foot firmly planted in each existence, and to not let mythology take over my life entirely."

"I think that's pretty common knowledge within our world. Why bring it up?" He looked confused, but the good stuff was just getting started as far as I was concerned.

"I need you to understand that if I fail, and become more seated in the mythological world, I won't be able to go back to my humanity when my twelve years are up."

Hellion sat staring at me uncomprehending of the import of this tidbit of information. I started counting slowly and reached fourteen before I saw understanding dawn across his features. He looked horrified. "But—"

I gently laid three fingers over his lips, and his reaction was to kiss them. It broke my heart a little because I couldn't think of a single time I'd reacted the same way to this familiar gesture of his. I'd just shut up, not taken the opportunity to turn it into easy affection. Shying away from the reality of my emotional dysfunction, I told him the truth as I understood it. "If I can't be human, and I'm not mythological, then I'll have nowhere to exist, and history will consider me to have never existed at all. I'll fade from both realms, and a preselected storyteller will immortalize me in print as a sort of consolation prize, I suppose. The bottom line is that I'll cease to be. So when I tell you I really need to work on the case, I'm not being overly dramatic. If I don't work at balancing the two worlds and my place in each of them, I worry I'll fail. Then I run the risk of losing myself, literally."

Hellion stared at me, his eyes pulsing as strongly as they had in the park. Finally he raised a hand to continue to hold my fingers against his lips as he spoke. "There was speculation among the Council members about the Niteclif's responsibilities, as well as rewards and consequences, but it's always been this way. The prophecy is all we've ever been given, and the Niteclif has been historically silent as to the rest." He pulled his hand away from mine and laced our fingers together. "What happens if you fail to solve a case?"

"I would imagine I begin to fade, just more slowly, because I won't be serving a purpose for either world at that point."

"And knowing this, Bahlin has left you to solve these murders yourself?"

I jerked as though I'd been shocked. I hadn't thought of it that way. "I suppose he has." The acknowledgement felt pulled forcibly out of me. What sick part of me insisted on holding on to his innocence? I wasn't sure, so I put that away to examine later. "Regardless, I don't want to talk about him anymore tonight. We looked at a couple of sites, I got attacked by some corporeal projection of the killer's psychotic self and I learned next to nothing. I want to go inside, have a bath and a glass of wine, and plot out our next steps before crawling into bed and sleeping eight straight. That is, if you're not opposed to working with me on this?"

Hellion was recovering nicely. "The only thing I'd ask you to do differently is change the wine to whiskey, neat, and have it in the bath, which we'll take together. And if you think I'd not agree to work with you..."

"I'm glad to hear it."

We got out of the car and held hands as we rode the elevator up to his flat.

Hellion and I got out of the bathtub nearly an hour later. I was slightly tipsy from the whiskey taken on an empty stomach, but I don't think I was alone in the feeling. He had consumed about three times as much alcohol in half the amount of time I had. *Irish refortification*, he'd called it. He had taken the time to treat my bruising with some type of tincture, and while it smelled really bad, the bruises were already fading. I'd be a little sore tomorrow, but he assured me the majority of the damage would be healed in twenty-four hours.

Hellion insisted on drying me off, head to toe, and I found myself blushing at the inordinate amount of attention he paid to my breasts, lower belly and the juncture of my thighs. He was kissing my hips, licking along the top of my pubic bone and making my legs feel like cooked pasta when a loud knock sounded at the bedroom door.

"Sir?" called Mark.

Hellion laid his cheek against my bare stomach and let out a soft string of inventive curses.

I stroked his damp hair and whispered, "I'm not sure that's physically possible, Hellion." I felt his smile against my skin. "He wouldn't have come to the room if it weren't important, would he?"

"Mark's a bit of an overachiever, so it could be anything." He sighed. He stood and wrapped a towel around his waist, but there was no hiding his erection. He gave it a look of consternation, and I laughed out loud.

"I'll get the door," I said, still smiling, "and we can shock him senseless." I could imagine Mark's horrified expression if he realized what he'd—almost—interrupted.

"You get in bed and cover that luscious body up. I'll get the door and be done with him."

I scurried to the bed, crawling under the covers and tucking them up to my chin while enjoying the view of Hellion's body as he stalked across the hardwood floor to yank the door open.

"Sir—" Mark began.

"Quickly, Mark, unless you've a desire to watch me weep like a lad," Hellion said, looking over his shoulder pointedly at me.

I smiled at Mark and did a little finger wave. The man blushed so ferociously I thought he ran a very good chance of passing out. I watched Hellion pinch the bridge of his nose and try not to laugh. He reined in his expression before turning back to face the young butler.

Mark cleared his throat and said, "Sir. The mundane police are at the door. They claim to want to ask you some questions regarding the recent murders."

I felt my stomach fall as I watched Hellion pull himself to his full height, his relaxed demeanor gone. "Hellion?"

He turned to me, his gaze guarded and his face friendly but neutral.

"How did they know we were here?" I asked.

"They claim to have seen the car at the park this evening where they watched you return to the scene of the crime with an unidentified female."

Hellion ripped his towel off and stormed for the closet. I didn't even have the opportunity to get embarrassed about him shedding the towel in front of Mark before he was in the closet with the door closed. We could hear him rustling about, undoubtedly getting dressed.

"Mark? Give us a minute, would you?"

"Yes, madam. The police don't know you're here."

"I'll stay upstairs for now," I said. He nodded and went to shut the door. "Mark?"

"Madam?"

"Did anyone come to the house tonight?"

"No, madam. The wards held, and no alarm indicated they were attempted by any other than you and Hellion."

"Thanks." He shut the door quietly, and I got up and headed to the closet just as the door opened. "You look nice," I managed after taking in the gloriousness of Hellion in a businessman's navy power suit, complete with silk handkerchief.

"This is going to complicate things," he muttered, stalking to the chair in the corner of the room and sitting to put on his shoes. Yanking at the laces, he snapped one off in his hands. "Fuck," he muttered, taking the shoe off and hurling it across the room.

I walked to him, still nude, and crouched on my knees in front of him. "Hellion, you've got to stay calm." I shook my head as he began to answer me. "No, you've got to hear me out. Do you want me to come down to the parlor with you? Because I can, I *will*, if you need the support."

Hellion traced the line of my temple and jaw, smiling just enough to thaw the chill in his black eyes. "No, *anamchara*, I shall be fine. I'm just angry, though it will pass. I should have considered that the police would be watching the crime sites." He pulled me to him and kissed me thoroughly. "Stay here, love, and I'll be back in no time." He strode to the closet and emerged a minute later with a different pair of shoes, these without laces. "The gold coin?" he asked, looking around the room.

"On the bureau," I said, pointing to the dresser top.

He retrieved it and tossed it to me. This time I caught it. "Keep it hidden, no matter what."

I nodded and he left the room.

Hellion was gone for nearly an hour, during which time I tried first to read and later to watch TV. No dice. I couldn't get involved in anything, my mind constantly wandering down to the parlor below. It was too nerve-wracking to sit and wait, so I put myself together and even toyed with a touch of makeup. I sat on the bed waiting for Hellion to return, turning the gold coin over and over in my hands. It felt like I should be making some ambiguous connection regarding the coin, but it was just out of my mental reach.

Hellion looked haggard when he finally returned to the room. "Mark's showing them out now. I've been named a person of interest in the case and advised not to leave the city."

I leapt up off the bed and went to him, leaving the coin on the bed. Wrapping my arms around him, I asked, "What do they have against you? Is there anything they're claiming as evidence?"

"It's all circumstantial. The worst of it is that I was seen at one crime scene with a woman who looked remarkably like the victim profile." The irony wasn't lost on me. I was the target, he was helping protect me, and now the mundanes were interested in him.

"Sounds like a Hollywood made-for-TV movie," I teased, smoothing his lapels. He looked confused and I just shook my head. "Look, I'd like to ask you to do something for me."

He nodded.

"I want to have you check the gold coin for anything resembling magic. Don't you think it's odd that they came to see you after you received it?"

"Son of a bitch," he muttered, walking to the closet. I heard a series of beeps and then a heavy lock give way. He came out of the closet holding the other gold coin Darius had given him at the circle. "Let me see both of them, love."

I tossed him the other coin and he set them on the dresser. He took off his jacket, rolled up his sleeves and began mumbling something over the coins. A wisp of smoke came from each coin, and Hellion lifted his eyes to me. The blackness had spread so his irises were almost half again as large as a normal man's. It set me back a bit, but I didn't say anything.

"They're sister coins," he said. "They come from the same collection. Whatever has been done to them, I suspect they're being used as a tracking mechanism, not unlike a LoJack you'd use on a car. This way the killer knows what information is in whose hands."

"Clever," I mumbled, closing my eyes and taking a deep breath. "Hellion, what if this is the blue weyr's responsibility? Aiden indicated they had magic available to them."

Hellion brushed my cheek and I opened my eyes, watching him walk to the closet as he began to take his clothes off. "Sweetheart, I think they had Conor available to them. If that's the case, he wasn't capable of this level of magic. It will take me some time to sort out who's responsible for this, but even if it was Conor, his active spells would have released when he was killed."

"Ah. I see. We need to get the coins to another location then. Where do you think they would be safe?" I asked.

"I'll send them with Amaly. I trust her completely to figure out what's going on and to be discreet about everything." He emerged from the closet for, hopefully, the last time tonight and was wearing a pair of flannel pajama pants and nothing else. I went to my knees on the bed and followed his movements around the room. His hair had dried and was a multitude of colors, waving past his shoulders in thick locks. He was lightly tanned all over and looked delicious in his pajamas.

"I think we're going to have to start moving about as Tyr suggested," he said, unaware I was watching him with such avid interest.

"That's fine. We can leave in a little while," I said softly. "Hellion?"

He turned to answer me and froze at the look on my face. "Maddy?"

I slid off the bed and walked toward him, peeling my T-shirt off and shimmying out of my underwear as I went. "Take me back to bed,"

I suggested, running my hands up the planes of his stomach.

His muscles clenched and he rolled his shoulders forward. He slipped my arms up around his neck and kissed me slowly, gently, and with great care. "With great pleasure, my Madeleine."

He was entirely right—it was a great pleasure.

We lay with arms and legs tangled together. He languidly ran a hand up and down my back, and I curled into his body. Small aftershocks of pleasure made me smile against his chest.

"Where would you like to go tonight since we've got to move about anyway?" he asked.

"Do you think we could go out to dinner?" I asked. "Like a... Never mind. We can go wherever you want." I buried my face into his shoulder and enjoyed the warm smell of his skin.

"'Like a' what, love?" He turned me so I faced him, and he slid down so we were nose to nose. "Out with it, then."

"A date," I whispered, feeling somehow like I was both trivializing this intimate moment with talk of dinner and dates and disrespecting the dead girls by worrying about my stomach when there was work to do.

He kissed my forehead and stroked a hand down my side. "I think that sounds like a right fine idea. We need to be seen together outside the immediate area, so we'll pop to the other side of London and go out to a nice meal and then spend the night...where? Where would you like to stay?" A look of pure delight overtook him and he said, "No, never mind. I've got it figured out, though it directly breaks the orders of the guarda. We'll spend the night at a place special to me. Now go get your nicest clothes, and we'll be off to Amaly's place, then to dinner and later our night together."

He looked so thrilled with his little planned surprise that I couldn't help but respond to his enthusiasm. "Give me thirty minutes and I'm all yours." Shocked at my casual statement, I turned away quickly, scampering out of bed before he could say anything. I heard him sigh as I shut the bathroom door behind me.

I emerged thirty minutes later in the only nice dress I'd brought with me—an above-the-knee little black silk wrap and black knee-high boots with a three-inch heel. I'd reapplied my makeup, and I felt beautiful when Hellion looked at me and said, "Screw going out, Maddy. Let's stay right here."

I did a little pirouette for him. "I take it you approve."

"More than approve, love. I feel like a starving man who's been given the keys to the kitchen. Lucky, lucky, lucky me." He had changed to a black suit with a garnet-colored silk shirt. We'd look like a normal couple out for a night on the town if no one recognized Hellion or caught a glimpse of his black eyes. I guess the "if" was still part of the rub with me, just as it had always been with Bahlin. I hadn't fully integrated into this world of "other" and I wasn't sure if I ever would...or if I even wanted to.

Hellion moved toward me and held out an arm. "Let's go out so we can come back in," he said suggestively, sliding his free hand down my back and grasping my ass as he pulled me in close.

"Don't mess up my lipstick," I murmured, caught up in the passion in his eyes.

"I won't," he said softly, bending me backward and dipping his lips into my cleavage while he held me at an impossible angle. I shivered as he nuzzled my breasts. Hellion stood me back up and let me rearrange my clothes.

Hellion and I dematerialized and came back into being in a small but well-decorated living room with definite feminine touches here and there. The furniture was smaller and, while it was all solid and gender-neutral beige fabric, there were chintz pillows decorating the ends, stained glass lamps on the sofa table, and a beautiful oriental rug on the floor. The art on the walls was modern but held undeniably feminine attributes, as well.

"Amaly?" Hellion called out, turning to look around the room, never letting go of my hand.

"Hellion," purred a voice from behind me. I released Hellion's hand and turned to face a stunning blonde woman as she entered the room through a side door. Her timing was too impeccable to have been anything other than planned. She was wearing a caftan that did nothing to hide the shape of her curvaceous body or the fact she wasn't wearing anything *but* the semi-transparent robe, the blues and greens and browns complementing her peaches-and-cream skin tone and light blue eyes. She held out a hand to me and I took it, feeling the now-familiar invasive push of power race up my arm. "You must be Madeleine, the infamous Niteclif," she said, openly raking me with her eyes and giving me the once over as only another woman can do, taking in my short hair, high heels and everything in between.

"I am, though I strongly prefer to go by Maddy. And you're Amaly?" I shook her hand firmly and refused to let her energy intimidate me when we touched.

"I am. Hellion, welcome. I've not seen you since the fight at Tarrek's," she said, laying a proprietary hand on his arm. I suddenly wanted to scratch her eyes out and lay her bloodied head out for the crows to pick over. *Yikes.*

Hellion slid his arm around me, effectively dislodging Amaly's hand. "Amaly, this is the Niteclif. I trust Mark relayed to you what we need?" he asked, all business.

"He did. I'll be setting protective wards around my flat to prevent anyone tracing me. You'll need to leave me a few hairs when you go so I may allow you to come and go as you please. I'm going to get to work on this immediately. I'll also need a few drops of the Niteclif's blood on the off chance the coins are tracers for her and her alone." Amaly spoke in crisp, disgruntled tones, not at all pleased to have been displaced from Hellion's side so easily, and by the man himself. He and I were going to have to talk about her.

"What are tracers exactly?" I asked.

"Remember the LoJack example I gave you earlier?" he asked, looking down at me and stroking his hand up and down my back. The glide of his rough hands over the silk of my dress sounded like a muted zipper being pulled down slowly, over and over.

The fine muscles in my back and shoulders shuddered. My eyes found his, and his hand stopped at my lower back. "I remember." My voice sounded deeper, concupiscent. Hellion stared at me and his lips turned up in a half smile as if he knew what I was thinking. I looked away, suddenly hyperaware of the heat generated at the base of my spine and the warmth pooling between my legs, legs which felt as supportive as a stiff pudding parked under a truck.

"Then you'll remember that it's just a magical way of discussing a tracing system that's been created for a specific being—in this case, you." He turned into me and lowered his head, kissing my temple softly. I regretted my early admonishment to spare the lipstick.

A throat was cleared to my immediate right and I jumped, having forgotten entirely about Amaly. "Obviously you two need some private time. If you'll excuse me, I'll take my leave and encourage you to do the same." Intentionally ignoring me, she inclined her head to Hellion as if she were royalty before stalking out of the room in a billow of fabric and attitude that nearly left the air crackling behind her.

"Oops."

"Don't mind her," Hellion muttered, looking thoroughly disgusted, though whether it was at Amaly's behavior or her interruption of a promising kiss I wasn't sure. He leaned close and whispered, "She's been sour since I rejected her advances in 1887." My eyes were wide enough I could just see their white reflection in Hellion's reflective black ones as he bent to give me a quick bus. "Amaly?" he called out. "I'm leaving the envelope with my hair on the countertop. I'll have my driver, Stearns, come back for a blood sample for Maddy. Set your wards when we leave." Turning back to me, he asked with total casualness, "Ready to go to dinner?"

I braced myself for the disconcerting dematerialization process but he just tucked my hand up under his arm.

"We'll walk. Black & Bleu is a steakhouse just around the corner. Besides, if we *were* traced here, it will help to be seen leaving. Can you manage four blocks in those heels?" he asked, looking skeptically down at my boots.

I scoffed at the question. "Manage? Hell, for a real steak I can out-walk you in your *best* shoes. It's part and parcel of being a woman, baby." I sashayed out of the room, hoping like hell I was headed in the direction of the front door. Nothing ruins a good sashaying exit more than having to turn around and ask for directions.

Chapter Sixteen

Dinner was a lovely candlelight affair amid very chic diners. Modern art adorned the walls, and subdued laughter mixed with the clink of silverware in the smoky, charbroiled air. We sat holding hands, chatting quietly. It felt so much like a real date that I found myself relaxing enough to trace the toe of my boot along his leg and to flirt a little over the first glass of wine.

Hellion was insatiable in his desire to know everything about me, from likes and dislikes to passions and neutralities. He wanted to know about my childhood, and he was most curious about my parents. I found myself discussing them with great affection and fond memories colored only lightly with loss. It was a first for me since their deaths, to talk about them without experiencing debilitating grief, and I was profoundly grateful for that turning point.

I was equally curious about him, and found myself hugely relieved to find that I thoroughly enjoyed Hellion's personality when we were removed from the stresses and realities of paranormal life. He was charming and highly intelligent, with an appreciation for the finer things life had to offer. When I asked him about his love of finance, he answered simply, "When you grow up in the shadow of gross poverty, wealth becomes your sun." He'd had nothing as a child—no shoes, little food, rarely a roof over his head. Abandoned by his parents at the age of seven, he'd lived on the streets for two years before he'd been taken in by an old mage seeking an errand boy and, later, an apprentice. Hellion had proven himself a hard worker and quick learner, rapidly amassing levels of power that surpassed his teacher's and, later, his teacher's teacher. He'd followed his love of magic across Europe and parts of Asia, learning from every great master he could find, searching out old tomes and spell books, learning anywhere there was someone willing to teach. Arcane or modern for the times, it all interested him. He talked about the changes he'd seen in his long life, and the things he hoped to see in the future.

"No hope for world peace?" I asked, only partially teasing as he discussed his hopes for mankind.

"If I've learned anything over the last three hundred plus years it's that mankind has no hope for peace. History is cyclical, and wars are fought with disturbing predictability. The only thing that truly changes is the inventive ways the mundanes come up with to kill each other."

I thought about that before answering, chewing my steak slowly and following it with a sip of wine. "I don't believe it's limited to the cruel creativity of mundanes," I said softly, looking around to ensure we hadn't picked up any eavesdroppers. "I believe, after the last several weeks, that anything that walks on two legs at any time, whether human or not, is capable of unparalleled violence."

"You're right. Of course you're right. I've just watched from the sidelines of humanity long enough now that I feel closer to the paranormal than the..."

"Normal?" I teased, smiling softly to ensure he caught the teasing.

"Normal," he replied. He reached over and tugged on my bangs, his eyes growing somber. "You are magnificent tonight, gilded in the light of a hundred candles. I'm beginning to believe that of the two of us, you're the bewitching one." His fingers traced down my neck and slid across the upper swells of my breasts as he withdrew his hand.

Desire breathed across my skin. Hellion's eyes fell to heavy-lidded insinuation and my breath caught, my hand pausing with my wine glass halfway to my lips. The sound of the restaurant seemed to fade until it was only the two of us and I swear, I *swear*, I heard his breath catch in return.

He leaned forward, holding out a hand to me. "Shall we go?"

"Yes. Please."

He took my wine glass from my trembling fingers and set it on the table, his movements careful and deliberate. He stood and set his napkin on the table. I followed suit, not offering him the opportunity to pull out my chair. I was either too liberated or in too much of a hurry, or both. I compromised, though, and took his proffered arm, and we walked toward the back of Black & Bleu without a word to each other.

At the back of the main dining area there was a short, dark hallway whose entrance was delineated from the patrons' tables by a row of old phone booths that housed art for sale instead of old telephones, the retro among the modern making the Naugahyde seats trendy instead of worn and tired looking. Beyond the booths were the restrooms and doors to the managers' offices.

Hellion bent to lay his lips to my ear. "Go into the women's room and leave the door unlocked, provided you're alone. I'll follow you inside in just a moment, and we'll dematerialize from there."

I nodded and walked inside without looking back. I checked the two stalls and found I was alone so I unlocked the door. Hellion slipped inside and pulled me to him, turning as his arms wrapped around me. We were already fading out when the door flew open and Gaitha, Queen of Faerie, rushed into the room.

We came back together with an inaudible pop. The little jaunt had left me with temporary vertigo, and Hellion caught me as I staggered, my heels sliding precariously across an uneven stone floor, snagging in the wide seams.

"Sorry, love. The longer the trip, the longer it will take you to gather your bearings once we arrive. I should have warned you, though you managed the trip to Ireland quite well."

I shook my head, clutching his arm as the room righted itself and I regained my feet. "No problem. I'm going to assume you didn't see our visitor just as we left the bathroom. If you did, you're being very calm."

Hellion's whipped around to face me, grabbing me by my shoulders. "What visitor?" He gave me a little shake before I could answer.

"Easy," I said, reaching up to pry his hands from my shoulders lest they become welded there. "Where are we, Hellion?"

"Ballinlough Castle, Maddy. For the love of country, if you don't tell me what you've seen, I'm going to—"

"What, exactly, are you going to do?" I growled. "Get your hands off me if you're tending toward violence, Hellion."

He finally relaxed his grip but he didn't remove his hands.

"Gaitha opened the bathroom door just as we began to"—I wiggled my hand through the air—"whatever it is exactly that happens when we dematerialize. But we were far enough gone that she couldn't seem to reach us, and I couldn't say anything."

"You can't speak during dematerialization?" he asked, curious.

"Nope. I would have screamed bloody murder at you and Odin if I'd been able to gather my voice. I'm totally at your mercy when you move me through space like that." *Never thought about it that way*, I mused.

"Hm. I'll have to take more care. Did you get a good look at Gaitha?" he asked, finally relaxing just a bit.

"Hardly, but she looked mad, Hellion, and I don't mean angry. She looked deranged—eyes wide and wild, hair knotted and dirty, clothes ragged. You saw her at the henge at the meeting?"

He nodded, solemnity settling over his features. "Aye, I did that."

"She looked the same." I shivered at the thought of madness claiming my mind. What would it be like to find yourself trapped inside a dysfunctional psyche and have reality consumed and destroyed like that? Never having given it much thought before, I found it terrified me. I stepped into Hellion and slid my arms around his waist. He drew me close and settled his chin on top of my head.

Sighing deeply, his voice rumbled through my ear when he spoke. "She's mad, all right. Any member of the *Tuatha Dé Danann* with as much power and natural magic as she has, who has lost her mind to the craze, scares the hell out of me. I'm not sure how to best protect us from her."

I pulled back from him and looked up to find him staring blankly across the room, his words not uttered for sake of discussion but rather, I thought, to verbalize his fear so we might face it together. "We're not sure it's her, Hellion. I still need to speak to Bahlin about the suspicious activity surrounding the gold coins, the gouged dirt, and the shadow-mist that attacked tonight. I absolutely hate to think of him as a suspect, but I have to rule him out, not just dismiss his possible involvement." My heart constricted, but it wasn't the same breath-stealing pain that had grabbed me every time I thought of him when I'd believed him dead. "Do you know where Bahlin is?"

"No. I tried to scry for him as you got ready to go out this evening, to see if he was still at his sister's home in Scotland, but there was no resolution to the search. He's cloaking himself or being cloaked by someone of significant magical ability if they can hide from me." It wasn't said with arrogance but rather as a statement of simple fact. Was Hellion one of the most powerful magi in the world? Yes. Did he know it? Yes. Did that make him arrogant? Justifiably.

I wondered at the significance of Bahlin hiding himself from me, and I didn't like the way the short hairs at the base of my skull stood up. I'd begun to learn not to dismiss those things I seemed to intuit because they were often founded in logic and survival. Did it give me answers to the murders? No, but it helped me cull out legitimate worries, fears and, on occasion, clues. I reached back to massage my tense neck muscles, taking the same opportunity to look around the room we were in. It was a long hall that had been converted to a family room with a large television, gaming tables, a full-size snooker table, multiple sofas and overstuffed chairs. The plaster and beam ceilings were marked with smoke scars above the two hearths. The crystal chandelier was on low, casting dim but glittering light across the uppermost part of the room that became diffused as it drifted lower down the pale walls. Everything about the room combined to speak of immense wealth, yet it was comfortable enough to not be off-putting.

Neither of the two fireplaces was lit. Noticing my interest in the cold hearth nearest us, Hellion casually flung out a hand, and the fireplace lit with a great *whoosh* of flame. Taper candles flickered to life around the room, and I flinched. Hellion chuckled.

"It's only my Boy Scout badge after all, Maddy."

I hunched my shoulders a little, warding off the guilt. "Yeah, sorry about that. Why are we here exactly?"

"Because I thought taking us to the bedroom directly would have been slightly crass, so I thought it more gentlemanly if we start here and watch a movie together. We can canoodle on the sofa like teenagers if you'd like."

I turned, smiling, to look at Hellion, and found him watching me with that same heavy-lidded look he'd given me at the restaurant. Apparently "canoodling" was serious to the Irish. My smile faltered a bit as I stared at him.

Hands in his pockets, he rocked back and forth slowly, heel to toe, toe to heel, and watched me without comment. When I said nothing, he stopped. "Was I wrong?"

"No, I appreciate coming here. Did you really say 'castle'?" I asked, looking around.

"I did. It was built back in the 17th century. It's generally rented out for weddings and other private events, but it was available tonight." He glanced around the room, proprietarily assessing the condition and quality of the environment as a whole.

I reached down and unzipped my boots, stepping out of them and wiggling my toes in the plush oriental rug. "A movie would be great. Something funny, maybe? I'm not really one for anything violent."

Hellion chuckled. "Wrong line of work for your lifetime, then, *hmm?*" He kicked his shoes off and stretched, curling his toes, arching his back, arms over his head and muscles vibrating as the tension built then released.

"Well, yeah."

His hand snaked around my waist and pulled me close to his body. "What would you like to watch?" he asked, nuzzling my neck.

I snuggled back into him. "Surprise me."

"I can do that." He nipped down the length of my neck to that soft spot between the neck and shoulder and bit me.

I was instantly aroused.

His hands slithered up my front and cupped my breasts, rubbing my nipples through my bra.

I needed to sit before I fell. I raised my hands to cover his over my breasts and moved us toward the longest sofa. Seeing where we were going, he swept me up and carried me to the divan, gently laying me down and kneeling beside me as I shifted my body toward his.

"No," I murmured. "I need you closer than this." I tugged at the front of his shirt, and he shed his jacket as he moved forward. I began unbuttoning his shirt and, in frustration, tore off the last two buttons. "Sorry." I leaned up to kiss my way from the hollow of his throat down to his navel. His erection twitched and punched out from his slacks as I drew closer to his belt with my lips. I smiled into the skin of his belly, nipping it and causing him to shudder. I leaned back on the sofa, grasped the edges of his shirt and pulled him toward me. I met his eyes as he moved over me, still kneeling on the floor.

He whispered, "Maddy," and leaned down to kiss me gently. "It's the first time ye've looked at me like that," he said in a heavy brogue. "*Tá grá agam duit,* my Madeleine," he whispered.

I stared up into his fathomlessly dark eyes, feeling an answer in my soul. It was too powerful to ignore, too significant to disregard, and suddenly I knew. "I don't understand it but I'm terrified I could fall in love with you, Hellion," I answered in a shaky voice. My heart felt like it was cleaved into two unequal pieces, overjoyed for the promise of everything that might be and anguished over those things that would never be again.

He pulled me gently to him, his body shaking with fine tremors. "Maddy," he choked out. "I'll be honest, *mo chroí,* I'm not sure why it matters so much so soon, but damned if it doesn't."

I sat as still as unmoving as a stone guardian, afraid to re-engage with the scene that was playing out in front of me.

Shock, it's just shock, Niteclif. That and the fact that you're switching lovers, and loves, faster than the willing men around you are dropping their pants. Besides, you said you could see yourself falling for him, not that you were in love with him. Big difference. Yeah, right.

I thought of Bahlin and it was the final rending of my heart. I began to sob, realizing a part of my past was just that—past. Hellion held me tight as I broke apart, knowing for whom it was that I grieved. In the small part of my mind that still functioned, I later remembered thinking at the time that he was a damn fine man to put up with so much at the beginning of a relationship. Any other man would have dumped me and run as fast and as far as he could.

For one very selfish moment, I just couldn't find it in myself to care.

We lay together in front of the fire, neither of us speaking. He'd insisted I rest, retrieving a handful of warm cloths for me to use and freshen my face. It was still undoubtedly blotchy from my breakdown, but he said nothing of it. Instead, he cradled me close to his chest, stroking my bared arm and murmuring to me in Gaelic every now and then. I heard a door open and close, and before I could lift my head to see who had entered the room, Hellion said, "Hello, Mark."

"Sir."

"I assume you've come bearing news," Hellion said. Holding my hand, he helped me to sitting and we both faced the butler.

"Gaitha came to the house tonight, sir."

"She *what?*" I gasped, pulling away from Hellion and pushing myself to standing.

"She arrived tonight shortly after Darius. I refused to answer the door, as instructed, but Darius felt none of the compunction to follow the same orders." It was obvious Mark thought little of Darius's apparent lack of respect for Hellion's wishes.

I rubbed my upper lip to hide a smile. I really liked Darius, all the more for his disregard of the rules.

Hellion sighed. "And?"

"Gaitha handed him this and then she left." Mark held out his hand, and I snatched the gold coin out of it.

"Holy crap!" I exclaimed, looking at the now familiar raised monarch and horseman. The gold felt heavy in my hand, and I didn't object when Hellion lifted it from my palm and examined it closely.

"Is it the same, then?" he asked me.

I nodded grimly. "Yeah." I turned and walked over to the sofa and flopped down, discouraged at the implications. I leaned forward and dropped my head into my hands.

"Anything else, Mark?" Hellion asked, pocketing the coin.

"Another note arrived after you left, sir." He pulled out a long white envelope with an "H" scrawled on the front in blue ink.

"How was it delivered?" I asked, watching Hellion walk to the antique secretary sitting in the corner and dig around, finally coming up with a letter opener shaped like a miniature claymore.

"It was shoved in the mail slot," Mark answered. "It was just lying on the floor. I came to you instead of calling because I knew you'd want to see the coin and the letter."

Hellion walked slowly back to Mark, every step calculated and heavy, as if he was dreading reading this letter as much as I was. He accepted the missive and sliced it open, carefully keeping his fingers away from the sharp edge of the little sword. He tossed the letter opener carelessly on the coffee table and pulled out the letter, glancing through it quickly before handing it to me and turning to face the fire to gather his thoughts, hands clasped behind his back. Before I could lift the letter to read, Hellion abandoned the fire to stalk to the bookshelf. He searched for a moment before pulling down a large tome and, sitting down at a nearby table, began thumbing through it hastily before finding what he was looking for. As he read, so did I.

Hellion,

Every fool can be led astray by their wandering cock, and for that you can be forgiven. What will not be forgotten is the history you incur with the whore at your side, who is as Catherine Howard was to Henry Manox—neither wife nor consummated lover. Stand aside and let the whore fall for treason or face a similar fate.

I was too shocked and angry to hold the paper still in my trembling hands. I made my way to Hellion's side and stood, dropping a hand on his shoulder, not entirely sure what to make of the note. I needed answers to that riddle before I could form intelligent questions about the rest of this mess.

"Who is Catherine Howard, sir?" Mark surreptitiously wiped the bead of sweat from his upper lip and stood straighter.

"Just a moment, Mark." Hellion scanned pages before finding what he was looking for. Summarizing as he read, Hellion said, "Catherine Howard, wife of Henry VIII, was tried for treason and beheaded on February 13, 1542. Her crimes were charges of adultery. Henry Manox was her music teacher when she was a young girl, and while they never consummated their relationship, it was improper for the times and he never married her. When her indiscretions came to light, Henry had her tried for treason and then beheaded." Hellion pushed his hands through his hair and dropped his forehead to the table, banging it lightly against the wood. Sighing, he pushed himself to standing and turned to me, quickly and unapologetically pulling me to him for a scorching kiss.

Confused, I kissed him back until I remembered Mark was standing there waiting on us to do, well, *something*. I disentangled myself from Hellion's embrace and buried my face in his chest while I regained some semblance of control. After a few seconds, I turned out of Hellion's arms and faced the other man. "Did Darius say anything when you left him?"

"Only that he wasn't going to leave me behind when he came to deliver your love note," came the midnight voice from the corner.

I turned to find Darius sprawled on the sofa, watching us with interested eyes.

"You're not nearly jaded enough, old man," Hellion snarked, "if watching two people snog is entertainment."

"And you, chap, need to pull your pants out of your bum crack. They seem wedged high enough you should be able to taste the worsted wool."

Hellion frowned, rubbing at the wrinkles in his brow. "I believe you're right. Apologies, Darius." Hellion took my hand and walked over to the opposing sofa and took a seat, waving at the lamps so they turned on enough to supplement the room's candlelight. "Mark, have a seat."

The butler look surprised but quickly took a seat near Hellion. "I insisted he remain behind, sir, but he wouldn't be swayed—"

Hellion waved off the man's apology. "I just want to know what happened between Gaitha's visit and the arrival of the letter." Hellion leaned back, extended his arm across the back of the sofa and stretched his legs out in front of him, crossing his sock-clad feet at the ankles.

I slid closer to him, curling up under his arm.

"Literally, sir, Gaitha arrived and demanded to see you. I wouldn't open the door and was preparing to contact the new fae High Council member, Praen, but Darius opened the door."

Hellion lifted his hand off the back of the sofa and motioned for Darius to pick up the story.

"Arrogant bastard," Darius muttered, leaning forward in his seat.

Hellion just smiled. "Worsted wool, was it?"

"Screw you. The queen stood there, shocked, I think, that it was me standing under the lintel. She demanded to know where you were, saying it was a matter of vengeance. Naturally I refused, and she became more agitated. Frightening woman, really, though she does inspire some pity. I was getting ready to forcibly remove her from the stoop as we'd drawn some attention from neighbors and passers-by—"

"Shit," muttered Hellion.

"—when she seemed to scent something. Acted like an animal, raising her face to the wind and then she was gone, running up the street faster than any human could track."

"She likely picked up our trace since we left from the house," Hellion groused. "I'd imagine she found Amaly's general vicinity but was forced to resort to canvassing the neighborhoods on foot looking for us since we'd blocked Maddy's tracers as we left. Thanks for handling her, Darius." The vampire inclined his head. "And the letter, Mark?"

"I found that too," Darius said. "I walked by the foyer about an hour later, bent on sending you a text despite your admonishment to leave you free this evening. I'd fretted about it like a damned schoolgirl, and figured you'd both ignore it if you didn't need to know. The letter was lying on the floor and smelled odd, like burning hair."

Burning hair... "Shit," I gasped, pushing away from the comfort of Hellion's side and sitting up quickly. "The night Bahlin came to the window I smelled a similar smell in your bedroom, Hellion."

"And you didn't think to mention it because...?"

"It was one of those fleeting things, there and gone. I forgot about if after I got the eerie sensation of being watched at the window." I thought back to that night and wracked my brain for anything else I might have forgotten. It was all so vague except the sense of being watched and that distinctive smell. "I suppose she could have been at the house that night, but then why did the smell show up so long after she left tonight? Could she have come back and dropped the note off, using some type of magic that generates the smell? No, it doesn't make sense. Not with what we have so far."

"I agree," Darius said before the other men could disagree. "Maddy's right. If it had been Gaitha, I'd have smelled it on her when she first showed up tonight. It was a wretched smell, wasn't it?"

"Like very *fresh* singed hair." Without thinking, I reached up and fingered the small stubble where the hair had been shorn as I slept. I turned to Hellion with a feeling of horror snaking its way through my belly.

"Fair enough," Hellion said, not seeing the look on my face.

Darius, though, saw me and stood quickly. "Maddy?" he asked, taking a step toward me.

"No," I whispered and shook my head slowly. "No, no, no."

Grasping that something was wrong from Darius's movement toward me, Hellion turned and took me by the shoulders. "Maddy? What is it, love?" he demanded, giving me a small shake again.

I felt like a rag doll, even though he'd been gentle, my head lolling about on my shoulders. "Did you cut my hair?" I asked.

He looked at me like I'd lost my mind. "What? When?"

"When you sent the roses."

He looked disturbed. "I'm not quite clear what you're asking, love. I've never cut your hair, and I've never sent you roses." Looking closely at me, he sat up straight. "You're not suggesting—"

"The roses weren't from you?"

"What bloody roses?" Hellion demanded.

"Remember? The ones in the hotel room when you came to get me the first time, and you pulled Clay out of bed?"

Disturbed, Hellion shook his head.

"Oh. They really weren't from you," I said softly.

"I'm not clear—"

"No? Okay. But what was you it you said about the dirt? The gouges at the park?"

His eyes searched my face. "You're not making any sense, *anamchara*."

"You said the magic was elemental, right?" He nodded. "You said you should be able to do something with it as far as a revelation spell because it was elemental and, as dirt, didn't really belong to anyone. What could you do with hair?"

Hellion's eyes widened as he began to understand what I was after. "Hair is a personal element, Maddy. It could be used in a thousand upon a thousand different spells, for equally as many reasons. Are you suggesting... I hate to sound dense, but what *are* you suggesting?"

I stood and walked on wooden legs to the fireplace, no longer feeling the warmth of the fire or seeing the leaping flames. Instead what I saw were the faces of the potentially damned. "I'm sorry, Mark, but I've got to ask you to leave," I whispered. Hearing no movement behind me, I turned and repeated the request, more firmly this time. "Please," I added with more pleading than I'd like to have had in my voice.

"Go," Hellion said, "but stay here tonight. I may yet need your help."

"Sir. Darius. Niteclif." Mark bowed briefly to each of us. He walked out of the room and shut the door behind him.

I turned back to the fireplace, and all I could see were flames dancing merrily to the tunes of murder and vengeance playing through my mind.

Chapter Seventeen

Darius looked at me very carefully, watching as my fingers worried a loose thread on a throw pillow I'd pulled into my arms. I needed to have something to do with my hands. My heel bounced against the floor in rapid bursts of fidgety activity before I became aware of the behavior and willed the foot to stillness. His voice was gentle when he asked, "Should I stay or go, Maddy?"

"I'd like you to stay. Please." This was firmer, and I was glad I didn't sound quite so desperate.

He stepped up to me and wrapped me in a strong hug. "For you, anything." Hellion cleared his throat and Darius turned to him, keeping his arm draped casually over my shoulder. "You'll have to accept that I'm crazy about your lover, Hellion. Treat her well," he said, a trace of jest in his voice but, underlying that, a note of heavy seriousness. "I'll be here if you don't."

"We've been friends too long for you to threaten me," Hellion said softly, standing up and lording his height over the shorter man.

"We have, but you've a real gem here, and for the first time in many centuries I find myself coveting the life of a mortal." Darius kissed me quickly on the temple and slid back into his chair, lounging for all the world like there was nothing serious happening.

What the hell? Was I emitting some kind of pheromone? I cleared my throat. "The hair." Both men nodded at me but never took their eyes off each other. I continued. "What could you have done with my hair if you'd kept it, Hellion?"

"Truthfully? Nearly anything involving your person. For example, I could have fabricated spells of lust, hatred, binding, wealth—"

"Tracing?" I interrupted.

"Tracing," he said, nodding.

"What about breaching wards? Could hair allow you to do that?"

"The hair would either have to be taken from the warding source or else it would have to be taken from the magic practitioner and stationed inside the wards to provide grounding inside the magic. So yes, it could be used to breach wards."

"Do you recall who admitted to us that they had a magus in their employ?"

"No, I don—*son of a bitch*," he bellowed, turning to the table and swiping at the lamp so that it flew across the room and smashed into the wall in an explosion of glass. His chest heaving, Hellion turned back to me. "Aiden and the blue weyr," he growled, low and fierce. He sank back to the sofa and dropped his head back against the high cushion.

I cleared my throat and swallowed hard. "Yes." I began to step toward him and Darius was suddenly there, lifting me off my feet.

"No need to run the risk of getting glass in a foot," he said softly. He deposited me carefully on the sofa next to Hellion, who stared at him unblinking before reaching out and gently taking my hand.

"It seems, again, I owe you an apology, Madeleine. So I'll tell you with all sincerity that I'm sorry." He lifted my hand to his lips and asked, "Forgive me?"

"I do. But you need to keep better control of your temper or I'm going to hesitate to share things I can't afford to hold back, Hellion. I need to know you've got a level head and will keep it, at least while you're working with me."

"I won't be so foolish as to make that promise, Maddy, but I'll promise to truly try."

I shrugged. I couldn't fault his honesty. I let myself slip backward into the depression he made in the sofa, and he dropped his arm around me, kissing the opposite temple Darius had bussed. "So if we're dealing with elemental magic, does that preclude a warlock from being a possibility?"

Hellion's face softened and he closed his eyes, cupping the back of my neck and then gently moving his forehead to rest against mine. "No. Maddy, I think there's an elephant in the room we need to address."

"I don't want to," I whispered, closing my eyes and rolling my head back and forth against his.

Darius stood and looked down at the two of us. "I suspect I know where this is going. However, I'd like plausible deniability so that if you need more time to work out the specifics, I can honestly give it to you as a Council member. If I participate in this discussion, I can't do that. So I'll bid you goodnight and take myself off to find some entertainment."

By the time I lifted my head and opened my eyes, the door was shutting behind Darius as he left the room.

"Do you ever get used to him moving so quickly?"

Hellion opened his eyes and squeezed my neck. "You're asking someone who can move across space?"

"I suppose I am. What am I going to do, Hellion?" My voice inched back toward the precipice of grief's canyon.

"As hard as it is, you're going to do the right thing. You're going to toss this around a little with me, privately, and then you're going to get a good night's sleep so you're fresh to tackle it first thing in the morning. Tell me, please, what made you put the pieces together." He pushed gently on my shoulders until I lay back on the sofa and propped my feet in his lap. He began to rub my arches with long, deep strokes and I groaned. "Better than sex?"

"Don't ask me that right now," I said in a sleep-heavy voice.

He chuckled and pulled my big toe. "Fair enough. Then tell me why you've gone down this road."

I sighed. "Your talk of elemental magic has been bothering me. Limited elemental magic would narrow down its practitioners, right?"

"*Mmm hmm.*" He lifted a foot to his mouth and kissed along the toes, his breath tickling the sensitive skin so that I jerked slightly. He grasped my ankle and held it firm as he laid kisses along the arch and licked the ankle. "Focus." Dropping that foot, he picked the other up and began repeating the process.

"Um, from what I've learned, elemental magic is powerful stuff. There are only a handful of creatures that can successfully wield it, and each with limitations. Except for magi. So I started thinking about access to the most powerful wizards and witches in the paranormal world. Who had those connections?" He hit a particularly sensitive spot and I shivered, goose flesh breaking out on my lower body. "Uh, so, who had the connections and, equally important, who could afford to buy it if they needed it?"

Hellion ran a hand up my leg and stopped at the back of my knee, his fingers pressing lightly against the skin as they rubbed back and forth and circled around to the front of the leg. "Is it a matter of wealth, then?"

"No, not only wealth. Like you said earlier, wealth is something that runs easily among all of you who have the time, and an inclination, to amass it. No, it's a matter of connections and, even more, intentions." I pulled my feet from his lap and sat up, tucking them under me and effectively ignoring the minute trembling that shook me from head to toes. Scrubbing my hands through my hair, I continued. "I think what I need to know is the structure of the magi hierarchy. You said Amaly is your second, so she must be powerful, right?"

Hellion nodded, shifting to face me with guarded eyes. "Aye, she's fiercely powerful, nearly so much as I am. But she's also equally loyal and wouldn't have thrown me over for a chance at power or wealth. She's got plenty of both."

"A bit defensive, aren't you, over someone who means nothing more to you than a business partner should?"

Hellion instinctively reached up to tug his collar before realizing it was unbuttoned. He shrugged out of his shirt altogether, as if the weight of the material was too much. "No, I'm not defensive. Frankly I just don't want to believe one of my people could be involved."

I sighed. We were *really* going to have to talk about her at some point, but even I knew this wasn't the time to do it. I stuck out a foot and pushed at his thigh. "No, I don't think it's anyone in your coven. I just want to understand a few things. First and foremost, what's the balance of, well, light versus dark magi?" Watching Hellion shed his shirt had a direct result. Now I wanted to shrug out of my own clothes too. While it held a lot of promise for later, right now it seemed uncomfortably inappropriate. Another pound of proof that logic and lust didn't belong in the same room together.

Hellion snickered, and it turned into a full-blown laugh. "'Light and dark' forces, Maddy?" He guffawed, and I bristled. Wiping the tears from his eyes he snorted in mirth, his eyes shimmering madly in the firelight. "Gods and goddesses, I needed that."

I had to force myself to keep from hunching my shoulders. "Glad to help."

"No, no, sweetheart. Don't be cross with me. It was wonderfully adorable—"

"I'm not a child, Hellion."

"No, you're definitely not." He let his gaze fall over me, and the weight of his eyes seemed to rake my nipples and make them stand on end, caress my cleft and make me gasp, and trace down the outside of my thighs and make me twitch.

"How...?" I asked, reveling in the lingering weight of his unseen touch.

"Oh, love, we've only just begun to explore each other's talents."

I felt a punch of lust, sure Hellion felt his own version of it too. We stared at each other for several long seconds before I managed to get out, "We need to finish this, Hellion, so we can go to bed."

"That we do," he said so quietly his voice was forced to compete with the hiss of the fire's flames.

I cleared my throat and began to stand up, but Hellion quickly stopped me by grabbing my arm. "The glass," he muttered. "I'll have a maid come clean it up later. For now, won't you just sit with me?"

"Fine, but stop distracting me." I smiled at him gently to soften the harsh words and scooted a little farther away.

He nodded at me, licking his lower lip before catching it between his teeth.

"That! That's what you have to stop!"

"What?" he asked with sincere innocence.

"Hell, you don't even realize you're doing it, do you? Forget it. Just forget it. Back to the topic at hand. What do you call good wizards and bad wizards?"

He smiled and shook his head, obviously thinking me daft. "'Good wizards' are referred to as wizards, or magi. Females are witches. 'Bad wizards' are warlocks, while bad witches are *heaxags*. The clearest definition between the two is that one is focused on first harming none, while the other side is into the preservation of one. But the thing to always remember is that wizards and witches all begin as humans, regardless of where they end up. It's how we choose to use our gifts that define us." Hellion leaned forward and grasped my ankle, and heat crawled up the leg and pooled between my thighs.

I gasped and clamped my legs together, unsure how he could invoke such feelings in me.

"A very important thing to remember, Maddy, is that we cannot create something that is not there. So I can conjure a storm because a storm exists somewhere for me to pull energy from. I can make a rose appear"—he mumbled something softly and held out one perfect, long-stemmed red rose—"because I've taken it from somewhere else. I cannot make you feel lust that you don't already harbor, though I can redirect that which you have. By my oath, I cannot take without offering something in return. So by my nature, I seek balance.

"There are those, though, who do not hold themselves to higher codes of conduct. They take that which is elemental and taint it with darkness that isn't inherent to the element's nature." I must have looked confused because he clarified it for me on the most basic level. "If I call a thunderstorm, it's just a storm. But if I call the storm and direct the lightning to destroy or kill, I've harnessed a darkness not inherent to the storm, because the storm would never seek out a person or place to destroy. Do you understand?"

It made perfect sense, and I nodded. "You said to me once that you had both wizard and warlock within you."

Hellion thought about his answer before speaking. "Doesn't every man have the potential for good and evil?"

"Yeah, I suppose so. It's just that most don't come with the ability to back up their promise or, I suppose, their threat, so effectively."

"Is this what you imagine has happened with the blue weyr?" he asked gently.

I shrugged, feeling like a traitor. But I knew this had to be discussed, and Darius had been right to leave Hellion and I to discuss it together, without witnesses. The implications were too great to risk such weighty allegations. "I don't know." I stopped myself and shook my head again. Justice weighed heavily on my shoulders, and I knew that if I didn't get this right, someone ran the risk of being labeled a suspect. Shit. Who was I kidding? Bahlin ran that risk. "No, that's not right. I do know. I *do*," I emphasized, seeing his skepticism. "I may not want it to be so for a thousand different reasons, but I know that if I make this connection, the Glaaca runs the risk of being labeled a suspect."

"Can you not even say his name?" Hellion's face was curiously blank.

"What? Who? The Glaaca's?"

"I suppose that's my answer." Hellion closed his eyes and took a deep breath, pulling his hand away from my ankle to rub the back of his neck.

Guilt washed over me like a wave rolling in to shore. "Bahlin," I whispered.

Hellion froze, and movement only came back to him in stages. His eyes opened first, then his fingers flexed on his free hand, followed by the slow lifting of his chin and a relaxing of his stress-wrinkled brow.

"It's difficult, but not impossible. Just bear with me." I looked away from him and took a shaky breath.

"Let's abandon emotion, Maddy, and pursue logic," he said gently, laying his hand back on my ankle. "It will probably help us both where he's concerned. Is that fair enough?"

I took a shuddering breath, held it, and let it out with a whoosh. "Yeah." I lifted a trembling hand to my face and covered my eyes for a moment while I breathed through a near anxiety attack. While they'd been prevalent right after the death of my parents, I hadn't had one in the last eight weeks despite what life's little revelations had thrown at me. But one broken engagement compounded by a fractured heart and here I was, nearly hyperventilating in my effort to get air into lungs that felt surrounded by a steel band.

"Hey." Hellion's gentle voice broke through the labored sound of my breathing. "I won't force you to do this, Maddy."

I flashed back to my first Council meeting, the one held in the faes' sithen, when I'd suggested to Gaitha that she not sit through the meeting if it was too hard for her. She'd barked at me that her station didn't allow her to avoid things because they were simply too painful. At the time I'd been confused at her statement. Now it was perfectly clear. I stiffly stood, stepping around the worst of the glass and moving toward the fireplace despite Hellion's sounds of objection. I let my arms hang at my sides and I shook my head, quick and harsh. He shut up. I rolled several ideas around, seeing which ones felt wrong in my head, disregarding my heart as nothing more than an organ that pumped blood for the good of my other organs.

In a low, tight voice I said, "I believe the blue weyr may, and I emphasize *may*, have hired a warlock to carry out inappropriate, if not illegal, acts of violence against me. I believe there's a very good chance that the mist that attacked me in the park is a byproduct of this magic, and I'm relatively certain my death is the intended goal." I cleared my throat once, twice. "I am beginning to believe that either Bahlin or Clay cut the hair off my head while I slept in order to give it to their hired magi. This may well have been done to create questionable circumstances for the killer who was, at the time the roses arrived, unknown. Clay had no idea it was another Council member he was framing. Further, I believe it's highly possible this warlock has engaged either one or more of the blue weyr, or some other creature with claws, to attempt to behead the girls being killed, marking each mistaken woman a traitor, leaving a gold coin as a sort of calling card for the weyr. And I think it may have all been done with Bahlin's knowledge and involvement." I felt cold to the core, anger warring with despair at naming Bahlin a suspect. But too many pieces of evidence fell into place when I took my emotions out of the picture. So lost in thought was I that I didn't hear Hellion approach from behind. When he touched my hip, my ass clenched and I jerked to one side. "Sorry," I mumbled, but I didn't move closer to him.

"Maddy, I've been afraid for you to get there in your mind, but I think it's better that you see the potential for what it is. I'll not tell you you're right or wrong because I don't believe I've the proper perspective on this to be impartial. I will tell you that I'll set a curse on both this house and anyone in it who shares any information gained while we stay. That way you may be free with your thoughts as they come to you, and maybe we'll be able to make some headway tonight. Anyone maliciously gossiping will have his tongue shrivel in his head until I deem the punishment sufficient."

"That should make the culprits easy to identify." I turned back toward Hellion and stared up at him, one side of his face bathed in firelight while the other was cast in dark shadows. The irony that his light and dark halves were presented so literally tonight was not lost on me. Unaware of my internal observations, he continued to stare back at me.

"Would you like—" he began.

"Would you take me—" I started.

We both stopped and stared at each other. I stepped forward and took one of his huge hands in mine. "I'll go first?"

He shrugged. "Whatever suits you, Maddy."

I closed my eyes and stepped out on destiny's narrow ledge of faith. "Take me to bed, Hellion."

"If you're tired. That's what I was going to—"

"Take. Me. To. Bed." I opened my eyes and quirked a brow at his mental lethargy. "I need a night of forgetting how screwed up my life is getting. Give me one night of nothing but great memories." Lifting his longest finger to my lips, I sucked the tip into my mouth and swirled my tongue around the whorls of the finger pad. I pulled back and was secretly thrilled that he unconsciously followed my mouth with that finger. "Now, please," I breathed. "I know you can't be that obtuse."

Hellion nodded and yanked me roughly to him. I crashed into his body with enough momentum to force him to take a step back to maintain his balance. I slowly tipped my head back and our eyes met, and I gasped at the heat reflected in his ebony gaze.

"Don't worry tha' I don't understand, Maddy," he growled at me, his Irish brogue deepening. "Yeh just be sure yehr aware that yehr playing with fire, *síorghrá*." His hands low on my back heated and seared me through the silk, forcing me to involuntarily arch forward onto his thigh.

I ground my mound into the hard muscles of his upper leg in a parody of the sex act. I leaned forward and hooked that leg behind him, sliding it slowly up and down, the scent of my arousal marking him and hanging in the air between us.

He grasped the back of my neck and drew me up on my tiptoes as he pulled me toward his lips. I went like a flame drawn to air. His erection twitched behind the heavy fabric of his trousers, and I smiled into his lips, running my fingernails down his chest and causing him to shiver under my touch. This was definitely touching with intent. He dropped both hands to my hips before stooping lower, crossing his arms under my ass, and lifting me so I was actually slightly taller than him.

I braced one hand on his shoulder and, with the other hand woven through his hair, I took control of the kiss. Our tongues dueled with each other, but I always seemed to have the upper hand, beating him to the next move by a millisecond, so it was I who licked the roof of his mouth first, it was I who nipped his lower lip, and it was I who sucked on his tongue as if it were his cock. In response to my aggressive onslaught, Hellion moaned into my mouth, and I had to force my breathing to slow down.

Hellion slid me down the front of his body, breaking the kiss as I neared the floor. He was panting like a buck in full rut. I ran my palms down his chest, across his stomach and to his belt where I curled my fingers over the waistband of his pants. I was able to hide the shocked pleasure of finding he was going commando again tonight. *Sexy.* I tugged him forward as I backed up, making my way—I hoped—toward the door Darius had exited earlier.

"Where's the bedroom?" I asked in a throaty voice more suited to hot phone sex than paranormal detective work.

"Pick one. The master's always off limits to guests, so we can go there or we can use one of the closer rooms." I grinned up at him, and he forced a small, answering smile on lips flushed with kisses.

"Let me guess—you own this place too?"

"Guilty. But can we discuss my real estate holdings later? Hell, I'll give you my whole fucking portfolio if you'll just take your dress off." His eyes were slightly wild. He bent over and pulled me forward slowly so that his lips latched onto the silk of my dress, and the nipple beneath, in a rush of moist heat.

I stumbled, and only his hand at the small of my back kept me from landing on my ass. I stopped walking and closed my eyes, letting my head fall backward and reveling in the skill of the man's mouth, even through layers of cloth. I threaded my fingers gently through his hair so I cupped his skull, my fingers stroking and massaging the small ridges and knots of bone beneath skin. I held him close to my breast, my chest rising and falling rapidly enough that he had to make an effort to keep up with the movement of my nipple, which was, at this point, fully distended and as hard as a dried pea. "I have two," I gasped. "Two..."

"So you do," he whispered before moving to my other breast, snaking his free hand up under my dress so he could grasp my bare cheek. Tracing the crevice of my ass with one finger and running up and down the split, he encouraged me to move my legs farther apart and allow him to reach my center. Hellion bit my through the cloth of dress and bra and I squeaked, jerking forward as he speared me with his thumb. He massaged me, nestling his free fingers into my crevice so he could massage me deeper internally. "Maddy," he whispered, his breath blowing cool across my damp nipple and causing it to pebble impossibly harder.

"Hellion, you'd better get me to that bedroom *now* because I don't want to have sex on a hard floor when there's a perfectly good bed nearby," I choked out, caught between laughter and begging.

He released me completely and I whimpered involuntarily. Standing and twisting in one swift motion, Hellion materialized with me in his arms in a lavish master suite.

"Remind me to be more specific next time," I gasped, still somewhat unnerved when I wasn't given warning that we were going to dematerialize so quickly. "I meant *walk*, not pull a wandering Houdini!"

Hellion said nothing, just unbuckled his belt then unsnapped the top button of his pants and slid the zipper down. I could clearly make out the head of his penis under the fabric of his pants. As if in slow motion, I reached out and traced the crown and he held his breath, trembling with need. I glanced up through my lashes and quickly looked back down. His eyes were closed and his head tilted to one side, as if he were listening for my movements. I dropped my hand and turned so my back was to him, reaching across my waist to untie the knotted waist of the wrap dress. I felt the air move as he stepped close to me, his hands coming around and taking over the untying of the sash. Before I could get to the hip button that held the dress in place, he grasped the two pieces and pulled, popping the button off. The button arced through the air and clattered to the floor. Hellion ran his hands up under the shoulders of the dress and gently lifted the material off my skin.

I turned out of the dress so I stood facing him in only my bra and panties. Both of us were breathing hard, unable to tear our eyes from each other. Passion wove us together tighter than daylight is to dusk as we moved with each other in the ageless ritual of mating.

Hellion stepped in to me and, starting at the backs of my upper thighs, ran his rough palms up my back until his nimble fingers reached my bra clasp. He undid the hooks and let my breasts spring free. Unfettered by the confines of damp fabric, my nipples felt even more sensitive in the open air. He bent low and paid equal attention to each nipple. At turns gentle and then almost bruising, he brought me nearer to begging for simple penetration than I'd ever been.

Pulling out of his mouth, I went to my knees in front of him and pulled his pants down his legs. He stared down at me from his towering height, watching me carefully, as if afraid to hope for what he wanted most from me in that moment. I leaned forward and ran my hands between his spread legs, cupping his ass, and I drew him forward. His erection was intimidating as it bobbed and twitched with excitement, a bead of moisture running down the underside of the head. I snaked my tongue out and licked the tip quickly and he hissed, involuntarily arching forward to place himself closer to my mouth. I took advantage of the movement and grasped the broad head between my lips and sucked him in, working as much of his length into my mouth as I could. His width made it a poor effort, but it was effort all the same. I worked my way back to the tip, then back down several times before he roughly hauled me to my feet and kissed me using every mad skill he possessed, kicking off his pants as he shredded my underwear with his bare hands.

"Hey—" I started to protest, but I was silenced as he spun me around and bent me over the edge of the bed. He held me down by the shoulder, kicking my feet apart, and I felt him position himself at my entrance.

"Do you object?" he ground out in between hard breaths.

"No," I moaned into the duvet, insanely turned on by the submissive role he'd put me in.

Without apology, Hellion slammed home in one hard thrust, and I screamed in shock and pleasure and pain. I hadn't been entirely ready for such a brutal invasion, but it didn't matter: he was there now. He set a bruising pace, fucking me so hard he had to release my shoulder and hold on to my hips lest he force me across the bed. I clawed at the duvet, cursing Hellion with one breath and begging for more with the next. The sound of our skin slapping together was loud and rhythmic, erotic and unapologetic. Slicked with sweat, we were sliding all over each other as we fought to get closer, fuck each other harder, and find just that right spot. Hellion lifted my hips up fractionally, and suddenly he was hitting my sweet spot with every push and pull. I nearly wept with gratitude, so intense was the feeling, and I screamed at him, "Harder, damn it!"

I'll never know how he managed it without causing himself permanent damage, but he managed "harder" and my orgasm crashed over both of us without any warning. I stiffened up and grunted, unable to speak or scream, my body shaking so hard Hellion had to fight twice as hard to maintain his grip. He pounded me six, seven, eight more times and he came with a guttural shout, unintelligible words and sounds coming from him as he pushed into me. My orgasm faded and I went completely limp. Hellion followed my state of relaxation within the next minute, and we slid to the floor bonelessly where we lay immobile.

I probably would have stayed that way indefinitely if Darius hadn't moved.

Chapter Eighteen

I opened my mouth to scream, and the vampire shook his head so quickly he was little more than a blur of motion. He stopped and held a finger up to his lips, then dropped it and put his hands together in pleading supplication.

"*Out. Now,*" I mouthed at him. Hellion was lying on the floor still panting, his eyes closed, one knee cocked up and a hand splayed loosely over his belly. I forgot my own nakedness for just a moment as I stared at him. I was around him enough that I often forgot just how beautiful he really was. Thinking of the vampire, I rolled my head back his way and found him watching me with something akin to longing. I loosely flicked a hand toward the curtains, and he slid behind them without seeming to even disturb the air.

I rolled my head back to find Hellion watching me, a wary look on his face.

"What?" I asked, uncomfortable with the level of scrutiny he was laying on me. Had he seen me waving at Darius?

"Are you angry?"

"What? Angry? No. Why would I be angry?" I was at a total loss.

"I was, ah... How can I be concerned with delicacy *now*?" He flopped a long arm over his eyes, and his mouth thinned into a thin line, his jaw flexed, and I heard his teeth grind together, all actions combining to very effectively convey his annoyance. But with whom?

"Hellion? Just tell me why I would be angry."

His voice exploded out of him in a rush. "Because, Maddy! I was rough bordering on violent just now. That's the second time I've acted such with you. You asked me for memories, and these aren't the ones I'd leave you with in relation to our first real night together!" He raised his other arm and dropped both hands to his face, scrubbing vigorously. "I'm a fool." He worked his loose body to sitting, and his head hung dejectedly.

Inexplicably touched, I reached over and laid a hand tenderly on his bare thigh. "Hellion?" No response. "Baby?"

His head whipped down and he looked at me, confusion reigning. *Ah, there he is.*

He turned his whole body toward me, brows drawn together and his body softened from loving. "Aye?" he answered quietly.

"Look." I didn't want to have this conversation with Darius in the room, but I couldn't see a way around it. "I..."

"You needn't make excuses for my behavior, Madeleine," Hellion said, forcing his still-loose muscles to support his large frame as he stood. "I apologize for—"

"For what, exactly?" I demanded, reaching out from my prone position on the floor and grabbing his ankle. I wasn't sure how else to keep him from leaving the room. "For giving me exactly what I wanted, maybe even what I needed tonight? Why in the world are you apologizing for that?" I held out a hand, and he reacted automatically, helping me first to sit and then to stand. "I needed to forget, Hellion. I needed to leave old memories and new torments behind. What you gave me tonight did exactly that."

"Didn't I hurt you?" he asked, reaching down and placing his hand on top of the reddened mark of a large handprint on my hip. It would, undoubtedly, be blue come morning.

I reached for his wrist and pressed it into the young bruise. "Maybe a little." He tried to gently pull away but I pressed myself into his hand. "The point is, you didn't hurt me any more, *or any less*, than I wanted you to." I blushed a little at this intimate revelation.

"You're joking."

"Not so much. I'm, um, finding I like it a little energetic at times." I swear I heard a snort from behind the curtain. "The point is, you asked me if you should stop. I said no, knowing full well you intended on being rough. With foreplay like that, it wasn't going to be classical music and tender glances, now was it?" I teased. "More like Nine Inch Nails and serious—"

"Fucking," he finished for me, and a huge grin split his face.

"Yeah, that." I turned away to hide my blush, and he caught my chin in his hand, turning me back to face him. I glared, uncomfortable with this level of intense scrutiny. Couldn't he just back the hell off and let me be a little embarrassed? I'd tried to assuage his guilt. Couldn't he respect mine? "What?" I snapped, whipping my head out of his grasp.

"Don't be ashamed of what you like, *anamchara*. Not now, not ever. Not when it comes to me. I want your honesty, all of it. But for now, come hide your face," he said, taking my hand and pulling me in close so I could press my forehead to his chest.

I rested there for a few minutes, allowing him to soothe me by running his hands up and down my bare back, completely forgetting that Darius was waiting to exit the room until I saw a pale hand wave at me from near the window.

"Shit!" I exclaimed, jumping back from Hellion's arms.

"What?" He looked around to see what had scared me.

"Uh, I need to clean up. Now. Would you go start the shower for me?" I asked, using his body as a shield while I crawled under the covers on the bed.

"Sure." He looked at me curiously but didn't say anything else. He bent to kiss me and padded out of the room, the twin globes of his ass rolling as he swaggered into the bathroom, confidence restored.

I winced, feeling the first pangs of discomfort as the endorphins officially left. "Get. Out." Fury rang true in my voice, even though it was low to prevent Hellion's overhearing me.

Darius stepped out from behind the curtain and strode to the bed, each step measured and graceful.

"What are you doing here?" I hissed. "I meant it: get out." I pulled the covers up higher and glared at him. Unfortunately it's hard to look mean when you're rumpled and smelling of sex...that was witnessed. Oh crap. I covered my face in my hands just as the sound of the shower started, and cool hands grasped my wrists.

"I stepped in moments before you two appeared. The lovely lady who agreed to spend the evening with me entered a doorway down this hall, and I was to meet her there." He pulled a hand down his face. "I clearly ended up in the wrong room." Darius lifted his chin a bit and looked at me very seriously. "I meant it earlier, Maddy. If it doesn't work out—"

"You damned voyeur! Do you really think it's not 'working out'?"

"I must admit I'm impressed, but—"

"Out, Darius. Just leave, and don't you ever mention this again. Ever."

He inclined his head toward me and flashed to the door, pulling it open and shut in one seamless movement.

Hellion stepped out of the bathroom, his head cocked to one side, his eyes roaming the room. "Who were you talking to, Maddy?"

"No one. Shower ready?" I asked with forced cheerfulness as I crawled out from under the covers.

Hellion watched me carefully before looking around the room one last time. He grabbed my arm as I tried to sneak by him and I flinched. "I'll not hurt you, but I'll ask you for the truth. Did I cause you harm?"

Thanks to all the appropriate powers. I thought he was going to push about my behavior. Instead he was worried about whether or not I was okay. I smiled and reached up to tuck a stray strand of hair behind his ear. "I'm fine. I'll undoubtedly be sore tomorrow, but it will have been well earned."

He looked down bashfully, long eyelashes rimming guarded eyes. "So you aren't too sore now?"

"Now? No, not really. Why do—"

He swept me up, hooking one arm behind my knees and one behind my shoulders and carried me into the enormous bathroom. "Then there's a load of time before tomorrow gets here. Come, Maddy," he whispered, stepping into the steaming shower. And I did. Repeatedly.

The morning light crept across the bedroom floor, lighting first a sock, then a pair of pants, and, eventually, the rest of our clothes as they had been strewn with enthusiastic abandon across the hardwoods and antique rugs. Fresh light played hide and seek with the shadows and coaxed dust motes into a lazy, uncoordinated dance. And for all its cheerfulness, I watched the creeping of the light with an unexpected sense of foreboding ambiguity, as if the coming day was nothing more than an exercise in frustration and dubious plotting by a person, or persons, unknown.

Too true, I thought.

The bed shifted as Hellion rolled over, but I didn't move. His breathing settled back into an indolent rhythm, and I eased myself out of bed. I needed to walk a bit, to have a few minutes to myself. I picked up my dress and slipped it on without undergarments, only holding it together until I was out in the hall and could tie the sash appropriately. I wandered down the long hallway, stopping now and again to mindlessly admire some relic or another, or to peruse a painting, eventually finding my way back to the main hall and the doorway to the family room we'd used last evening. Stepping inside, I located my boots and fetched them, noticing in passing that the glass had been cleaned up.

I exited the room through the nearest French doors and stepped into the breezy morning. The partly cloudy sky felt like a game of roulette—it could go either way. We could end up with a lucky spin and sunshine or the more predictable outcome of rain. I wandered down toward the waterside, thinking back over the clues and my decision to both organize and formalize my thoughts about Bahlin's potential involvement in the crime. It was so frustrating to realize that the dragon himself had planted a kernel of doubt. How could he abandon me when I needed his help and he'd promised to always be there for me? How could he abandon me *period*? I'd been so convinced I was falling in love with him, and I'd rushed headlong into that mess, agreeing to marry him when I still had my reservations. I'd never make that mistake again. Never.

I picked up a flat stone the size of my palm and chucked it out across the water, watching it skip across the agitated surface several times before sinking away. I ran the clues back through my head, summarizing what I knew to be true. First, the killer was right-handed. I began to walk along the shoreline, paying little to no attention to where I was going but, rather, doing my best not to twist an ankle on the rocky terrain.

Second, the killer was using a weapon of some type that had a wickedly sharp, smooth edge. It could be a knife, or it could be a claw. The cuts had been clean, though, so we knew with relative certainty that whatever wielded the weapon had both the experience and the strength to get the job done.

Third, the killer was attacking at night. I rolled my head around my shoulders, feeling the muscles knotting up already. This third point was a real sticky issue for me. I couldn't count the number of times Bahlin had emphasized to me that he couldn't use his cloaking skills except after the sun went down. So if he was hiding from, or stalking, a potential victim, nighttime was the time for him to be most effective.

Fourth were the gold coins, and they posed a real problem for me. Bahlin surely wasn't the only individual in the world to have those same coins. *Think, Maddy,* I chastised myself. *Who else would be a prime candidate?* It could be his mom, or even his little brother, Aiden. What had Bahlin told me? Something about a dragon's parents making an initial contribution to the young dragon's treasure cache when he or she came of age, and then the young dragon had to amass his or her own fortune. Bahlin's gold coins had been given to him by his father. So realistically, I was going to have to focus on Bahlin's family as the source of the coins because he would have given Bahlin's brother and dead sister deposits in the same currency. *Shit.*

Pausing in my list making and my leisurely morning stroll, I grabbed a handful of stones and began throwing them, one at a time, as hard and as far as I could. I made it through a half a dozen throws before I had to reach for more stones. Settling in to continue tossing the small rocks, I kept on with my mental compilation.

Fifth, the killer was targeting women who looked like me as he, or she, tracked my movements around London. Bahlin had known where I was at all times. It would have been a matter of simple deduction to determine I was with Hellion after we disappeared from the fall together.

Sixth, the blue string tied around the hair—

A hand dropped onto my shoulder and I screamed, spinning around and striking out at my assailant as my boot heels dug into the rocky soil and dumped me on my ass. I was unable to stop my right hook before it glanced off Hellion's chin and snapped his head back.

"Bloody hell!" he shouted, grabbing the side of his jaw and slowly shaking his head. "What was that for?"

I sat on the ground, the water from the lake's shore seeping through my dress, and I looked up at him. It suddenly struck me as funny, and I began to laugh, trying to get my feet under me so I could stand. I finally ended up taking my boots off before being able to get vertical again, albeit with Hellion's proffered hand as help.

"Sorry," I hiccupped, wiping at the tears that had leaked down my cheeks. "Oh, you should have seen your face."

"Likewise," he said, a smile lurking in his voice under the frustration and mock anger. "What in the saints' names were you thinking of that had you so—ah, murder. Don't I feel foolish?" We walked hand in hand back toward the house. I was surprised I'd come so far. "I've always felt this was a good place for thinking. Did you come to any profound conclusions out here on the water's edge, then?"

"No." I pulled him to a stop and he turned to face me, effectively blocking out the sun. His hair was slightly wild this morning, loose and blowing in the breeze, and the light created a nimbus of gold around his head, making him look like a fallen angel. Why fallen? Because no angel could do what he could do in a bedroom and maintain their holy standing. No way. I blushed and looked down, remembering last night and early into the hours of this morning.

He chucked me gently under the chin and said, "And why does it embarrass you, what we shared last night?"

My head snapped up and I asked, "How in the world did you know what I was thinking?"

"Nothing makes you blush except sex, Maddy, and it's usually either right before or right after the main event that leaves you most vulnerable. So really, it's just a matter of deduction."

"And you didn't think you were a detective," I muttered, turning to walk back toward the house. "I was thinking about last night and..." I paused, unsure how to say what I really wanted to say.

"Are yeh hurt, then?" His voice barely carried over the sound of the wind and I was forced to stop and turn back to him. He hadn't moved with me as I continued on toward the manse.

"Not really. What I wanted to say was thank you." I held my head up and met his gaze despite the heat I could feel crawling up my neck and staining my cheeks. "I asked you for memories and you gave me just what I wanted."

He tilted his head to the side, and a strange look passed over his face. He turned to face the water, sticking his hands in his pants pockets and looking out across the water. "You make it sound like it's the last we'll be together." He didn't look at me.

"No, that's not what I meant." I took a couple of tentative steps toward him and stopped, unsure of his reserved mood. "Is something wrong?"

"Not wrong, per se. I was just curious why you saw fit to get out of bed without saying anything." He turned to look at me, capturing his hair in his hands and holding it back from his face so he could see me without impediment. "I woke to find yeh gone, your clothes and shoes missing. No note, nothing. I suppose..." Now it was his turn to look awkward and uncomfortable. "I suppose I was concerned."

"I'm sorry. It never occurred to me to leave a note or to wake you. Frankly I needed a few minutes to sort out the clues I've got, and I wanted to get out of the house to get some fresh air to do it. I've been cooped up inside since we left Ireland, and I wanted a little country air and some solitude." I took the last few steps back to him and dropped my boots near his feet. I stepped into him and wormed my way under his arms, and they instinctively wrapped around me. "Thanks." His shirt was still missing the buttons I'd ripped off last night, so I had access to his smooth chest. I nuzzled his skin and laid my head against his chest so I could hear his heart beating in my ear. "I'll try to be more considerate."

He tightened his hold around my shoulders. "And I'll try to be more trusting." He bent and kissed the top of my head, and I tilted my face back so he had access to my mouth. He kissed me tenderly and I relaxed into him, following his direction as the kiss morphed into a more serious moment. He broke from it first, and his eyes pulsed softly. "We've both had a hard go of it in the relationship department."

I nodded, unsure what to say.

"All I want from you is the true opportunity to give this a shot. I'm not asking you for your confession of undying love, but do you think you can give me something? I'm ashamed to need the reassurance, but I promised you honesty, and there it is." He laid his forehead against mine, his eyes closed and the fine lines more pronounced in this moment than in quite a while.

"I want nothing more than to be loved, to have a home, to belong to one person wholly and completely. I thought I had that."

He flinched and began to pull away. I held tight.

"It apparently wasn't real, so I'm naturally going to be cautious. But I can tell you this, Hellion. We want the same things, you and I. I'm willing to give this a shot if you are, so long as you don't push me to commit in any way other than this." I pulled his head down to me, meeting his lips as I went up on tiptoes. He was reserved at first, and I wondered if I'd blown it. He slowly gave in to my perseverance and I let loose a breath I hadn't known I was holding.

Again, Hellion ended the kiss, pulling back to stare at me intently. "*Tá grá agam duit*, Maddy. I'll not apologize for feeling as I do, and I won't expect you to profess the same until you're ready. But know that I'm here, and I'm waiting, and I will continue to wait so long as you need me to. I want nothing more than your happiness, and I only pray to Odin that you find it with me."

Impossibly moved, I nodded, looking away. "I appreciate that."

I saw him look over my shoulder toward the house, and his brows drew together. "What in the world is Mark doing?"

I turned to see the butler, who was also a member of Hellion's coven, racing down the hill as fast as his legs would carry him. The totally irreverent thought crossed my mind that the Grim Reaper wouldn't appreciate his message bearer to comport themselves with such haste.

I turned back to Hellion with a sense of impending doom. "Someone else has died."

Chapter Nineteen

Mark was still shaking, his breathing shallow and too rapid. He'd reached us and delivered news we'd never expected to hear: Amaly was dead.

Hellion had sagged against me, nearly taking us both back to the ground. Only Mark's quick reflexes had kept the large man from crushing me as he went to his knees. Mark had helped Hellion to the ground and I stroked his hair as he clung to my waist and wept. That man and the vision of rage in front of me now seemed worlds removed in a very short amount of time.

Hellion was a column of barely contained fury. His skin was pale and taut, his irises had expanded again and were pulsing furiously, and his movements were condensed and precise. A faint wind was generating around him without his awareness, blowing his hair about. The fourth time the wind blew his hair into his face he cursed, then retrieved a leather strip and tied his hair back with harsh but controlled motions. Pulling his hair back only revealed more of his savage countenance, and I wasn't sure it was an improvement for me. He scared me a little bit.

He finally turned to Mark and said simply, "Tell me."

Mark was sweating and shivering, and I grabbed a small blanket off the back of the sofa as I walked past it, headed for Mark. Reaching him, I dabbed at the sweat running down his temples and then slung the blanket around his shoulders and tucked in the loose edges.

He tried to smile but his face couldn't make the small motion. Instead his lips twitched and he said, "Thanks."

I nodded. "Can you tell us what happened? And how did you find out?"

He cleared his throat, and I asked Hellion to pour him a small whiskey. "For medicinal purposes," I said, encouraging him to accept the glass from Hellion.

He did, and sipped it slowly. The alcohol flushed his cheeks a bit and took the harsh edge off his movements. Of course, my mellowed observation wasn't at all influenced by the two-finger shot Hellion had handed me that I'd thrown back like a seasoned bar patron.

Mark set his glass down and pulled the blanket closer. "I tried to call Amaly this morning to see if she'd had any luck with the tracers you left her. She didn't answer." He began to shake, and I reached over and pressed the glass back into his hand. He took a larger sip, bordering closely on a mouthful, and gasped as the liquid seared his throat and gullet going down. Eyes watering and voice a bit strained, he continued. "When she didn't answer after the third phone call, I called the London house and asked Stearns to go over and see if there was anything wrong. He said that her front door was open an inch or so, and there were no signs of warding in her area. The second fact dawned on him only after the first fully registered. He called out for her and..." Mark downed the rest of the whiskey as a fortifier and choked, eyes streaming, but he didn't complain. Hellion approached with the bottle but Mark just shook his head and set his glass to the side. "Anyway, she was on the floor in the living room, her throat cut and, and—" Mark began to cry softly. "There was blond hair scattered around her, sir, as if she'd been trying to use your hair for—"

"Hellion!" I gasped, a horrible possibility dawning on me. "The hair." The reality of the death hadn't hit me because Amaly hadn't been important to me at all, but Hellion, he was a different story. I looked at him over my shoulder and found him staring at me with something akin to horror on his face.

"We never tested it before we left," he whispered.

"The killer's a blond," I thought aloud. "Blond, with long hair. That narrows it down somewhat." I stood and paced the length of the room, the gentlemen watching me carve out a path in the enormous room. The only sounds were those of the men's labored breathing, the soft slap of my feet as they went from carpet to stone and back again, and the rustle of my silk dress moving over my body as I walked.

Blond hair, blond hair... Most of the dragons I knew were darker haired, browns and auburns and blacks. I didn't know if I'd ever met a blond dragon. *The dragons were darker...* It meant it couldn't be Bahlin's hair. The invisible weight of guilt I'd been carrying since naming him a person of interest partially lifted off my shoulders as I realized that, while this wouldn't completely absolve him from suspicion, it did remove a certain level of consideration from his person. Of course, I supposed he could have hired someone to do it; he didn't like to get his hands dirty. And just like that, the guilt's tonnage settled back over me like a saddled burden.

"I'll find the killer and petition the Council to be the one to dispense justice," Hellion growled, watching the play of emotions across my face. Undoubtedly he realized the mental gymnastics I was doing regarding Bahlin. "You'll not ask me to refrain from vengeance on behalf of Amaly." It was a question posed as a statement.

"Don't ask this of me at this point, Hellion. You know I can't answer you. Not now." My voice was the firmest in the room, the most rational. If justice came down to the dragon and the wizard, I didn't know what I'd do. Two men with one holding a little more than half of my heart. How would I choose where my loyalty would lie? *You'd do the right thing, the* honorable *thing, and support justice,* my internal voice said. I shivered at the thought. If one killed the other, whether in cold blood or in an act of Council justice, I wasn't sure I'd ever forgive the one who delivered the killing blow.

Hellion stood watching me for a moment and then he was gone, dematerializing in front of me.

"He's probably going to Amaly's flat," Mark said in a flat, toneless voice. "He'll make sure there's nothing for the mundane police to find before placing a call to alert them to the murder."

My blood chilled in my veins. *Police.* Oh shit. "Mark, did anyone see Stearns come or go from the flat?" I asked, desperation creeping into my voice like frost creeping into a cold morning. *Please say no, please say no.* I recognized the exact moment Mark realized what this meant.

If someone had seen the chauffeur in Hellion's car, it placed him at the scene of the crime. And if the police had already been called and Hellion showed up at the flat, he'd likely be caught there by the police. He was already being considered as a possible suspect after being seen with me at the scene of a crime in the park. And even worse, if he were to be caught *in* the home of a new victim...

I turned and raced for the phone on the desk while Mark began dialing his own cell phone. "Stearns? Mark here. Were you observed entering or exiting Amaly's place? I'm just wondering. She did? What did you say?" Mark paused to listen to Stearns's response as I dialed Hellion's number frantically. One ring, two, three, four: voicemail. *Shit!* I slammed the phone down and took a deep breath. Picking up the receiver, I dialed again, only to meet with the same response.

Mark's voice had become subdued as I grew more frantic. I heard the snap of his cell phone closing, and I turned to face him. His young face was grim. "The neighbor saw him and attempted to question him extensively. Stearns tried to deflect her, but she was insistent. He's concerned she may have already called the police."

I stumbled to the nearest sofa and sank down, letting my head fall back to the cushions and my hands flop to my sides. I needed to reach Hellion. If he had materialized in a roomful of mundanes, he was screwed.

"Mark, Hellion said there were a handful of people who could materialize and dematerialize. Is there anyone else in the coven who can—"

Mark's cell phone rang. He fumbled it getting it open, but he finally managed. "Hello! Hello!" he nearly shouted. His face paled, and I began imagining the worst-case scenarios. There were some doozies. Mark held the phone out to me without a word, and I took it woodenly.

"Hi," I said, knowing who would respond.

"Niteclif," said a garbled voice that was neither male nor female, high nor low in tone or pitch.

"Yeah?" I answered, sitting up and forcing myself into the moment. I needed to take notes. I stood and made my way to the desk.

"Your champion is removed." The voice chuckled. "And the other fellow you are so desperate over is now a suspect." *Hellion and Bahlin.*

"And?" I asked, taunting the owner of the voice just a bit. "What do you want? And what do you mean my champion is removed? He's just fine." I was certain of it. He hadn't been gone a half hour yet.

"Think, you fucking imbecile," the voice spat.

"Hey!" I said, offended. The other line beeped in. Out of habit I looked and saw Hellion's number. Did I answer it? Not? I didn't feel like I had a good choice. Without warning, I clicked over and said, "Hellion?"

"Maddy, this will have to be brief. I've been arrested and am being taken to the nearest processing facility. I'm not sure where it is. I need you to call Ben and make arrangements for bail. I need you to—"

"Off the phone, lover boy," came a gravelly voice within a few feet of Hellion. "You can make a phone call once you're processed and in the gaol. Off the phone, I said. Now."

Wrath

"Hellion?" I asked, hating the pleading in my voice. "Hellion?" But the line had gone dead.

I clicked back over and found that the killer was gone too. I'd apparently received the message he wanted me to receive.

Fortunately, Mark had known exactly what Hellion had meant when he said to "call Ben." Ben Raines was Hellion's solicitor. *Un*fortunately, he'd not been able to remember contact information off the top of his head, and the firm was an elite, private-list firm that wasn't advertised since it dealt with the city's wealthiest patrons. To obtain representation there was apparently like a club membership. But that was all secondary. The first thing I had to do was get back to London. We were about two hours by car, which was how Mark had arrived last night, so I drafted a note for Darius before we headed back as fast as we dared.

Hellion's townhome seemed silent and empty of all life without the man himself in residence. I went straight to his office, flipping on lights as I went. "Mark? Make sure the wards are still set and do whatever it is you do to strengthen them. I need to get into his checkbook and see if I can find any checks written to Ben and track down the law firm. Can you help me with this?"

"Of course, madam," he said formally.

"Just Maddy, please."

"But, madam, with Hellion gone, you're the head of his household now."

"What?"

"Just as I said. He's professed his level of commitment, he's, ah, taken you to bed, and—"

"I get it, I get it," I said, blushing like mad and trying to ignore the fact that Mark may have intimate auditory knowledge of my relationship with Hellion. *Yikes. Okay, think, Niteclif.* "Does he have any financial software?"

"Yes, and the passwords are kept in the safe. I'll retrieve them." He was off, moving quickly and with purpose, his hopeful youthfulness restored by action.

Funny, I thought, *I consider him 'youthful' when he's probably my age.*

199

I sat at Hellion's desk and did my best not to panic. The thought of him depending on me to get him out of this mess was daunting. I thumbed through his ledger, astounded at some of the deposit amounts and equally astounded at some of the money the man spent. Then I got to the last line and I blanched. He'd spent an exorbitant sum at a jewelry store. The note on the ledger entry just said "My Love." I traced the letters he'd written with my fingertip, feeling the slight impression the ballpoint pen had made in the paper. Mark cleared his throat and I snapped back to reality, dropping the ledger closed.

"He'd not want you to see that before he was ready, Maddy."

"I understand."

"He'd be very hurt if he thought the surprise was ruined. Please understand I'm not making demands, only asking you to respect his privacy in this one thing and be surprised when the time comes."

My stomach felt to my ankles, which felt oddly detached from the rest of me. "Is it a ring?" I croaked.

"I'll not answer that. All I'll say is that it would be better to consider your answer to him than to give him the response you just gave me." He looked disappointed in me, and my shoulders hunched in automatic response. Years of conditioning, I suppose. Much as I had loved my parents, they had a tendency toward being critical. I'd spent my childhood years always striving to be good enough, smart enough, pretty enough. Most of the stresses were probably self-imposed, but they had to have come from somewhere. Shaking my head, I stepped back into the present.

I nodded my head toward the folder Mark was holding. "Let's get to it."

"He has four solicitors that I'm aware of, each managing a different part of his personal and professional needs. I just don't know which firm is Mr. Raines's."

"If I have to, I'll call them all." I took the folder Mark offered, and I logged into Hellion's financial tracking software. I about fainted when I saw some of the other ledger balances. I'd dreamed of money like this, usually in terms of "if I ever win the lottery...six times," but never had I imagined people actually lived with this much in their accounts. Shaking off the shock of enormous dollar signs and plentiful commas, I began searching for the tab or folder he used for solicitor services and finally found it under "Legal." *Common sense, you abandon me.* I found the number in his electronic Rolodex and called. Navigating the secretaries, I finally made my way to Mr. Raines by weight of serious threat.

"Ben Raines," he snapped as he answered the phone.

"Mr. Raines, please accept my apology for my rudeness but I need your help. I'm—"

"Who the hell are you to come in here bullying my people?"

"Hellion Markalon's, um, well, his partner. Life partner." Somehow "fuck buddy" just didn't seem appropriate here.

"I see," Ben said, his manner changing entirely. "What can I do for you, Ms.—?"

"Madeleine Niteclif, but please just call me Maddy."

"Then call me Ben."

"Thanks. Look, I'll be nice next time. Right now I need your help. Hellion's been taken by the police to be questioned for murder." My voice quavered just a bit, and I forced back the emotion that was threatening to spill over into my voice. Stress and panic would have to take a number. I'd get to them when I could.

"He *what*?" Ben yelled.

"Questioned. For. Murder," I ground out. "I need you to find out what precinct he's being held in and get to him quickly. He'll give you the details."

"Kara," Ben bellowed. "Get me the damned police commissioner on the phone *now*."

I sagged in Hellion's chair as the reality of Ben's position, connections, and force of personality hit me. I had help. Finally, someone who could make things happen. "Ben?"

"One moment, Maddy."

I could hear him talking to someone, but it sounded like his hand was over the phone receiver. I leaned back in the chair and swung it back and forth slowly, the rocking motion lulling me into a state of relaxation.

"Maddy? Sorry to keep you waiting." Ben was typing away at a keyboard madly. "I'm going to get this sorted out, call in some favors, and I'll get back to you. Is there a good number to reach you at?"

I thought about that. My cell phone was somewhere in all the stuff that had been moved over from the hotel. "Mark? Can we use your cell phone as our primary contact number?"

"Absolutely." He handed me the cell phone without question and then gave me the number. I repeated it to Ben, and he promised to call as soon as he knew anything at all.

Getting off the phone, I realized I needed a shower. I thanked Mark and kissed his cheek, and he blushed and stammered that it was no trouble at all. I headed for the master bathroom, and it wasn't lost on me the level of comfort I'd found here in Hellion's house. It felt suspiciously like home.

I put myself together following a long, hot shower then crawled into bed just to smell the scent of Hellion on the sheets. I lay there thinking about how it seemed that the solitary wish I'd made for an altered reality had set a multitude of things into motion that I'd never, ever fathomed as possible. I didn't intend to doze, but it happened, and Tyr took the opportunity to visit.

I felt him sit on the edge of the bed and I whipped my head around, hoping to find that Hellion had somehow made it home. But it was only the god. I snorted. *Only.*

"What's so funny, child?" he asked gently, reaching out to stroke my hair.

"I was thinking about you as just a god. It struck me as funny. Sorry."

He smiled indulgently. "Forgiven. You've had a very hard day. Hellion isn't holding it together too well. He'll need you when he gets out of there."

"Is he getting close?"

"His legal advisor, no, what do you call them now? Praetors? No, that was the Romans. Solicitation? No, that's not quite right. Ah! Solicitor. That's it. His solicitor is down at the gaol now and is serving them with papers to release him. He'll be home within the next two hours."

"How goes it with the investigation?"

I shrugged, uncomfortable at being questioned by someone who *knew* the outcome of things already. "Can't you just divine the future and find out whether I succeed or fail?"

"In all things but you, yes. Odin has taken away my gift of sight when it comes to you. Doesn't trust me, I imagine," he chuckled.

"Oh. Well, I've got some solid clues, but I need to figure out the thing with the hair. Hellion's second, Amaly, was found with the blond hair all over her. Why would the killer cover her in blond hair?"

Tyr rolled his eyes and scrubbed his face with his hands. Turning so he better faced me he said, "Maddy, you've got to learn to really assess clues, not just take them at face value. What I want you to consider is that Amaly wasn't 'covered' in hair, but rather there was blond hair at the scene. Ask Hellion where it was, then think about it. You've got to stop jumping to the first conclusion you come to."

I bristled at the criticism. "And who the hell do I have helping me with this? I know it's *my* job, but my on-the-job training has totally *sucked*, Tyr! My familiar's abandoned me, I can only reach you randomly, and my, my, well *whatever* Hellion is, he's in jail for a murder he didn't commit." I bounded out of bed and stood facing him, my chest heaving with righteous indignation, my hands bunched in the fabric of my pants as I did my best not to wave my arms around like a mad woman. "I need help. I don't like to admit it. In fact, I hate to ask for help. But I'm not getting this done fast enough, and women are dying because I'm too damn slow to figure this out on my own!" Tears trailed down my cheeks, and I swiped at them angrily. I hate that I cry when I get really mad, but there you go. "Who am I supposed to ask? You tell me and I'll do it, because I don't want any more women dying." The fight went out of me and I sank to the floor, leaning back against the bed and putting Tyr at my back. I felt the bed shift and heard Tyr walking around the foot of the bed. He sat down next to me and gathered me in his arms. I was stiff for a moment before relaxing into my many times great-grandfather's arms.

"I'm sorry, child. Truly. What you're suffering is enough to try the nerves of a seasoned justice dealer. I wish desperately that I could just give you what you need, but I cannot."

"Can you answer questions for me?"

"Some. Ask, and if I can answer, I will." He stroked my hair, and I relaxed a bit more.

"Where was the blond hair found?"

"Next."

"I've discerned, with the help of some outside information, that the killer is right-handed and is using a non-serrated blade. Can you confirm this for me?"

"Very good. I can confirm that your deductions are correct."

"Hm. All right. Is the blond hair related to the blue dragon weyr?"

He scrunched his eyes up in thought and then said, "Not exactly."

"Can't you give me any more than that?" I asked in exasperation.

"No. Not without saying too much, and you clearly know I can't do that." Tyr met my eyes. "Ask more careful questions. Working within the rules, I'll tell you everything I can."

So I thought about how to phrase the next question to get the most out of Tyr. "How about this—was Amaly's killing the same as all the other girls'?"

Tyr hugged me tighter. "Yes, it was. Unfortunately, her killing was due to her relationship with Hellion."

"By relationship I assume you mean her position in the coven?" I asked. Despite my attempt at a nonchalant tone of voice, my stiff back, rigid muscles and the tic in my jaw gave the truth away.

He rubbed my back with long, gentle strokes. "Ease down, sweetheart. I did indeed mean her relationship with him in relation to the coven. Do you doubt him so soon?"

And there was the other rub. Maybe I did doubt him already. Maybe I wasn't as confident with him as I wanted to be. Maybe I was uncomfortable with the thought that I'd had wild and crazy circus sex with someone I wasn't confident I could trust. And maybe, instead, I needed to figure out why I had such issues with trust, because though I blamed Bahlin's recent behavior, it went back a lot farther than him. He was just the most recent wound.

I rubbed my stomach, the ache making me slightly nauseous, even in the astral plane. I really needed to figure this out if I was going to attempt a serious relationship with Hellion. It wasn't fair that I was admitting my developing feelings for him if I wasn't going to follow through. "I'm no better than Bahlin," I mumbled, shaking my head back and forth in general disgust. I pulled away from Tyr and scooted to sit independent of his touch.

"Maddy?" he asked, reaching over and running his hand down the back of my head until it rested on my shoulder and cradled my neck. "There are differences in who you and Bahlin are and the different ways you've behaved. The biggest difference is that you haven't hurt Hellion yet."

"Yet?" I latched onto that one word. "What do you mean yet?"

"I mean that you have choices to make in how you comport yourself, just as Bahlin did. You will continue to learn things about yourself and your duties as Niteclif that will challenge you, at times pushing you to the point of breaking. How you respond to the challenges is on you, no one else, just as how Bahlin responded is on him, and no one else. You are not responsible for his choices."

"Then he chose not to love me." There it was, one of my darkest fears related to my time with Bahlin. And now it was out there and I couldn't take it back. I sighed and dropped my head into my hands, willing the nausea back down. In my sleep, my physical body shifted and I held my stomach. Great—nauseous on two different planes. At times life could really suck.

"Explain." Not a question but a command.

"No."

"Don't make me force it out of your mind. If you think you're sick now, you won't like the aftereffects of me—"

"What? Pillaging about in my thoughts? You're right. Fine, you want to know? I think I'm most afraid that I did something that *made* Bahlin stop loving me. Because he turned it off awfully fast. Engaged one minute, abandoned the next. How could he ever have really loved me if he could turn it off that fast? Unless..."

"You may as well finish the thought."

I shot him the dirtiest look I could muster, but he just looked at me blandly. "Unless he was playing me the whole time like his family seemed to think, and he was only after the power."

"And if he was? If that's true, and Bahlin wanted to secure his power base, what does that mean Hellion wants from you?" He stared at me hard, and his eyes flashed in the dim light.

"I don't know, and that's part of what scares me." I leapt up from the floor to prowl around the room. I pulled on my hair and groaned in frustration. "I don't know. What do I have left to give?"

"I think that's a question that's easier for me to answer than it is for you to accept."

I turned and looked at Tyr. He rose to his substantial height and looked down at me. "You stand to lose the most you've ever lost, Madeleine: your heart. And you're too much a coward yet to face the reality that in losing the most you've ever lost, you stand to gain more than can be measured and weighed."

"I'm not a coward!" I slapped my hand over my thundering heart and turned my back on him so he wouldn't see how close to home the blow had struck.

"What has Hellion ever done to you, Maddy, that wasn't fair or just?"

"He tried to kill me."

"He came to you to tell you he'd discovered that Gretta was having an affair and to find out if it changed your version of events. Wouldn't you expect to be avenged by him if Bahlin killed you?" Tyr asked.

As the Voice of Reason he was really pissing me off. My back still to him, I shrugged.

"Before that, or even since, has he done anything to you? Anything at all?"

I thought about it. If I was going to be fair, he never had. Gretta had attempted to kill me, but she'd been in league with Tarrek. Hellion hadn't had anything to do with it. Huh. "He...he..."

"Yes? He what, Maddy?" Tyr asked, pushing harder for me to justify my answers.

"Just shut up, Tyr," I sighed. I refused to turn around and watch him gloat since he'd made his point so effectively.

There was no response from behind me, not even the sound of his breathing.

Without turning around I said, "Look, maybe we should just stick to the case. I'd like to know if the gold coins are all from the same lot."

When Tyr still didn't comment, I turned around prepared to have it out with him, but it was pointless. He was gone.

Chapter Twenty

I woke up still feeling sick to my stomach and angry with Tyr. "He doesn't know shit about what I'm going through," I muttered, getting up and wandering into the bathroom to see about digging up some antacids of some sort. I wasn't picky. Anything would help at this point. I heard voices coming from the hall, and I wandered out to the bedroom before finding anything, curiosity more important than my sour stomach. I was almost to the bedroom door when it opened and Hellion walked in, followed closely by his butler, his driver and a well-dressed gentleman who could only be Ben Raines.

Hellion looked horrible, with dark circles under his eyes, eyes that were...what the hell? They were a beautiful light brown. I stared at him, arrested mid-step. He shook his head and rolled it on his shoulders as if stretching his muscles but I recognized his nod toward Ben. So instead of commenting, I walked forward and hugged Hellion, my eyes shut tight against the room's other occupants. For the moment, I just needed Hellion.

As if he'd read my thoughts, he said, "Give us a moment, gentlemen."

I heard the shuffling of feet and the quiet click of the door, and I started to lean back to ask him how he really was, but he wouldn't let me go. He clung to me, his breathing harsh, and never spoke a word. Finally relaxing his grip, he took my shoulders and leaned me back so he could kiss me gently. "I need a quick shower. Will you let the men know I'll meet them downstairs? Then I'd appreciate it very much if you'd come keep me company."

"Sure." I trotted downstairs and into the parlor where Mark was fixing drinks for everyone. Approaching Ben, I held out my hand and said, "Ben Raines?"

He nodded.

"I didn't get a chance to introduce myself. I'm Madeleine Niteclif."

He grasped my hand and said, "But you strongly prefer to go by

Maddy."

My grin was grim, but I thought I should get points for effort. "I do. Thank you for getting him out so fast."

"It wasn't cheap or neat, but it's done. He'll probably be watched carefully, but he's aware of that. He should—"

"Probably be here for this conversation," I said, interrupting him. "But he's grabbing a quick shower and clean clothes. I'll be down with him within a half an hour. Please, make yourself at home while we're gone." Before anyone could argue or question me, I turned and power-walked out of the room, breaking into a trot the minute I cleared the doors. Making it back to the room, I went straight to the linen closet and got Hellion a clean towel and then headed for the shower. He was just turning it off as I rounded the corner. I stopped, swaying slightly from my halted momentum. It was times like this, when I came on him unaware, that I was struck by his sheer size and attractiveness.

Water dripped down his muscled frame. With his back to me, I watched as the water found its way down the column of his spine and disappeared between his butt cheeks. He reached back to squeeze out his hair, and his shoulders bunched under the effort, the globes of his ass tightening as he kept his balance. Tyr had asked what Hellion had ever done to me, and maybe the answer was nothing. But maybe the better answer was what I faced here and now—he'd made me want him with abandon, respond to him without thought and care for him before I was ready. He'd wormed his way into my life by being kind, caring and just frustrating enough to be attractive. He'd loved me without compromise, and I didn't know how to deal with that. I had always said it's what I'd wanted from Bahlin, but was it? Really? I wasn't sure anymore.

Hellion turned around and saw me holding the clean towel. He smiled, and I was lost to him all over again, my conversation with Tyr forgotten.

"I, um...here." I shoved the towel around the corner of the glass shower door, and Hellion took it.

"Thanks, *mo síorghrá*. Is something wrong?" He toweled off slowly, watching me watch him. Concern gathered at the corners of his eyes in the way of little lines, and I was touched. The man just got out of jail, and he was asking about me?

"I'm good. Much better now that you're home." *Home.* I blanched. I'd made myself comfortable and, well, at home during his absence.

"Does it bother you that I'm living here?"

His brows shot halfway to his hairline. "Bother me? Why in the world would it bother me?" He stepped out of the shower and pulled me into his arms so that I snuggled into the damp heat of his skin and sighed. "Maddy, *mo chroí*, knowing you'd be here when I got here was what made coming home a bonus. Otherwise I'd be out looking for Bahlin right now." He ground his teeth together, and I cringed at the sound as it reverberated through his chest. "That bastard will pay for what he did to Amaly."

"What if it's not him?" I asked.

Hellion stepped back from me, his movements slow and deliberate. "You're not going to do this again, are you?" When I didn't answer him, his face locked up and his eyes began to pulse. "Madeleine, if you are still in love with Bahlin I need to know, because you and I can't build our own relationship on your broken foundation. It's all or nothing. I've said that before."

"I know about your ultimatums, Hellion. And I've told you I don't respond well to them. Do I still love Bahlin? It's not something I could just turn off like he did, any more than I could turn off what I feel for you if you left me tomorrow." Turning away from him, I wrapped my arms around my center. Was this what Tyr had been talking about? This fear of losing everything—my control, heart, life, individuality, even my clear sense of self? Because that's what it felt like Hellion wanted—*all of it*. Before I could work through the thought, Hellion sighed and gently pushed past me as he headed to the closet to get dressed.

"Do you want me to move out, or do you want to?" he asked from the recesses of his giant clothes vault.

"What?" I squeaked. "I don't think we need to—"

"Because I won't do this, Maddy. I know I promised to wait, but I won't continue to wait on a maybe that you tie all your terms to, I won't continue to put myself out there for you unconditionally and I won't continue to risk the lives of my coven when you're afraid to commit to even me. They swore fealty to you, and any one of them would lay down their life for you. In fact, one has." Pain etched his features like a rime formation, and was just as cold when he walked out of his closet. He stopped in front of me and stepped out of my reach when I tried to take his hand, shaking his head. "I won't ask you to choose to stay or leave your new home, to love or not love me, or to attack or defend your former fiancé. But I won't stand by and let your indecision cause anyone other than me any harm. I love you, Madeleine. I'm absolutely crazy about you, but you need to work out your issues before someone else gets hurt, or worse." He walked toward the door, leaving me standing in the middle of the room.

"Amaly was killed because of her connection to you," I murmured, hating that I defended myself with such a lack of compassion, but he needed to know.

"What did you just say?" His voice had taken on a volatile edge, and I knew I had moments to salvage this conversation, maybe even this relationship, before things were said and done that could never be taken back.

I turned to faced him slowly, staring at his knees. "Tyr visited before you got home. He and I discussed the crimes and, well, other stuff, but we talked about Amaly in particular. He said she was killed because of her relationship with you. The women who died because they looked like me. They were all strangers. The only connection Amaly had to us was you."

"Oh. Oh shit," Hellion gasped, running for the bathroom. The sound of his retching nearly made me lose the contents of my stomach but, for the first time ever, his well-being trumped my status as a sympathetic vomiter. I walked into the bathroom, scared to say what I knew had to be said. I grabbed a washrag, wet it with cold water and carried it over as a peace offering, meager as it was.

Hellion reached back and took it, scrubbing his face, and I bent down to hold his hair back as he spit into the toilet.

"I'm sorry. I thought it was important to be honest about the why of things, particularly if you were thinking I'd been the cause of her death." I loosened my hold on his hair as he nodded and I stroked his head. "Hellion, you didn't cause her death. The killer is the responsible party. Whoever it is, they'll be brought to justice. Period. If it's Bahlin, I'll accept that. But I don't want you hunting him down and killing him, or running the risk of him killing you, when there's a chance he may be innocent."

Hellion moved away from me and I released his hair. He turned and sat on the marble floor, his knees bent and his hands dangling between them. His head fell forward, and his shoulders relaxed some before beginning to shake. "I'll ask the Council to allow me to mete out justice, Maddy. I don't care who's found guilty. Their head is mine." He looked up and, for the first time, I saw the warlock in him. The whites of his eyes had given way completely to the black, making his eyes emotional pits of rage. I could feel the malevolence rolling off him in waves, and it made my stomach clench in fear. I didn't believe he'd strike out at me, but I knew with an indescribable clarity that he was more powerful, more *deadly*, than I'd given him credit for being. And my hurt over Bahlin's actions seemed paltry when compared to Hellion's seething fury. Bahlin had wounded me, making me want to curl up and die. But whoever had wounded Hellion, whoever this killer was, had made Hellion want to retaliate in kind. I wasn't dismissing my feelings toward Bahlin, but rather was looking at them in a new light.

I sank to the floor where I stood, leaving several feet between us. "I don't want you to leave, Hellion."

"I won't." He closed his eyes and rubbed his brow, his lips turning down at the corners. "I'll just move to another bedroom. I won't leave you, Maddy, especially now when you need me the most."

And there, *there* was the rub. "When you need me the most," he'd said. I did need him. And where the hell was Bahlin? He'd left me in order to either sulk somewhere out of site or to have the freedom to kill me for not falling back into line.

Hellion was a good man, and I'd treated him with a lack of respect and consideration. Sure, I'd taken him to bed several times, but that was truly more the result of my late-blooming sexuality and the fierce physical attraction between us. But sex wasn't enough to sustain him. He needed, even demanded, more.

I thought about what Tyr had said. Hellion hadn't done anything to hurt me, even when he'd come to the hotel. Sure, he'd freaked me out, but he was still pissed. He wanted me scared so I might slip up and change my story, but he'd recognized the truth for what it was once he'd calmed down enough to see it.

Hellion had given me unconditional love, with no power plays or political maneuvering. My fear was that it had come as a result of the prophecy. But even when I'd wept for Bahlin, Hellion had held me. He'd shown me nothing but compassion until moments ago when he'd basically said he'd had enough.

Hellion had asked me to give it a chance, to love him in return. And what had I done? Balked. Screwed his brains out. Treated him like a bedroom commodity to be used and exchanged in the event Bahlin came back. But he'd not complained. He'd made it clear what he wanted, and I dismissed it all as if it, and maybe he, was inconsequential.

The longer I sat here, the more I realized what a royal bitch I'd been. I'd treated Hellion no better than Bahlin had treated me, though for different reasons. Bahlin's reasons had been personal, and I had begun to convince myself that a power play was at the center of his manipulation of me. I'd used my neuroses as layered excuses, claiming I couldn't love or trust Hellion for a number of reasons. None of the reasons was good enough. It was time to stop being a coward. Oh yeah. Tyr had been right. I was a chicken shit.

I'd sat immobile during this whole internal revelation. Hellion, however, had begun to shift as if to get up.

"They'll be waiting for us downstairs, and I need to get my power under control so I can cloak my eyes for Ben's sake. No need to scare the poor fellow." He used the wall to push himself to standing. As angry as he was at me, he still offered me a hand to stand.

I accepted it and refused to let go.

"Maddy," he said, his voice laced with a warm warning.

"No, Hellion. I need five minutes of your time. Give me five minutes, and then if you want to walk out that door, I'll not say another word." I hated pleading with him, but I would do what I had to do.

"Five minutes, but then I need to go see to my guest." He purposefully removed his hand from mine though I tried to hold on. "No, Maddy. Say what you need to say and let's get it over with."

I swallowed hard. "Can we sit on the bed?"

"I think it's best we have this conversation somewhere other than the bedroom, don't you?"

I realized then that he expected the worst from me. What else had I taught him, though? He expected me to balk because it was getting difficult and I wasn't getting my way. Well, this time he was wrong. "Fine, if you want to stand here next to the toilet and talk, we'll stand here."

He sighed and dropped his chin to his chest. Crossing his arms and leaning back against the wall he said, "Just get it over with."

I took a deep breath in through my nose and exhaled slowly through my mouth, trying to gain control over my stampeding pulse.

"I'm sorry." I paused, and Hellion quirked an eyebrow at me.

"Okay." He stood and began to walk by me and I grabbed his arm.

"No! It's not okay," I snapped, pulling his arm hard enough to force him to either turn around or drag me along with him.

He stopped.

"Don't you get it? It's *not* okay. None of this is okay. But it's my new life, and one I've got to master. I've been given a really crappy deal in the form of the prophecy, because I feel like it doesn't give me any choice." I scrubbed my hands through my hair, making it stand on end. I grabbed it and pulled, groaning. "I hate the idea of destiny. I don't want to believe everything is preordained and nothing I do matters. Don't you see?"

"No," he whispered. "I don't see, Madeleine. What I see is that you've been given some amazing opportunities as well as a strong, guaranteed love, and all you've done is bitch. And what of me? What of my destiny that the prophecy has touched? Have you wondered how I feel? Have you ever even asked what I wanted before meeting you? No. Most people would give anything for the opportunities you've been given, but all you can see is the heartache dealt *you*. Instead of embracing the man standing in front of you, the proud man you've reduced to nearly begging for your affection, you mourn for and rage against the man who abandoned you and left you to essentially die."

As far as blows to the heart, his was a direct hit I was sure I'd feel for a while.

Hellion closed his eyes and shook his head in apparent disgust. "In addition to finding your killer, you need to find some happiness, Maddy. That's really what I want for you. Because while you'll fade if you don't solve the crimes, you won't ever live, *really* live, if you don't figure out how to be happy."

The back of my throat got tight and I nodded quickly, trying desperately to hold on to my composure. "You're right," I choked out. "I know you're right."

"Your five minutes is up," he said gently, and he turned to walk away.

"Wait!" I cried. "Please wait. I..." I paused, unsure how to get around the lump in my throat and the bands of terror wrapped around my chest. I was a historical failure at love, yet here I was, willing to try again if it meant not losing this man.

"Yes?" he said patiently, his back still toward me.

"Just answer me this. Do you truly want me? I mean *want* want. As in can't-live-without-me want. Because I'll not settle for anything less than that." I couldn't believe I was doing this. I felt giddy and sick.

He turned and looked at me, his face so serious it looked as if it might never smile again. For a moment I worried I'd misjudged this situation as badly as I'd misjudged Bahlin. Then Hellion spoke. "I cannot imagine a day without you in it. And while I would miss you horribly in such an event, it's the small things that would haunt me." He stepped up to me and tenderly took me by the shoulders, his face softening almost imperceptibly. "The texture of your lips"—he bent and grazed them with his own—"the timbre of your laugh"—he stroked my throat—"the dip in your lower back"—he caressed it with his hands—"the sweet spot behind your knee that makes you whimper when kissed"—he bent and touched it with his fingertips and took the opportunity to kiss my collar bone—"your generous smiles"—he traced my lips with his thumbs—"and the look in your eyes when you first wake up and see me watching you." He looked at me so earnestly. "I'd grieve you, Maddy. It's part of what being in love truly is, and I never thought to feel this way about anyone, particularly you. It's terrifying and exhilarating and maddening all at once."

"I know the feeling," I said, finding myself strangely, erotically, turned on to hear how much he loved me. For love I believed it was, more now than ever before.

He gave a small smile and looked so sad. It was clear he thought he had his answer, and that my "knowing" involved Bahlin, not him.

I stepped up to him and reached for his hands, never breaking eye contact. "I love you too," I breathed, leaning forward to kiss his lips.

The world tilted, just like it had that fateful night at the stones, and we clung to each other. Time stopped, and we were suspended in being before the words, "*Thar gach ni eile, a chuisle, a chroí*" whispered across our skin, and we were slammed back into our bodies. *Above all else, my pulse, my heart.* Something in me let go. We both went to our knees on the hard floor, the fall jarring me and making my teeth clack together.

Hellion grabbed my face and held me too tightly. "Are you all right?"

I tried to nod but only managed a small movement between his clutching hands.

He dragged me to him, crushing his lips to mine as he lay down with me, his body covering mine, forearms pushed up under my armpits and behind my shoulders so his hands cupped the back of my head. I clung to him like the sky clings to the horizon. He ravished my mouth, breaking away only to nip at my jaw and neck, gripping my hair and pulling my head back for better access.

I gasped. My body ached. I wanted him in every way, in every possible way a woman can want a man. "Take me to bed, Hellion," I whispered, licking the outer shell of his ear and then biting his neck hard enough that he gasped.

"We've a guest to attend to and then I'm all yours. But first, tell me again," he pleaded, pushing back and looking into my eyes. "Please, say it again."

"I love you," I gasped, my voice hardly more than a whisper.

"Why? Why now?" he demanded, gripping my head between his enormous hands.

"I'm tired of fighting what I feel. I know that destiny's at play in my life to a point, but I still have free will in some of my choices. One of those choices is how well I love you, and I want to do it right. So I choose to love you well, Hellion. *I. Choose.*"

He crushed his lips to mine once more in a blood-boiling kiss and then he stood, pulling me up with him. "If I didn't run the risk of being charged as a serial murderer, I'd tell Ben to take a bloody hike. As it is, I need him."

My stomach fell at the thought of Hellion charged with crimes I knew he hadn't committed. "Can't I act as a witness? I mean, I know you were home on more than one occasion when a murder occurred."

"We'll see. You know what? I'm going to tell Ben we'll meet with him Monday. That gives us the rest of today and the weekend to get the two of us sorted out, and that's got to be my first priority." He strode out of the bathroom and came right back in to kiss me once more before jogging out of the room.

I sat on the edge of the counter, contemplating the strange feeling in my chest. *I love Hellion,* I thought, and it gave me butterflies and made me feel breathlessly hopeful. Smiling a bit to myself and rubbing my lips where he'd last kissed me, I turned to straighten the bathroom counter from where he'd put himself together after his brief shower. Picking up his brush, I was struck by the blond hairs stuck in the bristles. Hellion's hair was naturally that blond that women pay for:

brown, gold, platinum, and copper. It was rich and vibrant and...*holy mother of Moses.*

I turned and sprinted out of the bathroom and through the bedroom door, straight into Hellion, who was charging back into the room after having said his farewell to Ben. He grunted, staggering back from the impact. I threw my arms around him to steady myself.

"What is it?" he demanded, setting me behind him and away from whatever threat he thought was in the bedroom.

I scrambled around in front of him, waving his brush around. "No! Don't you see? It wasn't your hair!" I shouted.

"Beg pardon?" he asked, watching me carefully.

"Come here." He let me drag him into the bathroom and turn on the recessed lighting. It shined down on us, brilliantly illuminating the calico hair in the brush. "See? Your hair is multi-colored, right? What color was the hair in your letter and the hair found at Amaly's?"

Hellion's face clouded over and he looked down at his feet. "I'm still not entirely clear, Maddy. It was blond, like mine."

"But that's where you're wrong, Hellion. The hair in your letter and, I'm betting, at Amaly's was a true, solid blond. Not the multicolored pelt you sport. It couldn't have been your hair!" I pumped my fist in the air then hugged the brush to my chest, a sense of satisfaction spreading through me.

Hellion finally looked up and he smiled a small smile, but his eyes were shadowed with grief. "So I really did kill her."

"Huh?"

"Amaly. I really did kill her," he said. He hung his head and locked his hands behind his neck. "Shit."

"No, you didn't. The killer did." Tossing the brush on the counter, I stepped forward and grabbed his arms, pulling his hands down and sliding my own into his. Hellion's hands were cold, and I began rubbing them to warm him, though I wasn't sure it would help. "Hellion, what could a witch or wizard do with hair?"

"We talked about this, Maddy. Hair is an incredibly personal item and could be used to do any number of things. The list is too long to possibly go through, and even if we did I'm sure we'd miss things. No, I don't think it's possible."

I gently slapped a hand to his chest, making him raise his eyes.

"Any reason you're hitting me?" he asked in a flat voice. His eyes were drawn and bruised looking, his lack of sleep and ricocheting emotions finally catching up to him.

"I need your attention. This is critical." Reaching up, I ran my fingers through his hair. "We don't need all the possible solutions regarding what hair can be used for. We need one probable solution. What we need to know is what *this* hair was used for." Taking a handful of his hair, I tugged and pulled his face down to me for a kiss. He came willingly, and his lips moved against mine in a sweet joining that left us both breathless and Hellion's eyes a little brighter.

"What could this hair have been used for?" he asked absently as his gaze softened and he dug through his mental files, biting his bottom lip and holding it between his teeth. He ran a hand over his chest slowly where I'd slapped him, unconsciously massaging his pectoral muscle.

"Think of it this way," I said. "Is there some benefit for getting the hair into a person's home, or even hotel room? Does having hair inside a dwelling do anything for the person whose hair it is? Or was? Or—"

"I get it," he muttered, switching to rubbing his jaw as he thought. I saw the moment he had the answer because he paled further and swayed. "Holy goddess," he croaked. "I did kill her, Maddy."

"Hellion! No, you didn't. You—"

"Stop," he commanded in a deep voice, and I did.

I hated it when he pulled magic shit like that against me, even if it was small.

"Just listen. Hair is a very personal thing, unique to its owner. That individuality makes hair a powerful addition to any spell or magic performed. If strong wards are set—for example, around this house—and a person cannot break the magic in order to get inside, she, or he, can choose to get something of theirs that is highly personal and unique to them *inside* the place that's warded. In this case, the killer used hair. Once the hair is inside, the person can call themselves to that piece of, well, themselves. Only one or two wards are strong enough to keep someone out when they are calling themselves back together." He pressed his hands against his temples and pushed, the muscles on his arms flexing and releasing as he pushed then relaxed over and over again. Opening his eyes, he stared at me and asked, "Why would someone want inside these places?"

"For me," I whispered. "Each place has been somewhere I was or had been. So if anyone killed Amaly, it's me." I hadn't liked her, but I hadn't wished her dead, either. It was hard on the conscience to realize your simple existence caused someone else's death. "I'm so sorry."

"No, you said it yourself. The killer is responsible here." Hellion gathered me up in a bone-crushing hug then released me and grasped my shoulders. "Now I need you to think. Put that inherited logic to use, Maddy. What is the killer after?"

"Seriously, Hellion, it's got to be me. Think about it. At the hotel, the hair was put into the card on the flowers and delivered to my room. The killer wanted to be able to get into rooms she, or he, assumed were heavily warded, so he sent the hair. Then at your place, he sent the letter with the hair because he was sure your home was warded against intruders. We made the mistake of carrying the hair to Amaly's and then—"

"Walking to dinner," he finished for me, and I nodded. "We walked to dinner and the killer likely saw us, so after he knew we'd gone, he returned to Amaly's and killed her."

"Yes." A feeling of dread was blossoming in my stomach, unfurling like a flower on a time-lapse camera, one petal at a time on fast-forward. "Hellion, Gaitha was here at the front door that night, remember? Darius said she left in a rush when she caught a whiff of something. I'm proposing it was magic that drew her away. Gaitha was at Avebury Henge the night the waitress was killed. And Gaitha saw us leave Black & Bleu." I looked at him, my breathing suddenly shallow and too fast. "I think we may have our killer."

Chapter Twenty-One

Hellion and I walked dazedly back into the bedroom. Sitting on the edge of the bed, he pulled me to stand between his legs and laid his head on my chest. There was nothing remotely sexual about the action. This was about comfort.

"How in the name of all the gods will we stop her?" he muttered, eyes closed as I ran my fingers through his hair. "She's a bloody *queen* and fae to boot."

I was quiet, partly because I had no answers for him and partly because I was lost in thought. Was she the killer? It would have taken an inordinate amount of strength to nearly cut the heads off the girls, and if they struggled, it would have been all the worse for the attacker. Did Gaitha have that kind of strength? I wasn't sure. "Hellion?"

"Hmm?" His voice was subdued, and he didn't lift his head. Needing him more alert, I stopped rubbing his scalp and pulled his face up to look at me. He slowly opened solemn eyes and blinked.

"How physically strong are the fae? Particularly female fae."

"Well, I'm not sure entirely since they're so secretive. I know they're stronger than the average human, and incredibly fast, though not as fast as a vampire." He looked at me, brows drawing together. "Why? Does it make a difference if we've already figured out she's guilty?"

"No, I suppose not. I just want to be sure."

He stroked my arms and then stood, scooped me up and laid me down on the bed. Flipping up the foot blanket, he crawled in beside me and held me close. "The burden of justice is great. Plato said, 'Not to help justice in her need would be an impiety'."

I turned into him and buried my face in his chest as his arms came around me. "A man who quotes Plato? I'm a lucky girl," I teased.

"Damn straight, and don't you forget it, chit." He stilled. "Of course, I believe we're both lucky to have been brought together. Maddy, I—"

A knock at the door interrupted him, and he sighed and dropped his head to my shoulder in resignation. It seemed there was always someone at the nearest door when we had something significant to say to one another.

"What?" he snapped out in a loud voice.

"No need to growl, mate, it's just me."

Darius was here.

We sat in the parlor sipping a variety of drinks. Either vampires were quite fond of a glass of wine or what Darius was drinking *wasn't* red wine. In that case, I didn't want to be "paranormally enlightened." Friendship would only take me so far. Hellion and I had opted for whiskey. Surprisingly, I'd developed quite a taste for the stuff of late.

"So how goes the investigation?" Darius asked from the corner where he lazed by the fire. He was well dressed as usual in fitted black pants that fell over buttery leather boots, a midnight blue silk shirt and a black leather coat that hung to his knees.

"Well enough," Hellion answered. He was tense, and I wasn't clear what the problem was. I knew *I* was tense because Darius had watched me get nasty with Hellion, and there's nothing that says uncomfortable like being an unwilling victim of voyeurism. I sure as hell wasn't going to bring it up now, though, not with Hellion already acting strange.

"Not willing to talk about it?" Darius pressed.

"Not yet," I answered, glancing between the two men. "Besides, I thought you wanted plausible deniability."

"Oh, I did." He picked up his glass of wine and ran a finger around the rim, watching me closely. "That was until I found out Bahlin has been employing a certain wizard with questionable morals. Now I'm wondering if we shouldn't take a closer look at things before someone else dies."

"But..." I wasn't sure what to say. Inexplicably, I still didn't want Bahlin to be guilty. It was one thing to be disgusted with someone and entirely another to rain certain death down upon them.

Hellion thought to ask the more pertinent question. "Who's the wizard?" His voice was cool and detached, not the friendly one I was used to hearing when these two spoke to each other.

"Hellion?" I asked.

"Later. Who's the wizard?" he asked again.

"Connell Darach."

Hellion clenched the glass he was holding so tightly I was scared he'd break it. I reached to remove it from him and he snapped, "Leave it."

I jerked my hand back as if he'd struck it. "I'm not a damned dog, Hellion. Set the glass down before you shatter it or don't, but don't expect me to help pick glass out of the hand if you cut it up." I stood and walked to the bookcase, leaving my back turned toward the men as I fought to gain control of my anger and self-doubt. Like Bahlin, was Hellion going to change the way he behaved since I'd admitted I loved him?

Darius's voice was like a hand brushed across velvet when he spoke, saying, "He's angry because Connell is one of his primary adversaries. He's probably the one man on the planet who could challenge Hellion for his position as Europe's Coven Master and his position on the High Council...and win." His voice went from soft to sharp, taunting.

"He'd try but he'd no succeed," Hellion snarled, his brogue slipping into the conversation.

"What's with you two?" I asked, turning around to find they'd both stood up and taken a step toward each other. I pointed at Darius. "You need to stop being a prick. Seriously." Turning to Hellion, I said, "And you, you need to stop rising to the bait." I shook my head and muttered, "Everyone needs one asshole, and I was born with mine. How did I suddenly end up with two extra?"

Darius snorted and said, "My apologies, Maddy." He sat back down, dropping his head into his hands as if he had a headache. "I'm not sure what's come over me lately. It's true I desire you, and greatly, but Hellion's been my friend for too long to allow things to escalate to such a point, and so quickly." He rubbed his forehead and I looked down, belatedly realizing his coat had fallen open. Darius was sporting a serious...*whoa*.

He snorted, and I belatedly remembered his little gift of mind reading. *Get out of my mind, you giant tick*, I thought, concentrating on mentally pushing him away.

He tipped his wine glass toward me and flashed fang when he smiled.

What was it with everyone jockeying for position where I was concerned? I felt like a queen on a chessboard, with everyone circling

221

around me and trying to figure out how to find the best way to knock me down, knock me out or take me off the board for good. I shook my head, disgusted.

"I want to know what's going on that has you so, um, wound up," I said, blushing and waggling a hand in Darius's general direction. "Something clearly isn't right here. If you take a second to tone down the testosterone, you'll see it too."

"'Right' how, Maddy?" Darius moved a step back and set his glass down before lacing his hands behind his head.

"You're acting like I'm a prize to fight over. I'm not sure what brought this on, but you need to quit." I looked at Darius, pointedly holding his gaze.

Hellion quietly watched the byplay. He startled us when he spoke. "Something is clearly out of sorts. I believe it has to do with you, *anamchara*, though I'm not sure what it is. Darius, I'll ask you as a friend to respect the relationship I have with her. She's off limits."

"I'm well aware of that," Darius muttered. "And I'll agree something is out of sorts. It centers around you, Maddy, like some sort of primal pull. I've never felt anything like it." Shaking his head, he stood and shoved his hands in his pockets. "I'm fine."

In an effort to get the conversation back on track, I turned it back to Darius. "So where is this Connell guy?"

"At the risk of sounding like a smartass, I'll say he's likely wherever Bahlin is." Darius rubbed his forehead and took several deep breaths. It took me a moment to realize what was wrong with that picture. Vampires don't have to breathe more than a few times a minute unless they were talking or scenting. We were talking, but not that much.

Hellion stood and moved up behind me, wrapping his arms around me so quickly I jumped. Darius stopped rubbing his head and stared at us.

"Darius, whatever is happening is beyond your control at the moment. I believe it's in your best interest to leave and let me and Maddy sort this out."

"Right. I know exactly what you'll be 'sorting out'," Darius bit out, grabbing his glass and hurling it into the fireplace where it exploded into a million fragmented pieces. "You'll be sorting out who's on top." His voice was low and threatening.

Wrath

A breeze rustled through the room as Hellion breathed deeper and gathered his power around him. He roughly set me aside as he faced the vampire. "Darius, Child of Lilith, I will not ask you again to leave this place," Hellion said, his voice booming around the room as if amplified.

"Stop!" I bellowed, stepping between the two men. Hellion's power danced across my skin like thousands of tiny, painful pinpricks, but it was secondary to my memories. Flashbacks of the fight that had, ultimately, permanently separated me from Bahlin flashed across my mind like snapshots: Hellion entering the room; Bahlin fighting with him; the two of them going out the window; the feeling I'd had when I thought Bahlin was dead. "Stop," I said softly, and Hellion's power abated as he realized what I was reliving. Darius, however, didn't back down. Instead, he bared his fangs and hissed at Hellion, his humanity folding away as the creature he was sought to satisfy some wrong it thought done to it.

Hellion snapped his hand out and a small orb hung between us, pulsing like a heart beats. "Do not make me do this, Darius," Hellion said gently. But Hellion's blood was pumping too hard and too fast for Darius to let go of its siren's embrace.

Darius must have made some movement because Hellion grabbed me and turned, putting himself between the orb and me just as it flashed to a blinding light. A heartbreaking scream rent the air, and I grabbed onto Hellion as the light extinguished. Seeing spots, I tried to get my bearings. A horrible smell was creeping through the room, rising lazily like heat off pavement, and I realized what had happened. The light that had been given off had burned Darius, and it was his cooked skin I smelled. Pushing away from Hellion, I tried to get to Darius but Hellion wouldn't let me go.

"Mark!" he yelled. "Bring the first aid kit and a blood donor." How he knew Mark was in the vicinity was anyone's guess.

"Let me go, Hellion." I pulled but he wouldn't release me.

"No, *anamchara*. I won't have you see him like this. He'll heal; you might not. I'll feed him my own blood if I have to, and with the blood and a night's rest he'll be restored completely. Trust me. Please. The next thing to have happened would have been a fight. I would avoid that at all costs because I can't restore him to what life he has left him." His voice was pleading.

I didn't really want to see Darius, only to help him. If Hellion promised me he'd see him well, there was no reason for me to look other than to torture myself. But I was curious about the argument itself. "What happened?"

"I don't know, but rest assured I'll be finding out. We've never come against each other before, so this makes no sense." He sighed and ran his hands through his hair before holding them out to look at them critically. "They hold such power, and power in the wrong hands is deadly. Connell's hands are the wrong hands." Hellion bent and kissed me quickly as Mark walked into the room. "Go now, Maddy. I'll see him taken care of, and he'll stay here to heal. I promise you this."

"Come to me as soon as you're able?" I turned to leave the room, making an effort to keep my eyes from the corner where Darius lay. Already Mark and another coven member were taking care of him.

"As soon as Darius is well-situated, *mo chroí*. Nothing will keep me away."

I nodded and left the room, feeling all the while like a coward.

I rode the elevator to the master bedroom, not feeling like fighting two flights of stairs, and in my current condition it would have been a fight. I was contemplating the consequence of the weyr choice of magus, wondering how that might change the suspicion that Gaitha was the killer. It definitely changed things.

The smell of the burned skin and clothing clung to the inside of my nose and mouth so that it was omnipresent. That's the only excuse I had for not identifying the smell of singed hair. Had I caught it, it would have saved me a lot of misery.

Chapter Twenty-Two

I was barely through the bedroom door when it slammed shut behind me and the lock snicked into place. Before I could react, I was shoved to the ground, and a heavy weight slammed into my lower back, arching my spine to the point I felt like it would snap before it gave another millimeter. The pressure all but rendered me paralyzed with pain. A second weight—a knee?—settled between my shoulder blades, and I couldn't move at all. My lungs burned with the need to expand more with each breath, and I couldn't get enough air to scream, but it didn't really matter. The knife at my throat pretty much purchased my silence.

"Murdering bitch," said a vaguely familiar deep voice. "You've been hard to catch up to, but only because you had your trick pony around to pop you in and out of different locations so easily."

Why was this voice so familiar? Recognition flitted around the edges of my consciousness but frustratingly wouldn't come within reach.

"All those pretty girls, they were such wasteful sacrifices, don't you think? Their deaths are on your hands." He grabbed me by the hair at the crown of my head and hyper-extended my neck so badly that my eyes watered and I began to hyperventilate as I sought enough air to scream in pain. The knife pressed harder against my throat, and I felt my skin split under the pressure of the sharp blade. Warmth trickled down, pooling between my breasts.

I rolled my eyes to the left and right, trying desperately to pick up some clue to his identification. On the off chance I lived through this, I wanted to be able to finger the bastard. I saw golden skin and darker hair, and my heart fell.

But it wasn't him. *It wasn't him!* my mind shouted. I made a gurgling sound in lieu of a whimper and my breathing grew harsher, causing the blade to cut into my skin even farther. I grunted in pain.

"I see you think you know who I am, whore. Too bad I'm going to kill you before you get closure." Then he reached down and licked my ear, and his brown hair fell into my field of view.

Black spots danced in my vision; I saw the hand draw away and his grip shift on the knife just as I heard voices coming down the hall. They say that a victim's life will pass in front of her eyes in the final moments of life, but that wasn't the case for me. Time slowed so that it ebbed and flowed like the shifting of a glacier— the sound of his hand on the knife handle and his labored breathing, the unseen movements from the men in the hall, the unfamiliar rustling of something in the corner of the room. Nothing happened until the knife began to descend. I yanked my head down with all my might and felt hair tear from the top of my head in a white-hot pain, and suddenly I could breath. The knife slammed through the hand that was spread out on the floor. I thought I heard a woman scream just before I passed out, but it could have been me.

I woke to the feel of my hand being seared over an open flame, and I tried to plead for mercy only to find my voice was gone. All I could manage was a mild rasping sound. I rolled my head and found Hellion bent over my hand and Mark and Stearns, the driver, holding my arm still. Several other coven members gathered around, some mumbling unintelligible words while others looked on with a mix of curiosity and horror. I felt nausea building hot and bitter in the back of my throat, and I rolled toward the edge of the bed where the men were working. Despite my best efforts to hold my stomach, I lost its contents all over the floor and the shoes of those closest to me, namely the men. Mark and Stearns glanced my way but no one said anything. That scared me. Panting and wanting nothing more than a cold rag and a sip of water, I tried to fold my fingers up to get Hellion's attention.

"Easy, *mo shíorghrá*, you'll not want to push too hard. The wound is healing, but slowly." His voice was like salve to my battered body. In it resided love and safety. I closed my eyes and nodded, but my brow must have creased because he said, "This is normal when other magic is part of the injury process. Just like when you couldn't heal the fae's curse?"

I nodded slowly once again. I'd never used the word "weary" to describe myself before, but for the first time it felt entirely appropriate.

"We're nearly done, Maddy. One last push and you're through. Be brave, my heart."

I wasn't sure if he was speaking to me, or if he was literally asking his heart to be brave. Either way, the sentiment made me smile.

Another blast of raw heat seared my hand, and I screamed and started to thrash about involuntarily, but someone grabbed my ankles and pinned me down. Looking down, with tears flowing down my face, I saw Darius and I froze. He was burned everywhere that leather hadn't covered his body. His clothes had been removed from the waist up and his chest, neck, face and hands were a series of oozing blisters and split skin. Closing my eyes seemed cowardly, but I just wasn't up to dealing with his pain as well as mine.

Darius's voice was raspy when he spoke. "Rest easy, *mia cara*, rest easy."

"*I didn't know you spoke Italian,*" I thought at him.

"Ah, yes. Telepathy is quite handy," Darius answered, clearing his throat. "I speak several languages, as a matter of fact. How did you know it was Italian?"

"*I honestly don't know. Tyr said I'd have a gift for languages.*" I rolled my eyes and shook my head, grateful for the conversation that was keeping my mind off my hand.

"Tyr? So he's really your great grampy, huh?"

"*I can't believe you just said grampy, you mean-ass metrosexual, you.*"

He bared his fangs at me again, and they were wicked sharp, but I'd bought that ticket and been to that show when I'd saved his life in Ireland. I wasn't impressed anymore.

"Can't even intimidate the damned locals," he muttered, and I laughed. It was nothing more than the whooshing of air, but it was a genuine laugh.

"Thanks," I thought at him. "*I wasn't sure if I'd laugh again after that little nightmare come to life.*"

"You'd be surprised, *cara*, what one can and will live through. Fear is a fierce weapon, and violence acted upon is equally effective, but the human spirit is amazingly resilient." He stroked my ankles now that I wasn't struggling, and I relaxed some. "You were amazing."

"*Right. Once again I ended up getting my ass handed to me on a platter, and I'm a fucking hero? Uh huh.*" I shook my head and rolled my eyes. "*If you were American, I'd ask if you'd ever sold used cars for a living because you wade through bullshit with amazing aplomb.*"

He chuckled then hissed as his skin cracked. "If I were American, I'd have asked you to just let me die earlier instead of letting Hellion save my so-called life."

"Don't hate on America, Darius. You're just mad because you fry up faster than an unlucky turkey at Thanksgiving." I grinned, and he shook his head again.

"Ah, you mean the holiday you Yanks celebrate where you invaded a foreign land, introduced disease and then took the land, lives and liberty away from the natives?" he asked, all pious innocence.

I squinched my eyes at him and thought very clearly, *"Don't hate on me for what happened well before I was born. Besides, you're just pissed because we threw your sorry British asses out of the country...twice."*

He chuckled again and shook his head then hissed again at the pain.

"If you two are done yukking it up over here, I think we're through with you," Hellion said gently. He laid his hand over my throat and, without his even uttering the words this time, my voice was restored.

"Thanks," I whispered. Mark reached over my shoulder and handed me a glass of water, which I started to take with my right hand before I remembered it was wounded. I looked down and saw it wrapped in a mountain of gauze, and I looked back to Hellion.

He took the glass of water from Mark and sat next to me, helping me sit up. He held it to my lips and I took a small sip, reveling in the cool relief of such a rarely appreciated resource. "The gauze is just a precaution. It shouldn't need to be wrapped up any longer than the rest of this evening. Then we'll be able to remove it, and you should have the use of your hand back." He cleared his throat and looked away, taking a deep, shaky breath. I started to reach for him but he got up and walked out of the room without seeing my gesture. He handed Mark the glass of water as he passed through the doorway, and Mark made his way back to my bedside.

Looking over at the vampire, Mark said, "Darius, you should probably go rest, yourself. Dawn isn't that far away, and I know you need to feed again and be bedded down before daylight breaks. You're too weak to fight the sunrise today."

"You're right, Mark. Thank you. Will you look after our girl here?" Darius's fingers lingered, and he stroked the small node of the tibia on the inside of my ankle. His eyes were warm as he looked at me, and I blushed, feeling that same strange sexual tension I'd felt before he was magically flambéed.

I pulled away from him and sat up, embarrassed. "Thanks, Darius. I'll, uh, see you tonight." Gathering my wits about me and shielding my mind as hard as I could, I slid off the bed and stumbled to the bathroom. Behind the safety of the closed door, I could hear the men and the few remaining coven members gathering the flotsam of their visit and getting the hell out. I sat on the closed toilet and cradled my throbbing hand in my lap. I hadn't had time to break down after the assault, and now I found myself shaking and dizzy.

Slow down, Niteclif. Think about what you know for certain, I coaxed myself. But my brain just wouldn't engage. It was partly because I was afraid of what it might confirm for me. That dark hair....

No! Not going there. Pick another train of thought, my mind demanded. I complied.

I tapped my good hand against my thigh, anxiety beating against me like a thumping bass speaker at a nightclub, but it was my heart that set the rhythm.

Get a grip. What's the one thing that immediately stands out, the thing that is most irrefutable? I made a conscious effort to stop the nervous movements and focus, but I couldn't help but continue to worry my bottom lip with my teeth. Replaying the scene as I'd walked in the door, the most relevant fact broadsided me. The assailant was a man. I knew there were supes who could perform glamours to either appear to be something they weren't or else enhance what they were, but this? No. He had clearly been a man. And I had thought I'd recognized the voice despite his efforts to keep it low and gruff.

But if the assailant was a man, how was he connected to the blond hair in the letter and at Amaly's? Because unless it *was* glamour, his hair hadn't been the true blond of the hair left behind. That would confirm an accomplice. I'd have to ask Hellion about the probability of a wizard capable of dematerialization being able to both carry a passenger *and* breach wards. If one was rare, the combination should take truly remarkable skill. That should narrow the list.

And if my assailant was a man, where did that leave Gaitha, Queen of the Fae? Was she a suspect or just a crazed and grieving mother?

The door opened slowly and Hellion stepped through. He looked so dispassionate that I was concerned for a moment he might be upset

229

with me. Then understanding blew across my skin. Hellion was struggling with the typical alpha male hero complex. That just wasn't going to work.

"You realize that there's nothing you could have done, right?"

"How well you already know me." He took several long strides into the room and dropped to his knees in front of me, taking my one good hand into his. "If I'd come to the bedroom with you when you asked—"

"Then we would have both been taken by surprise."

"Not necessarily."

I pulled my hand back. "I *know* you're not saying you would have defended us successfully whereas I only managed to get a beat-down."

"Maddy, *a mhuirnín*, how can you ask me to not regret anything that brings you harm?" He stood up and stomped to the mirror, his frustration palpable. "I'd have taken every blow. The one to your hand..." He paused, seeming bothered.

Pretending I was brave, I held it up so he saw the bandage reflected over his shoulder. He glanced at it and then looked quickly away. "I'll live, Hellion. In fact, I'm only alive right now because you came down the hall when you did. So thanks for saving my life yet again."

Hellion looked at me with a studied look, as if determining what was true and what was false in my words. He finally accepted my gratitude and nodded in response. "Do you love me?"

"Yes, I do."

His gaze was unwavering, his black eyes still and deep. I stood then sat again, shifting on the toilet seat and trying unsuccessfully to get comfortable. I continued to squirm and he finally asked, "You're sure?"

"Yes, Hellion, I love you. I sincerely, honestly love you." The words still caused a thrill to run through me. I stood and walked toward him, carefully gauging his response. Just like earlier in the parlor, something was out of balance. This time, however, it was between the two of us. "Is there something you want to discuss?"

He turned and leaned against the counter, ankles crossed and hands clutching the edge of the counter. "Was it Bahlin, Maddy? I need to know."

"I don't think so." Hellion shook his head and started to gather himself to leave but I grabbed his arm and snapped, "We seem to be doing this an awful lot, and I'm getting tired of it."

He stopped and looked at me, clearly confused.

"Don't you even see it?" I asked, shaking my head and squeezing his arm. This blind ignorance was a source of frustration for me. "You've done this over and over, and it's getting old. You ask me a question, I answer, and you either don't believe me or you dislike my answer so you prepare to walk away. I'm forced to nearly beg you to have faith in me, and I'm not doing it anymore." He looked at me like I'd bitch slapped him with a Louisville Slugger. Tough shit—the truth throws a wicked curve ball. "I know Gretta lied to you. I know she betrayed you in the worst possible way. But you need to understand that I'm not Gretta." I let go of his arm and waved toward the door. "Go if you need to make some sort of statement by walking out on me. But when you've gone, I want you to think about what kind of statement it really is." I waved toward the door a second time but he just stood there.

"If I'm honest, I've got to admit I'm not exactly sure what to say to you right now." He reached across his chest and rubbed his shoulder, looking at a point on the floor somewhere between us.

"Then there's really nothing to say, is there?" I asked gently. "I'll gather a few things and go to a spare bedroom for the night."

"No! I—"

"I think you need to spend the evening determining how long you're going to punish me for Gretta's indiscretions and lies." I squeezed passed him and went to the bedroom to grab one of his T-shirts and a clean pair of underwear. I'd shower before I left.

He walked up behind me and laid a hand softly on my arm just above my elbow. Heat spread through my wounded hand and up the arm, through the shoulder and across to my heart.

"Stop, Hellion."

"No, Maddy. You had your say, now I'll have mine. You asked how long I'd punish you for Gretta's indiscretions, and the first thing that popped into my head was a denial. I know that's not right, but it's the truth. But you want to know the second thing I thought?"

I shrugged and stayed facing the wall. "If it will help you sleep better."

"I thought to myself, 'I'll keep it up as long as you keep punishing me for Bahlin's mistakes'." He gripped my arm and stopped me from storming out. "Now who has a statement to make by walking out?" he whispered, bending close to my ear. "Be careful how you answer."

"Fuck. You. Careful enough for you?" I ground out between clenched teeth. "Get your hands off me."

"And here's where we differ, Maddy. I walk away, whereas you strike out *then* walk away. So if you want to leave things on such a note, go on with yourself." He let go of my arm and stepped back.

I stood there shaking with rage and some other emotion I didn't want to examine too closely for fear it would look like anguish. Hellion was right, and I knew he was right. "What kind of relationship can we possibly hope to have if we can't get beyond our collective pasts?" I asked, finding myself chilled. I refused to turn around and meet Hellion's gaze. His arm slithered around my waist, winding its way up the front of my T-shirt and cupping my breast. I laughed but it sounded more like a strangled sob. "This has never been the hard part, Hellion." I tried to dislodge him but he was stuck to me like a barnacle to a boardwalk.

He pulled me close to him and bent to whisper in my ear. "No, this has been disturbingly easy for you, Maddy, you who has never been casual in her lusts. I think that's part of what bothers you about me."

Tears burned my eyes and I blinked furiously. "Yeah," I said through the chokehold my emotions had on me.

"I punish you to keep you from getting any closer. You punish me to keep me from getting close at all." His voice sounded as strangled as mine, and I realized we'd reached a pivotal point in our fledgling relationship much sooner than either of us had anticipated we would.

"So we're screwed..." I started to say, and he tightened his hand on my breast and made me involuntarily arch my back.

"Oh no, *grá mo chroí*, we're no' screwed." The heavy, emotional brogue rolled off his tongue and danced across my skin only to be followed by his tender lips. "No, no' screwed. Yeh said yeh love me, an' I believe yeh. I hope yeh'll believe me when I tell yeh the same, an' that yeh've shamed me. Yeh deserve better'n I've given, Maddy. We'll start tonight teh let go o' the ghosts, living and dead, who haunt our dreams. Because yeh're mine as much as I'm yehrs, *a mhuirnín.* An' I'm all yehrs." He hugged me tight to his front, resting his chin on my shoulder. "Yeh'll stop this business o' believin' we're doomed too."

I nodded, a strange and unexpected feeling of genuine relief clutching at my heart and mind. I hadn't realized until that moment how much I'd expected him to leave me, and sooner rather than later.

Sighing deeply, Hellion closed his eyes and shook his head. "I'm no' yehr da, Maddy, and I'm definitely no' Bahlin. I need yeh to accept me as *me*, no' overlay me with the sins of my predecessors." He lifted his head slightly and opened his eyes to see if I was listening. He stared at me, deep and hard, and I smiled tentatively.

Wise man, Hellion. He'd recognized what I'd been doing all along when I, myself, hadn't completely understood it. I was blaming him for the men I'd loved who had left me, one by death and the other by choice; one involuntarily and one voluntarily. And I'd not forgiven either of them. In this single moment he had helped me see it while offering me a chance to change my behavior instead of bailing on me. My parents would have loved him, and the thought that they'd never meet him just slayed me.

His head cocked to the side and he said, "There's a look of shock and sadness on yehr face. What're yeh thinking, *an duine dorcha.*"

"That's new. What does it mean?" I asked softly.

"My dark one. Yehr hair, Maddy, and sometimes yehr soul." He reached out to stroke my head, soothing the area where the murderer had taken his liberty with me.

"I'm thinking I'm guilty of all the things you said." I held up a hand to stop his interruption. "I never looked at it directly or intentionally because I felt like it would hurt too badly. But in only a few moments, you laid it all out in front of me, and I'm suddenly looking at it, and I'm not dying or crumbling. It feels like I should thank you." I laid my good hand on his arm and followed it by turning toward him. Our bodies touched, nearly head to toe, my injured hand long forgotten as I laid it across his heart. Tilting my head back, I looked at him, taking in the masculine beauty that defined his face.

"Tell me," he said with great tenderness, "tell me like yeh mean it, *mo chroí.*"

"I love you, Hellion Markalon," I said, the glowing ember of love coaxed to flame.

"Spend yehr life with me, Madeleine. Be mine, now and always. Marry me, and let me call yeh my own." He dipped his head toward me and our lips brushed together. The tenderness of the moment gave way to passions and lusts we never had a hard time conjuring.

This is why he kept his distance during the discussion, I mused, *so that we said what needed to be said instead of falling back on this, the thing we do so well.* Thinking became increasingly difficult as he nipped at my neck, and I groaned at the searing heat that flowed seemingly straight to the crux of my thighs.

"What the hell are you *doing*?" I panted.

He laughed ominously and said, "Just earning another Boy Scout badge, my love." He bent and secured his arms under my ass cheeks and lifted, turning me around and setting me on the counter.

"Somehow I don't think they're teaching this to the little guys," I gasped as he laid his hands on my lower back and pulled me to the edge of the counter. Everywhere he touched me seemed to draw a hot, lingering line to my center. "Why haven't you done this before?" I asked in a quivering voice.

Nestling himself between my legs, he grasped my chin and tilted it up for another kiss. Just before our lips made contact, so close that his brushed mine as he spoke, he said, "Because I didna want yeh to run, my fair Madeleine." His tongue licked out along my bottom lip, and I instinctively opened my mouth. He nibbled at my lips, coaxing me into the kiss, before using his undeniable skills to lay ruin to what little self-control I had left. Being such a tall man, Hellion had had the counters in his bathroom custom built so they were as tall as those in most kitchens. Convenient, really, in that when he pulled me forward I was now at groin level with him. Convenient for whom? Definitely me.

He rocked against me so that I rode the ridge of his erection gently, moaning as he shifted this way and that, always touching me with his hands so the feel of nearly unbearable heat never left my core. He hissed as the temperature saturated his pants and he shuddered against me, his rhythmic motions interrupted as our passions had us moving in different directions, each seeking to move against the other but at such different angles that nothing was being accomplished. And I *wanted* something accomplished. I wanted it badly.

I pushed against him with my good hand and slid off the counter. Hellion watched me with hungry, heavy-lidded eyes as I landed lightly on the floor, and my legs wobbled slightly. My head hurt where my hair had been pulled out, and I reached up with my good hand to rub my scalp before heading into the bedroom. I stopped to turn back and say something undoubtedly provocative to my lover only to find him inches away, stalking me as I headed toward the bed.

My breathing hitched as I thought of all the things he could do with this newly displayed skill of his, but one came to mind that would be mutually pleasurable.

"Do you trust me?" I asked, my voice sounding loud in the silent room.

"With my life."

"Heat up my mouth," I whispered, and his eyes flared.

"Gods above, you're trying my control! This is supposed to be for you, love—about you. You don't have to—"

"Heat. It. Up." I ran my tongue over my upper lip, and his breath caught as he watched the tip of my tongue touch the bow of my upper lip. Suddenly I felt as if I'd just sipped a cup of extremely hot coffee. I bent forward and flicked my tongue over his nipple, and I felt rather than saw his stomach and pecs clench.

"Odin's balls, Madeleine," he ground out through tightly clenched teeth.

"Oh, I'm not sure he's got much use for them." My tone was deceptively conversational as I rained kisses over his chest, running my tongue across sensitive skin only to follow by blowing on it to rapidly cool it off. I made it to the waistband of his pants and traced the outline of his cock with my thumbs, pressing under the crown and making him groan.

Unable to stand the escalating suspense, Hellion ripped his pants down and said in a choked voice, "I've never in my three hundred thirty-eight years had to ask a woman to suck my cock, but I'm going to... That is, if you don't, Madeleine—"

His pleading became a choked gasp as I sucked in as much of him as I could manage. I had to push against his hips to help regulate the involuntary pumping motion, and it took me a moment to understand what he was saying as he caressed my head. His thrashed voice was pleading with me to not stop one minute and apologizing for who knew what the next. I renewed my efforts to swallow more of him, but there was only so much I could do before I simply choked. He tried to pull out of my mouth, but I was anticipating the chivalrous reaction. I grabbed him by the balls and tugged forward. His knees buckled. Only the slap of his palms on his thighs keeping him from pitching forward. He moaned, and I rolled my eyes up to find him watching me with a new franticness I'd never before seen on his face. He trembled as he held still and praised me effusively. If I hadn't had to concentrate on what I was doing, I'd have been mightily entertained. New at this or not, I was obviously doing something right.

He tried to pull out of my mouth but I grunted and shook my head, redoubling my efforts.

"I can't, Maddy. Oh, sweet Freyr, I can't stop. I'm going to... I'm..." he panted. "Maddy!" he hissed harshly, but I ignored him, tightening my hold on his balls so he couldn't pull away without pulling against my hold on them. I slipped a finger along the firm ridge behind the furry pouches, and he let out a roar. It was over in moments, and he sank to the floor in front of me and drew me into his arms.

Burying my face in his chest, I asked, "Have you ever, um, with another... That is, is this first time you've used your magic this way with..."

He shook his head and said, "I'd change everything and nothing in my past. 'Everything' because I'd love to share the joys of new experiences with you and you alone, *mo shíorghrá*. 'Nothing' because to change even one thing might mean I wasn't where I needed to be to experience what you and I are building together." He dropped a kiss to my forehead and shifted to sit by my side and draw me onto his lap. I curled up and he rested his chin on my head, causing me to jerk involuntarily. And then it hit me.

"Holy shit," I whispered, a sick feeling in the pit of my stomach. "Holy shit!" I scrambled out of his lap, and he grunted in discomfort as my hand or elbow or something made contact with some soft part of his anatomy. "Sorry! Oh shit, Hellion. Get up."

He leapt to his feet and grabbed me by the shoulders. "Maddy, slow down. What is it, love?" He pulled me into his arms and I fought him, shaking my head.

"I know how to find the murderer. He took my hair."

Hellion just stared at me and said, "Yes. And?"

"Don't you see? You can dematerialize with me to wherever my hair ended up and then we can leave immediately if it's not safe." I was rushing around the room gathering up clothes when Hellion's arm snaked out and grabbed me around the waist, snugging me up to his body.

His voice, gentle but firm, was right next to my ear. "No, Maddy. I won't have you go into this with some half-assed idea of what will or won't happen."

"You don't understand, Hellion. This could be the simple solution to solving the cases. I can't let another woman die—"

"Then we'll go out with Darius and some of his people tonight, but we'll not go blindly, following some unknown killer across the gods only know how much time and space on the hopes we catch him unaware." He spun me around, and his face was as grave as I'd ever seen it. "I won't risk you, *anamchara*, not for all the young women's lives in London. I'm sorry, but no."

"But don't you see? The sun's coming up. If the killer is power-bound by the night, the daytime is the best time to hunt for him," I argued. "Darius and his people won't be able to help us because they're night-bound too."

"I mean it, Maddy, when I say that there are no arguments you can make that will convince me it's worth risking you. Understand that pushing is just going to make me push back harder. And while I admire your enthusiasm, you're not thinking logically."

I began to argue but stopped mid-breath. Hellion was right, and I sagged with the burden of knowledge. Not knowing what was on the other end of a rematerialization could spell disaster. Hadn't he already been arrested for just such a move only hours ago? No, I knew he was right and it wasn't feasible. But still... "Is there a way to trace the hair? Scry for it maybe?"

He shook his head and rubbed his forehead. "Scrying can't be your answer for everything, love." He looked up, and I was glad to see he had relaxed some once he'd realized I wasn't going to fight with him about running off all helter skelter after the madman. "For what it's worth, scrying can only be done on living things."

"Vampires?"

"Not living, so no."

"Uh, what *are* they?"

"Best anyone can tell, they are reanimated corpses affected by creation magic. There are a hundred different theories on the how and why of it all. Do you really want to discuss this now?"

I shrugged, tossing the clothes I'd grabbed back onto the dresser top. "No. I was just curious." I walked to the bed and slid under the covers, having become chilled as the initial adrenaline rush wore off.

Hellion followed me to his side of the bed and crawled in, lying on his side and propping his head in his hand. "There are some things we can do today if you'd like to get a feel for the magic that was at work while the killer was here. Or, if you'd like, we can get some sleep and then go out and see what else there is to learn about the most recent murders."

"That's a good idea. I suppose one of the first things we should do is see if he struck again last night," I mumbled, suddenly exhausted.

"I'll make you a deal. I'll let you come in and hang out while I work on testing the bedroom's resonance, or magical footprint, if you'll get some rest now and work on the murders in just a little while." He reached over and ran a warm hand up and down my arm, and I slid under the covers.

"I can't seem to think," I said around a yawn. "I don't know how much good I'd be now anyway." I rolled my head on the pillow so I met his eyes. "Give me your word that we'll work on this as soon as we're up in a little while."

"On my honor, we'll work on this and nothing else." He looked guilty, and I couldn't help but worry at the doubt that sprang up unwelcomed.

"What?"

He half-shrugged, and I tucked the covers under my chin, fighting the pull of sleep as I warmed up and my muscles relaxed.

"What is it?" I asked again. "Don't shrug me off. This new honesty policy is working out all right for you so far," I teased, running a finger down his nose and touching his lips.

Hellion rolled over on his back and dropped his arms behind his head. "Is there anything you want from me? I feel I took advantage of you just a bit ago."

"Want? Oh. Uh, I'm okay." Suddenly I felt awkward and shy. "Is there anything else you want from me?"

"Yes," he said softly. His head lolled to the side, and his eyes were pulsing like crazy. "I'd like to know how long you're going to avoid the fact that I've asked you to marry me."

Chapter Twenty-Three

Sleep was suddenly a wishful commodity I knew I wouldn't be getting any time soon. My stomach knotted and I curled around my free arm, afraid yet again that I would say or do something that would potentially make Hellion abandon me. I fought the quaking fear but it built relentlessly, and I found my mouth watering excessively as my stomach pitched and rolled. I clenched my eyes shut and held my midsection, breathing shallowly through my nose as I fought the feeling.

Hellion reached out and touched my forehead and the nausea eased, so I let my eyes open incrementally. The volatile queasiness passed and I took a deep, shaky breath.

"Thank you," I breathed. There was little I hated more than puking.

"I suppose your physical reaction to my proposal is telling enough," Hellion said softly, his disappointment hanging invisibly in the air between us. "I'll not bring it up again." He rolled over and laid on his back, eyes closed, fine lines etching his countenance and aging him perceptibly.

"I just can't," I whispered. "Not yet."

"I'm not proposing we post banns and hire a priest, Maddy. I'm asking you to commit to me and wear my mark so the world knows you're mine and, equally, that I'm yours." His voice was low and soft, not angry like I'd expected. But anger would have been more welcome a reaction than the dejection I felt from him. The proud, arrogant, decisive man I was falling in love with was not the same insecure and rejected man who faced me now. Or maybe he was, and I'd brought him this low.

Bingo, I thought, and guilt took over where the nausea had left off. I wasn't sure what to say or do to make this better, but I knew I had to do something. He'd told me in Ireland he'd only ask me once, and he'd broken that promise and asked me twice. It was telling for him to put himself out there, to make himself vulnerable, twice. I wouldn't get a third opportunity.

I reached over and traced the edge of his jaw, ending at his ear, and I tugged. "Hellion?"

"Hmm."

"Look at me. I need you to have this discussion with me face-to-face. I won't allow either of us to hide from this, because we both have needs here." I was almost shocked at the rational approach I was taking. I definitely hadn't expected it of myself. Arm waving, tripping over my feet, and totally irrational was more my historical style.

With a great upheaval of the covers, he ended up lying on top of me, and I squeaked in alarm. "Close enough for you?" His voice was still low, but it was laced with a new menace that hadn't been there before. He was working himself up to a self-righteous fit of temper.

"I imagine this will do." I laid a trembling hand on his heart and felt it pounding traitorously, revealing his angst as equal to, and possibly greater than, mine. His building arousal twitched against my thigh and I sighed. *Men.* They'd get a cockstand over anything. And Hellion was definitely all man. He was horny enough that I imagine the daily stock reports gave him a hard-on.

He wiggled and pushed until he was lying between my thighs and was well situated to make the most of his condition, but I definitely wasn't going to respond to being bullied.

"You're making this into something it's not supposed to be," I said gently, pushing his hair back so it was out of his face.

"No, Maddy, that's your job. You wanted a physical relationship with an option for love, and I gave you that. You professed you loved me. Time itself stood still, and I believed you. But it's not enough to convince you. So I'll make my point"—he pushed at my entrance—"however I believe you'll see it. We're meant, you and I, and damn if I'm not getting tired of trying to convince you."

Just as quickly as he'd been about to slip inside me, he was gone, striding across the room to his closet. I heard him rustling about, and he came back out with a small, blue velvet box. His movements were slower, more contained, as he approached the bed. He knelt down on one knee, his erection an odd flagship before him. My stomach lurched and he spoke softly but urgently. "I hadn't meant to ask again, truly, for I'd promised you I wouldn't. But I saw this the night we walked to Black & Bleu and had Mark go back and purchase it. It's yours, whether you choose to marry me or not, because I bought it as a gift, not a sentence." He folded the lid open, and inside winked the most beautiful diamond and tanzanite ring I'd ever seen. The center stone was an asscher-cut diamond of highly respectable size, framed on either side by simple but brilliant tanzanite trillions. Set in white gold—or was it platinum?—the ring winked at me from its velvet nest.

Tears blurred my vision, and I felt such compassion and empathy for this proud man, kneeling naked on the floor in front of me. He had put himself out there a final time, willing to confess to all his intent to love me forever, and still I held back, despite what I knew to be true. I loved him. Looking down, several tears broke free and slid down my face to drip onto the duvet.

What the hell is wrong with you, Niteclif? my conscience demanded.

All I knew was that it was too soon after Bahlin's rejection for me to make promises of forever again, no matter what I felt to be true. Maybe we could compromise. I cleared my throat and looked up.

Hellion looked heartbroken, and I reached out to touch his face. He shook his head and sat back on his heels, just out of my reach, the ring box hanging loosely in his grasp. Once again, he expected me to disappoint him.

"I have a proposal of my own," I rasped, clearing my throat yet again. His eyes snapped up and I shook my head, holding out a hand. He took it tentatively. "I will accept your ring," I said, and his eyes flashed to my face, "*but*, and this is a big but, Hellion. I'll accept it as a symbol of my commitment to you, but not as an engagement ring. I'm not ready to take that step yet, and I think pushing me into it is the wrong way to start our married lives together, don't you?" I held my breath, hoping he'd take my olive branch.

"I have no wish to tie you down, Madeleine Niteclif, only to love you as no woman has been loved before by man." He leaned forward so he was on one knee. "Let me modify my proposal then. Madeleine Niteclif, will you wear this ring as a symbol of the promise we make to each other here and now, to love each other to the best of our abilities, individually and as a mated pair, to stay committed and true to each other in spite of the absence of a spoken vow, and as a means of letting the world know that you are my beloved?" He looked at me with such naked hope, and I knew this was the compromise I sought.

"I would be honored." And while my response was almost entirely true, I inwardly flinched when I realized my right hand was still bandaged so my left hand was the only option.

Hellion, though, nearly blazed with triumph at the realization, and his large hands shook as with one hand he held my wrist while with the other he slid the ring on my ring finger. The band grew hot and heavy, but the feeling was fleeting. He looked up and grinned, and I was touched by the look of joy on his face.

I reached out a trembling hand and laid it against his cheek. "I have a favor to ask."

"Anything. Just don't ask me to take the ring off, please. That would hurt me."

"The thought honestly never crossed my mind." And it hadn't. It was the putting it on at all that had given me pause. "No, what I'd like to ask is that you wear a ring, too. Because it's always seemed a little sexist that the woman wears a token and the man still runs around and 'looks' free to other women." I rolled my shoulders at the discomfort that lodged between my shoulder blades. "I know it's sort of hypocritical—"

"I'd be so damned honored, Madeleine Niteclif," he whispered, choked with emotion. He swallowed hard and I reached out to stroke his throat.

"Wait here." I couldn't believe I was about to do this. I went to my small jewelry pouch and dug through the little bit I had, and emerged with a titanium band. On legs that felt as firm as well-cooked pasta, I made my way back to the bed and sat on the edge. *This is the strangest freaking way this could have happened,* I thought to myself. My hands were shaking so hard Hellion had to take the band I held.

Grasping my good hand and rubbing the ring newly situated on my hand, he watched me with such openness that I followed my heart and leaned in to kiss him. He stood and leaned me back onto the bed, covering me with his body, kissing me with a newfound tenderness I'd never experienced from him. He lifted his head and smiled such an angelic smile, but it was countered by the fierce pulsing of his obsidian eyes.

"Will you wear my ring, Hellion? Will you let the world know we've taken the first steps in declaring out commitment to each other?" I asked in a tight voice.

"If it's what you'd ask of me, I will."

The ring was too small for his ring finger on either hand, so I slid it onto the pinky finger of his left hand, where it fit well. "When did you have the opportunity to buy a ring, Maddy?" he asked, and then froze, horror dawning on his face as his lips drew tight. "Please tell me this isn't something you bought for Bahlin."

The small remaining wound in my heart pulsed, and I squashed it. The dragon had no place in this room. "No! No, Hellion. The ring was my dad's. It's the only thing that I got back after the accident." I suddenly couldn't breathe. I began to gasp, trying to force air back into my lungs, and I panicked. I stood and began to pace the room, turning as I reached the bedroom door only to find that Hellion had followed me silently.

"Slow down, Maddy. I'll take it off and we'll find something else, okay?" He went to remove the ring, and I shook my head violently.

"No!" I wheezed. "No, Hellion. Keep it on. Please. I just had a flashback to the day the ring arrived. The police *mailed* the thing to me. The last piece of my father, and it arrived parcel post." Tears raced down my cheeks but my breathing slowed. "Parcel post," I whispered, "with no warning. I saved it, knowing someday I'd meet a man worthy of the most valuable personal possession I owned."

If ever someone had looked shell-shocked, it was now. Hellion went down on one knee in front of me and, grasping my good left hand, made an impassioned speech in Gaelic. I caught the words forever, always, promise and a few others. He kissed my hand and stood.

"Come to me, Maddy. Let me take you to bed, *muirnuin*, and show you what it is to be loved. It will be the first day of the rest of our days."

I walked into his open arms and he swept me up, carrying me to the bed where, for the very first time, I laid my ghosts to rest and made love to my intended.

We slept for six solid hours and would have likely slept longer if Mark hadn't come to the door. Hellion stretched and called for the butler to enter. The young man entered as if hell's hounds were on his heels, slamming the door behind him.

"What the blazes is your problem, Mark?" Hellion demanded as he took in the butler's disheveled appearance.

"Sir, I—er, I—" he stammered, pulling at his shirt collar and rolling his shoulders around in the suit jacket he wore.

"Spit it out, Mark," I said, sitting up. I felt the top of my head and was grateful to find it healing. Getting hair pulled out hurts.

"Bahlin's here!" he said quickly and with something that sounded suspiciously like fear.

"What?" I demanded as Hellion exploded out of bed.

"I'll kill that sorry son of a bitch," he swore as he stormed across the floor, his erection once again an awkward flagship as he strode away from me and toward the stuttering coven-member-turned-house-servant.

"Hellion," I called, terrified this was about to turn irrevocably violent. When he didn't stop but had reached the door, I bellowed, "Hellion son of Markalon, stop!"

He stopped so hard he stumbled as he swung around to face me, his chest heaving and splotched an angry red. The blacks of his eyes had again eaten the white, and his hair whipped about. He was no less aroused, though I imagined it was something similar to what old reports say would happen to warriors headed into battle. Other heads got involved as the testosterone skyrocketed. Shaking my head, I turned to Mark and barked, "Out! Stand by the door and give me five minutes. If he comes out that door, you are going to stop him or so help me I will rain fury down on you, Mark."

The little man nodded and scampered out of the room.

"How *dare* you interrupt me," Hellion boomed, his chest heaving and muscles quivering. "He killed Amaly, and he came for you last night. You will *not* deny me my vengeance."

"What did you just say to me?" I asked in a soft voice as I stalked closer to him, slowly advancing and circling him where he stood immobile. "Don't you *dare* speak to me as if you'll command me, Hellion. Don't. You. Dare!" I spat as I came full circle around him.

"Tell me you'll defend him again, Madeleine. Say it," he hissed back at me, bending down and getting in my face. "Say it," he bellowed.

A strange sense of self washed over me, and I was aware of every hair on my body as it went on alert, and every square inch of skin as it puckered not with cold but with power. Knowledge flowed over me, and the words I spoke were strangely mine but not my own. "The vengeance you seek so desperately is not yours to dispense, Hellion. No amount of rage and punishment will change the fact that Amaly is dead, and your best efforts failed to keep me safe." I jerked like a marionette whose puppet master had sneezed before continuing. "You will allow me to do my job and I, not you but *I*—I pounded my chest—

"will render judgment. This is not the burden of your heritage. It's mine. You will not attempt to take it from me—not now, not ever." I sagged as whatever it was that had empowered me left, and Hellion let me stumble.

His eyes we flat black, and I knew he was at his most dangerous when they became fathomless like this. "So you'll choose him again," he said in a bitterly cold voice. "Don't do this to me, Maddy. Don't do this to us."

"I don't have enough evidence to convict him, Hellion. If I did, I'd take it straight to the Council. But there are holes in the logic, holes you made me see. I can't let you go blowing in there to kill him. I'm not convinced it's right."

Hellion closed his eyes and the wind around him eased down. When he opened his eyes, the whites had returned, but they were still flat and his face was expressionless. He walked to the closet and I heard him dressing, and then I heard nothing at all. I waited until Mark knocked on the door, and I ran back to bed and jumped in, pulling the covers to my chin.

"Come in!" I called.

"It's been almost ten minutes, madam," Mark formally announced, his composure restored.

"Thanks. Hellion?" I called. "Come out here."

There was no response save an echoing silence.

"Hellion?" Nothing. "Mark, hand me my robe and wait outside for a few seconds while I sort this out." He tossed me the robe that lay across the foot bench and shut the door quietly behind him. "Hellion?" I called one last time as I walked to the closet. But I could call all I wanted to.

Hellion was gone.

Unsure what to do, I dressed and made my way downstairs to the parlor. Someone had set it to rights since Hellion's impromptu flash grenade had been set off last night. The furniture had even been polished so the smell of burned flesh was overpowered by the tang of lemon oil. I nearly choked.

The slight sound I made had Bahlin turning to meet my gaze as I came into the small room. I held my breath and waited for the worst of the pain to subside, but it didn't. It just hurt. I didn't know how long it would be before I could look at him without wanting to claw my heart out of my chest to make the pain of betrayal feel less like a mortal wound. Apparently a handful of weeks, the divine word of Odin and two marriage proposals weren't enough. *Fabulous.*

"Madeleine," he said, inclining his head toward me as he held out a hand to shake.

"Council Leader," I said in return, ignoring his gesture. I didn't want to touch him.

"Fair enough. I've come, as promised, to help you solve these recent crimes."

"Who's Connell Darach?" I asked, and I was pleased when Bahlin paled. "I see you know him."

"He's an old family friend," he answered smoothly.

Going out on a limb I said, "You shouldn't lie, Bahlin. It's not becoming." I walked over to the sideboard and poured a stiff three fingers of whiskey neat and didn't offer Bahlin a drop. He wouldn't be staying. I looked over my shoulder and found Bahlin a couple of steps closer to me and watching me in a predatory way. "You'll need to keep your distance, Glaaca. It would be a shame for the blue weyr to lose another leader so soon." It was a vicious blow, but I wasn't going to play games with him.

Bahlin reacted as if I'd slapped him, taking a full step back. "What in Grenla's name has he done to you?" he asked. "You weren't such a bitch when you left me."

"*I* left *you*? Is that how you remember it?" I snorted in bitter amusement. "You need to lay off the gold dust, dragon boy. It's going to your head." I threw the whiskey back, grateful for the burn as it washed through my stomach.

"You had the opportunity to come home with me in Ireland and, as I recall, you threatened to kill me." He quirked a brow at me, and my heartbeat sped up at the familiar gesture.

"Why have you come, Bahlin? It's obviously not to help. You're days late for that. So own up and then get out."

He turned and walked to the bookshelf and perused the knickknacks of several lifetimes. "I'm amazed he let you come down by yourself. If you were mine, I wouldn't have let you near him without me as a chaperone." When I didn't answer, he continued. "I also wouldn't allow you to be injured."

A chill ran up my spine, and I felt like a pair of cold lips had been laid at the base of my skull. "What would you know about the injury?" I asked.

"Nothing other than you weren't hurt when you were with me."

I turned slowly and stared at him in disbelief. "I was shot when I was 'with' you, as you say, I got my ass thoroughly kicked, I was cursed, I *died* and then you broke my heart! In a matter of only a few *weeks*, Bahlin!" I bellowed the last, and Mark and Stearns came racing into the room. I waved them off and didn't turn to see if they left. "Your track record isn't spotless, Bay, so cool it." The easy nickname I'd coined for him fell off my tongue before I could stop myself.

Bahlin turned back to face me, and a look of remorse passed over his features. "I've missed you, Maddy. Won't you come home?" He approached me very slowly and reached for my good hand. Static jumped between us and, lifting my hand to his lips, he never took his eyes off my face. But when his lips met the cold weight of the stones, he glanced down.

I choked on a sob and shook my head. "I *am* home, Bahlin."

"Gods alive, I swore to Aiden you wouldn't do this," he said, visibly reeling from the shock the ring had brought. "I swore you were just punishing me, but that's not it, is it?"

"No, it's not." I shook my head and gently took my hand back.

"I was wrong to come."

"Particularly if you only thought to try to coerce me to leave."

"I was actually showing up for duty," he said, bitterness tingeing what should have been benign words. "Seems you've got everything under control, so I'll just be going." He grabbed his leather motorcycle jacket and headed for the parlor door but he couldn't go without one parting shot. "Connell Darach is my magus, Madeleine. At least I didn't have to fuck mine to keep him."

I stood quietly until I heard the front door slam, and then I folded in on myself and sank to the carpet, my one good hand clamped firmly over my mouth so I wouldn't scream in rage or pain. I was too far gone emotionally to give over to angry tears, so I lay there, curled on my side, thinking of all the things I would have loved to have said. Unfortunately, there was no one there to hear me.

Darius wandered into the parlor a while later and froze when he registered the heartbeat in the otherwise silent, dark room. Looking around, he saw my prone form on the floor, and he took a half a dozen large steps to my side and lay cool fingers on the side of my neck. "Maddy? Darling?" he said softly. "Sweet Cain, what is going on in this house while I sleep?" Scooping me up in his arms, he headed for the stairs.

"I don't want to go back to the master," I rasped, my voice rough after the tension it had been under.

"That's fine, love. What kind of man would I be if I were to try to get you into bed in another man's room?" he teased, but I wasn't sure there wasn't some underlying truth to his words. He carried me passed the curious staff and, in particular, a goggling Mark, and headed for the second floor. I hadn't explored the house, so I wasn't sure what the second floor held beyond a couple of bathrooms and bedrooms. Darius held me easily, and I curled into his arms, strangely comfortable with my head tucked under the vampire's chin. Opening the door to a room I wasn't familiar with, he stepped inside confidently and kicked it closed. Darkness enveloped us like a shroud, and I felt inexplicably safe, as if the world couldn't see me because I couldn't see it.

"Foolish girl," Darius chastised, but there wasn't an ounce of malice in his voice. "Don't you know to be afraid of me?"

"How do you know I'm not?" I whispered into the front of his soft silk shirt.

"Your heart rate slowed when the door closed behind us, and you took a deep breath and just…just…well, I suppose you sighed."

"I suppose I did."

He stopped and held me out from him but I clung tightly, turning so I wrapped my arms around his neck. "Would it bother you terribly, Darius, if I asked you to just hang on to me for a moment?"

"Oh, Maddy. I don't mind, my little chick. What will you say if Hellion finds us cuddled up on the sofa?"

"To hell with Hellion," I whispered harshly. I imagined the look on Darius's face and I shook my head and said, "Just pretend he doesn't exist."

"You don't want me to do that, love. Trust me."

"I don't know, Darius. You're the only one who's been honest about just wanting to get into my pants."

He snorted out a laugh, and I felt him sink down into a deep sofa with my weight still held comfortably in his arms.

I turned my face into his chest and whispered, "If I asked you for a favor, would you do it?"

"I've been alive too long to blindly agree to anything, Maddy. But I will agree to help you if it's a reasonable request." He was silent as he waited on me to decide whether to ask or not. I slipped off his lap and settled into his side, and his arm wrapped around my shoulders in a casual manner.

"I'm close to catching the killer, and Hellion and I were going to go out with you and some of your people tonight to hunt. But now Hellion's gone, and Bahlin's been here—"

"Oh sweet hell," Darius snapped, pulling his arm away from me and sitting forward to turn on the lamp.

I squinted into the sudden brightness.

"When were you going to mention this?" he demanded.

"Which part?" I snapped. "Because a lot happened while you were out." I waved my hand under his nose, and he snatched it out of the air.

"Is it official then?" he asked quietly.

"No," I answered, equally quiet. "It's not. It's more a promise now that we'll make bigger promises later. But it wasn't twelve hours this time before it all went to hell." I took my hand back and slipped the ring off, intent on putting it in my pocket.

Faster than thought, Darius snatched the ring out of my hand and was slipping it back on my finger before I could react. "I can't believe I'm doing this," he muttered. "You're going to turn me into a flippin' bleeding heart yet. Look, don't take it off, Maddy. Hellion may be quick-tempered at times," he said, and I snorted, "but he's a good bloke. I've known him since he was a lad. If he saw fit to commit to you, it's for the right reasons. He's a strong sense of right and wrong for all he's a hot-headed prick." He rolled the ring back and forth on my finger and looked at it speculatively. "I've envied him a time or two, Maddy, but never so much as the first time I met you." He looked up, and the depth of feeling in his normally aloof eyes startled me. Darius tightened his hand around mine and lifted it to his mouth for a kiss. "If it had been different, if the Fates had seen fit to put me on the Council before Imeena's disappearance, I like to think destiny would have offered you a third choice." He leaned forward and brushed firm, cool lips over mine and I gently kissed him back. It was superficially platonic, but words went unspoken between us in the seconds he held his lips to mine.

I gently disengaged from the sweet kiss. "You're a good man, Darius." He shook his head, and I reached over to still his face. "You are. Which is why I know you'll honor what I can offer you now instead of looking back at what might have been. I have two suitors, which is one too many. What I don't have, though, are friends. And friendship is what I need the most."

Darius slid off the sofa and pulled me to my feet. Holding my hand over his still heart, he said, "My voyyen is at your disposal, Madeleine Niteclif, whether in an official capacity or a private one." *Ba-boom!* His heart pounded once under my hand and it felt like the house shook. My fingers clutched at his shirt as a primal sexual response was pulled from me at the noise. His eyes widened and he hissed, "No."

"What the hell was that?" I demanded, embarrassed at the moisture collecting between my thighs.

Darius closed his eyes and scented the air, and when he opened his eyes to gaze at me I gasped. They had gone the color of the night sky, that deep purplish-black. "You made my heart beat. It's a mythical talent."

"What—"

"I'll not answer anything else tonight, Maddy. Please, for the sake of our friendship, don't push me on this. All I'm willing to say is that it explains the draw I feel toward you." He rubbed his chest and took a short breath. "Do you want me to gather members of my voyyen and help you hunt tonight?"

I watched him carefully and was surprised to see his movements were far from smooth. Deciding to honor his request to leave it be—didn't I have enough trouble without seeking more out intentionally?—I answered him as strongly as I could. "Yeah, I want to catch the bastard."

"Do you have a plan?"

"Sort of. But I could use a real predator's help."

"Then you've come to the right monster." His arctic smile and dagger-like fangs told me I had, indeed.

Chapter Twenty-Four

The plan was that we would contact the Council and ask for three warriors from each sect. The vampires would provide more because Darius was going to partner with me on point. With Hellion missing and Amaly dead, I had no one to approach and ask for help within the magical sect, so I went to Mark. The poor man nearly had a heart attack.

"I'm not qualified to make those determinations, madam," he said, sweat popping out at his hairline.

I rubbed my forehead and frowned, staring at my shoes. "Mark," I said in exasperation, "the name's Maddy, not madam. Look, just tell me who to ask, because Hellion's MIA, and I'm not waiting on him to get over his temper tantrum."

"I can't, Maddy. I just can't." I suddenly realized what a horrid position I'd unwittingly put Mark in, and I felt like an ass. I'd indirectly asked him to pick a side in the fight Hellion and I were having, and it wasn't his job to do that.

"I'm sorry," I said, and reached out to take his hand. The middle-aged driver and footman, Stearns, who was quite the healer within the coven, had taken the bandages off my right hand, and it was healed with the exception of a small, pink scar where the knife had gone through. "Forget I asked."

His hand shot out and grabbed my arm. "Devlin is Hellion's third. He'd know." He dialed a number on his cell, and I reached out and closed it before the call went through.

"I don't want to put anyone in the coven between Hellion and me. So I'll do without."

"But, Maddy—"

"No, Mark. It's okay. I'd rather not create any hard feelings anywhere."

"Thank you."

I nodded and walked back to the second floor where Darius was having a small, impromptu meeting with ten of his most lethal vampires.

While I felt safe with Darius, these vamps gave me pause. Efein was there along with nine others, all males save one. Introductions were made, and Darius broke down where we were.

"Sarenia can't get here in time, but she will be contacting some of her people and having them meet us at Hyde Park near the fountain. We'll coordinate our efforts by spreading out around the park. It's very important that you stay strictly with the plan, Maddy, because there will only be a few of us nearby to watch you, as you've requested." The tone of his voice made it clear he still didn't agree with me. We'd argued and I'd won, but only when I'd threatened him with rock, paper, scissors. He'd been so shocked he'd laughed and finally acquiesced. Drawn back into the present, I heard Darius giving final instructions to his vampires, and they slid from the room like wraiths to go assume their positions around the park.

Darius came up behind me and rested his hands on my shoulders. "Are you sure about this? You don't want to wait for Hellion?"

"I'd love to wait, but I'm back in London, and another woman's going to die if I don't get this right, Darius." I didn't mention my own consequences should I fail. Shaking my head, I tilted it back to rest on the vampire's shoulder. "No, I can't wait."

"Then let's away, Maddy, before he gets home and threatens to disembowel me with his bare hands."

I nodded, my stomach in my throat. It was easier to be brave when the person with you didn't realize what a coward you really were.

We headed down the stairs when I thought to ask about the shape-shifters' sect. "Did you get in touch with Bahlin?"

"I did. He said he'd send people, but he won't be there himself. I take it whatever happened between you this afternoon was bad."

"Bad enough." If he could be vague about his heartbeat, surely I had the right to be equally vague about my love life.

"Punishing me for not answering you, huh?"

"Shit!" I'd forgotten he could read minds. "Stay out of my head, leech."

"Sure, flower, if you'll stay out of my heart."

I had no idea what he meant, so I kept my mouth shut. I rarely got in trouble when I stuck to that edict.

We got to the park's main entrance along the A4, and I realized what a motley crew we were. At a distance I was sure we looked like a rather normal group of friends, but up close the vampires were lethally beautiful, the weres seemed to have slightly animalistic traits, the random species were smaller and more reserved and the fae were just somehow wrong when you stared at them too long. What they all had in common with each other was that at least one member of each group stared at me with undisguised hostility.

Kelten, king of the fae, walked up to me and bowed slightly at the waist. "Maddy," he said by way of greeting.

"Kelten. How is Gaitha?"

His eyes clouded over, his eyes tightened and his breathing changed slightly. "She's not well, Maddy. I'm afraid there's naught to be done for her at this point. I'll keep her contained as well as I may, but if it comes to it, she'll have to be executed."

I reeled with shock at his heartfelt pronouncement. First the loss of his son, then the potential loss of his wife. It seemed so unfair. I held out my hand and he took it, looking at me with grief clearly marring his otherwise lineless skin. "I'm so sorry, Kelten."

"Thank you, Maddy. It means a great deal to hear." He moved away and Praen, his niece, approached.

"Niteclif," she said, holding out her hand to shake in a more modern greeting than her uncle's.

I froze with a smile on my face though I managed to briefly shake her hand.

Darius laid his hand at the small of my back. "Praen. How do you fare?" he asked the fae.

"Well, though Aunt Gaitha is not. I'll tell her you asked after her, Niteclif."

"Do that," I said softly, and she inclined her pale blonde head before walking away. I turned to Darius, my eyes undoubtedly wide. "Do you think—" I began.

"It's possible. She's very brazen in coming here if it's her."

"True." I relaxed and felt him lean in closer. Turning my head toward him, I met his sharpened gaze. "I'm still bothered by the peripheral sound I heard when I was attacked. I'm pretty damn sure there was another person in the room. If I'm right, the person watched the assault and did nothing to intervene. Do you think Imeena could be a part of this?"

"Hm. I suppose it's possible, though she's never been the type to passively sit and watch violence occur." He idly ran a hand up and down my arm. "She's much more inclined to participate."

I shivered and closed my eyes briefly.

Darius stopped stroking my arm and tightened his hand on my bicep. "I'll be near all night, Maddy."

"Thanks." I stood straight and saw a shorter woman with long, brown hair weaving through the foot traffic as she made her way toward me. The towering younger man who followed in her wake had eyes only for me.

"Darius, stay here," I commanded. "Don't leave me."

"Wouldn't dream of it."

The petite woman stopped in front of me, and I had no doubt she would have done me physical harm had we been locked in a room together.

"Adelle," I said, greeting Bahlin's mother. "Aiden."

"You are *not* good enough for my son, you...you..." she sputtered, stepping well inside my personal space. She raised her hand to slap me, and I grabbed it in an instinctive block before letting my hand fall away from hers. Aiden reached out and grabbed my arm as it fell away.

"Hands off, junior," I said quietly, aware that most of the supes were watching us, either openly or indirectly. Either way, we had an audience.

"You're going to want to back off, madam," Darius said, and his voice was cold enough that it felt like the air just before a heavy snow, the bitter promise of a storm held in check. He stepped up next to me and laid a hand on her arm. "Step back. Now."

"You bitch," she hissed. "You've cost me the last you'll cost me you...you...*whore!*" she spat. Spinning out from under Darius's arm, she stalked off, taking Aiden with her. They stopped at the edge of the fountain area, and Aiden looked back at me like I was a delicious treat he'd get to carve up later.

"Okay, this is just getting freaky," I said, slipping under Darius's outstretched arm and tucking into his side. "I'm seeing murder suspects everywhere I look, and I'm not liking it."

Darius bent his head to whisper in my ear, his voice tickling as it skated across my skin. "Tell me what you see."

"Kelten's got darker hair, and his skin is darker than most of the fae's, though I'm not sure it's dark enough. But his wife, Gaitha? Blond hair, wicked powers and bat-shit crazy enough he's considering executing her for everyone's safety. Praen's got the hair, the skin tone, the power and the ability. I'd bet my life on it." I paused, thinking that might not be the best bet to make. Darius rubbed my back briskly and I continued. "Adelle referred to me as a whore, just like in the letter, and obviously thinks of me as a traitor. She's got the hair and skin color of my attacker, and is undoubtedly strong enough. Aiden's just a kid, but he's turning into a violent little shit, and he'd do anything for his brother or his mother." I looked around, taking into consideration all the other hostile glances I was gathering. "Too many suspects," I whispered, shaking my head. "I don't know, Darius..."

"Don't doubt yourself." He pulled me in for a tight hug and then set me back from him. "You've been clear you're living at Hellion's, Hyde Park is near his home, and we expect the killer to have followed you out. He, or she, will see you out with a bunch of supes and either run, and we'll catch him, or he'll attack, and we'll catch him. Go out and know I'm watching over you."

Something wasn't sitting well with Darius's logic, but the plan had been mine so out I went. It was going to be a long night.

I walked the dark bike path slowly, truly lost in thought. I saw and heard no one, but I knew they were there. The sounds of the night were hushed, even the smallest insects silenced with the knowledge predators moved among them. And that's really what the supes were—superior predators.

A twig snapped and I froze, afraid to turn around. I had to trust Darius and the others would keep me safe, and those who truly wanted me dead wouldn't converge on me all at once. I began walking again and slipped off the bike path, hoping that if the killer was out there, he'd make his move.

Thinking over all the clues as well as the attack last night, I wondered if I'd been right in assuring both Hellion and myself that the attacker had been a male. The voice had been deep, but that meant nothing. Voices were easy to disguise. And I'd just acknowledged the superiority of the supes as predators, so to think one could hold me down and take me out—well, it was entirely reasonable it could have been a woman.

What about the attacker's hands? I wondered. I hadn't seen much after I'd been stabbed. Unconsciously I curled my fingers over the scar that marred the palm. And before that? What had I seen? Not enough to say for sure.

The coins in each body were really bothering me. Why was the killer leaving a calling card? Who would have access to those coins? The basic answer was anyone in Bahlin's family. But with his dad and sister dead, it left the mother and two brothers as suspects. Could Adelle kill? For either of her sons, or her dead daughter, I was willing to say that she not only could, but would.

Then there was the method of attack: from the back, with a sharp instrument of some type. The killer expected me to recognize him or her, so surprise was an element of necessity. I shook my head and kept walking.

I couldn't figure out where the blond hair would come in to play, either. The killer had thought to accomplish something specific in leaving it first at Hellion's and then at Amaly's. What if it was as simple as being able to materialize in their homes? It made the most basic sense, because where Hellion was, so was I. Being able to circumvent the protective wards around the houses—well, that was a huge bonus. It gave the killer the ability to bypass some of Hellion's most important safeguards.

The smell of burning hair was another stumper, and as I walked and considered it, it was almost as if I could smell it again. I shook my head and smiled at my overactive imagination. I had to chill out about this stuff. I was working myself into a real—

Like before, the blow came from behind and sent me sprawling into the dirt. I rolled over and threw my hands up as silver flashed toward my face. The slashing pain of the blade cutting into my left arm was wicked, and I screamed, kicking out with my legs. I swung my good arm out and connected with the knife hand, and I knocked the knife loose, sending it skittering across the gravel. The black, smoky mist began to coalesce into the form of a human and, then it scattered to the breeze as Darius grabbed me up off the ground and ran with me at frightening speed. It wasn't until we came to a stop and I wiped my streaming eyes that I realized we'd made it all the way home.

The front door flew open and Mark ushered us in, pointing us toward the kitchen and calling for Stearns. The magus appeared quickly, carrying a small first aid kit. Ripping my sleeve away, he sighed. This was heavy conversation for the normally silent man. I smiled at him and was about to offer him some light-hearted banter until he began to clean the wound. I instinctively tried to snatch my arm away but Darius wasn't having any of it. He held me in place as Stearns cleaned me up and bandaged the arm.

"Hellion's going to kill you," Stearns said, looking squarely at me for the first time as he put the final wrap on the Ace bandage holding the butterfly bandages and gauze in place.

"He'll have to get in line," I muttered.

"I'm already there."

Hellion was home.

Darius stood and moved between us. While I appreciated the gesture, this was between Hellion and me.

"Darius?" I said gently. "Can you give me some time with Hellion, please? I'd like you to stay here tonight and help gather information about the events that happened, particularly after I was attacked."

"You were *what*?" Hellion yelled.

"You weren't here, mate, so she had to go it with her secondary players," Darius said in the voice I was beginning to think of as his Glacial Voice. He'd used it a lot lately, and always on my behalf.

Hellion said nothing, just stood glaring at the wound on my arm.

"I'm going back to the park to clean up any mess left behind, and I'll meet with you either just before sunrise or first thing this evening." Darius bent and bussed my cheek before turning and rushing out of the room without another word to Hellion.

"Care to bring me up to speed?" Hellion asked cautiously. I looked up and realized all the other coven members had left when the vampire did. We were alone in the kitchen.

"Sure." I flexed my arm and grimaced at the tight, raw feeling of the wound. I told Hellion about the plan and the park, and calling the Council together, and his face grew more and more grim, the lines around his mouth become deeper, the black of his eyes broader, and his breaths shorter. I finished with my arrival here in Darius's arms. Hellion stood there, unspeaking.

"Do you realize I could have lost you tonight?" he asked, trying to master the emotions leaking into his voice.

"Don't you realize you could have lost me when you left?" I fidgeted with the edge of the bandage, refusing to look at him for fear it would be my undoing, and I'd either beg him to stay or demand that he go.

He stepped close to me, the tips of his shoes quickly breaking the plane of my vision. A hand reached out and lifted my chin and I let him, though I closed my eyes.

"Please, Maddy. Look at me." I hesitated and he squeezed my chin. "Please."

I slowly opened my eyes and stared at him.

"I will get down on my knees, I will lay prostrate on the floor, I will abject myself in whatever way you deem necessary, if you will only forgive me." True to his word, he went to his knees, but I was somehow unmoved, my heart guarded against his pleas for absolution. "Do you want me to beg? Because I'll do that too."

Swallowing hard, Hellion reached out and took my hands, fingering the ring I still wore though it was now coated in my dried blood. "When I left, I went to Ballinlough and spent the day at the lake, thinking. I was so angry with you for denying me my vengeance, not only on Amaly's behalf, Maddy, but also on yours. You crucified me when you said I'd failed in my best efforts to keep you safe." He rubbed his jaw and sat back on his heels, finally resting his fidgety hands palm down on his thighs. "I'd failed you, Maddy, after doing what I'd considered my best. I was terrified that if I couldn't protect you in our own home I'd stand no chance in the outside world. I've been so powerful for so long that it was debilitating to realize what I have, what I *am*, might not be enough." He reached out a hand and gripped my ankle, bending forward to lay his forehead on my knees. I didn't touch him, but he continued anyway. "I thought of the million ways I might lose you, Maddy, but it wasn't until I watched the sun set across the lake that I realized the biggest threat came from within our own home."

I fought to keep from reaching out and stroking his head. "And what's the biggest threat, Hellion?"

"Me. My tendency to walk away in anger may find me coming home one day to an empty house. I nearly died at the thought, Maddy, and then when I got home and you weren't here... I nearly went berserk. I'd only been back a few minutes when Darius came in with you."

Wrath

I nodded and gave in to the urge to lay my hand on his head. "You can't leave me every time I make you mad, Hellion, or we'll never spend any time together."

He snorted with laughter, and his shoulders shook slightly with an emotion his hidden face protected. "I'll give you my word, Maddy, that I'll never walk out on you again. Forgive me, I'm begging you. Forgive me, and I'll show you a staying power you've not experienced from me. Just...forgive me." He lifted his face and met my eyes.

I reached down and grabbed his face with my hands, ignoring the pain in my arm, and said, "Don't you ever, *ever*, leave me again, Hellion. The next time you walk out on me in anger will be the last time. Do you understand?"

"I do. But I'll ask the same of you. Don't you ever walk out on me. I'll covenant with you now to stay, but you must do the same. I may be your destiny, Madeleine Niteclif, but so are you mine. And even destiny leaves room for choices made of free will. Do you choose to fight with me, not against me?"

I nodded, unspeaking. *Destiny leaves room for choices made of free will.* Hellion might be my destiny, but I'd reaffirmed that destiny by choosing him in every way that would tie me to him permanently—by wearing his ring, publicly moving into his home, dismissing my dragon in Ireland and again last night in London, and confessing my love for this magus. I'd exercised free will in my decision-making, though it had all been done in his favor.

So how much is actually free will, then? my subconscious asked yet again.

I sighed and admonished myself to, for once, just shut the hell up. Scrubbing my good hand over my face, I nodded at him. "I don't want to fight with you, Hellion. There will be so many times I can imagine we won't agree, particularly when it comes to my function as Niteclif, but you have to remember justice is mine to interpret, though not necessarily to administer. You can have a hand in the second, and influence the first, but it's ultimately mine to determine. If you take that from me, you may doom me to an existence worse than death. I love you, but I won't choose to fade for anyone. I deserve more consideration than that from you."

He started in surprise, and fresh hurt flashed across his features. "I never considered my demands to be a choice you had to accept or decline, Maddy, but you're right. And to potentially cause you to fade?

Gods and goddesses alike would have to fight me to keep me from following you. I don't know how I'd manage, but I'd find a way. I won't leave you again."

I had a horrid question to ask, but if I could face Bahlin down alone, I should be able to confront Hellion. "I'm going to ask you one time, because I have no choice, and I expect you to answer me without arrogance or anger. Are we clear?"

He nodded, curiosity decorating his face. "Anything, Maddy."

"You were gone tonight when I was attacked, then you were here as fast as we were. The mist that struck me was just like the mist that hit me in the park when we were separated but you were near. Hellion, do you have any part in these attacks and/or murders?" I held my breath, anxiety beating on my back so it was hard to draw a lungful of air, but I wouldn't give my fear over to it. I sat still, waiting for his answer.

He stood slowly, his eyes pulsing and his face pale and taught, pulled tight over the bones of his skull. "I will answer you this one time, Madeleine, in your capacity as Niteclif. I swear on the magic and capability within me that I did not do these things. I swear I have never, nor will I ever, raise a hand to you with harmful intent. I swear I have been honest and genuine in my desires to help solve this case." He voice was formal and cool, though not nearly as frigid as the vampire's.

I nodded and stood, weaving slightly with exhaustion and hunger. Still behaving in a reserved manner, Hellion was solicitous and careful with me as I returned to our bedroom, going so far as to order dinner be delivered to my room since I hadn't eaten tonight. Once there, he sat next to me on the covers and waited on the food. The silence was heavy and uncomfortable, and I knew he felt it too because he was unable to sit still, forever moving around and straightening things: the front of his shirt, the duvet, the clock on the nightstand. It was driving me nuts.

A knock at the door had us both yelling, "Come in."

Mark entered, carrying the dinner tray, and I was relieved to see him until I realized he was avoiding looking at me. Apparently there would be no camaraderie from that corner. He set the tray down and left, the click of the door as he closed it seeming to smash through the room.

At my wit's end, I finally broke. "Look, are you going to speak to me or just hover? Because, frankly, it was easier when you were gone than it is to endure what's going on now."

Hellion jerked as if I'd slapped him. "You want me to leave?"

"For such an intelligent man, you are such a moron sometimes," I bitched, lifting the lid off the tray and finding my favorite meal: a McDonald's burger and fries. I sighed. I'd have to kiss Mark full on the lips for this one.

He stood and towered over me. "I'm not leaving. I'm just banjaxed that you'd consider it of me."

I set my fries down slowly and laid my hands one on each side of the tray. "I'm going to say this slowly so you'll process it clearly. If you'd been here when the attacks happened, would I have had to ask?" I answered my own question before he could. "No. I wouldn't. I don't understand you sometimes. For such a logical guy with an alchemist's mind, you allow your arrogance and emotions to impede your vision. You're angry at me for having to ask, when my actions are a direct result of yours. Why is it my fault?"

His shoulders slumped some as she stood at the end of the bed, one hand hooked behind his neck and the other in his pants pocket. "I'm sometimes disturbed I understand you. You make me feel like such a gouger, love."

"Gouger?" I asked around a mouthful of burger. I was frustrated but I was also hungry, and I wasn't letting my burger go to waste.

"Irish slang for an aggressive asshole."

I raised one eyebrow and kept eating, not disagreeing with his sentiment.

"Fair enough," he muttered, and sat down on the edge of the bed. "I'm sorry. Again. I just don't want to believe you'd think these things of me!" he shouted, making me jump.

I smashed my hamburger down on the tray and scrambled out of bed, furious. "I don't *want* to think these things! They come to me, like I'm logic impaired with a gift of vision! Half the time I don't know what the hell to do with the thoughts that come into my head. Do I share them, and risk looking the fool, or do I sit on them and risk someone else dying? And if I *do* share them, and the wrong conclusions are drawn, who am I condemning to death with my ignorance!" I screamed, shaking with rage and terror. I'd just unwittingly vocalized my deepest fears since this whole life evolution had begun.

Hellion stood in front of me, gobsmacked at my outburst. He opened his mouth several times as if to begin to say something only to close it and start again. Finally, he sat down on the foot bench and bent forward, dropping his elbows to his knees and letting his hair hide his face as it fell forward.

I stood there shaking, angry and scared that I'd just bared this piece of my soul to him and he'd been unsure what to make of it. I needed him to help me build a foundation for this responsibility, not wonder where to put the next stone.

A strange sound, similar to wind whipping through tall pines, caught my attention. Without any other warning than that, I collapsed to the floor in a boneless heap as I was lifted from my physical self into the astral plane.

Tyr drew me into his arms and hugged me so tight I couldn't move. I could hear Hellion yelling at me, and my astral self even twitched as he shook me, but Tyr never let go. "Madeleine Niteclif," he whispered into my ear, "do you have any idea how close you came to death tonight?" He held me back at arm's length and looked me over carefully. I turned to look at Hellion, frantically trying to wake me, and I saw other coven members barge into the room en masse. "They are going to pull you back into your body, so I must be fast. I apologize for the abrupt meeting, but I had to speak to you. Things are progressing quickly with some of the killer's decisions tonight. You must act fast to stop him or you will lose one of your heart's own, Maddy."

"My heart's... Do you mean Hellion?" I gasped, terrified at the thought. A strange sensation of having my bellybutton tugged at from the inside began, and it was gross. I shuffled around and found the coven standing, hands joined, in a circle around my fallen physical body.

"To say you love only Hellion is a falsehood. A piece of your heart is Bahlin's, which is why you couldn't commit to marrying Hellion just yet. You must resolve that piece first for the union to last, Madeleine."

"Just Maddy, Tyr," I growled, and he glowered at me.

"Fine. You're about to be ripped back into consciousness, and it's disorienting, so I'll leave you with this. You touched the killer tonight, Maddy. Narrow it down, and fast."

The tugging on my bellybutton changed to a burning feeling as I was slammed back into my body. I involuntarily arched my back off the floor and gasped for air, my heels digging for purchase. I fell back to the floor and, breathing heavily, demanded, "What the effing hell was that?"

"Maddy!" Hellion fell to his knees, gathered me up in his arms and clutched me to his chest, rocking back and forth. "Odin save me, I didn't know what happened."

"Tyr pulled me aside for a little pep talk," I murmured into his chest. I leaned my head back to find him looking down at me, his eyes entirely black with the power he'd wielded. "Can you not tell when I'm in the astral plane?"

"Normally I can and, on occasion, I may even be able to project myself along with you. But it takes time and concentration, and I'm afraid to say I had neither available to me tonight." He refused to let go of me, and I snuggled into him. "Thank you, everyone," Hellion said to the crowd still hanging around. "I think we're done with emergencies this evening, so feel free to go home and tend to your own lives." The smile in his voice was clear. "Your allegiance and support are much appreciated."

"Thanks." My voice was still muffled by his shirt but it was intelligible. Seriously, he was going to have to let me breathe. I pushed back and found him watching me, even as he addressed the few remaining hangers-on personally as they left the room.

Hellion finally let me up, and I went to the sofa and sank down, holding out a hand to him in a silent offer to join me. He came to me quickly and took a seat, dropping his arm around me and laying his chin on my head. "I'm incredibly sorry," he whispered, "for everything. I'm going to expand my covenant to promise you I'll work on humility."

I thought of all the times he'd held me as I cried for Bahlin, his sticking power through an investigation that made him as uncomfortable as it made me, and his willingness to take a long-term chance on someone who listed "potential to fade to non-existence" as a job hazard, and I forgave him all of it. "The effort would be appreciated, but don't change for me, Hellion. I've fallen in love with the man you are, not the man you might be."

He tilted me head back and laid his forehead against mine. "I'd like nothing more than to kiss you, to reestablish our connection in a way we both know and understand."

I rested a hand on his cheek and shifted my lips so they angled over his. He kissed me long and slow, and the tensions of the last twelve hours faded. I pulled away reluctantly, but I knew my window of opportunity here was small. "Tyr told me I'd touched the killer tonight."

"Touched how?"

"I didn't have the chance to ask. I just assumed he meant touched-touched, as in 'laid my hand on' somehow." I rubbed my sweaty right palm against my pants unconsciously and shook my head. "I'm sure he meant physically touched. He admonished me to hurry, Hellion, or risk..." I paused, not wanting to admit the last of Tyr's warning.

"Risk what, love?"

I swallowed hard and closed my eyes before answering. "You or Bahlin."

"Ah, so the dragon's a factor then. I suppose that means he's innocent."

I pushed away from him and stood, stunned I hadn't made the connection. Tyr had given me the biggest clue he could, and I'd fumbled it. I was a walking catastrophe. Shaking off the chains of self-punishment, I said, "I suppose he is."

"I'll accept that, Maddy. Despite my earlier actions, I do want the right person brought to justice." He stood and walked to the fireplace and picked up a picture on the mantle that I'd never paid attention to. It was an old, sepia-toned photo, and I wandered over to see what was so intriguing to him about it.

The photo was cracked, obviously having been folded at some point in its long life, and the edges were split, dirty and frayed. The glass frame that currently held and protected it was probably the kindest thing that had been done to the photo since it had been taken.

Hellion traced a finger down the front of the glass, and I saw where his eyes rested, on a woman with pale hair and bright eyes who looked up at the man standing next to her in the group shot with open adoration. Amaly.

"You must miss her," I said, laying my hand on his back.

"I grieve her like I've lost a sister, a blooded member of my family," he said. I could taste his grief like the bitterest of pills swallowed, and I hurt for him.

He sighed and turned away from the photo. "I sincerely want to catch her killer, Madeleine, and I will be petitioning the Council to allow me to carry out the execution." His voice was nearly flat, monotone, as if he expected me to fight so he'd taken the fight out of the words as they were spoken.

"Okay."

He lifted his head and looked at me, and the look on his face said I wouldn't have shocked him more if I'd asked his butler to be part of a spontaneous ménage. Shivering with the ickiness of that mental image, I stepped even closer to him and met his astonished gaze. "You need this, Hellion. I get that. Just promise me you'll take precautions and make it a quick kill. No dragging it out in the name of vengeance, whether for Amaly or for pride."

"My word." The oath was as filled with emotion as his words moments ago had been devoid of it.

I nodded. That was settled.

Now we had to catch the bastard.

Chapter Twenty-Five

We grabbed a fast four hours of sleep and were sitting down to lunch when Stearns came in. He walked slowly, his narrow shoulders hunched like he was burdened with heavy news. Unfortunately I didn't realize how right I was.

"Sir, Niteclif." He looked anywhere but at me. "There's news."

Hellion set his napkins down on the table and reached for my hand. "Best get it over with, Stearns. Was it someone we know?"

He shook his head, and I released a breath I hadn't realized I was holding. "Three women were killed last night, their heads completely severed. London's in an uproar, sir, and the police are at the door."

Shit. We'd completely forgotten the police.

"If they see me sitting here, they're going to assume you're acting out some passive-aggressive rage issue that you have with me." I stood and looked quickly around the room. I could go through the kitchen and maybe out the back door—

"Stop, Maddy. I've done nothing wrong." He stood and offered me a hand.

"Now who's being naïve?" I snapped, fear giving my words a nasty bite. "Haven't you ever watched *American Justice*?" I shook my head. "Dumb question. I don't suppose you have. It's just, well, the police need someone to pin the fears of the commonwealth on, and you're it." I tugged at my hand and tried to get free of his grasp, but he wouldn't let go.

"I've made up my mind not to leave you, *mo chroí*, so here's where I'll stay." He turned to Stearns and said, "Show the guarda in, then you and Mark bar the front door in the event something goes wrong."

Stearns's eyes rounded and he nodded quickly, backing out of the room and never breaking his wide gaze from Hellion's calm face.

"Hellion," I said, warning lacing my voice. "What could go wrong?"

"I'd hate to make a misstep, so I'll take a simple precaution. Do you wish to stay or go?" he asked, rolling up his sleeves. He glanced over at me, and once again his eyes were a light brown. While his black eyes had creeped me out at first, and made his face feel cold and hostile, now they were just his eyes. Seeing the artificial brown felt entirely wrong.

I looked away and said, "I'll stay."

"You'll be an accomplice, love. Be sure."

"I want it noted that I think you're taking this 'not leaving me' thing a little far, but it's fine. I'll stay. Will there be blood?" I asked, my voice squeaky.

"No," he chuckled. "No blood. Just loosely harnessed power, and it takes people funny sometimes. Gives me a terrible cockstand."

The door swung open, and the two inspectors walked into the room with clear intent. They weren't leaving without Hellion. I backed away, and my movement drew their attention. Neither of them could hide their reaction at finding the perfectly profiled victim in their suspect's home. I gave them a little finger wave of acknowledgment.

"Have you been harmed, madam?" the taller of the two asked.

"Nope. I'm good." I scooted further along the wall that was now at my back, intent on getting closer to Hellion.

"Stop there, sweetheart," he said.

I froze.

I heard one of the men gasp, and I looked up just as the wind of Hellion's power roared over me in a fiery wash that went straight to the juncture of my thighs. It was like an hour of really good foreplay in an instant. I groaned and found myself anchored to the wall by the invisible bonds of his will. It infuriated me. I tugged and struggled, but the strength of his will alone held me.

The two inspectors were suffering similar fates, and dimly I recalled Hellion saying he couldn't create something that wasn't there. Clearly these men had sufficient lusts to be drawn on, but the curious question was to whom were they drawn?

Hellion's voice seemed to whisper through my head. *"Unam oblvionis, oblivion duo, memoriam tuam accipio ut ad tenebrosam caliginem mentem." Oblivion for one, oblivion for two, I take your memories to the dark and make it the mist of the mind.*

The power in the room increased, and the chandelier swung in the breeze as napkins and papers blew about. The men stood rooted to the floor, unable to take their eyes off Hellion. I was suffering a similar fate, but there was no question from where my lust generated. One of the officers was rapidly rubbing his erection through his pants, and I watched in fascination as the other seemed to want to fight off the magic that threatened to consume him. Hellion's voice came again through my mind, repeating the same words with more conviction. With each word he loosed in my subconscious, my consciousness reached for him.

I looked up and was almost frightened of the man he'd morphed into. He felt larger than the simple capacity the room could contain. His power made the air crackle, and it felt like the room itself was trying to conduct lightning with aluminum foil—too much power insufficiently harnessed inside such a little space. This power was elemental and belonged in the wide-open spaces of the cliffs of Ireland, where the power could commune with the sea and the sky. Hellion's eyes had disappeared, and in their place were hollows of black that appeared to be vacant until you looked closely and realized things moved just beneath the surface of that obsidian gaze, things you dared not look straight at for fear they might see you, recognize you, want you.

Hellion threw out an arm and pointed at the two men. He made a harsh slashing motion with his right arm and said sharply, "*Est perfectus.*" *It is done.*

The bonds that had held me to the wall let go, and I slid to the floor on legs as reliable as democracy. I trembled with need and mewled when Hellion's hand reached for me. I shook my head in denial, terrified at the purely sexual need I felt for him.

The shorter of the two officers looked down and realized he was still rubbing his fading erection, but the stain on the front of his pants said it was post-masturbation kindness he was showing himself. His partner looked over and stared at the man's groin, and I wondered again what lusts Hellion had raised that this man, wearing a timeworn wedding ring, didn't want to recognize.

The short officer was flame red in the face and ears when he said, "You'll have to excuse us. I seem to have had an accident." His partner didn't seem so inclined to believe it had been an accident, but he didn't question it out loud. Instead, they filed out of the room, looking curiously over the chaos of the room. They'd forgotten the wind as much as they'd forgotten the reason they'd been there at all.

The dining room door swung shut behind them, and I launched

myself up off the floor, clawing my way up Hellion like he was a mountain to be scaled. "Please, please, please," I begged between kisses, wrapping my legs around his waist and grinding against him.

He took five large steps to the dining room table and swept off the dishes and silverware with one pass of his arm. He peeled me off him and flipped me over on my stomach, ripping my cotton lounge pants down around my ankles. I cried out as the cool air hit my inflamed lips, and suddenly he was there. The broad head of his penis penetrated me without apology, stretching me to the point where pain and pleasure converged, my natural lubricant so abundant that he slid home with one push despite my tight channel.

Hellion groaned and I began to push against him, encouraging him to find a rhythm that would help me get to the crescendo.

He didn't give me a choice. Hands gripping my hips, Hellion began to move in a way that bordered on contained violence, pounding into me mercilessly. I grunted with each slamming stroke, and I could feel my orgasm building immediately. The dregs of magic seemed to swirl and stroke all my most private places, and he coaxed it with words I couldn't understand so it seemed there were suddenly a dozen hands pinching and tugging at my clit and my nipples, stroking my lips and tracing down my spine. I couldn't form intelligent words as I scrabbled with my hands against the wood to gain some handhold that would let me be more than just the recipient. But it was useless. Hellion rode me hard, fast and deep, his thrusts bruising my hips as they hit the edge of the table over and over. I screamed as my orgasm tore through me, lighting me up from the inside. I felt Hellion's response and he thrust once more, buried as deep as he could get, shaking with the power of his release.

He kept making small mini thrusts, as if he couldn't quite let go of the pleasure, and so long as his continued, so did mine.

I felt him slip from me, and I grunted in response to the sensation. Lifting my head, I was horrified at the state of the room. Broken dishes and food were slung across the floor where Hellion had swept them with his arm. Napkins and paperwork were all over the place, chairs were overturned and the chandelier was still swinging. I pushed myself to standing then bent gingerly to pull up my pants, only to find them in tatters around my ankles. I'd been going through a lot of clothing since I'd a) become involved in the supernatural world and b) started having sex with the supes. My mind closed off at the track that was taking, doing what it could to protect the few shreds of what I considered decency I had left. I blushed furiously, those last few shreds sending up the white flag of surrender.

"What is it, *a mhuirnín?*"

"What is it?" I choked out. "The entire household is going to know what we've been doing! Adelle was right. I'm a whore." I shook my head, frustrated despite the lingering effects of mind-blowing sex.

"She said *what?*" Hellion stood and tucked himself back into his pants. He was white with rage, and I worried a little that I was going down a road I didn't want to travel.

"Can we just go to the bedroom? Do that dematerialize thing and save me from having to face the coven just yet?" I pleaded.

Hellion dropped his head forward and placed his clenched fists on his hips. "You're embarrassed again." It was a statement of fact, and one I wouldn't deny. "Maddy, the supernatural world has an entirely different take on sex than the mundane world. Sex is a natural thing between adults. We're fortunate we're very much in love, because it makes it better, and our species focuses on consent."

My head whipped around and I said, "What do you mean 'our species'?"

"You're right. *My* species of magi is concerned with consent. For some creatures of the supernatural, taking by force is as reputable as taking by seduction." His brows drew together, and he seemed to struggle with a question for a moment before asking, "Do you see us as so different, then?"

"No, it's just the consent thing that stumped me."

"You should have realized even dragons don't always consider consent essential, Maddy."

I groaned and thumped my head against the wall. "You're right. Great super sleuth I'm turning out to be."

He dropped a heavy hand gently to my shoulder and turned me around, offering me his opened arms, which I gladly accepted. He hugged me and set his lips just above my ear and whispered, "You've done an amazing job. Let's get you cleaned up, and we'll see if we can't put an end to this."

I nodded, tears inexplicably burning the back of my throat. Solving this case was going to put him in direct jeopardy because I knew the killer wouldn't just accept judgment for the crimes committed against the presumably "inferior" mundanes. No, the killer would have guilt determined and be taken down outside the safety of a stone circle. It wasn't going to be quiet or easy.

Hellion wrapped me in his arms and I clung to him, suddenly scared my time with him might be running out.

The day's light was fading as we wandered downstairs to meet Darius when he rose for the night. We'd read the online news reports of the most recent murders, discussed the locations of the bodies as they'd been found in the tony neighborhoods surrounding Hyde Park, and dissected every clue we'd uncovered in the course of the investigation. Nothing was gelling for me in the face of my blossoming fear that Hellion was going to end up fighting a bloody battle to see his vengeance served.

Mark and Stearns had been very solicitous in the wake of the dining room debacle, more impressed with Hellion's borderline dark magic than the resultant orgasmic earthquake and the mess we'd made. I tried to find reasons to leave the room every time they were around until, finally fed up with my doorway sprints, Hellion snagged me around the waist and pulled me into his lap. I struggled ineffectually and finally just gave up.

Darius strolled into the room looking delicious in black leather pants, combat boots and a tight cashmere turtleneck, also in black. He was completely healed. I couldn't help the once-over I gave him. Misinterpreting my careful perusal, he arched his brow and turned, striking a pose that gave me a perfect view of his ass. "Like what you see, Maddy?" His voice was teasing but there was still an undercurrent of something unidentifiable there, and it made me stop the easy rejoinder that was on the tip of my tongue and just make a noncommittal noise. "Hellion," Darius said, inclining his head. Tensions between the men were still higher than when I'd first met them, and the only denominator their strange behavior seemed to have was me.

"So," I said, desperately casting about for a way to direct the conversation. "Tyr pulled me into a little impromptu visit early this morning." The vampire never took his eyes off mine as he poured himself a glass of wine, so I continued. "He said I 'touched the killer' last night, and it was important that I get this tied up quickly." I swallowed the lump of fear building in my throat, and I closed my eyes,

271

concentrating on keeping him out of my thoughts.

He looked at me hard, and I felt the fingers of his mind poking around mine.

I shook my head and the feeling subsided. "Do you remember who I touched? I've gone over everyone I met, but most supes don't shake hands, and I was able to rule them out in groups. I've got Praen, who did shake my hand, Adelle, who went to slap me and I stopped her—"

"Come again?" Hellion demanded.

"Leave it alone. It's done." I ran my hand across his shoulder, and he trapped my hand with his, bringing it to his lips for a kiss. Remembering the way he and Darius had gone at each other only a couple of nights ago, I took my hand away and patted his knee, sliding off his lap to sit beside him. If it bothered him, he said nothing. "So there's Praen, Adelle and who? Who else that fits with the clues we know to be factual and not speculative?"

"You're forgetting me," Darius said, his voice making me shiver involuntarily as I thought of silk sheets and whipped cream and... Obviously there were residual effects from this afternoon's power surge. Hellion stroked my hand, and suddenly all I could think of was the silk sheets, whipped cream and these two men undeniably at my service. Darius's eyes widened almost imperceptibly, and he took a breath. When he didn't say anything, I realized he'd been scenting my arousal. Hellion must have suspected as much because he started to open his mouth, and I laid my hand on his thigh, close to his groin. He unconsciously shifted so my hand grazed his testicles, and they tightened in response. There was too much sexual energy in this room for this to be normal. Someone had to tone it down, and the way the men were looking at me made it clear neither of them would take the initiative.

So I cleared my voice loudly and said, "Who. Else. Someone throw in some ideas, now, before this pisses me off. And no, I'm not forgetting you. You aren't doing this."

Darius took a long sip of his wine and looked down, seeming to gather himself. "There are two others you're dismissing, though one touched you and you touched one. The first is Aiden, Bahlin's brother. When you stopped his mother from striking you, he grabbed your arm."

"But does that count? I mean, technically, he touched *me*, I didn't touch *him*."

"Because only you spoke to Tyr, I believe we're going to have to defer to your interpretation of his words to you," Hellion said, sitting forward and reaching for his whiskey glass. I'd elected a Coke tonight in lieu of alcohol. I needed the caffeine.

"I'm going to say he's not at the top of the list because he touched me, not the other way around." I tapped my fingers against my teeth as I thought, and Hellion finally reached over and grabbed my hand to make me stop.

"Thanks, Hellion," Darius drawled. "I was about to ask you to roast me again just to get her to quit." And with that jab at my expense, the men seemed to ease down and things were back to normal.

"Sorry," I murmured, watching them as they interacted. I envied the easy friendship that seemed to usually exist between them, and I hoped Darius and I would be able to develop that same comfortable familiarity over time. I thought we were well on our way. "Sorry," I said again, stronger this time. "My mind was wandering." I shook my head as if to clear the imaginary cobwebs, and I turned to Darius. "Who else, Darius? You said I was dismissing two others. Aiden's one. Who's the—" My stomach clenched and I grabbed it, bending over. "Oh shit. Oh shit. Oh shit. I know who it is."

Darius stood and stepped toward me, hand outstretched, but Hellion was closer. He swept me up in his arms and cradled me close to his chest. "Who, love?"

I shook my head violently, whispering, "No," over and over under my breath.

"Just tell me, Maddy." Hellion's arms tightened around me and held me protectively.

Darius opened his mouth to speak the name, and I screeched at him, "NO! Don't you dare say it, Darius."

Darius's voice cracked across the small room like a gunshot and was as effective as a physical slap to knock me out of my panic. "Madeleine Niteclif, you are not a coward, so stop behaving as such. Hellion, set her down."

Hellion looked thunderous but I took a shaking breath and nodded, standing on my own feet as Hellion released me. Shaky, but I'd do. "I'll thank you later."

"Care to elaborate on why the name fills you with dread?" Darius looked pointedly over my shoulder at Hellion, who was still hovering.

I rubbed the tight feeling that was gathering between my breasts and nodded. "Hellion said..." I had to stop and breathe.

"Whatever I said, Maddy, it can't be this bad." Hellion wrapped long arms around my waist and rested his chin on my shoulder. I laid my cheek against his and he whispered, "We'll handle it together."

"But that's just it. You didn't know if we could handle it. You said, oh Hellion, you said that if it was...Gaitha, you didn't know how we'd stop her."

"The mad queen was at the park?" he asked, clearly confused.

"No, but if she would have been hard to stop, how hard will it be to stop her husband? Kelten's our killer."

Chapter Twenty-Six

The house was a flurry of activity as phone calls were made and vampires came and went. We'd decided not to notify the Council because of Kelten's connections. Praen was new enough that there was little way to judge what her reaction would be. If she wanted to forewarn her uncle, he could hide in the fae's sithen until the end of time, and no one would be able to pull him out. From there he'd be able to coordinate my death among his loyalists or take care of it himself. A lifetime was a long time for me to be looking over my shoulder.

The men had been completely silent as I laid out what I was certain were the facts. The day I'd returned with Clay to the hotel, I'd seen someone in the hotel lobby who I thought I'd recognized. I'd been certain he was fae, but I'd been in enough pain, and had met enough of the fae over the previous weeks, that I wasn't certain I'd know his name, so I'd dismissed the thought of calling out a hello. In civilian clothes of jeans and a T-shirt, and out of his spot in my mind, it just hadn't dawned on me that it was Kelten.

The flowers had been from him. He'd stuck the hair inside the card to prove how close he had come to me while I was unaware of him, though how he'd obtained the hair from my head still stumped me.

The fight with Bahlin that resulted in his violent disappearance would have shown up on the Council's radar, and probably the fae seer's beacon. We knew that, at the very least, Sarenia's seer had picked it up. How? Bahlin's admission of Aiden's frantic call to him.

Kelten would have known of our general movements around England and Scotland because he had watchers of his own. It had been his lackey who had followed us to Avebury Henge and the restaurant that day. Kelten had killed the waitress before attending the Council vote, believing me to still be in the area. In fact, I'd already been at Hellion's London home or well seated inside the henge when the killing occurred. I regressed into speculation at that point, believing Kelten had had his wife, Gaitha, forcibly if not violently locked up and abused, hence the claw marks on his face and the scratches and bruises around her throat. She'd tried to warn me that night at the henge but I'd seen only what Kelten counted on me seeing when he brought her, and that was the countenance of a woman driven mad by grief.

That same night, we'd moved on to Hellion's estate in Ireland. Hellion's large country home hadn't been on his scope at the time and had been generally well warded enough to keep us hidden from all but Bahlin, who had Conor on the inside advising him of our movements. Had Conor figured out Kelten was the source of power he'd really sought, our stories would have likely all ended there. Instead, the power-hungry magus had followed the clearest source of power presented—the blue weyr—and his betrayal had been short-lived though high priced.

The murders followed me, always seemingly one step behind, until the blond hair showed up at Hellion's home. I was guessing the hair was Gaitha's, and Kelten had used it to bind her powers to him. If we learned she was able to dematerialize and corporally cloak herself, we'd be able to prove this conjecture.

Amaly's murder had been committed with the sole purpose of crippling Hellion. Kelten had likely followed the hair inside the ward, just as Hellion had speculated . Arriving at Amaly's, she either saw him and he killed her, or he waited her out and he killed her to hurt Hellion. Either way, it had been a true blow.

With Kelten busy that night, Gaitha had broken free of his bonds and made her way to Hellion's London home to warn us, later tracking us to Black & Bleu. She'd missed us by less than a second, and I was nearly physically ill to realize it could have all been stopped if we'd only taken a moment longer at the table, or if Hellion had decided to use the restroom before leaving, or if she'd been able to get to the restaurant any sooner. But what was done was done.

Kelten had firm knowledge we were basing ourselves out of London and had followed us closely. The night in the park, when Hellion left me to blow off some steam, Kelten had nearly had me. Only Hellion's fast return had saved my life. As a result, we suspected Kelten tipped off the mundane police in an effort to complicate our lives. It had worked.

The night Kelten had made it into our bedroom and waited on me, I'd sensed another person. This was, again, speculation, because I couldn't know for sure, never having seen her, but I believed it was Gaitha. With the blond hair out of the house, he'd needed the original magic, not magic he'd stolen, to help him travel to the room. Again, if Hellion's timing had been a moment off, things would have ended differently.

Finally, last night in the park had been the snapping point for Kelten. Alerted to the hunting activity by his niece, he'd been unable to stay away. He had come to see what would happen when the killer couldn't be located. Likely intending to stay to the shadows, he hadn't been able to pass up the opportunity to finish me. He'd been denied too many times and didn't believe he'd really be caught. So he'd followed along as a corporeal mist and had taken advantage of my step off the path to attack. He hadn't expected me to fight back, and I was sure I wasn't going to catch him off guard a second time. That meant that, whatever happened tonight, we had to end this thing.

Darius left with Hellion to go plan how to track Kelten down and lure him out for the kill. There would be no trial. The men had asked surprisingly few questions, instead keeping me on track when the shaking got too bad and became a physical distraction.

I was lying on the leather sofa, eyes closed, when I felt my companion move. Even though Hellion had strengthened his warding, no one wanted to leave me alone in the house. And because I wasn't ready to listen to violence being plotted like a street map, I'd begged off the planning part. It would be a cold day in Hell before I'd stay home tonight, but for now, I needed some time to myself.

"Maddy?" Efein said, rubbing cool fingers along the arch of my foot. "Are you awake, love?"

"*Mmm hmm.*"

He rested his hand on my ankle, and I opened my eyes. I had met Efein twice before, but I'd never really spoken to him much. Tonight I'd found the soft-spoken, auburn-haired vampire to be pleasant, undemanding company. He was one of Darius's best warriors, though he refused to tell me where he'd honed his battle skills. His carriage and comfort with a sword made me believe he wasn't a recent recruit.

"Will you call Bahlin?" he asked, his voice hardening some on the other supe's name. "Because as much as I despise the bastard, I think he deserves to be involved."

"You're right," I said on a sigh as I sat up. "Did you mention this to Hellion or Darius?"

Efein looked uncomfortable before he schooled his rugged face into the smooth, lineless visage I was used to. "I did. They want to handle it without calling the dragons."

"Why?"

"I believe it's to do with you."

"Figures." I pushed myself up off the sofa and stretched, my back cracking. "I think we should probably call him and his people in, but the more we open this up to Council, the more we run the risk of tipping Kelten off. I'll defer to them unless, well, unless I don't." I smiled at Efein and offered him a hand up off the floor where he'd sat by my feet. He took it and stood, and his disproportionate weight had me stumbling into him as he gained his feet. His arms instinctively wrapped around me, and he sighed. "They are lucky men to hold your favor as they do," he whispered before letting me go.

I stepped back, a little uncomfortable. I mean, seriously, what the hell was it with all the guys seeming to sprout mature wood in my vicinity lately? I'm not a prize. I'm average looking, slightly neurotic, clumsy as hell, prone to fits of temper compounded by panic attacks, and I am, apparently, a real cover hog. It made no sense.

Shaking my head, I stepped away from him and squeezed his hands before letting go. "You're kind, Efein, but I'm no catch."

"I respectfully beg to differ, Maddy." He seemed so easy-going and gentle in that small moment in time that it was hard for me to reconcile this vampire with the one who had participated unquestioningly in draining Conor of his life that night in Ireland.

Just shows how hard it is to really know people, I thought to myself. I gave a small smile and headed down the hall to the library, Efein on my heels. Still more than fifteen paces away, I could hear the angry, raised voices of the men as they argued about how they'd draw Kelten out. I realize it was open eavesdropping, but I stopped to listen anyway, convinced they'd dumb it down if I made myself known. *Men.*

Hellion's voice was loudest as he opposed the plan which, from what I could gather among the arguing, called for me being used as bait. He thought it was too great a risk to use me and instead proposed sending in a different decoy, one who maybe didn't entirely understand the risks—i.e. didn't have a clue what was going on. He wanted Darius to pick up a woman who looked like me and take her for a stroll in Hyde Park, or pull her down an alley to make a meal of her, or something. It was evident he wanted anything, would support anything, that kept me safely locked up with a gaggle—flock? passel?—of vampires for protection. Voices suddenly died down, and I strained to hear what had happened. The answer came easily enough. I'd been discovered.

"Come in, Maddy," Darius called. "You might as well have a say in our planning."

"No! She is *not* going to come in here and tell me—"

"What? I'm not going to tell you *what*?" I asked in a soft, menacing voice as I walked around the corner and into the room. "Because I know we're not going to have this conversation again, Hellion, the one where I explain to you what my job is." My voice was sharp but not hostile, though it could have been pushed that way in a second.

"Maddy," Hellion pleaded, "this is insane. I can't allow you to—"

"And *there's* the rub, Hellion. I'm the Niteclif, so ultimately it's not up to you." Out of sheer stubbornness and poor judgment skills, I turned to Darius. "Here's what we're going to do."

London's predictable afternoon showers had left the night air so heavy with moisture it felt dense and unbreathable. Gutters still trickled with the last dregs of the day's rain, carrying away at least two layers of the city's grime and depositing them in places best not thought about. Hellion and Darius argued as they walked down the front stairs, their footsteps muffled in the opaque fog that was beginning to materialize as the evening air rapidly cooled under suspiciously clear skies. Stars struggled to shine through the lights of the city, winking against the purplish-black canvas of the night. I loved nights like this.

I leaned out the door and watched the men argue as they walked, the sounds of a raucous game of cards bleeding through the open doorway at my back. No, this wasn't part of the plan, but I couldn't seem to stop myself.

"Maddy?" Efein called. "Shut the door, love. You know Hellion doesn't want you anywhere near the doors or windows."

I looked down the street as the men came to a stop, still arguing. This was going too far, but there was nothing I could do to stop it.

I slammed the door loudly as Efein came around the corner. "Join us?" He jerked his head toward the library.

"No, thanks. I think I'll go up and read for a bit." I rubbed his arm as I walked passed him and squeezed his hand. He gave no indication of having noticed, or cared.

I jogged up the two flights of stairs and headed for the bedroom, a little nervous about entering alone after the attack only a couple of days ago. Hellion had assured me the house was warded more heavily than ever before, but my security had been shaken. I eased through the door instead of walking straight in, my eyes sweeping the bedroom. No madmen. No smell of burning hair. All clear.

I went to the closet and repeated my easing in, back-against-the-wall routine with the same result. I grabbed my sweatshirt and headed for the window. This was going to be one of the most difficult things I had to do. Taking a deep breath, I opened the window at the back of the closet and let the emergency ladder roll down the side of the building. I couldn't help the increased breaths per second or the spike in heart rate. I took a shuddering deep breath and, with sweaty palms, I eased my way down from the third story and stopped. No one followed me, so I made my way down to the first story with the same result. At this point a fine sheen of sweat decorated my neck, hairline and upper lip and I'd sweated through the T-shirt I wore under my sweatshirt. I had to leap the last five or six feet to the ground, but I did so without complaint, grateful for the feel of terra firma under my sneakers. I adjusted all of my clothes to make sure I was comfortably arranged before taking off at a slow jog in the general direction the men had gone.

Slipping through a small opening in a manicured boxwood hedge I emerged on Lee's Place and turned toward Wood's Mews, headed for Hyde Park. The street was quiet this late in the evening with most households tucked in for the night. Slipping along like an exceptionally tall specter, I imagine I looked like an over-bundled cat burglar. If the police caught me, I'd have a lot of explaining to do. People just didn't hoof it around this neighborhood dressed in all black and looking scared. Money like this bought insulation from intent.

I reached the end of the street where the men had last been seen arguing. Crossing Park Street, I continued on, no sign of the men anywhere. I heard distant shouting, someone calling my name. *Efein.* I picked up the pace, knowing the vampires would catch me if I didn't gain some distance.

"Oy! You there!" came a man's voice.

I looked up and saw a foot patrolman stepping it toward me. I waved and shouted, "Out for an evening run!" and I sprinted off, convinced this evening had been doomed since I took over planning and the men had walked out. The sound of galloping feet followed, and a stitch in my side began to grow as I pounded pavement. I hit the A4202 and dashed across amid the sounds of squealing brakes and blaring horns, praying all the way that Tyr would carry me into the park unharmed. Clutching my side, I made it through the northeastern main entrance, keeping my eyes peeled for any of the supernatural creatures I sought, and who sought me. Looking back, I realized the foot patrolman was gone. He was either calling in backup or backtracking to ensure his residential areas were secure. I stopped and bent at the waist, one hand on the ribs that felt as if they were being sawn open to allow more air directly into my lungs.

If you survive this, Niteclif, you will start exercising again.

I took the path toward the Serpentine. There were more lights along the path, lending a sense of false security to the park. There were still quite a few people out and about despite the rash of killings. I shook my head at the risks people took in the name of It Won't Happen to Me and kept going. I heard familiar voices coming from behind me, and I darted off the path, diving into the underbrush where I went as still and quiet as the animals around me.

"Damned woman," Efein growled, several of his compatriots echoing the sentiment in much more colorful, less flattering ways. I tried to memorize faces so I knew whom to bitch at. Again, it was all contingent on my survival. They passed by on the path, never slowing down.

I crawled out from under the brush after several minutes and took an alternate path, still heading toward the Serpentine.

It took me another half an hour and one final dive under the bushes to make it to the lake. There were fewer people this deep in the park, and I looked around, wondering what I'd expected. This wasn't it. The entire area, even the landing at the marina, was landscaped and perfectly maintained. There was no trash, and the water reflecting the light of the moon promised rare clarity in the sunshine.

I walked down to the edge of the water and looked around, but there were no signs of any of the men. I sighed, frustrated. I must have lost them.

A scream tore the air. It was a high, panicked noise cut off far too quickly for my comfort. I sprinted toward the noise, kicking hard to get to the—

Body. I rounded the corner and tripped, sprawling in the dirt. What took me down? The body. The head lay ten feet away, the eyes closed and the mouth open, as if the scream had followed her into death. It took me only a moment to process that her hair, though matted with blood, was far from my dark brown/black color. Hers was the color of straw spun to silk. *Oh shit.* It was Praen.

Scrambling to my feet, I spun around, looking at all the shadows as potential hiding places for the mist Kelten assumed. There were too damn many for me to cover all my bases. Blood seeped across the ground, and I stepped farther away from the body to keep her blood off my shoes.

Every shadow held menace as I bent over and found in her hands strands of blond hair braided together and bound by a blue ribbon.

"She was guilty, Niteclif, and I had no choice but to kill her."

I spun around to face my manifested fear.

Kelten stepped out from the murky shadows. He was carrying a long knife, his hands gloved to protect them from the metal that, as fae, would burn him. Praen's blood decorated the wickedly sharp weapon, and threads of blond hair hung from it in matted clumps.

I reached back under the guise of scratching my back and felt for the cold-forged iron dagger strapped to my lower back. I had practiced with this particular knife on several occasions and could draw it relatively quickly. Of course, "relatively" was the operative word when up against supernatural creatures.

He cocked his head to one side like a curious dog and said, "You don't believe me."

"Kelten, I have to ask you—did you kill the other women?" My voice was low and steady. Point to me. He started to walk toward me, and I backed up a step. "Stop, Kelten."

He kept coming, his hand tightening on the handle of the knife.

"Kelten, I'm asking you one last time. Stop and discuss this with me."

His eyes shifted, literally changing color from dark blue to what—

in the dark—appeared to be a steely gray, and the insanity peeked out from the depths. "You killed my only son, you traitorous bitch. You toyed with him, making him believe he stood a chance with you while you were whoring around with the dragon. You drove him to madness, forcing him to go to extreme lengths to gain your affections!" He sliced through the air, flinging blood and hair toward me.

"Are you nuts?" Why the hell was I even *asking*? He was as crazed as the devil at an all-you-can-eat soul buffet.

"Do *not* insinuate I didn't know what was going on!" he screeched, spittle flying from his mouth. He moved quickly and slashed out, his blade laying open my sweatshirt and leaving a thin, horizontal gash on my stomach.

I gasped, my hand automatically going to the cut, and he flashed in to nick my shoulder next. Ignoring the cuts, I dropped my hand and in one motion drew the iron dagger. Compared to his knife it looked a little pathetic, but it was what I had. Besides, the cavalry was supposed to come storming in at any moment.

"Tell me," I said conversationally, "what's the blond hair for?"

"It's Gaitha's. One of her gifts is mist dissipation. One of mine is borrowing others' magic if I can take one of the creature's elements. With her hair, I can dematerialize as mist. All it takes is a pairing of elements. For this? Fire."

Ah, the singed hair smell. The thought that he'd been so close every time I'd smelled it creeped me out a little.

We continued to circle each other slowly. "What's with the blue thread?"

"It's symbolic of the other element: air. The blue thread represents air, since you can't exactly harness air." He darted and cut me again, and I grunted in pain. The cut to my thigh was deeper than the others. Shit, that hurt.

"What was with the deep gouges in the dirt at the park?" I moved more slowly now, working to keep him facing me as he circled the clearing.

He paused. "What gouges?"

"Must've been nothing." Keeping him talking gave me extra time to get the backup in place, because without them I was doomed. Playing to his ego, I said, "The gold coins were a brilliant calling card. Where'd you get Bahlin's coins?"

He snorted. "They weren't Bahlin's, you prat. They were his sister's. She'd left a number of things at Tarrek's residence. After you killed my son..." He began to breathe hard, distracted. He darted in and cut me across the other thigh, and I hissed.

Shit. I hadn't even seen him move. Where the hell were Darius and Hellion?

"When Tarrek died, I went through his home, and she'd left a handful of things there, among them a small cache of gold coins. I took them." He shrugged. "It seemed appropriate to leave a calling card that would haunt the dragon who'd killed his sister, and would remind you of what you'd lost when he left you."

"Smart move," I acknowledged, unsure what to say. We were fast winding down. "How did you get to me to cut my hair?"

"You were at Bahlin's and he'd left the wards down. I'd seen him come and go, and I knew you wouldn't be far from wherever he was. I took a chance and dissipated, coming back together in his flat. You were asleep—"

"Why not just kill me then?" I asked, stunned to immobility that he'd been so close to me, and I'd been so incredibly vulnerable.

He dashed in and sliced me again, this time just above my dagger wrist, and said, "Don't interrupt me, you treacherous bitch. I will cut your damnable tongue out of your mouth when this is through," he hissed, seeming to draw great pleasure from the threat. I shuddered involuntarily and he laughed. "Coward. You should at the very least die well, like I know Tarrek did." His eyes misted at the thought of his son, and that seemed to be the end of the games.

Kelten shifted the knife in his grip and began to stalk straight toward me. I backed up, one hand out behind me as I felt my way along, too intent on Kelten's advance to take my eyes off him for even a moment.

"I wish you'd let your hair grow like a proper woman. Beheading is harder when you have to hold the head by the ears or the jaw." His teeth flashed as he grinned.

"Hellion!" I screamed. "Darius! Efein!"

"Don't pretend to call for help, whore. I saw you sneak out of the house, saw you hide from the vampires who chased you, so I know no one knows where you're off to." He leapt forward and I swung out, out blades clashing. I pushed at the same time with my free hand and hit his shoulder, spinning him off balance so my blade was able to gain additional purchase. I pushed the blade and pricked him with it. I was shocked at the ease with which the blade slid through his tunic and straight into his skin.

Taking advantage of my shock, he backhanded me, splitting my lip and inner cheek against my teeth, filling my mouth with blood.

I stumbled backward, my head ringing. I spit at his feet and he grinned. That look, man, that *look*. It made my stomach clench and my bowels feel loose. For the first time, I began to genuinely doubt I'd get out of this alive.

"Why Praen?" I said, my torn up mouth making my words slightly distorted.

"She's my wife's niece, and she began to suspect something was amiss. She followed me"—he darted in, and I swung too late to defend myself from the second slice across my abdomen—"and I had to kill her. She left me no choice." His voice was calm, as if he were discussing a bakery order and not a beheading.

A flutter of movement behind him caught my eye, but the slight hesitation gave him another opening, and he stepped in quickly and pierced my side.

I cried out, holding the bleeding wound, the others suddenly lighting up as if on fire. It wasn't magic, just my body acknowledging that there was little left it could do, even with an endorphin dump, to mask the pain I was in. It's what he had counted on, toying with me. I didn't expect to die easily, but I'd do what I could to take him with me. My vision swam, and I fought to stay on my feet, clutching my dagger.

How poorly I misjudged her. It took a moment for me to understand what I was seeing when a blade erupted out of Kelten's chest. He looked down, confused.

"Addoed wedi d yn galw pryd 'ch bacia chorddir, anwylyd g." *Death has come calling while your back was turned, dear husband.*

Gaitha wrenched the blade, turning it one hundred eighty degrees and effectively shredding his heart. He went to his knees and she went with him. Blood bubbled from his mouth and ran down his chin as his lungs rejected the air, and he gasped, blood and spit decorating the ground in front of him. Gaitha shoved once more, and Kelten fell face-first into the dirt. She pulled the sword from his chest and turned her attention to me, and her eyes were as cold as a starless night sky.

I sank to my knees, unable to stand any longer. My head was alternately heavy and light, and I wondered how long it would be before

I blacked out.

"I never thought myself to be in a position to thank you, Niteclif, but your wounding of him allowed me to break free of his cursed chains and come to claim my vengeance. I'll never forgive you the death of Tarrek, so I'll leave you wounded, whereas I could heal you were I so inclined. But I will owe you a debt of gratitude for helping me see to his death." She dispassionately toed Kelten's body with her slipper-clad foot.

"How did wounding him help?" I slurred around my torn mouth.

Her smile was glacial and I shivered. She chuckled. "Wise girl. I cursed him, that I'd be drawn to the first battle in which his blood was shed, and it just happened to be here."

"Lucky me," I whispered.

"Indeed. I'll leave you to either make it home or not. If you survive, let Bahlin or Hellion know I'll be taking over rule of the fae. It may take me a while to weed out the traitorous fae who enabled my husband, but I will find them all. Your services for dispensing justice won't be needed." She faded away to a mist and was gone.

Chapter Twenty-Seven

I lay on the ground, breathing hard. Where the hell was my backup? I held my side where his knife had pierced me, the blood seeping through my fingers.

A sound drew my attention, and I turned my head to face whatever emerged from the shadows and greenery. If it was bigger than a squirrel, I was fucked. If it was a rabid squirrel, I was fucked.

Stunned, I was slow to find my voice but when I did, it was harsh. "What the hell are you doing here?"

Bahlin stepped fully from behind the tree where he'd been hiding. "I followed you from Hellion's home. Sneaking out with all this going on wasn't your best idea. I was just about to step in when Gaitha showed up and spit Kelten like a fatted pig." He moved closer to me. "You clearly had this figured out, if not under control. You're getting better. The only clue you sincerely misinterpreted was my fault."

I couldn't do more than grunt my curiosity as I shifted and looked for a more comfortable position. On the ground. As I bled. Clearly, delusion was setting in.

"The gouged earth was my fault. I went to the crime scene at the park and was forced to leave in a hurry. I shifted and pushed off, and I must have drug my talons through the dirt with the force of the launch." He ran his hands through his hair and pulled it back in a familiar gesture.

"Makes sense. I'm glad you looked in on the scenes." I took a deep breath and his smell, that of the sweet night, blew through me, a memory not distant enough to give me perspective. My breath caught in my throat and I swallowed hard, closing my eyes.

"Maddy?" His voice was threaded through with longing. The close rustling of fabric and the movement of air were accompanied by a soft *thump* as he went to his knees at my side.

A single finger traced down my cheek.

"Maddy?" he asked again.

I shook my head and tried to scoot backwards, but I was too weak. "Son of a bitch," I gasped, grabbing again for the wound in my side. "I feel like the heroine in a horror movie who finds herself fallen on the ground at the feet of the bad guy and all she does is lay there and scream like a damn ninny. I'm *not* screaming." *Was I making sense?*

Bahlin froze. "So I'm the bad guy?"

"How about the questionable dragon?" I asked, twisting to look at the wound on my side. It burned horribly to twist far enough to the side to see it, but I'd have done anything to keep from looking at him.

"I suppose I've earned that."

"'Suppose'? Bahlin, you absolutely shattered my heart." My voice was choked with emotion, and I had to close my eyes and pretend he wasn't looking at me with passionate regret. "You promised me a fairytale I'd never believed in, and I finally bought the whole thing. Then you..." I gasped, rubbing my heart. "You used me, knowing the prophecy. If you'd waited to pursue me, even if I'd been with Tarrek for some unfathomable reason, you would have known there was a good possibility that I'd end up with you forever." And suddenly there it was, the reason I couldn't get over him. If he'd just waited, waited a few measly weeks, maybe things would have been different. I was getting tired, and my vision was going gray at the edges.

Bahlin sat all the way down in front of me. "If you believe in destiny, Maddy, you would have ended up with Hellion anyway, and I would have missed out on the opportunity for even the brief time we had together," he whispered. "I didn't want to miss one minute."

"And if I believe in free will?"

"Then you've chosen Hellion."

"Too right, mate." Hellion stepped out of the darkness, his eyes entirely black.

Fuck.

Bahlin surged to his feet and backed away from me, giving himself room to maneuver if necessary.

Hellion didn't come any closer to us. He trembled with rage, his heartache visible in the depth of his eyes. I'd hurt him with this indecision of mine, and to hear the regret I'd been unable to mask with Bahlin...

"Hellion," I said softly, holding out a hand to him.

He shook his head, turning to stare out over the lake. Praen's body lay forgotten mere yards away, the drama of the shattered dreams of the living more relevant than the dead who held no hope of resurrection.

I couldn't contain the sob that broke from my chest. Looking from man to man, dragon to warlock, I made a decision that would haunt me for a lifetime. It hurt me in every way possible, but I had to put an end to this indecision, this constant, unbearable heartache. These two men had been set against each other in a fight for my love, and there could only be one winner. I turned myself to the west and, with my toes pushing and my fingers ripping at the grass, I dragged myself across the ground toward my salvation.

He watched me, his face riddled with pain and doubt as his eyes slid from me to the man behind me. It was clear he thought I'd come to say goodbye. Shaking, he bent and helped me stand. I was hurt enough that I couldn't do it without his support as the stab wound in my side throbbed and the slices and cuts all over my body burned, pulling apart as I moved. My skin twitched. Endorphins from the fight could kick back in any time now. I didn't know how much longer I'd be able to hold it together, but this had to be done before I lost it—both my nerve and consciousness—because the man behind me was suffering, and I knew it.

Standing on legs as shaky as a newborn foal's, I clung desperately to my hope. He was aloof, reserved, as if by keeping himself distanced he could stop the momentum of the moment. But he was wrong. I stroked his face and pushed his hair out of his eyes and smiled tentatively, tears coursing down my cheeks. There would be no wavering any longer, no going back and forth between the two, and I knew it.

"I love you," I said.

"But is it enough?" he whispered in a rough, emotion-choked voice.

"It will have to be. It's all I've got to offer you."

He raised a hand to my face and I wobbled without the support of both of his arms. *Prophetic?* I wondered. It was too deep a thought for me to consider here and now.

"Is this what you want, Maddy? Because I won't have less than all of you." He looked over my shoulder at the other man.

I could hear his breathing escalating as he understood what was happening, that I hadn't crawled across the grass to say goodbye to his competition but to offer my heart to the other man.

"No," said the voice from my back. "Maddy, no, don't do this. Don't throw this away."

I turned and looked at Bahlin, my heart shattering and the tears flowing faster. "I'll always love you, Bahlin."

"But not enough to choose me." He shook his head, and bitterness sang down the lines of tension between us.

I lifted a trembling hand, covered with blood and dirt, to my face to wipe the tears away. "I don't think we're entirely good for each other, Bay. I'm so sorry." My voice cracked on the last word, and strong hands supported me as I stood facing my old lover.

"Give me a chance, Maddy. Just one more chance. Please," he asked, holding out a hand to me.

I shook my head quickly and nearly collapsed, but Hellion's arms were there to catch me.

"Maddy, love, we need to go home and get you tended. Your side is bleeding profusely," Hellion said softly, keeping his eyes cast down and away from the other man.

"Please don't make this harder, Bay. If you ever loved me—"

"I never stopped," he choked out as his first tears fell. "I never stopped."

A gasping sob escaped me, and I bit my hand to keep any further sound from betraying my heartbreak. I knew that if I lost it now, I'd be done for. I would completely break down, and neither man needed that. Hellion didn't need the doubt. Bahlin didn't need the false hope that I could be persuaded to change my mind.

I reached out a hand to Bahlin, and he shook his head. "Don't do this, Maddy." His words were guttural and deep, and I wondered if his dragon was begging me or if it was the man. Did it matter? No. It only hurt more. I beckoned to him with my hand, and I took a shaky step away from Hellion.

"Bahlin," I whispered.

He strode forward and crushed me to him, and I grunted in pain. His mouth came down on mine, and I kissed him as if he was the air I needed to breathe. I broke the kiss and he didn't let go.

"Bahlin," I whispered, "I have to go. I'm hurting—"

"Me too," he said with a small smile.

I nodded quickly and whimpered, and he handed me back to Hellion.

In a hard voice, he said, "Love her well, because if you don't, I will *always* be right there, waiting for you to make that one unforgivable mistake that sends her back to me."

"I know," Hellion said, lifting me up and cradling me in his arms. He turned to go and I stopped him.

I looked at Bahlin one last time, and then Hellion turned back to dematerialize and take me home. I allowed myself one final moment of terror. *Was I making the right decision?* Only time would tell.

The last thing I heard was Bahlin's anguished roar as he took to the air. Then we were gone.

About the Author

Denise Tompkins lives in the heart of the South where the neighbors still know your name, all food forms are considered fry-able and bugs die only to be reincarnated in aggressive, blood-craving triplicate. Thrilled to finally live somewhere that can boast 3 ½ seasons (winter's only noticeable because the trees are naked), her favorite season is definitely fall. It's the time of year when the gardens are just about to pass into winter's brief silence, and the leaves are out to prove that nature is the most brilliant artist of all.

A life-long voracious reader, Denise has three favorite authors. Why three? Because favorite authors are like chips: a person can't have just one. Her little house was so overrun with books last year that her darling husband bought her an e-reader out of self-preservation. He was (legitimately) afraid she might begin throwing out pots and pans to make room for more books, and he didn't want to starve.

You can find out more about Denise by visiting her website, www.denisetompkins.net, or by following her on Twitter, @DeniseJTompkins.

When Fate makes you her bitch, accept it and adapt. Or die.

Legacy
© *2011 Denise Tompkins*
The Niteclif Evolutions, Book 1

Looking back on the wish she made on Midsummer's Eve, Maddy Niteclif should have been more specific. She only wanted to escape the shadowy nightmares that plagued her nights, not to be thrust into a completely altered reality.

If a strangely familiar, sexy dragon-shifter named Bahlin, who causes a never-to-be-mentioned-again fainting spell, isn't enough to make her question her sanity, his insistence she's *the* Niteclif ought to do the job. Prophesied super-sleuth of the supernatural world—a world that desperately needs her help—isn't a job she's remotely qualified for no matter *what* her family tree says.

Catapulted into a very different London ruled by dark mythology, mystery and murder, Maddy makes a few startling discoveries. Paranormal creatures exist. Getting shot really sucks. And her body responds remarkably well to dragon magic—in more ways than simple wound healing.

But in this kill-or-be-killed world, reality bites. And Maddy must choose to go back to what she knows…or stay and fight for the man she knows she can't live without.

Warning: This book contains a shape-shifting dragon with a Scottish accent, modern and archaic weapons, global inter-species politics that make democracy seem mild, some very steamy sex underground, a severed head, murder, and…oh yeah…a woman caught in the middle of it all.

Available now in ebook and print from Samhain Publishing.

The gods play…and mortals pay.

Bad Blood
© 2011 Lucienne Diver
Latter-Day Olympians, Book 1

Tori Karacis's family line may trace back to a drunken liaison between the god Pan and one of the immortal gorgons. Or…maybe it's just coincidence that her glance can, literally, stop men in their tracks. While her fear of heights kept her out of the family aerobatic troupe, her extreme nosiness fits right in with her uncle's P.I. business.

Except he's disappeared on an Odyssean journey to find himself. Muddling through on her own, she's reduced to hunting (not stalking, because that would just be weird) brass-bra'd Hollywood agent Circe Holland to deliver a message…only to witness her murder by what looks like the Creature from the Black Lagoon.

Suddenly, all of her family's tall tales seem believable, especially when Apollo—*the* Apollo, who's now hiding out among humans as an adult film star—appears in her office, looking to hire her. She knows the drill: canoodling with gods never works out well for humans, but she's irresistibly drawn to him. Maybe it's her genes. Maybe not.

Given her conflicted feelings for one hot and hardened cop, it's a toss-up which will kill her quickest. The danger at her door…or her love life.

Warning: Contains pot-boiling passion between a heroine who may—or may not—be a descendant of Medusa, and a hot god and a hunky cop with the…equipment…to handle her, even on her worst bad-hair day. Beware of killer kisses, trickster gods and bearded grandmothers Who Know Everything.

Available now in ebook and print from Samhain Publishing.

www.samhainpublishing.com

*Green for the planet.
Great for your wallet.*

It's all about the story...

Romance

HORROR

www.samhainpublishing.com

CPSIA information can be obtained at www.ICGtesting.com
Printed in the USA
LVOW131741060113

314510LV00001B/30/P